The Silkworm

ALSO BY ROBERT GALBRAITH

The Cuckoo's Calling

The
Silkworm

Robert Galbraith

MULHOLLAND BOOKS

Little, Brown and Company

New York Boston London

Copyright © 2014 Robert Galbraith Limited

Mulholland Books / Little, Brown and Company
Hachette Book Group
237 Park Avenue, New York, NY 10017
mulhollandbooks.com

First North American Edition: June 2014
Published simultaneously in Britain by Sphere, June 2014

Mulholland Books is an imprint of Little, Brown and Company, a division of Hachette Book Group, Inc. The Mulholland Books name and logo are trademarks of Hachette Book Group, Inc.

The publisher is not responsible for websites (or their content) that are not owned by the publisher.

The Hachette Speakers Bureau provides a wide range of authors for speaking events. To find out more, go to hachettespeakersbureau.com or call (866) 376-6591.

"Oh Santa!": Words and Music by Mariah Carey, Bryan Michael Paul Cox and Jermaine Mauldin Dupri © 2010, Reproduced by permission of EMI Music Publishing Ltd., London W1F 9LD / © 2010 W.B.M. MUSIC CORP. (SESAC) AND SONGS IN THE KEY OF B FLAT, INC. (SESAC) ALL RIGHTS ON BEHALF OF ITSELF AND SONGS IN THE KEY OF B FLAT, INC. ADMINISTERED BY W.B.M. MUSIC CORP. © 2010 Published by Universal/MCA Music Ltd.

"Love You More": Words & Music by Oritsé Williams, Marvin Humes, Jonathan Gill, Aston Merrygold, Toby Gad and Wayne Hector © 2010 BMG FM Music Ltd., a BMG Chrysalis company / BMG Rights Management UK Ltd., a BMG Chrysalis company / EMI Music Publishing Ltd. All Rights Reserved. International Copyright Secured. Reproduced by permission of Music Sales Limited. Reproduced by permission of EMI Music Publishing Ltd., London W1F 9LD.

ISBN 978-0-316-20687-7 (hc) / 978-0-316-41071-7 (lp) / 978-0-316-37747-8 (intl pb)
LCCN 20149381832

10 9 8 7 6 5 4 3 2 1

RRD–C

Printed in the United States of America

To Jenkins,
without whom…
he knows the rest

… blood and vengeance the scene, death the story,
a sword imbrued with blood, the pen that writes,
and the poet a terrible buskined tragical fellow,
with a wreath about his head of burning match instead of bays.

The Noble Spanish Soldier
Thomas Dekker

1

QUESTION
What dost thou feed on?
ANSWER
Broken sleep.

Thomas Dekker, *The Noble Spanish Soldier*

"Someone bloody famous," said the hoarse voice on the end of the line, "better've died, Strike."

The large unshaven man tramping through the darkness of pre-dawn, with his telephone clamped to his ear, grinned.

"It's in that ballpark."

"It's six o'clock in the fucking morning!"

"It's half past, but if you want what I've got, you'll need to come and get it," said Cormoran Strike. "I'm not far away from your place. There's a—"

"How d'you know where I live?" demanded the voice.

"You told me," said Strike, stifling a yawn. "You're selling your flat."

"Oh," said the other, mollified. "Good memory."

"There's a twenty-four-hour caff—"

"Fuck that. Come into the office later—"

"Culpepper, I've got another client this morning, he pays better than you do and I've been up all night. You need this now if you're going to use it."

A groan. Strike could hear the rustling of sheets.

"It had better be shit-hot."

"Smithfield Café on Long Lane," said Strike and rang off.

1

The slight unevenness in his gait became more pronounced as he walked down the slope towards Smithfield Market, monolithic in the winter darkness, a vast rectangular Victorian temple to meat, where from four every weekday morning animal flesh was unloaded, as it had been for centuries past, cut, parceled and sold to butchers and restaurants across London. Strike could hear voices through the gloom, shouted instructions and the growl and beep of reversing lorries unloading the carcasses. As he entered Long Lane, he became merely one among many heavily muffled men moving purposefully about their Monday-morning business.

A huddle of couriers in fluorescent jackets cupped mugs of tea in their gloved hands beneath a stone griffin standing sentinel on the corner of the market building. Across the road, glowing like an open fireplace against the surrounding darkness, was the Smithfield Café, open twenty-four hours a day, a cupboard-sized cache of warmth and greasy food.

The café had no bathroom, but an arrangement with the bookies a few doors along. Ladbrokes would not open for another three hours, so Strike made a detour down a side alley and in a dark doorway relieved himself of a bladder bulging with weak coffee drunk in the course of a night's work. Exhausted and hungry, he turned at last, with the pleasure that only a man who has pushed himself past his physical limits can ever experience, into the fat-laden atmosphere of frying eggs and bacon.

Two men in fleeces and waterproofs had just vacated a table. Strike maneuvered his bulk into the small space and sank, with a grunt of satisfaction, onto the hard wood and steel chair. Almost before he asked, the Italian owner placed tea in front of him in a tall white mug, which came with triangles of white buttered bread. Within five minutes a full English breakfast lay before him on a large oval plate.

Strike blended well with the strong men banging their way in and out of the café. He was large and dark, with dense, short, curly hair that had receded a little from the high, domed forehead that topped a boxer's broad nose and thick, surly brows. His jaw was grimy with stubble and bruise-colored shadows enlarged his dark eyes. He ate gazing dreamily at the market building opposite. The nearest arched entrance, numbered two, was taking substance as the darkness thinned: a stern stone face, ancient and bearded, stared back at him from over the doorway. Had there ever been a god of carcasses?

He had just started on his sausages when Dominic Culpepper arrived. The journalist was almost as tall as Strike but thin, with a choirboy's complexion. A strange asymmetry, as though somebody had given his face a counterclockwise twist, stopped him being girlishly handsome.

"This better be good," Culpepper said as he sat down, pulled off his gloves and glanced almost suspiciously around the café.

"Want some food?" asked Strike through a mouthful of sausage.

"No," said Culpepper.

"Rather wait till you can get a croissant?" asked Strike, grinning.

"Fuck off, Strike."

It was almost pathetically easy to wind up the ex–public schoolboy, who ordered tea with an air of defiance, calling the indifferent waiter (as Strike noted with amusement) "mate."

"Well?" demanded Culpepper, with the hot mug in his long pale hands.

Strike fished in his overcoat pocket, brought out an envelope and slid it across the table. Culpepper pulled out the contents and began to read.

"Fucking hell," he said quietly, after a while. He shuffled feverishly through the bits of paper, some of which were covered in Strike's own writing. "Where the hell did you get this?"

Strike, whose mouth was full of sausage, jabbed a finger at one of the bits of paper, on which an office address was scribbled.

"His very fucked-off PA," he said, when he had finally swallowed. "He's been shagging her, as well as the two you know about. She's only just realized she's not going to be the next Lady Parker."

"How the hell did you find *that* out?" asked Culpepper, staring up at Strike over the papers trembling in his excited hands.

"Detective work," said Strike thickly, through another bit of sausage. "Didn't your lot used to do this, before you started outsourcing to the likes of me? But she's got to think about her future employment prospects, Culpepper, so she doesn't want to appear in the story, all right?"

3

Culpepper snorted.

"She should've thought about that before she nicked—"

With a deft movement, Strike tweaked the papers out of the journalist's fingers.

"She didn't nick them. He got her to print this lot off for him this afternoon. The only thing she's done wrong is show it to me. But if you're going to splash her private life all over the papers, Culpepper, I'll take 'em back."

"Piss off," said Culpepper, making a grab for the evidence of wholesale tax evasion clutched in Strike's hairy hand. "All right, we'll leave her out of it. But he'll know where we got it. He's not a complete tit."

"What's he going to do, drag her into court where she can spill the beans about every other dodgy thing she's witnessed over the last five years?"

"Yeah, all right," sighed Culpepper after a moment's reflection. "Give 'em back. I'll leave her out of the story, but I'll need to speak to her, won't I? Check she's kosher."

"*Those* are kosher. You don't need to speak to her," said Strike firmly.

The shaking, besotted, bitterly betrayed woman whom he had just left would not be safe left alone with Culpepper. In her savage desire for retribution against a man who had promised her marriage and children she would damage herself and her prospects beyond repair. It had not taken Strike long to gain her trust. She was nearly forty-two; she had thought that she was going to have Lord Parker's children; now a kind of bloodlust had her in its grip. Strike had sat with her for several hours, listening to the story of her infatuation, watching her pace her sitting room in tears, rock backwards and forwards on her sofa, knuckles to her forehead. Finally she had agreed to this: a betrayal that represented the funeral of all her hopes.

"You're going to leave her out of it," said Strike, holding the papers firmly in a fist that was nearly twice the size of Culpepper's. "Right? This is still a fucking massive story without her."

After a moment's hesitation and with a grimace, Culpepper caved in.

"Yeah, all right. Give me them."

The journalist shoved the statements into an inside pocket and gulped his tea, and his momentary disgruntlement at Strike seemed to fade in the glorious prospect of dismantling the reputation of a British peer.

"Lord Parker of Pennywell," he said happily under his breath, "you are well and truly screwed, mate."

"I take it your proprietor'll get this?" Strike asked, as the bill landed between them.

"Yeah, yeah ..."

Culpepper threw a ten-pound note down onto the table and the two men left the café together. Strike lit up a cigarette as soon as the door had swung closed behind them.

"How did you get her to talk?" Culpepper asked as they set off together through the cold, past the motorbikes and lorries still arriving at and departing the market.

"I listened," said Strike.

Culpepper shot him a sideways glance.

"All the other private dicks I use spend their time hacking phone messages."

"Illegal," said Strike, blowing smoke into the thinning darkness.

"So how—?"

"You protect your sources and I'll protect mine."

They walked fifty yards in silence, Strike's limp more marked with every step.

"This is going to be massive. Massive," said Culpepper gleefully. "That hypocritical old shit's been bleating on about corporate greed and he's had twenty mill stashed in the Cayman Islands ... "

"Glad to give satisfaction," said Strike. "I'll email you my invoice."

Culpepper threw him another sideways look.

"See Tom Jones's son in the paper last week?" he asked.

"Tom Jones?"

"Welsh singer," said Culpepper.

"Oh, him," said Strike, without enthusiasm. "I knew a Tom Jones in the army."

"Did you see the story?"

"No."

"Nice long interview he gave. He says he's never met his father, never had a word from him. I bet he got more than your bill is going to be."

"You haven't seen my invoice yet," said Strike.

"Just saying. One nice little interview and you could take a few nights off from interviewing secretaries."

"You're going to have to stop suggesting this," said Strike, "or I'm going to have to stop working for you, Culpepper."

"Course," said Culpepper, "I could run the story anyway. Rock star's estranged son is a war hero, never knew his father, working as a private—"

"Instructing people to hack phones is illegal as well, I've heard."

At the top of Long Lane they slowed and turned to face each other. Culpepper's laugh was uneasy.

"I'll wait for your invoice, then."

"Suits me."

They set off in different directions, Strike heading towards the Tube station.

"Strike!" Culpepper's voice echoed through the darkness behind him. "Did you fuck her?"

"Looking forward to reading it, Culpepper," Strike shouted wearily, without turning his head.

He limped into the shadowy entrance of the station and was lost to Culpepper's sight.

2

How long must we fight? for I cannot stay,
Nor will not stay! I have business.

Francis Beaumont and Philip Massinger,
The Little French Lawyer

The Tube was filling up already. Monday-morning faces: sagging, gaunt, braced, resigned. Strike found a seat opposite a puffy-eyed young blonde whose head kept sinking sideways into sleep. Again and again she jerked herself back upright, scanning the blurred signs of the stations frantically in case she had missed her stop.

The train rattled and clattered, speeding Strike back towards the meager two and a half rooms under a poorly insulated roof that he called home. In the depths of his tiredness, surrounded by these blank, sheep-like visages, he found himself pondering the accidents that had brought all of them into being. Every birth was, viewed properly, mere chance. With a hundred million sperm swimming blindly through the darkness, the odds against a person becoming themselves were staggering. How many of this Tube-full had been planned, he wondered, light-headed with tiredness. And how many, like him, were accidents?

There had been a little girl in his primary school class who had a port-wine stain across her face and Strike had always felt a secret kinship with her, because both of them had carried something indelibly different with them since birth, something that was not their fault. They couldn't see it, but everybody else could, and had the bad manners to keep mentioning it. The occasional fascination of total strangers, which at five years old he had thought had something to do with his

7

own uniqueness, he eventually realized was because they saw him as no more than a famous singer's zygote, the incidental evidence of a celebrity's unfaithful fumble. Strike had only met his biological father twice. It had taken a DNA test to make Jonny Rokeby accept paternity.

Dominic Culpepper was a walking distillation of the prurience and presumptions that Strike met on the very rare occasions these days that anybody connected the surly-looking ex-soldier with the aging rock star. Their thoughts leapt at once to trust funds and handsome handouts, to private flights and VIP lounges, to a multimillionaire's largesse on tap. Agog at the modesty of Strike's existence and the punishing hours he worked, they asked themselves: what must Strike have done to alienate his father? Was he faking penury to wheedle more money out of Rokeby? What had he done with the millions his mother had surely squeezed out of her rich paramour?

And at such times, Strike would think nostalgically of the army, of the anonymity of a career in which your background and your parentage counted for almost nothing beside your ability to do the job. Back in the Special Investigation Branch, the most personal question he had faced on introduction was a request to repeat the odd pair of names with which his extravagantly unconventional mother had saddled him.

Traffic was already rolling busily along Charing Cross Road by the time Strike emerged from the Tube. The November dawn was breaking now, gray and halfhearted, full of lingering shadows. He turned into Denmark Street feeling drained and sore, looking forward to the short sleep he might be able to squeeze in before his next client arrived at nine thirty. With a wave at the girl in the guitar shop, with whom he often took cigarette breaks on the street, Strike let himself in through the black outer door beside the 12 Bar Café and began to climb the metal staircase that curled around the broken birdcage lift inside. Up past the graphic designer on the first floor, past his own office with its engraved glass door on the second; up to the third and smallest landing where his home now lay.

The previous occupant, manager of the bar downstairs, had moved on to more salubrious quarters and Strike, who had been sleeping in his office for a few months, had leapt at the chance to rent the place, grateful for such an easy solution to the problem of his homelessness.

The space under the eaves was small by any standards, and especially for a man of six foot three. He scarcely had room to turn around in the shower; kitchen and living room were uneasily combined and the bedroom was almost entirely filled by the double bed. Some of Strike's possessions remained boxed up on the landing, in spite of the landlord's injunction against this.

His small windows looked out across rooftops, with Denmark Street far below. The constant throb of the bass from the bar below was muffled to the point that Strike's own music often obliterated it.

Strike's innate orderliness was manifest throughout: the bed was made, the crockery clean, everything in its place. He needed a shave and shower, but that could wait; after hanging up his overcoat, he set his alarm for nine twenty and stretched out on the bed fully clothed.

He fell asleep within seconds and within a few more—or so it seemed—he was awake again. Somebody was knocking on his door.

"I'm sorry, Cormoran, I'm really sorry—"

His assistant, a tall young woman with long strawberry-blond hair, looked apologetic as he opened the door, but at the sight of him her expression became appalled.

"Are you all right?"

"Wuzassleep. Been 'wake all night—two nights."

"I'm really sorry," Robin repeated, "but it's nine forty and William Baker's here and getting—"

"Shit," mumbled Strike. "Can't've set the alarm right—gimme five min—"

"That's not all," said Robin. "There's a woman here. She hasn't got an appointment. I've told her you haven't got room for another client, but she's refusing to leave."

Strike yawned, rubbing his eyes.

"Five minutes. Make them tea or something."

Six minutes later, in a clean shirt, smelling of toothpaste and deodorant but still unshaven, Strike entered the outer office where Robin was sitting at her computer.

"Well, better late than never," said William Baker with a rigid smile. "Lucky you've got such a good-looking secretary, or I might have got bored and left."

Strike saw Robin flush angrily as she turned away, ostensibly organizing the post. There had been something inherently offensive in the way that Baker had said "secretary." Immaculate in his pinstriped suit, the company director was employing Strike to investigate two of his fellow board members.

"Morning, William," said Strike.

"No apology?" murmured Baker, his eyes on the ceiling.

"Hello, who are you?" Strike asked, ignoring him and addressing instead the slight, middle-aged woman in an old brown overcoat who was perched on the sofa.

"Leonora Quine," she replied, in what sounded, to Strike's practiced ear, like a West Country accent.

"I've got a very busy morning ahead, Strike," said Baker.

He walked without invitation into the inner office. When Strike did not follow, he lost a little of his suavity.

"I doubt you got away with shoddy time-keeping in the army, Mr. Strike. Come along, please."

Strike did not seem to hear him.

"What exactly is it you were wanting me to do for you, Mrs. Quine?" he asked the shabby woman on the sofa.

"Well, it's my husband—"

"Mr. Strike, I've got an appointment in just over an hour," said William Baker, more loudly.

"—your secretary said you didn't have no appointments but I said I'd wait."

"Strike!" barked William Baker, calling his dog to heel.

"Robin," snarled the exhausted Strike, losing his temper at last. "Make up Mr. Baker's bill and give him the file; it's up to date."

"What?" said William Baker, thrown. He reemerged into the outer office.

"He's sacking you," said Leonora Quine with satisfaction.

"You haven't finished the job," Baker told Strike. "You said there was more—"

"Someone else can finish the job for you. Someone who doesn't mind tossers as clients."

The atmosphere in the office seemed to become petrified.

Wooden-faced, Robin retrieved Baker's file from the outer cabinet and handed it to Strike.

"How *dare*—"

"There's a lot of good stuff in that file that'll stand up in court," said Strike, handing it to the director. "Well worth the money."

"You haven't finished—"

"He's finished with *you*," interjected Leonora Quine.

"Will you shut up, you stupid wom—" William Baker began, then took a sudden step backwards as Strike took a half-step forwards. Nobody said anything. The ex-serviceman seemed suddenly to be filling twice as much space as he had just seconds before.

"Take a seat in my office, Mrs. Quine," said Strike quietly.

She did as she was told.

"You think she'll be able to afford you?" sneered a retreating William Baker, his hand now on the door handle.

"My fees are negotiable," said Strike, "if I like the client."

He followed Leonora Quine into his office and closed the door behind him with a snap.

3

...left alone to bear up all these ills...

Thomas Dekker, *The Noble Spanish Soldier*

"He's a right one, isn't he?" commented Leonora Quine as she sat down in the chair facing Strike's desk.

"Yeah," agreed Strike, sinking heavily into the seat opposite her. "He is."

In spite of a barely crumpled pink-and-white complexion and the clear whites of her pale blue eyes, she looked around fifty. Fine, limp, graying hair was held off her face by two plastic combs and she was blinking at him through old-fashioned glasses with overlarge plastic frames. Her coat, though clean, had surely been bought in the eighties. It had shoulder pads and large plastic buttons.

"So you're here about your husband, Mrs. Quine?"

"Yeah," said Leonora. "He's missing."

"How long's he been gone?" asked Strike, reaching automatically for a notebook.

"Ten days," said Leonora.

"Have you been to the police?"

"I don't need the police," she said impatiently, as though she was tired of explaining this to people. "I called them once before and everyone was angry at me because he was only with a friend. Owen just goes off sometimes. He's a writer," she said, as though this explained everything.

"He's disappeared before?"

12

"He's emotional," she said, her expression glum. "He's always going off on one, but it's been ten days and I know he's really upset but I need him home now. There's Orlando and I've got things to do and there's—"

"Orlando?" repeated Strike, his tired mind on the Florida resort. He did not have time to go to America and Leonora Quine, in her ancient coat, certainly did not look as though she could afford a ticket for him.

"Our daughter, Orlando," said Leonora. "She needs looking after. I've got a neighbor in to sit with her while I'm here."

There was a knock on the door and Robin's bright gold head appeared.

"Would you like coffee, Mr. Strike? You, Mrs. Quine?"

When they had given Robin their orders and she had withdrawn, Leonora said:

"It won't take you long, because I think I know where he is, only I can't get hold of the address and nobody'll take my calls. It's been ten days," she repeated, "and we need him home."

It seemed to Strike a great extravagance to resort to a private detective in this circumstance, especially as her appearance exhaled poverty.

"If it's a simple question of making a phone call," he said gently, "haven't you got a friend or a—?"

"Edna can't do it," she said and he found himself disproportionately touched (exhaustion sometimes laid him raw in this way) at her tacit admission that she had one friend in the world. "Owen's told them not to say where he is. I need," she said simply, "a man to do it. Force them to say."

"Your husband's name's Owen, is it?"

"Yeah," she replied, "Owen Quine. He wrote *Hobart's Sin*."

Neither name nor title meant anything to Strike.

"And you think you know where he is?"

"Yeah. We was at this party with a load of publishers and people—he didn't want to take me, but I says, 'I got a babysitter already, I'm coming'—so I hears Christian Fisher telling Owen about this place, this writer's retreat place. And afterwards I says to Owen, 'What was that place he was telling you about?' and Owen says, 'I'm not telling you, that's the whole bloody point, getting away from the wife and kids.'"

She almost invited Strike to join her husband in laughing at her; proud, as mothers sometimes pretend to be, of their child's insolence.

"Who's Christian Fisher?" asked Strike, forcing himself to concentrate.

"Publisher. Young, trendy bloke."

"Have you tried phoning Fisher and asking him for the address of this retreat?"

"Yeah, I've called him every day for a week and they said they'd taken a message and he'd get back to me, but he hasn't. I think Owen's told him not to say where he is. But *you'll* be able to get the address out of Fisher. I know you're good," she said. "You solved that Lula Landry thing, when the police never."

A mere eight months previously, Strike had had but a single client, his business had been moribund and his prospects desperate. Then he had proven, to the satisfaction of the Crown Prosecution Service, that a famous young woman had not committed suicide but had been pushed to her death from a fourth-floor balcony. The ensuing publicity had brought a tide of business; he had been, for a few weeks, the best-known private detective in the metropolis. Jonny Rokeby had become a mere footnote to his story; Strike had become a name in his own right, albeit a name most people got wrong...

"I interrupted you," he said, trying hard to hold on to the thread of his thoughts.

"Did you?"

"Yeah," said Strike, squinting at his own crabbed writing on the notebook. "You said, 'There's Orlando, I've got things to do and there's—'"

"Oh yeah," she said, "there's funny stuff happening since he left."

"What kind of funny stuff?"

"Shit," said Leonora Quine matter-of-factly, "through our letter box."

"Someone's put excrement through your letter box?" Strike said.
"Yeah."

"Since your husband disappeared?"

"Yeah. Dog," said Leonora, and it was a split second before Strike deduced that this applied to the excrement, not her husband. "Three or four times now, at night. Nice thing to find in the morning, I don't think. And there was a woman come to the door and all, who was weird."

She paused, waiting for Strike to prompt her. She seemed to enjoy being questioned. Many lonely people, Strike knew, found it pleasant to be the focus of somebody's undivided attention and sought to prolong the novel experience.

"When did this woman come to the door?"

"Last week it was, and she asks for Owen and when I says, 'He's not here,' she says, 'Tell him Angela died,' and walks off."

"And you didn't know her?"

"Never seen her before."

"Do you know an Angela?"

"No. But he gets women fans going funny over him, sometimes," said Leonora, suddenly expansive. "Like, he had this woman once that wrote him letters and sent him photos of herself dressed up like one of his characters. Some of these women who write to him think he understands them or something because of his books. Silly, innit?" she said. "It's all made up."

"Do fans usually know where your husband lives?"

"No," said Leonora. "But she could've bin a student or something. He teaches writing as well, sometimes."

The door opened and Robin entered with a tray. After putting black coffee in front of Strike and a tea in front of Leonora Quine, she withdrew again, closing the door behind her.

"Is that everything strange that's happened?" Strike asked Leonora. "The excrement through the door, and this woman coming to the house?"

"And I think I've been followed. Tall, dark girl with round shoulders," said Leonora.

"This is a different woman to the one—?"

"Yeah, the one that come to the house was dumpy. Long red hair. This one's dark and bent over, like."

"You're sure she was following you?"

"Yeah, I think so. I seen her behind me two, three times now. She isn't local, I've never seen her before and I've lived in Ladbroke Grove thirty-odd years."

15

"OK," said Strike slowly. "You said your husband's upset? What happened to upset him?"

"He had a massive row with his agent."

"What about, do you know?"

"His book, his latest. Liz—that's his agent—tells him it's the best thing he's ever done, and then, like, a day later, she takes him out to dinner and says it's unpublishable."

"Why did she change her mind?"

"Ask *her*," said Leonora, showing anger for the first time. "Course he was upset after that. Anyone would be. He's worked on that book for two years. He comes home in a right state and he goes into his study and grabs it all—"

"Grabs what?"

"His book, the manuscript and his notes and everything, swearing his head off, and he shoves them in a bag and he goes off and I haven't seen him since."

"Has he got a mobile? Have you tried calling him?"

"Yeah and he's not picking up. He never does, when he goes off like this. He chucked his phone out the car window once," she said, again with that faint note of pride at her husband's spirit.

"Mrs. Quine," said Strike, whose altruism necessarily had its limits, whatever he had told William Baker, "I'll be honest with you: I don't come cheap."

"That's all right," said Leonora implacably. "Liz'll pay."

"Liz?"

"*Liz*—Elizabeth Tassel. Owen's agent. It's her fault he's gone away. She can take it out of her commission. He's her best client. She'll want him back all right, once she realizes what she's done."

Strike did not set as much store by this assurance as Leonora herself seemed to. He added three sugars to the coffee and gulped it down, trying to think how best to proceed. He felt vaguely sorry for Leonora Quine, who seemed inured to her erratic husband's tantrums, who accepted the fact that nobody would deign to return her calls, who was sure that the only help she could expect must be paid for. Her slight eccentricity of manner aside, there was a truculent honesty about her. Nevertheless, he had been ruthless in taking on only profitable cases since his business had received its unexpected boost. Those few people who had come to him with hard-luck stories, hoping that his own personal difficulties (reported and embellished in the press) would predispose him to helping them free of charge, had left disappointed.

But Leonora Quine, who had drunk her tea quite as quickly as Strike had downed his coffee, was already on her feet, as though they had agreed to terms and everything was settled.

"I'd better get going," she said, "I don't like leaving Orlando too long. She's missing her daddy. I've told her I'm getting a man to go find him."

Strike had recently helped several wealthy young women rid themselves of City husbands who had become much less attractive to them since the financial crash. There was something appealing about restoring a husband to a wife, for a change.

"All right," he said, yawning as he pushed his notebook towards her. "I'll need your contact details, Mrs. Quine. A photograph of your husband would be handy too."

She wrote her address and telephone number out for him in a round, childish hand, but his request for a photo seemed to surprise her.

"What d'you need a picture for? He's at that writer's retreat. Just make Christian Fisher tell you where it is."

She was through the door before Strike, tired and sore, could emerge from behind his desk. He heard her say briskly to Robin: "Ta for the tea," then the glass door onto the landing opened with a flash and closed with a gentle judder, and his new client had gone.

4

Well, 'tis a rare thing to have an ingenious friend...

William Congreve, *The Double-Dealer*

Strike dropped onto the sofa in the outer office. It was almost new, an essential expense as he had broken the secondhand one with which he had initially furnished the office. Covered in mock leather that he had thought smart in the showroom, it made farting noises if you moved on it in the wrong way. His assistant—tall, curvaceous, with a clear, brilliant complexion and bright blue-gray eyes—scrutinized him over her coffee cup.

"You look terrible."

"Spent all night weaseling details of a peer of the realm's sexual irregularities and financial malfeasance out of a hysterical woman," said Strike, on a massive yawn.

"Lord Parker?" gasped Robin.

"That's the one," said Strike.

"He's been—?"

"Shagging three women simultaneously and salting millions away offshore," said Strike. "If you've got a strong stomach, try the *News of the World* this Sunday."

"How on earth did you find all that out?"

"Contact of a contact of a contact," intoned Strike.

He yawned again, so widely that it looked painful.

"You should go to bed," said Robin.

"Yeah, I should," said Strike, but he did not move.

"You haven't got anyone else till Gunfrey this afternoon at two."

"Gunfrey," sighed Strike, massaging his eye sockets. "Why are all my clients shits?"

"Mrs. Quine doesn't seem like a shit."

He peered blearily at her through his thick fingers.

"How d'you know I took her case?"

"I knew you would," said Robin with an irrepressible smirk. "She's your type."

"A middle-aged throwback to the eighties?"

"Your kind of client. And you wanted to spite Baker."

"Seemed to work, didn't it?"

The telephone rang. Still grinning, Robin answered.

"Cormoran Strike's office," she said. "Oh. Hi."

It was her fiancé, Matthew. She glanced sideways at her boss. Strike had closed his eyes and tilted his head back, his arms folded across his broad chest.

"Listen," said Matthew in Robin's ear; he never sounded very friendly when calling from work. "I need to move drinks from Friday to Thursday."

"Oh Matt," she said, trying to keep both disappointment and exasperation out of her voice.

It would be the fifth time that arrangements for these particular drinks had been made. Robin alone, of the three people involved, had not altered time, date or venue, but had shown herself willing and available on every occasion.

"Why?" she muttered.

A sudden grunting snore issued from the sofa. Strike had fallen asleep where he sat, his large head tilted back against the wall, arms still folded.

"Work drinks on the nineteenth," said Matthew. "It'll look bad if I don't go. Show my face."

She fought the urge to snap at him. He worked for a major firm of accountants and sometimes he acted as though this imposed social obligations more appropriate to a diplomatic posting.

She was sure that she knew the real reason for the change. Drinks had been postponed repeatedly at Strike's request; on each occasion he had been busy with some piece of urgent, evening work, and while the excuses had been genuine, they had irritated Matthew. Though he had never said it aloud, Robin knew that Matthew thought Strike was implying that his time was more valuable than Matthew's, his job more important.

In the eight months that she had worked for Cormoran Strike, her boss and her fiancé had not met, not even on that infamous night when Matthew had picked her up from the casualty department where she had accompanied Strike, with her coat wrapped tightly around his stabbed arm after a cornered killer had tried to finish him. When she had emerged, shaken and bloodstained, from the place where they were stitching Strike up, Matthew had declined her offer to introduce him to her injured boss. He had been furious about the whole business, even though Robin had reassured him that she herself had never been in any danger.

Matthew had never wanted her to take a permanent job with Strike, whom he had regarded with suspicion from the first, disliking his penury, his homelessness and the profession that Matthew seemed to find absurd. The little snatches of information that Robin brought home—Strike's career in the Special Investigation Branch, the plain-clothes wing of the Royal Military Police, his decoration for bravery, the loss of his lower right leg, the expertise in a hundred areas of which Matthew—so used to being expert in her eyes—knew little or nothing—had not (as she had innocently hoped) built a bridge between the two men, but had somehow reinforced the wall between them.

Strike's burst of fame, his sudden shift from failure to success, had if anything deepened Matthew's animosity. Robin realized belatedly that she had only exacerbated matters by pointing out Matthew's inconsistencies: "You don't like him being homeless and poor and now you don't like him getting famous and bringing in loads of work!"

But Strike's worst crime in Matthew's eyes, as she well knew, was the clinging designer dress that her boss had bought her after their trip to the hospital, the one that he had intended as a gift of gratitude and farewell, and which, after showing it to Matthew with pride and delight, and seeing his reaction, she had never dared wear.

All of this Robin hoped to fix with a face-to-face meeting, but repeated cancellations by Strike had merely deepened Matthew's dislike. On the last occasion, Strike had simply failed to turn up. His excuse—that he had been forced to take a detour to shake off a tail set on him by his client's suspicious spouse—had been accepted by Robin, who knew the intricacies of that particularly bloody divorce case, but it had reinforced Matthew's view of Strike as attention-seeking and arrogant.

She had had some difficulty in persuading Matthew to commit to a fourth attempt at drinks. Time and venue had both been picked by Matthew, but now, after Robin had secured Strike's agreement all over again, Matthew was changing the night and it was impossible not to feel that he was doing it to make a point, to show Strike that he too had other commitments; that he too (Robin could not help herself thinking it) could piss people around.

"Fine," she sighed into the phone, "I'll check with Cormoran and see whether Thursday's OK."

"You don't sound like it's fine."

"Matt, don't start. I'll ask him, OK?"

"I'll see you later, then."

Robin replaced the receiver. Strike was now in full throat, snoring like a traction engine with his mouth open, legs wide apart, feet flat on the floor, arms folded.

She sighed, looking at her sleeping boss. Strike had never shown any animosity towards Matthew, had never passed comment on him in any way. It was Matthew who brooded over the existence of Strike, who rarely lost an opportunity to point out that Robin could have earned a great deal more if she had taken any of the other jobs she had been offered before deciding to stay with a rackety private detective, deep in debt and unable to pay her what she deserved. It would ease her home life considerably if Matthew could be brought to share her opinion of Cormoran Strike, to like him, even admire him. Robin was optimistic: she liked both of them, so why could they not like each other?

With a sudden snort, Strike was awake. He opened his eyes and blinked at her.

"I was snoring," he stated, wiping his mouth.

"Not much," she lied. "Listen, Cormoran, would it be all right if we move drinks from Friday to Thursday?"

"Drinks?"

"With Matthew and me," she said. "Remember? The King's Arms, Roupell Street. I did write it down for you," she said, with a slightly forced cheeriness.

"Right," he said. "Yeah. Friday."

"No, Matt wants—he can't do Friday. Is it OK to do Thursday instead?"

"Yeah, fine," he said groggily. "I think I'm going to try and get some sleep, Robin."

"All right. I'll make a note about Thursday."

"What's happening on Thursday?"

"Drinks with—oh, never mind. Go and sleep."

She sat staring blankly at her computer screen after the glass door had closed, then jumped as it opened again.

"Robin, could you call a bloke called Christian Fisher," said Strike. "Tell him who I am, tell him I'm looking for Owen Quine and that I need the address of the writer's retreat he told Quine about?"

"Christian Fisher... where does he work?"

"Bugger," muttered Strike. "I never asked. I'm so knackered. He's a publisher... trendy publisher."

"No problem, I'll find him. Go and sleep."

When the glass door had closed a second time, Robin turned her attention to Google. Within thirty seconds she had discovered that Christian Fisher was the founder of a small press called Crossfire, based in Exmouth Market.

As she dialed the publisher's number, she thought of the wedding invitation that had been sitting in her handbag for a week now. Robin had not told Strike the date of her and Matthew's wedding, nor had she told Matthew that she wished to invite her boss. If Thursday's drinks went well...

"*Crossfire*," said a shrill voice on the line. Robin focused her attention on the job in hand.

5

There's nothing of so infinite vexation
As man's own thoughts.

John Webster, *The White Devil*

Twenty past nine that evening found Strike lying in a T-shirt and boxers on top of his duvet, with the remnants of a takeaway curry on the chair beside him, reading the sports pages while the news played on the TV he had set up facing the bed. The metal rod that served as his right ankle gleamed silver in the light from the cheap desk lamp he had placed on a box beside him.

There was to be an England–France friendly at Wembley on Wednesday night, but Strike was much more interested in Arsenal's home derby against Spurs the following Saturday. He had been an Arsenal fan since his earliest youth, in imitation of his Uncle Ted. Why Uncle Ted supported the Gunners, when he had lived all his life in Cornwall, was a question Strike had never asked.

A misty radiance, through which stars were struggling to twinkle, filled the night sky beyond the tiny window beside him. A few hours' sleep in the middle of the day had done virtually nothing to alleviate his exhaustion, but he did not feel quite ready to turn in yet, not after a large lamb biryani and a pint of beer. A note in Robin's handwriting lay beside him on the bed; she had given it to him as he had left the office that evening. Two appointments were noted there. The first read:

Christian Fisher, 9 a.m. tomorrow, Crossfire Publishing,
Exmouth Market EC1

ROBERT GALBRAITH

"Why's he want to see me?" Strike had asked her, surprised. "I only need the address of that retreat he told Quine about."

"I know," said Robin, "that's what I told him, but he sounded really excited to meet you. He said he could do nine tomorrow and wouldn't take no for an answer."

What, Strike asked himself irritably, staring at the note, *was I playing at?*

Exhausted, he had allowed temper to get the better of him that morning and ditched a well-heeled client who might well have put more work his way. Then he had allowed Leonora Quine to steam-roller him into accepting her as a client on the most dubious promise of payment. Now that she was not in front of him, it was hard to remember the mixture of pity and curiosity that had made him take her case on. In the stark, cold quiet of his attic room, his agreement to find her sulking husband seemed quixotic and irresponsible. Wasn't the whole point of trying to pay off his debts that he could regain a sliver of free time: a Saturday afternoon at the Emirates, a Sunday lie-in? He was finally making money after working almost nonstop for months, attracting clients not only because of that first glaring bout of notoriety but because of a quieter word-of-mouth. Couldn't he have put up with William Baker for another three weeks?

And what, Strike asked himself, looking down at Robin's handwritten note again, was this Christian Fisher so excited about that he wanted to meet in person? Could it be Strike himself, either as the solver of the Lula Landry case or (much worse) as the son of Jonny Rokeby? It was very difficult to gauge the level of your own celebrity. Strike had assumed that his burst of unexpected fame was on the wane. It had been intense while it lasted, but the telephone calls from journalists had subsided months ago and it was almost as long since he had given his name in any neutral context and heard Lula Landry's back. Strangers were once again doing what they had done most of his life: calling him some variation on "Cameron Strick."

On the other hand, perhaps the publisher knew something about the vanished Owen Quine that he was eager to impart to Strike, although why, in this case, he had refused to tell Quine's wife, Strike could not imagine.

24

The second appointment that Robin had written out for him was beneath Fisher's:

Thursday November 18th, 6.30 p.m., The King's Arms,
25 Roupell Street, SE1

Strike knew why she had written the date out so clearly: she was determined that this time—was it the third or fourth time they'd tried?—he and her fiancé would finally meet.

Little though the unknown accountant might believe it, Strike was grateful for Matthew's mere existence, and for the sapphire and diamond ring that shone from Robin's third finger. Matthew sounded like a dickhead (Robin little imagined how accurately Strike remembered each of her casual asides about her fiancé), but he imposed a useful barrier between Strike and a girl who might otherwise disturb his equilibrium.

Strike had not been able to guard against warm feelings for Robin, who had stuck by him when he was at his lowest ebb and helped him turn his fortunes around; nor, having normal eyesight, could he escape the fact that she was a very good-looking woman. He viewed her engagement as the means by which a thin, persistent draft is blocked up, something that might, if allowed to flow untrammeled, start to seriously disturb his comfort. Strike considered himself to be in recovery after a long, turbulent relationship that had ended, as indeed it had begun, in lies. He had no wish to alter his single status, which he found comfortable and convenient, and had successfully avoided any further emotional entanglements for months, in spite of his sister Lucy's attempts to fix him up with women who sounded like the desperate dregs of some dating site.

Of course, it was possible that once Matthew and Robin were actually married, Matthew might use his improved status to persuade his new wife to leave the job that he clearly disliked her doing (Strike had correctly interpreted Robin's hesitations and evasions on that score). However, Strike was sure that Robin would have told him, had the wedding date been fixed, so he considered that danger, at present, remote.

With yet another huge yawn, he folded the newspaper and threw it onto the chair, turning his attention to the television news. His one personal extravagance since moving into the tiny attic flat had been satellite TV. His small portable set now sat on top of a Sky box and the picture, no longer reliant on a feeble indoor aerial, was sharp instead of grainy. Kenneth Clarke, the Justice Secretary, was announcing plans to slash £350 million from the legal aid budget. Strike watched through his haze of tiredness as the florid, paunchy man told Parliament that he wished to "discourage people from resorting to lawyers whenever they face a problem, and instead encourage them to consider more suitable methods of dispute resolution."

He meant, of course, that poor people ought to relinquish the services of the law. The likes of Strike's average client would still avail themselves of expensive barristers. Most of his work these days was undertaken on behalf of the mistrustful, endlessly betrayed rich. His was the information that fed their sleek lawyers, that enabled them to win better settlements in their vitriolic divorces and their acrimonious business disputes. A steady stream of well-heeled clients was passing his name on to similar men and women, with tediously similar difficulties; this was the reward for distinction in his particular line of work, and if it was often repetitive, it was also lucrative.

When the news ended he clambered laboriously off the bed, removed the remnants of his meal from the chair beside him and walked stiffly into his small kitchen area to wash everything up. He never neglected such things: habits of self-respect learned in the army had not left him in the depths of his poverty, nor were they entirely due to military training. He had been a tidy boy, imitating his Uncle Ted, whose liking for order everywhere from his toolbox to his boathouse had contrasted so starkly with the chaos that had surrounded Strike's mother, Leda.

Within ten minutes, after a last pee in the toilet that was always sodden because of its proximity to the shower, and cleaning his teeth at the kitchen sink where there was more room, Strike was back on his bed, removing his prosthesis.

The weather forecast for the next day was rounding off the news: subzero temperatures and fog. Strike rubbed powder into the end of his amputated leg; it was less sore tonight than it had been a few months ago. Today's full English breakfast and takeaway curry notwithstanding, he had lost a bit of weight since he had been able to cook for himself again, and this had eased the pressure on his leg.

He pointed the remote control at the TV screen; a laughing blonde and her washing powder vanished into blankness. Strike maneuvered himself clumsily beneath the covers.

Of course, if Owen Quine was hiding at his writer's retreat it would be easy enough to winkle him out. Egotistical bastard, he sounded, flouncing off into the darkness with his precious book . . .

The hazy mental image of a furious man storming away with a holdall over his shoulder dissolved almost as quickly as it had formed. Strike was sliding into a welcome, deep and dreamless sleep. The faint pulse of a bass guitar far below in the subterranean bar was swiftly drowned by his own rasping snores.

6

Oh, Mr. Tattle, every thing is safe with you, we know.

William Congreve, *Love for Love*

Wads of icy mist were still clinging to the buildings of Exmouth Market when Strike turned into it at ten to nine the following morning. It did not feel like a London street, not with pavement seating outside its many cafés, pastel-painted façades and a basilica-like church, gold, blue and brick: Church of Our Most Holy Redeemer, wreathed in smoky vapor. Chilly fog, shops full of curios, curbside tables and chairs; if he could have added the tang of saltwater and the mournful screech of seagulls he might have thought himself back in Cornwall, where he had spent the most stable parts of his childhood.

A small sign on a nondescript door beside a bakery announced the offices of Crossfire Publishing. Strike buzzed the bell promptly at nine o'clock and was admitted to a steep whitewashed staircase, up which he clambered with some difficulty and with liberal use of the handrail.

He was met on the top landing by a slight, dandyish and bespectacled man of around thirty. He had wavy, shoulder-length hair and wore jeans, a waistcoat and a paisley shirt with a touch of frill around the cuffs.

"Hi there," he said. "I'm Christian Fisher. Cameron, isn't it?"

"Cormoran," Strike corrected him automatically, "but—"

He had been about to say that he answered to Cameron, a stock response to years of the mistake, but Christian Fisher came back at once:

28

"Cormoran—Cornish giant."

"That's right," said Strike, surprised.

"We published a kids' book on English folklore last year," said Fisher, pushing open white double doors and leading Strike into a cluttered, open-plan space with walls plastered in posters and many untidy bookshelves. A scruffy young woman with dark hair looked up curiously at Strike as he walked past.

"Coffee? Tea?" offered Fisher, leading Strike into his own office, a small room off the main area with a pleasant view over the sleepy, foggy street. "I can get Jade to nip out for us." Strike declined, saying truthfully that he had just had coffee, but wondering, too, why Fisher seemed to be settling in for a longer meeting than Strike felt the circumstances justified. "Just a latte, then, Jade," Fisher called through the door.

"Have a seat," Fisher said to Strike, and he began to flit around the bookshelves that lined the walls. "Didn't he live in St. Michael's Mount, the giant Cormoran?"

"Yeah," said Strike. "And Jack's supposed to have killed him. Of beanstalk fame."

"It's here somewhere," said Fisher, still searching the shelves. "*Folk Tales of the British Isles*. Have you got kids?"

"No," said Strike.

"Oh," said Fisher. "Well, I won't bother, then."

And with a grin he took the chair opposite Strike.

"So, am I allowed to ask who's hired you? Am I allowed to guess?"

"Feel free," said Strike, who on principle never forbade speculation.

"It's either Daniel Chard or Michael Fancourt," said Fisher. "Am I right?"

The lenses on his glasses gave his eyes a concentrated, beady look. Though giving no outward sign, Strike was taken aback. Michael Fancourt was a very famous writer who had recently won a major literary prize. Why exactly would he be interested in the missing Quine?

"Afraid not," said Strike. "It's Quine's wife, Leonora."

Fisher looked almost comically astonished.

"His wife?" he repeated blankly. "That mousy woman who looks like Rose West? What's *she* hired a private detective for?"

"Her husband's disappeared. He's been gone eleven days."

"Quine's *disappeared?* But—but then..."

Strike could tell Fisher had been anticipating a very different conversation, one to which he had been eagerly looking forward.

"But why's she sent you to me?"

"She thinks you know where Quine is."

"How the hell would I know?" asked Fisher, and he appeared genuinely bewildered. "He's not a friend of mine."

"Mrs. Quine says she heard you telling her husband about a writer's retreat, at a party—"

"*Oh,*" said Fisher, "Bigley Hall, yeah. But Owen won't be *there!*" When he laughed, he was transformed into a bespectacled Puck: merriment laced with slyness. "They wouldn't let Owen Quine in if he paid them. Born shit-stirrer. And one of the women who runs the place hates his guts. He wrote a stinking review of her first novel and she's never forgiven him."

"Could you give me the number anyway?" asked Strike.

"I've got it on here," said Fisher, pulling a mobile out of the back pocket of his jeans. "I'll call now..."

And he did so, setting the mobile on the desk between them and switching it on to speakerphone for Strike's benefit. After a full minute of ringing, a breathless female voice answered:

"Bigley Hall."

"Hi, is that Shannon? It's Chris Fisher here, from Crossfire."

"Oh, hi Chris, how's it going?"

The door of Fisher's office opened and the scruffy dark girl from outside came in, wordlessly placed a latte in front of Fisher and departed.

"I'm phoning, Shan," Fisher said, as the door clicked shut, "to see if you've got Owen Quine staying. He hasn't turned up there, has he?"

"*Quine?*"

Even reduced to a distant and tinny monosyllable, Shannon's dislike echoed scornfully around the book-lined room.

"Yeah, have you seen him?"

"Not for a year or more. Why? He's not thinking of coming here, is he? He won't be bloody welcome, I can tell you that."

"No worries, Shan, I think his wife's got hold of the wrong end of the stick. Speak soon."

Fisher cut off her farewells, keen to return to Strike.

"See?" he said. "Told you. He couldn't go to Bigley Hall if he wanted to."

"Couldn't you have told his wife that, when she phoned you up?"

"Oh, *that's* what she kept calling about!" said Fisher with an air of dawning comprehension. "I thought *Owen* was making her call me."

"Why would he make his wife phone you?"

"Oh, come on," said Fisher, with a grin, and when Strike did not grin back, he laughed shortly and said, "Because of *Bombyx Mori*. I thought it'd be typical of Quine to try to get his wife to call me and sound me out."

"*Bombyx Mori*," repeated Strike, trying to sound neither interrogative nor puzzled.

"Yeah, I thought Quine was pestering me to see whether there was still a chance I'd publish it. It's the sort of thing he'd do, make his wife ring. But if anyone's going to touch *Bombyx Mori* now, it won't be me. We're a small outfit. We can't afford court cases."

Gaining nothing from pretending to know more than he did, Strike changed tack.

"*Bombyx Mori*'s Quine's latest novel?"

"Yeah," said Fisher, taking a sip of his takeaway latte, following his own train of thought. "So he's disappeared, has he? I'd've thought he'd want to stick around and watch the fun. I'd've thought that was the whole point. Or has he lost his nerve? Doesn't sound like Owen."

"How long have you published Quine?" asked Strike. Fisher looked at him incredulously.

"I've never published him!" he said.

"I thought—"

"He's been with Roper Chard for his last three books—or is it four? No, what happened was, I was at a party with Liz Tassel, his agent, a few months ago, and she told me in confidence—she'd had a few—that she didn't know how much longer Roper Chard were going to put up with him, so I said I'd be happy to have a look at his next one. Quine's in the so-bad-he's-good category these days—we could've done something offbeat with the marketing. Anyway," said Fisher, "there *was Hobart's Sin*. That was a good book. I figured he might still have something in him."

"Did she send you *Bombyx Mori*?" asked Strike, feeling his way and inwardly cursing himself for the lack of thoroughness with which he had questioned Leonora Quine the previous day. This was what came of taking on clients when you were three parts dead of exhaustion. Strike was used to coming to interviews knowing more than the interviewee and he felt curiously exposed.

"Yeah, she biked me over a copy Friday before last," said Fisher, his Puckish smirk slier than ever. "Biggest mistake of poor Liz's life."

"Why?"

"Because she obviously hadn't read it properly, or not all the way to the end. About two hours after it arrived I got this very panicky message on my phone: 'Chris, there's been a mistake, I've sent the wrong manuscript. Please don't read it, could you just send it straight back, I'll be at the office to take it.' I've never heard Liz Tassel like that in my life. Very scary woman usually. Makes grown men cower."

"And did you send it back?"

"Course not," said Fisher. "I spent most of Saturday reading it."

"And?" asked Strike.

"Hasn't anyone told you?"

"Told me ... ?"

"What's in there," said Fisher. "What he's done."

"What has he done?"

Fisher's smile faded. He put down his coffee.

"I've been warned," he said, "by some of London's top lawyers not to disclose that."

"Who's employing the lawyers?" asked Strike. When Fisher didn't answer, he added, "Anyone apart from Chard and Fancourt?"

"It's just Chard," said Fisher, toppling easily into Strike's trap. "Though I'd be more worried about Fancourt if I were Owen. He can be an evil bastard. Never forgets a grudge. Don't quote me," he added hastily.

"And the Chard you're talking about?" said Strike, groping in semidarkness.

32

"Daniel Chard, CEO of Roper Chard," said Fisher, with a trace of impatience. "I don't understand how Owen thought he'd get away with screwing over the man who runs his publisher, but that's Owen for you. He's the most monumentally arrogant, deluded bastard I've ever met. I suppose he thought he could depict Chard as—"

Fisher broke off with an uneasy laugh.

"I'm a danger to myself. Let's just say I'm surprised that even Owen thought he'd get away with it. Maybe he lost his nerve when he realized everyone knew exactly what he was hinting at and that's why he's done a runner."

"It's libelous, is it?" Strike asked.

"Bit of a gray area in fiction, isn't it?" asked Fisher. "If you tell the truth in a grotesque way—not that I'm suggesting," he added hastily, "that the stuff he's saying is *true*. It couldn't be *literally* true. But everyone's recognizable; he's done over quite a few people and in a very clever way ... It feels a lot like Fancourt's early stuff, actually. Load of gore and arcane symbolism ... you can't see quite what he's getting at in some places, but you want to know, what's in the bag, what's in the fire?"

"What's in the—?"

"Never mind—it's just stuff in the book. Didn't Leonora tell you any of this?"

"No," said Strike.

"Bizarre," said Christian Fisher, "she must *know*. I'd've thought Quine's the sort of writer who lectures the family on his work at every mealtime."

"Why did you think Chard or Fancourt would hire a private detective, when you didn't know Quine was missing?"

Fisher shrugged.

"I dunno. I thought maybe one of them was trying to find out what he's planning to do with the book, so they could stop him, or warn the new publisher they'll sue. Or that they might be hoping to get something on Owen—fight fire with fire."

"Is that why you were so keen to see me?" asked Strike. "Have you got something on Quine?"

"No," said Fisher with a laugh. "I'm just nosy. Wanted to know what's going on."

He checked his watch, turned over a copy of a book cover in front of him and pushed out his chair a little. Strike took the hint.

"Thanks for your time," he said, standing up. "If you hear from Owen Quine, will you let me know?"

He handed Fisher a card. Fisher frowned at it as he moved around his desk to show Strike out.

"Cormoran Strike … *Strike* … I know that name, don't I … ?"

The penny dropped. Fisher was suddenly reanimated, as though his batteries had been changed.

"Bloody hell, you're the Lula Landry guy!"

Strike knew that he could have sat back down, ordered a latte and enjoyed Fisher's undivided attention for another hour or so. Instead, he extricated himself with firm friendliness and, within a few minutes, reemerged alone on the cold misty street.

7

I'll be sworn, I was ne'er guilty of reading the like.

Ben Jonson, *Every Man in His Humour*

When informed by telephone that her husband was not, after all, at the writer's retreat, Leonora Quine sounded anxious.

"Where is he, then?" she asked, more of herself, it seemed, than Strike.

"Where does he usually go when he walks out?" Strike asked.

"Hotels," she said, "and once he was staying with some woman but he don't know her no more. Orlando," she said sharply, away from the receiver, "put that *down*, it's mine. I said, it's *mine*. What?" she said, loudly in Strike's ear.

"I didn't say anything. D'you want me to keep looking for your husband?"

"Course I do, who else is gonna bloody find him? I can't leave Orlando. Ask Liz Tassel where he is. She found him before. Hilton," said Leonora unexpectedly. "He was at the Hilton once."

"Which Hilton?"

"I dunno, ask Liz. She made him go off, she should be bloody helping bring him back. She won't take my calls. Orlando, *put it down*."

"Is there anyone else you can think—?"

"No, or I'd've bloody asked them, wouldn't I?" snapped Leonora. "You're the detective, you find him! *Orlando!*"

"Mrs. Quine, we've got—"

"Call me Leonora."

"Leonora, we've got to consider the possibility that your husband might have done himself an injury. We'd find him more quickly," said Strike, raising his voice over the domestic clamor at the other end of the line, "if we involved the police."

"I don't wanna. I called them that time he was gone a week and he turned up at his lady friend's and they weren't happy. He'll be angry if I do that again. Anyway, Owen wouldn't—*Orlando, leave it!*"

"The police could circulate his picture more effectively and—"

"I just want him home quietly. Why doesn't he just come back?" she added pettishly. "He's had time to calm down."

"Have you read your husband's new book?" Strike asked.

"No. I always wait till they're finished and I can read 'em with proper covers on and everything."

"Has he told you anything about it?"

"No, he don't like talking about work while he's—*Orlando, put it down!*"

He was not sure whether she had hung up deliberately or not.

The fog of early morning had lifted. Rain was speckling his office windows. A client was due imminently, yet another divorcing woman who wanted to know where her soon-to-be-ex-husband was burying assets.

"Robin," said Strike, emerging into the outer office, "will you print me out a picture of Owen Quine off the internet, if you can find one? And call his agent, Elizabeth Tassel, and see if she's willing to answer a few quick questions."

About to return to his own office, he thought of something else.

"And could you look up 'bombyx mori' for me, and see what it means?"

"How are you spelling that?"

"God knows," said Strike.

The soon-to-be divorcée arrived on time, at eleven thirty. She was a suspiciously youthful-looking forty-something who exuded fluttery charm and a musky scent that always made the office feel cramped to Robin. Strike disappeared into his office with her, and for two hours Robin heard only the gentle rise and fall of their voices over the steady thrumming of the rain and the tapping of her fingers on the keyboard; calm and placid sounds. Robin had become used to hearing sudden outbreaks of tears, moans, even shouting from Strike's office. Sudden silences could be the most ominous of all, as when a male client had literally fainted (and, they had learned later, suffered a minor heart attack) on seeing the photographs of his wife and her lover that Strike had taken through a long lens.

When Strike and his client emerged at last, and she had taken fulsome farewell of him, Robin handed her boss a large picture of Owen Quine, taken from the website of the Bath Literature Festival.

"Jesus Christ almighty," said Strike.

Owen Quine was a large, pale and portly man of around sixty, with straggly yellow-white hair and a pointed Van Dyke beard. His eyes appeared to be of different colors, which gave a peculiar intensity to his stare. For the photograph he had wrapped himself in what seemed to be a Tyrolean cape and was wearing a feather-trimmed trilby.

"You wouldn't think he'd be able to stay incognito for long," commented Strike. "Can you make a few copies of this, Robin? We might have to show it around hotels. His wife thinks he once stayed at a Hilton, but she can't remember which one, so could you start ringing round to see if he's booked in? Can't imagine he'd use his own name, but you could try describing him . . . Any luck with Elizabeth Tassel?"

"Yes," said Robin. "Believe it or not, I was just about to call her when she called me."

"She called here? Why?"

"Christian Fisher's told her you've been to see him."

"And?"

"She's got meetings this afternoon, but she wants to meet you at eleven o'clock tomorrow at her office."

"Does she, now?" said Strike, looking amused. "More and more interesting. Did you ask her if she knows where Quine is?"

"Yes; she says she hasn't got a clue, but she was still adamant she wants to meet you. She's very bossy. Like a headmistress. And *Bombyx mori*," she finished up, "is the Latin name for a silkworm."

"A silkworm?"

"Yeah, and you know what? I always thought they were like spiders spinning their webs, but you know how they get silk from the worms?"

"Can't say I do."

"They boil them," said Robin. "Boil them alive, so that they don't damage their cocoons by bursting out of them. It's the cocoons that are made of silk. Not very nice, really, is it? Why did you want to know about silkworms?"

"I wanted to know why Owen Quine might have called his novel *Bombyx Mori*," said Strike. "Can't say I'm any the wiser."

He spent the afternoon on tedious paperwork relating to a surveillance case and hoping the weather might improve: he would need to go out as he had virtually nothing to eat upstairs. After Robin had left, Strike continued working while the rain pounding his window became steadily heavier. Finally he pulled on his overcoat and walked, in what was now a downpour, down a sodden, dark Charing Cross Road to buy food at the nearest supermarket. There had been too many takeaways lately.

On the way back up the road, with bulging carrier bags in both hands, he turned on impulse into a secondhand bookshop that was about to close. The man behind the counter was unsure whether they had a copy of *Hobart's Sin*, Owen Quine's first book and supposedly his best, but after a lot of inconclusive mumbling and an unconvincing perusal of his computer screen, offered Strike a copy of *The Balzac Brothers* by the same author. Tired, wet and hungry, Strike paid two pounds for the battered hardback and took it home to his attic flat.

Having put away his provisions and cooked himself pasta, Strike stretched out on his bed as night pressed dense, dark and cold at his windows, and opened the missing man's book.

The style was ornate and florid, the story gothic and surreal. Two brothers by the names of Varicocele and Vas were locked inside a vaulted room while the corpse of their older brother decayed slowly in a corner. In between drunken arguments about literature, loyalty and the French writer Balzac, they attempted to coauthor an account of their decomposing brother's life. Varicocele constantly palpated his aching balls, which seemed to Strike to be a clumsy metaphor for writer's block; Vas seemed to be doing most of the work.

After fifty pages, and with a murmur of "Bollocks is right," Strike threw the book aside and began the laborious process of turning in.

The deep and blissful stupor of the previous night eluded him. Rain hammered against the window of his attic room and his sleep was disturbed; confused dreams of catastrophe filled the night. Strike woke in the morning with the uneasy aftermath clinging over him like a hangover. The rain was still pounding on his window, and when he turned on his TV he saw that Cornwall had been hit by severe flooding; people were trapped in cars, or evacuated from their homes and now huddled in emergency centers.

Strike snatched up his mobile phone and called the number, familiar to him as his own reflection in the mirror, that all his life had represented security and stability.

"Hello?" said his aunt.

"It's Cormoran. You all right, Joan? I've just seen the news."

"We're all right at the moment, love, it's up the coast it's bad," she said. "It's wet, mind you, blowing up a storm, but nothing like St. Austell. Just been watching it on the news ourselves. How are you, Corm? It's been ages. Ted and I were just saying last night, we haven't heard from you, and we were wanting to say, why don't you come for Christmas as you're on your own again? What do you think?"

He was unable to dress or to fasten on his prosthesis while holding the mobile. She talked for half an hour, an unstoppable gush of local chat and sudden, darting forays into personal territory he preferred to leave unprobed. At last, after a final blast of interrogation about his love life, his debts and his amputated leg, she let him go.

Strike arrived in the office late, tired and irritable. He was wearing a dark suit and tie. Robin wondered whether he was going to meet the divorcing brunet for lunch after his meeting with Elizabeth Tassel.

"Heard the news?"

"Floods in Cornwall?" Strike asked, switching on the kettle, because his first tea of the day had grown cold while Joan gabbled.

"William and Kate are engaged," said Robin.

"Who?"

"Prince William," said Robin, amused, "and Kate Middleton."

"Oh," said Strike coldly. "Good for them."

He had been among the ranks of the engaged himself until a few months ago. He did not know how his ex-fiancée's new engagement was proceeding, nor did he enjoy wondering when it was going to end. (Not as theirs had ended, of course, with her clawing her betrothed's face and revealing her betrayal, but with the kind of wedding he could never have given her; more like the one William and Kate would no doubt soon enjoy.)

Robin judged it safe to break the moody silence only once Strike had had half a mug of tea.

"Lucy called just before you came down, to remind you about your birthday dinner on Saturday night, and to ask whether you want to bring anyone."

Strike's spirits slipped several more notches. He had forgotten all about the dinner at his sister's house.

"Right," he said heavily.

"Is it your birthday on Saturday?" Robin asked.

"No," said Strike.

"When is it?"

He sighed. He did not want a cake, a card or presents, but her expression was expectant.

"Tuesday," he said.

"The twenty-third?"

"Yeah."

After a short pause, it occurred to him that he ought to reciprocate.

"And when's yours?" Something in her hesitation unnerved him. "Christ, it's not today, is it?"

She laughed.

"No, it's gone. October the ninth. It's all right, it was a Saturday," she said, still smiling at his pained expression. "I wasn't sitting here all day expecting flowers."

He grinned back. Feeling he ought to make a little extra effort, because he had missed her birthday and never considered finding out when it was, he added:

"Good thing you and Matthew haven't set a date yet. At least you won't clash with the Royal Wedding."

"Oh," said Robin, blushing, "we have set a date."

"You have?"

"Yes," said Robin. "It's the—the eighth of January. I've got your invitation here," she said, stooping hurriedly over her bag (she had not even asked Matthew about inviting Strike, but too late for that). "Here."

"The eighth of January?" Strike said, taking the silver envelope. "That's only—what?—seven weeks away."

"Yes," said Robin.

There was a strange little pause. Strike could not remember immediately what else he wanted her to do; then it came back to him, and as he spoke he tapped the silver envelope against his palm, business-like.

"How's it going with the Hiltons?"

"I've done a few. Quine isn't there under his own name and nobody's recognized the description. There are loads of them, though, so I'm just working my way through the list. What are you up to after you see Elizabeth Tassel?" she asked casually.

"Pretending I want to buy a flat in Mayfair. Looks like somebody's husband's trying to realize some capital and take it offshore before his wife's lawyers can stop him.

"Well," he said, pushing the unopened wedding invitation deep into his overcoat pocket, "better be off. Got a bad author to find."

8

I took the book and so the old man vanished.

John Lyly, *Endymion: or, the Man in the Moon*

It occurred to Strike as he traveled, standing, the one Tube stop to Elizabeth Tassel's office (he was never fully relaxed on these short journeys, but braced to take the strain on his false leg, wary of falls), that Robin had not reproached him for taking on the Quine case. Not, of course, that it was her place to reproach her employer, but she had turned down a much higher salary to throw her lot in with his and it would not have been unreasonable for her to expect that once the debts were paid, a raise might be the least he could do for her. She was unusual in her lack of criticism, or critical silence; the only female in Strike's life who seemed to have no desire to improve or correct him. Women, in his experience, often expected you to understand that it was a measure of how much they loved you that they tried their damnedest to change you.

So she was marrying in seven weeks' time. Seven weeks left until she became Mrs. Matthew...but if he had ever known her fiancé's surname, he could not recall it.

As he waited for the lift at Goodge Street, Strike experienced a sudden, crazy urge to call his divorcing brunet client—who had made it quite clear that she would welcome such a development—with a view to screwing her tonight in what he imagined would be her deep, soft, heavily perfumed bed in Knightsbridge. But the idea occurred only to be instantly dismissed. Such a move would be insanity; worse than taking on a missing-person case for which he was unlikely ever to see payment...

And why *was* he wasting time on Owen Quine? he asked himself, head bowed against the biting rain. Curiosity, he answered inwardly after a few moments' thought, and perhaps something more elusive. As he headed down Store Street, squinting through the downpour and concentrating on maintaining his footing on the slippery pavements, he reflected that his palate was in danger of becoming jaded by the endless variations on cupidity and vengefulness that his wealthy clients kept bringing him. It had been a long time since he had investigated a missing-person case. There would be satisfaction in restoring the runaway Quine to his family.

Elizabeth Tassel's literary agency lay in a mostly residential mews of dark brick, a surprisingly quiet cul-de-sac off busy Gower Street. Strike pressed a doorbell beside a discreet brass plaque. A light thumping sound ensued and a pale young man in an open-necked shirt opened the door at the foot of red-carpeted stairs.

"Are you the private detective?" he asked with what seemed to be a mixture of trepidation and excitement. Strike followed him, dripping all over the threadbare carpet, up the stairs to a mahogany door and into a large office space that had once, perhaps, been a separate hall and sitting room.

Aged elegance was slowly disintegrating into shabbiness. The windows were misty with condensation and the air heavy with old cigarette smoke. A plethora of overstocked wooden bookcases lined the walls and the dingy wallpaper was almost obscured by framed literary caricatures and cartoons. Two heavy desks sat facing each other across a scuffed rug, but neither was occupied.

"Can I take your coat?" the young man asked, and a thin and frightened-looking girl jumped up from behind one of the desks. She was holding a stained sponge in one hand.

"I can't get it out, Ralph!" she whispered frantically to the young man with Strike.

"Bloody thing," Ralph muttered irritably. "Elizabeth's decrepit old dog's puked under Sally's desk," he confided, *sotto voce*, as he took Strike's sodden Crombie and hung it on a Victorian coat-stand just inside the door. "I'll let her know you're here. Just keep scrubbing," he advised his colleague as he crossed to a second mahogany door and opened it a crack.

"That's Mr. Strike, Liz."

There was a loud bark, followed immediately by a deep, rattling human cough that could have plausibly issued from the lungs of an old coal miner.

"Grab him," said a hoarse voice.

The door to the agent's office opened, revealing Ralph, who was holding tight to the collar of an aged but evidently still feisty Doberman pinscher, and a tall, thick-set woman of around sixty, with large, uncompromisingly plain features. The geometrically perfect steel-gray bob, a black suit of severe cut and a slash of crimson lipstick gave her a certain dash. She emanated that aura of grandeur that replaces sexual allure in the successful older woman.

"You'd better take him out, Ralph," said the agent, her olive-dark eyes on Strike. The rain was still pelting against the windows. "And don't forget the poo bags, he's a bit soft today.

"Come in, Mr. Strike."

Looking disgusted, her assistant dragged the big dog, with its head like a living Anubis, out of her office; as Strike and the Doberman passed each other, it growled energetically.

"Coffee, Sally," the agent shot at the frightened-looking girl who had concealed her sponge. As she jumped up and vanished through a door behind her desk, Strike hoped she would wash her hands thoroughly before making drinks.

Elizabeth Tassel's stuffy office was a kind of concentration of the outer room: it stank of cigarettes and old dog. A tweed bed for the animal sat under her desk; the walls were plastered with old photographs and prints. Strike recognized one of the largest: a reasonably well-known and elderly writer of illustrated children's books called Pinkelman, whom he was not sure was still alive. After indicating wordlessly that Strike should take the seat opposite her, from which he had first to remove a stack of papers and old copies of the *Bookseller*, the agent took a cigarette from a box on the desk, lit it with an onyx lighter, inhaled deeply then broke into a protracted fit of rattling, wheezing coughs.

"So," she croaked when these had subsided and she had returned to the leather chair behind the desk, "Christian Fisher tells me that Owen's put in another of his famous vanishing acts."

"That's right," said Strike. "He disappeared the night that you and he argued about his book."

She began to speak, but the words disintegrated immediately into further coughs. Horrible, tearing noises issued from deep in her torso. Strike waited in silence for the fit to pass.

"Sounds nasty," he said at last, when she had coughed herself into silence again and, incredibly, taken another deep drag of her cigarette.

"Flu," she rasped. "Can't shake it. When did Leonora come to you?"

"The day before yesterday."

"Can she afford you?" she croaked. "I wouldn't have thought you come cheap, the man who solved the Landry case."

"Mrs. Quine suggested that you might pay me," said Strike.

The coarse cheeks purpled and her dark eyes, watery from so much coughing, narrowed.

"Well, you can go straight back to Leonora"—her chest began to heave beneath the smart black jacket as she fought off the desire to cough again—"and tell her that I won't pay a p-penny to get that bastard back. He's no—no longer my client. Tell her—tell her—"

She was overtaken by another giant explosion of coughing.

The door opened and the thin female assistant entered, struggling under the weight of a heavy wooden tray laden with cups and a cafetière. Strike got up to take it from her; there was barely room on the desk to set it down. The girl attempted to make a space. In her nerves, she knocked over a stack of papers.

A furious admonitory gesture from the coughing agent sent the girl scuttling from the room in fright.

"Use-useless—little—" wheezed Elizabeth Tassel.

Strike put the tray down on the desk, ignoring the scattered papers all over the carpet, and resumed his seat. The agent was a bully in a familiar mold: one of those older women who capitalized, whether consciously or not, on the fact that they awoke in those who were susceptible childhood memories of demanding and all-powerful mothers. Strike was immune to such intimidation. For one thing, his own mother, whatever her faults, had been young and openly adoring; for another, he sensed vulnerability in this apparent dragon. The chain-smoking, the fading photographs and the old dog basket suggested a more sentimental, less self-assured woman than her young hirelings might think.

When at last she had finished coughing, he handed her a cup of coffee he had poured.

"Thank you," she muttered gruffly.

"So you've sacked Quine?" he asked. "Did you tell him so, the night you had dinner?"

"I can't remember," she croaked. "Things got heated very quickly. Owen stood up in the middle of the restaurant, the better to shout at me, then flounced out leaving me to pay the bill. You'll find plenty of witnesses to what was said, if you're interested. Owen made sure it was a nice, public scene."

She reached for another cigarette and, as an afterthought, offered Strike one. After she had lit both, she said:

"What's Christian Fisher told you?"

"Not much," said Strike.

"I hope for both your sakes that's true," she snapped.

Strike said nothing, but smoked and drank his coffee while Elizabeth waited, clearly hoping for more information.

"Did he mention *Bombyx Mori*?" she asked.

Strike nodded.

"What did he say about it?"

"That Quine's put a lot of recognizable people in the book, thinly disguised."

There was a charged pause.

"I hope Chard *does* sue him. That's his idea of keeping his mouth shut, is it?"

"Have you tried to contact Quine since he walked out of—where was it you were having dinner?" Strike asked.

"The River Café," she croaked. "No, I haven't tried to contact him. There's nothing left to say."

"And he hasn't contacted you?"

"No."

"Leonora says you told Quine his book was the best thing he'd ever produced, then changed your mind and refused to represent it."

"She says *what?* That's *not* what—*not*—what I s—"

It was her worst paroxysm of coughing yet. Strike felt a strong urge to forcibly remove the cigarette from her hand as she hacked and spluttered. Finally the fit passed. She drank half a cup of hot coffee straight off, which seemed to bring her some relief. In a stronger voice, she repeated:

"That's *not* what I said. 'The best thing he'd ever written'—is that what he told Leonora?"

"Yes. What did you really say?"

"I was ill," she said hoarsely, ignoring the question. "Flu. Off work for a week. Owen rang the office to tell me the novel was finished; Ralph told him I was at home in bed, so Owen couriered the manuscript straight to my house. I had to get up to sign for it. Absolutely typical of him. I had a temperature of a hundred and four and could barely stand. His book was finished so I was expected to read it *immediately.*"

She slugged down more coffee and said:

"I chucked the manuscript on the hall table and went straight back to bed. Owen started ringing me, virtually on the hour, to see what I thought. All through Wednesday and Thursday he badgered me ...

"I've never done it before in thirty years in the business," she croaked. "I was supposed to be going away that weekend. I'd been looking forward to it. I didn't want to cancel and I didn't want Owen calling me every three minutes while I was away. So ... just to get him off my back ... I was still feeling awful ... I skim-read it."

She took a deep drag on her cigarette, coughed routinely, composed herself and said:

"It didn't look any worse than his last couple. If anything, it was an improvement. Quite an interesting premise. Some of the imagery was arresting. A Gothic fairy tale, a grisly *Pilgrim's Progress.*"

"Did you recognize anyone in the bits you read?"

"The characters seemed mostly symbolic," she said, a touch defensively, "including the hagiographic self-portrait. Lots of p-perverse sex." She paused to cough again. "The mixture as usual, I thought ... but I—I wasn't reading carefully, I'd be the first to admit that."

He could tell that she was not used to admitting fault.

"I—well, I skimmed the last quarter, the bits where he writes about Michael and Daniel. I glanced at the ending, which was grotesque and a bit silly...

"If I hadn't been so ill, if I'd read it properly, naturally I'd have told him straightaway that he wouldn't be able to get away with it. Daniel's a st-strange man, very t-touchy"—her voice was breaking up again; determined to finish her sentence she wheezed, "and M-Michael's the nastiest—the nastiest—" before exploding again into coughs.

"Why would Mr. Quine try and publish something that was bound to get him sued?" Strike asked when she had stopped coughing.

"Because Owen doesn't think he's subject to the same laws as the rest of society," she said roughly. "He thinks himself a genius, an *enfant terrible*. He takes pride in causing offense. He thinks it's brave, heroic."

"What did you do with the book when you'd looked at it?"

"I called Owen," she said, closing her eyes momentarily in what seemed to be fury at herself. "And said, 'Yes, jolly good,' and I got Ralph to pick the damn thing up from my house, and asked him to make two copies, and send one to Jerry Waldegrave, Owen's editor at Roper Chard and the other, G-God help me, to Christian Fisher."

"Why didn't you just email the manuscript to the office?" asked Strike curiously. "Didn't you have it on a memory stick or something?"

She ground out her cigarette in a glass ashtray full of stubs.

"Owen insists on continuing to use the old electric typewriter on which he wrote *Hobart's Sin*. I don't know whether it's affectation or stupidity. He's remarkably ignorant about technology. Maybe he tried to use a laptop and couldn't. It's just another way he contrives to make himself awkward."

"And why did you send copies to two publishers?" asked Strike, although he already knew the answer.

"Because Jerry Waldegrave might be a blessed saint and the nicest man in publishing," she replied, sipping more coffee, "but even *he's* lost patience with Owen and his tantrums lately. Owen's last book for Roper Chard barely sold. I thought it was only sensible to have a second string to our bow."

"When did you realize what the book was really about?"

"Early that evening," she croaked. "Ralph called me. He'd sent off the two copies and then had a flick through the original. He phoned me and said, 'Liz, have you actually read this?'"

Strike could well imagine the trepidation with which the pale young assistant had made the call, the courage it had taken, the agonized deliberation with his female colleague before he had reached his decision.

"I had to admit I hadn't . . . or not thoroughly," she muttered. "He read me a few choice excerpts I'd missed and . . . "

She picked up the onyx lighter and flicked it absently before looking up at Strike.

"Well, I panicked. I phoned Christian Fisher, but the call went straight to voice mail, so I left a message telling him that the manuscript that had been sent over was a first draft, that he wasn't to read it, that I'd made a mistake and would he please return it as soon as—as soon as p-possible. I called Jerry next, but I couldn't reach him either. He'd told me he was going away for an anniversary weekend with his wife. I hoped he wouldn't have any time for reading, so I left a message along the lines of the one I'd left for Fisher.

"Then I called Owen back."

She lit yet another cigarette. Her large nostrils flared as she inhaled; the lines around her mouth deepened.

"I could barely get the words out and it wouldn't have mattered if I had. He talked over me as only Owen can, absolutely delighted with himself. He said we ought to meet to have dinner and celebrate the completion of the book.

"So I dragged myself into clothes, and I went to the River Café and I waited. And in came Owen.

"He wasn't even late. He's usually late. He was virtually floating on air, absolutely elated. He genuinely thinks he's done something brave and marvelous. He'd started to talk about film adaptations before I managed to get a word in edgeways."

When she expelled smoke from her scarlet mouth she looked truly dragonish, with her shining black eyes.

"When I told him that I think what he's produced is vile, malicious and unpublishable, he jumped up, sent his chair flying and began screaming. After insulting me both personally and professionally, he told me that if I wasn't brave enough to represent him anymore, he'd self-publish the thing—put it out as an ebook. Then he stormed out, parking me with the bill. N–not," she snarled, "that that's anything un–un–unus—"

Her emotion triggered an even worse coughing fit than before. Strike thought she might actually choke. He half-rose out of his chair, but she waved him away. Finally, purple in the face, her eyes streaming, she said in a voice like gravel:

"I did everything I could to put it right. My whole weekend by the sea ruined; I was on the phone constantly, trying to get hold of Fisher and Waldegrave. Message after message, stuck out on the bloody cliffs at Gwithian trying to get reception—"

"Is that where you're from?" Strike asked, mildly surprised, because he heard no echo of his Cornish childhood in her accent.

"It's where one of my authors lives. I told her I hadn't been out of London in four years and she invited me for the weekend. Wanted to show me all the lovely places where she sets her books. Some of the m–most beautiful scenery I've ever seen but all I could think about was b-bloody *Bombyx Mori* and trying to stop anyone reading it. I couldn't sleep. I felt dreadful…

"I finally heard back from Jerry at Sunday lunchtime. He hadn't gone on his anniversary weekend after all, and he claims he'd never got my messages, so he'd decided to read the bloody book.

"He was disgusted and furious. I assured Jerry that I'd do everything in my power to stop the damn thing… but I had to admit that I'd also sent it to Christian, at which Jerry slammed the phone down on me."

"Did you tell him that Quine had threatened to put the book out over the internet?"

"No, I did not," she said hoarsely. "I was praying that was an empty threat, because Owen really doesn't know one end of a computer from the other. But I was worried…"

Her voice trailed away.

"You were worried?" Strike prompted her.

She did not answer.

"This self-publishing explains something," said Strike casually.

50

"Leonora says Quine took his own copy of the manuscript and all his notes with him when he disappeared into the night. I did wonder whether he was intending to burn it or throw it in a river, but presumably he took it with a view to turning it into an ebook."

This information did nothing to improve Elizabeth Tassel's temper. Through clenched teeth she said:

"There's a girlfriend. They met on a writing course he taught. She's self-published. I know about her because Owen tried to interest me in her bloody awful erotic fantasy novels."

"Have you contacted her?" Strike asked.

"Yes, as a matter of fact, I have. I wanted to frighten her off, tell her that if Owen tried to rope her in to help him reformat the book or sell it online she'd probably be party to a lawsuit."

"What did she say?"

"I couldn't get hold of her. I tried several times. Maybe she's not at that number anymore, I don't know."

"Could I take her details?" Strike asked.

"Ralph's got her card. I asked him to keep ringing her for me. *Ralph!*" she bellowed.

"He's still out with Beau!" came the girl's frightened squeak from beyond the door. Elizabeth Tassel rolled her eyes and got heavily to her feet.

"There's no point asking *her* to find it."

When the door had swung shut behind the agent, Strike got at once to his feet, moved behind the desk and bent down to examine a photograph on the wall that had caught his eye, which necessitated the removal of a double portrait on the bookcase, featuring a pair of Dobermans.

The picture in which he was interested was A4-sized, in color but very faded. Judging by the fashions of the four people it featured, it had been taken at least twenty-five years previously, outside this very building.

Elizabeth herself was clearly recognizable, the only woman in the group, big and plain with long, windswept dark hair and wearing an unflattering drop-waisted dress of dark pink and turquoise. On one side of her stood a slim, fair-haired young man of extreme beauty; on the other was a short, sallow-skinned, sour-looking man whose head was too large for his body. He looked faintly familiar. Strike thought he might have seen him in the papers or on TV.

Beside the unidentified but possibly well-known man stood a much younger Owen Quine. The tallest of the four, he was wearing a crumpled white suit and a hairstyle best described as a spiky mullet. He reminded Strike irresistibly of a fat David Bowie.

The door swished open on its well-oiled hinges. Strike did not attempt to cover up what he was doing, but turned to face the agent, who was holding a sheet of paper.

"That's Fletcher," she said, her eyes on the picture of the dogs in his hand. "He died last year."

He replaced the portrait of her dogs on the bookcase.

"Oh," she said, catching on. "You were looking at the other one."

She approached the faded picture; shoulder to shoulder with Strike, he noted that she was nearly six feet tall. She smelled of John Player Specials and Arpège.

"That's the day I started my agency. Those are my first three clients."

"Who's he?" asked Strike of the beautiful blond youth.

"Joseph North. The most talented of them, by far. Unfortunately, he died young."

"And who's——?"

"Michael Fancourt, of course," she said, sounding surprised.

"I thought he looked familiar. D'you still represent him?"

"No! I thought..."

He heard the rest of the sentence, even though she did not say it: *I thought everyone knew that.* Worlds within worlds: perhaps all of literary London *did* know why the famous Fancourt was no longer her client, but he did not.

"Why don't you represent him anymore?" he asked, resuming his seat.

She passed the paper in her hand across the desk to him; it was a photocopy of what looked like a flimsy and grubby business card.

"I had to choose between Michael and Owen, years ago," she said. "And like a b-bloody fool"—she had begun to cough again; her voice was disintegrating into a guttural croak—"I chose Owen.

"Those are the only contact details I've got for Kathryn Kent," she added firmly, closing down further discussion of Fancourt.

"Thank you," he said, folding the paper and tucking it inside his wallet. "How long has Quine been seeing her, do you know?"

"A while. He brings her to parties while Leonora's stuck at home with Orlando. Utterly shameless."

"No idea where he might be hiding? Leonora says you've found him, the other times he's—"

"I don't 'find' Owen," she snapped. "He rings me up after a week or so in a hotel and asks for an advance—which is what he calls a gift of money—to pay the minibar bill."

"And you pay, do you?" asked Strike. She seemed very far from a pushover.

Her grimace seemed to acknowledge a weakness of which she was ashamed, but her response was unexpected.

"Have you met Orlando?"

"No."

She opened her mouth to continue but seemed to think better of it and merely said:

"Owen and I go back a very long way. We were good friends ... once," she added, on a note of deep bitterness.

"Which hotels has he stayed at before this?"

"I can't remember all of them. The Kensington Hilton once. The Danubius in St. John's Wood. Big faceless hotels with all the creature comforts he can't get at home. Owen's no citizen of Bohemia— except in his approach to hygiene."

"You know Quine well. You don't think there's any chance that he might have—?"

She finished the sentence for him with a faint sneer.

"—'done something silly?' Of course not. He'd never dream of depriving the world of the genius of Owen Quine. No, he's out there plotting his revenge on all of us, thoroughly aggrieved that there isn't a national manhunt going on."

"He'd expect a manhunt, even when he makes such a practice of going missing?"

"Oh yes," said Elizabeth. "Every time he puts in one of these little vanishing acts he expects it to make the front page. The trouble is that the very first time he did it, years and years ago, after an argument with his first editor, it worked. There *was* a little flurry of concern and a smattering of press. He's lived in the hope of that ever since."

"His wife's adamant that he'd be annoyed if she called the police."

"I don't know where she gets that idea," said Elizabeth, helping herself to yet another cigarette. "Owen would think helicopters and sniffer dogs the least the nation could do for a man of his importance."

"Well, thanks for your time," said Strike, preparing to stand. "It was good of you to see me."

Elizabeth Tassel held up a hand and said:

"No, it wasn't. I want to ask you something."

He waited receptively. She was not used to asking favors, that much was clear. She smoked for a few seconds in silence, which brought on another bout of suppressed coughs.

"This—this ... *Bombyx Mori* business has done me a lot of harm," she croaked at last. "I've been disinvited from Roper Chard's anniversary party this Friday. Two manuscripts I had on submission with them have been sent back without so much as a thank you. And I'm getting worried about poor Pinkelman's latest." She pointed at the picture of the elderly children's writer on the wall. "There's a disgusting rumor flying around that I was in cahoots with Owen; that I egged him on to rehash an old scandal about Michael Fancourt, whip up some controversy and try to get a bidding war going for the book.

"If you're going to trawl around everyone who knows Owen," she said, coming to the point, "I'd be very grateful if you could tell them—especially Jerry Waldegrave, if you see him—that I had no idea what was in that novel. I'd never have sent it out, least of all to Christian Fisher, if I hadn't been so ill. I was," she hesitated, "*careless*, but no more than that."

This, then, was why she had been so anxious to meet him. It did not seem an unreasonable request in return for the addresses of two hotels and a mistress.

"I'll certainly mention that if it comes up," said Strike, getting to his feet.

"Thank you," she said gruffly. "I'll see you out."

When they emerged from the office, it was to a volley of barks. Ralph and the old Doberman had returned from their walk. Ralph's wet hair was slicked back as he struggled to restrain the gray-muzzled dog, which was snarling at Strike.

"He's never liked strangers," said Elizabeth Tassel indifferently.

"He bit Owen once," volunteered Ralph, as though this might make Strike feel better about the dog's evident desire to maul him.

"Yes," said Elizabeth Tassel, "pity it—"

But she was overtaken by another volley of rattling, wheezing coughs. The other three waited in silence for her to recover.

"Pity it wasn't fatal," she croaked at last. "It would have saved us all a lot of trouble."

Her assistants looked shocked. Strike shook her hand and said a general good-bye. The door swung shut on the Doberman's growling and snarling.

9

Is Master Petulant here, mistress?

William Congreve, *The Way of the World*

Strike paused at the end of the rain-sodden mews and called Robin, whose number was busy. Leaning against a wet wall with the collar of his overcoat turned up, hitting "redial" every few seconds, his gaze fell on a blue plaque fixed to a house opposite, commemorating the tenancy of Lady Ottoline Morrell, literary hostess. Doubtless scabrous *romans à clef* had once been discussed within those walls, too…

"Hi Robin," said Strike when she picked up at last. "I'm running late. Can you ring Gunfrey for me and tell him I've got a firm appointment with the target tomorrow. And tell Caroline Ingles there hasn't been any more activity, but I'll call her tomorrow for an update."

When he had finished tweaking his schedule, he gave her the name of the Danubius Hotel in St. John's Wood and asked her to try to find out whether Owen Quine was staying there.

"How're the Hiltons going?"

"Badly," said Robin. "I've only got two left. Nothing. If he's at any of them he's either using a different name or a disguise—or the staff are very unobservant, I suppose. You wouldn't think they could miss him, especially if he's wearing that cloak."

"Have you tried the Kensington one?"

"Yes. Nothing."

"Ah well, I've got another lead: a self-published girlfriend called Kathryn Kent. I might visit her later. I won't be able to pick up the phone this afternoon; I'm tailing Miss Brocklehurst. Text me if you need anything."

"OK, happy tailing."

But it was a dull and fruitless afternoon. Strike was running surveillance on a very well-paid PA who was believed by her paranoid boss and lover to be sharing not only sexual favors but also business secrets with a rival. However, Miss Brocklehurst's claim that she wanted to take an afternoon off to be better waxed, manicured and fake-tanned for her lover's delectation appeared to be genuine. Strike waited and watched the front of the spa through a rain-speckled window of the Caffè Nero opposite for nearly four hours, earning himself the ire of sundry women with pushchairs seeking a space to gossip. Finally Miss Brocklehurst emerged, Bisto-brown and presumably almost hairless from the neck down, and after following her for a short distance Strike saw her slide into a taxi. By a near miracle given the rain, Strike managed to secure a second cab before she had moved out of view, but the sedate pursuit through the clogged, rainwashed streets ended, as he had expected from the direction of travel, at the suspicious boss's own flat. Strike, who had taken photographs covertly all the way, paid his cab fare and mentally clocked off.

It was barely four o'clock and the sun was setting, the endless rain becoming chillier. Christmas lights shone from the window of a trattoria as he passed and his thoughts slid to Cornwall, which he felt had intruded itself on his notice three times in quick succession, calling to him, whispering to him.

How long had it been since he had gone home to that beautiful little seaside town where he had spent the calmest parts of his childhood? Four years? Five? He met his aunt and uncle whenever they "came up to London," as they self-consciously put it, staying at his sister Lucy's house, enjoying the metropolis. Last time, Strike had taken his uncle to the Emirates to watch a match against Manchester City.

His phone vibrated in his pocket: Robin, following instructions to the letter as usual, had texted him instead of calling.

Mr. Gunfrey is asking for another meeting tomorrow at his office at 10, got more to tell you. Rx

Thanks, Strike texted back.

He never added kisses to texts unless to his sister or aunt.

At the Tube, he deliberated his next moves. The whereabouts of Owen Quine felt like an itch in his brain; he was half irritated, half intrigued that the writer was proving so elusive. He pulled the piece of paper that Elizabeth Tassel had given him out of his wallet. Beneath the name Kathryn Kent was the address of a tower block in Fulham and a mobile number. Printed along the bottom edge were two words: *indie author.*

Strike's knowledge of certain patches of London was as detailed as any cabbie's. While he had never penetrated truly upmarket areas as a child, he had lived in many other addresses around the capital with his late, eternally nomadic mother: usually squats or council accommodation, but occasionally, if her boyfriend of the moment could afford it, in more salubrious surroundings. He recognized Kathryn Kent's address: Clement Attlee Court comprised old council blocks, many of which had now been sold off into private hands. Ugly square brick towers with balconies on every floor, they sat within a few hundred yards of million-pound houses in Fulham.

There was nobody waiting for him at home and he was full of coffee and pastries after his long afternoon in Caffè Nero. Instead of boarding the Northern line, he took the District line to West Kensington and set out in the dark along North End Road, past curry houses and a number of small shops with boarded windows, folding under the weight of the recession. By the time Strike had reached the tower blocks he sought, night had fallen.

Stafford Cripps House was the block nearest the road, set just behind a low, modern medical center. The optimistic architect of the council flats, perhaps giddy with socialist idealism, had given each one its own small balcony space. Had they imagined the happy inhabitants tending window boxes and leaning over the railings to call cheery greetings to their neighbors? Virtually all of these exterior areas had been used by the occupants for storage: old mattresses, prams, kitchen appliances, what looked like armfuls of dirty clothes sat exposed to the elements, as though cupboards full of junk had been cross-sectioned for public view.

A gaggle of hooded youths smoking beside large plastic recycling bins eyed him speculatively as he passed. He was taller and broader than any of them.

"Big fucker," he caught one of them saying as he passed out of their sight, ignoring the inevitably out-of-order lift and heading for the concrete stairs.

Kathryn Kent's flat was on the third floor and was reached via a windswept brick balcony that ran the width of the building. Strike noted that, unlike her neighbors, Kathryn had hung real curtains in the windows, before rapping on the door.

There was no response. If Owen Quine was inside, he was determined not to give himself away: there were no lights on, no sign of movement. An angry-looking woman with a cigarette jammed in her mouth stuck her head out of the next door with almost comical haste, gave Strike one brief searching stare, then withdrew.

The chilly wind whistled along the balcony. Strike's overcoat was glistening with raindrops but his uncovered head, he knew, would look the same as ever; his short, tightly curling hair was impervious to the effects of rain. He drove his hands deep inside his pockets and there found a stiff envelope he had forgotten. The exterior light beside Kathryn Kent's front door was broken, so Strike ambled two doors along to reach a functioning bulb and opened the silver envelope.

Mr. and Mrs. Michael Ellacott
request the pleasure of your company
at the wedding of their daughter

Robin Venetia

to

Mr. Matthew John Cunliffe

at the church of St. Mary the Virgin, Masham
on Saturday 8th January 2011
at two o'clock
and afterwards at
Swinton Park

The invitation exuded the authority of military orders: this wedding will take place in the manner described hereon. He and Charlotte had never got as far as the issuing of stiff cream invitations engraved with shining black cursive.

Strike pushed the card back into his pocket and returned to wait beside Kathryn's dark door, digging into himself, staring out over dark Lillie Road with its swooshing double lights, headlamps and reflections sliding along, ruby and amber. Down on the ground the hooded youths huddled, split apart, were joined by others and regrouped.

At half past six the expanded gang loped off together in a pack. Strike watched them until they were almost out of sight, at which point they passed a woman coming in the opposite direction. As she moved through the light puddle of a streetlamp, he saw a thick mane of bright red hair flying from beneath a black umbrella.

Her walk was lopsided, because the hand not holding the umbrella was carrying two heavy carrier bags, but the impression she gave from this distance, regularly tossing back her thick curls, was not unattractive; her windblown hair was eye-catching and her legs beneath the loose overcoat were slender. Closer and closer she moved, unaware of his scrutiny from three floors up, across the concrete forecourt and out of sight.

Five minutes later she had emerged onto the balcony where Strike stood waiting. As she drew nearer, the straining buttons on the coat betrayed a heavy, apple-shaped torso. She did not notice Strike until she was ten yards away, because her head was bowed, but when she looked up he saw a lined and puffy face much older than he had expected. Coming to an abrupt halt, she gasped.

"*You!*"

Strike realized that she was seeing him in silhouette because of the broken lights.

"You fucking *bastard!*"

The bags hit the concrete floor with a tinkle of breaking glass: she was running full tilt at him, hands balled into fists and flailing.

"You bastard, you *bastard*, I'll never forgive you, *never*, you get away from me!"

Strike was forced to parry several wild punches. He stepped backwards as she screeched, throwing ineffectual blows and trying to break past his ex-boxer's defenses.

"You wait—Pippa's going to fucking kill you—you wait—"

The neighbor's door opened again: there stood the same woman with a cigarette in her mouth.

"Oi!" she said.

Light from the hall flooded onto Strike, revealing him. With a half gasp, half yelp, the redheaded woman staggered backwards, away from him.

"The fuck's going on?" demanded the neighbor.

"Case of mistaken identity, I think," said Strike pleasantly.

The neighbor slammed her door, plunging the detective and his assailant back into darkness.

"Who are you?" she whispered. "What do you want?"

"Are you Kathryn Kent?"

"*What do you want?*"

Then, with sudden panic, "If it's what I think it is, I don't work in that bit!"

"Excuse me?"

"Who are you, then?" she demanded, sounding more frightened than ever.

"My name's Cormoran Strike and I'm a private detective."

He was used to the reactions of people who found him unexpectedly on their doorsteps. Kathryn's response—stunned silence—was quite typical. She backed away from him and almost fell over her own abandoned carrier bags.

"Who's set a private detective on me? It's *her*, is it?" she said ferociously.

"I've been hired to find the writer Owen Quine," said Strike. "He's been missing for nearly a fortnight. I know you're a friend of his—"

"No, I'm not," she said and bent to pick up her bags again; they clinked heavily. "You can tell her that from me. She's welcome to him."

"You're not his friend anymore? You don't know where he is?"

"I don't give a shit where he is."

A cat stalked arrogantly along the edge of the stone balcony.

"Can I ask when you last—?"

"No, you can't," she said with an angry gesture; one of the bags in her hand swung and Strike flinched, thinking that the cat, which had drawn level with her, would be knocked off the ledge into space. It hissed and leapt down. She aimed a swift, spiteful kick at it.

"Damn thing!" she said. The cat streaked away. "Move, please. I want to get into my house."

He took a few steps back from the door to let her approach it. She could not find her key. After a few uncomfortable seconds of trying to pat her own pockets while carrying the bags she was forced to set them down at her feet.

"Mr. Quine's been missing since he had a row with his agent about his latest book," said Strike, as Kathryn fumbled in her coat. "I was wondering whether—"

"I don't give a shit about his book. I haven't read it," she added. Her hands were shaking.

"Mrs. Kent—"

"Ms.," she said.

"Ms. Kent, Mr. Quine's wife says a woman called at his house looking for him. By the description, it sounded—"

Kathryn Kent had found the key but dropped it. Strike bent to pick it up for her; she snatched it from his grasp.

"I don't know what you're talking about."

"You didn't go looking for him at his house last week?"

"I told you, I don't know where he is, I don't know anything," she snapped, ramming the key into the lock and turning it.

She caught up the two bags, one of which clinked heavily again. It was, Strike saw, from a local hardware store.

"That looks heavy."

"My ball cock's gone," she told him fiercely.

And she slammed her door in his face.

10

VERDONE: We came to fight.
CLEREMONT: Ye shall fight, Gentlemen,
And fight enough; but a short turn or two ...

Francis Beaumont and Philip Massinger,
The Little French Lawyer

Robin emerged from the Tube the following morning, clutching a redundant umbrella and feeling sweaty and uncomfortable. After days of downpours, of Tube trains full of the smell of wet cloth, of slippery pavements and rain-speckled windows, the sudden switch to bright, dry weather had taken her by surprise. Other spirits might have lightened in the respite from the deluge and lowering gray clouds, but not Robin's. She and Matthew had had a bad row.

It was almost a relief, when she opened the glass door engraved with Strike's name and job title, to find that her boss was already on the telephone in his own office, with the door closed. She felt obscurely that she needed to pull herself together before she faced him, because Strike had been the subject of last night's argument.

"You've invited him to the wedding?" Matthew had said sharply.

She had been afraid that Strike might mention the invitation over drinks that evening, and that if she did not warn Matthew first, Strike would bear the brunt of Matthew's displeasure.

"Since when are we just asking people without telling each other?" Matthew had said.

"I meant to tell you. I thought I had."

Then Robin had felt angry with herself: she never lied to Matthew.

"He's my boss, he'll expect to be invited!"

Which wasn't true; she doubted that Strike cared one way or the other.

"Well, I'd like him there," she said, which, at last, was honesty. She wanted to tug the working life that she had never enjoyed so much closer to the personal life that currently refused to meld with it; she wanted to stitch the two together in a satisfying whole and to see Strike in the congregation, approving (approving! Why did he have to approve?) of her marrying Matthew.

She had known that Matthew would not be happy, but she had hoped that by this time the two men would have met and liked each other, and it was not her fault that that had not happened yet.

"After all the bloody fuss we had when I wanted to invite Sarah Shadlock," Matthew had said—a blow, Robin felt, that was below the belt.

"Invite her then!" she said angrily. "But it's hardly the same thing—Cormoran's never tried to get me into bed—what's that snort supposed to mean?"

The argument had been in full swing when Matthew's father telephoned with the news that a funny turn Matthew's mother had suffered the previous week had been diagnosed as a mini-stroke.

After this, she and Matthew felt that squabbling about Strike was in bad taste, so they went to bed in an unsatisfactory state of theoretical reconciliation, both, Robin knew, still seething.

It was nearly midday before Strike finally emerged from his office. He was not wearing his suit today, but a dirty and holey sweater, jeans and trainers. His face was thick with the heavy stubble that accrued if he did not shave every twenty-four hours. Forgetting her own troubles, Robin stared: she had never, even in the days when he was sleeping in the office, known Strike to look like a down-and-out.

"Been making calls for the Ingles file and getting some numbers for Longman," Strike told Robin, handing her the old-fashioned brown card folders, each with a handwritten serial number on the spine, that he had used in the Special Investigation Branch and which remained his favorite way of collating information.

"Is that a—a deliberate look?" she asked, staring at what looked like grease marks on the knees of his jeans.

"Yeah. It's for Gunfrey. Long story."

While Strike made them both tea, they discussed details of three current cases, Strike updating Robin on information received and further points to be investigated.

"And what about Owen Quine?" Robin asked, accepting her mug. "What did his agent say?"

Strike lowered himself onto the sofa, which made its usual farting noises beneath him, and filled her in on the details of his interview with Elizabeth Tassel and his visit to Kathryn Kent.

"When she first saw me, I could swear she thought I was Quine."

Robin laughed.

"You're not *that* fat."

"Cheers, Robin," he said drily. "When she realized I wasn't Quine, and before she knew who I was, she said, 'I don't work in that bit.' Does that mean anything to you?"

"No ... but," she added diffidently, "I did manage to find out a bit about Kathryn Kent yesterday."

"How?" asked Strike, taken aback.

"Well, you told me she's a self-published writer," Robin reminded him, "so I thought I'd look online and see what's out there and"—with two clicks of her mouse she brought up the page—"she's got a blog."

"Good going!" said Strike, moving gladly off the sofa and round the desk to read over Robin's shoulder.

The amateurish web page was called "My Literary Life," decorated with drawings of quills and a very flattering picture of Kathryn that Strike thought must be a good ten years out of date. The blog comprised a list of posts, arranged by date like a diary.

"A lot of it's about how traditional publishers wouldn't know good books if they were hit over the head with them," said Robin, scrolling slowly down the web page so he could look at it. "She's written three novels in what she calls an erotic fantasy series, called the Melina Saga. They're available for download on Kindle."

"I don't want to read any more bad books; I had enough with the Brothers Ballsache," said Strike. "Anything about Quine?"

"Loads," said Robin, "assuming he's the man she calls The Famous Writer. TFW for short."

"I doubt she's sleeping with two authors," said Strike. "It must be him. 'Famous' is stretching it a bit, though. Had you heard of Quine before Leonora walked in?"

"No," admitted Robin. "Here he is, look, on the second of November."

Great talk with TFW about Plot and Narrative tonight which are of course not the same thing. For those wondering:- Plot is what happens, Narrative is how much you show your readers and how you show it to them.

An example from my second Novel "Melina's Sacrifice."

As they made their way towards the Forest of Harderell Lendor raised his handsome profile to see how near they were to it. His well-maintained body, honed by horseback-riding and archery skills—

"Scroll up," said Strike, "see what else there is about Quine." Robin obliged, pausing on a post from 21 October.

So TFW calls and he can't see me (again.) Family problems. What can I do except say that I understand? I knew it would be complicated when we fell in love. I can't be openly explicit on this but Ill just say he's stuck with a wife he doesn't love because of a Third Party. Not his fault. Not the Third Party's fault. The wife won't let him go even if it's the best thing for everyone so we're locked into what sometimes feels like it's Purgatory

The Wife knows about me and pretend's not to. I don't know how she can stnad living with a man who wants to be with someone else because I know I couldn't do it. TFW says she's always put the Third Party before everything else including HIm. Strange how often being a "Carer" masks deep Selfishness.

Some people will say its all my fault for falling in love with a Married man. Your not telling me anything my friends, mySsister and my own Mother don't tell me all the time. I've tried to call it off and what can I say except The Heart has it's reasons, which Reasons don't know. And now tonight I'm crying over him all over again for a brand new Reason. He tells me he's nearly finished his Masterpiece, the book he says is the Best he's ever written. "I hope you'll like it. You're in it."

66

What do you say when a Famous Writer writes you into what he says is his best book? I understand what he's giving me in way's a Non-Writer can't. It makes you feel proud and humble. Yes there are people we Writer's let into our hearts, but into our Books?! That's special. That's different.

Can't help loving TFW. The Heart has it's Reasons.

There was an exchange of comments below.

What would you say if I told you he'd read a bit to me? Pippa2011
You'd better be joking Pip he won't read me any!!! Kath
You wait. Pippa2011 xxxx

"Interesting," said Strike. "Very interesting. When Kent attacked me last night, she assured me that someone called Pippa wanted to kill me."

"Look at this, then!" said Robin in excitement, scrolling down to 9 November.

The first time I ever met TFW he said to me 'Your not writing properly unless someone is bleeding, probably you.' As follower's of this Blog know I've Metaphorically opened my veins both here and also in my novels. But today I feel like I have been Fatally stabbed by somebodywho I had learned to trust.

"O Macheath! thou hast robb'd me of my Quiet—to see thee tortur'd would give me Pleasure."

"Where's that quotation from?" asked Strike.

Robin's nimble fingers danced across the keyboard.

"*The Beggar's Opera*, by John Gay."

"Erudite, for a woman who confuses 'you're' and 'your' and goes in for random capitalization."

"We can't all be literary geniuses," said Robin reproachfully.

"Thank Christ for that, from all I'm hearing about them."

"But look at the comment under the quotation," said Robin, returning to Kathryn's blog. She clicked on the link and a single sentence was revealed.

I'll turn the handle on the f*@%ing rack for you Kath.

This comment, too, had been made by Pippa2011.

"Pippa sounds a handful, doesn't she?" commented Strike. "Anything about what Kent does for a living on here? I'm assuming she's not paying the bills with her erotic fantasies."

"That's a bit odd, too. Look at this bit."

On 28 October, Kathryn had written:

Like most Writers I also have a day job. I can't say to much about it for secuty reasons. This week security has been tightened at our Facility again which means in consequence that my officious Co-Worker (born again Christian, sanctimnious on the subject of my private life) an excuse to suggest to management that blogs e.tc should be viewed in case sensitive Information is revealed. Frotunately it seems sense has prevailed and no action is being taken.

"Mysterious," said Strike. "Tightened security ... women's prison? Psychiatric hospital? Or are we talking industrial secrets?"

"And look at this, on the thirteenth of November."

Robin scrolled right down to the most recent post on the blog, which was the only entry after that in which Kathryn claimed to have been fatally stabbed.

My beloved sister has lost her long battle with breast cancer three days ago. Thank you all for your good wishes and support.

Two comments had been added below this, which Robin opened. Pippa2011 had written:

So sorry to hear this Kath. Sending you all the love in the world xxx.

Kathryn had replied:

Thanks Pippa your a real friend xxxx

Kathryn's advance thanks for multiple messages of support sat very sadly above the short exchange.

"Why?" asked Strike heavily.

"Why what?" said Robin, looking up at him.

"Why do people do this?"

"Blog, you mean? I don't know ... didn't someone once say the unexamined life isn't worth living?"

"Yeah, Plato," said Strike, "but this isn't examining a life, it's exhibiting it."

"Oh God!" said Robin, slopping tea down herself as she gave a guilty start. "I forgot, there's something else! Christian Fisher called just as I was walking out the door last night. He wants to know if you're interested in writing a book."

"He *what?*"

"A book," said Robin, fighting the urge to laugh at the expression of disgust on Strike's face. "About your life. Your experiences in the army and solving the Lula Landry—"

"Call him back," Strike said, "and tell him no, I'm not interested in writing a book."

He drained his mug and headed for the peg where an ancient leather jacket now hung beside his black overcoat.

"You haven't forgotten tonight?" Robin said, with the knot that had temporarily dissolved tight in her stomach again.

"Tonight?"

"Drinks," she said desperately. "Me. Matthew. The King's Arms."

"No, haven't forgotten," he said, wondering why she looked so tense and miserable. "'Spect I'll be out all afternoon, so I'll see you there. Eight, was it?"

"Six thirty," said Robin, tenser than ever.

"Six thirty. Right. I'll be there ... Venetia."

She did a doubletake.

"How did you know—?"

"It's on the invitation," said Strike. "Unusual. Where did that come from?"

"I was—well, I was conceived there, apparently," she said, pink in the face. "In Venice. What's your middle name?" she asked over his laughter, half amused, half cross. "C. B. Strike—what's the B?"

"Got to get going," said Strike. "See you at eight."

"*Six thirty!*" she bellowed at the closing door.

Strike's destination that afternoon was a shop that sold electronic accessories in Crouch End. Stolen mobile phones and laptops were unlocked in a back room, the personal information therein extracted, and the purged devices and the information were then sold separately to those who could use them.

The owner of this thriving business was causing Mr. Gunfrey, Strike's client, considerable inconvenience. Mr. Gunfrey, who was every bit as crooked as the man whom Strike had tracked to his business headquarters, but on a larger and more flamboyant scale, had made a mistake in treading on the wrong toes. It was Strike's view that Gunfrey needed to clear out while he was ahead. He knew of what this adversary was capable; they had an acquaintance in common.

The target greeted Strike in an upstairs office that smelled as bad as Elizabeth Tassel's, while two shell-suited youths lolled around in the background picking their nails. Strike, who was impersonating a thug for hire recommended by their mutual acquaintance, listened as his would-be employer confided that he was intending to target Mr. Gunfrey's teenage son, about whose movements he was frighteningly well informed. He went so far as to offer Strike the job: five hundred pounds to cut the boy. ("I don't want no murder, jussa message to his father, you get me?")

It was gone six before Strike managed to extricate himself from the premises. His first call, once he had made sure he had not been followed, was to Mr. Gunfrey himself, whose appalled silence told Strike that he had at last realized what he was up against.

Strike then phoned Robin.

"Going to be late, sorry," he said.

"Where are you?" she asked, sounding strained. He could hear the sounds of the pub behind her: conversation and laughter.

"Crouch End."

"Oh God," he heard her say under her breath. "It'll take you ages—"

"I'll get a cab," he assured her. "Be as quick as I can."

Why, Strike wondered, as he sat in the taxi rumbling along Upper Street, had Matthew chosen a pub in Waterloo? To make sure that Strike had to travel a long way? Payback for Strike having chosen pubs convenient to him on their previous attempts to meet? Strike hoped the King's Arms served food. He was suddenly very hungry.

It took forty minutes to reach his destination, partly because the row of nineteenth-century workers' cottages where the pub stood was blocked to traffic. Strike chose to get out and end the curmudgeonly taxi driver's attempt to make sense of the street numbering, which appeared not to follow a logical sequence, and proceeded on foot, wondering whether the difficulty of finding the place had influenced Matthew's choice.

The King's Arms turned out to be a picturesque Victorian corner pub the entrances of which were surrounded by a mixture of professional young men in suits and what looked like students, all smoking and drinking. The small crowd parted easily as he approached, giving him a wider berth than was strictly necessary even for a man of his height and breadth. As he crossed the threshold into the small bar Strike wondered, not without a faint hope that it might happen, whether he might be asked to leave on account of his filthy clothes.

Meanwhile, in the noisy back room, which was a glass-ceilinged courtyard self-consciously crammed with bric-a-brac, Matthew was looking at his watch.

"It's nearly a quarter past," he told Robin.

Clean cut in his suit and tie, he was—as usual—the handsomest man in the room. Robin was used to seeing women's eyes swivel as he walked past them; she had never quite managed to make up her mind how aware Matthew was of their swift, burning glances. Sitting at the long wooden bench that they had been forced to share with a party of cackling students, six foot one, with a firm cleft chin and bright blue eyes, he looked like a thoroughbred kept in a paddock of Highland ponies.

"That's him," said Robin, with a surge of relief and apprehension.

Strike seemed to have become larger and rougher-looking since he had left the office. He moved easily towards them through the packed room, his eyes on Robin's bright gold head, one large hand grasping a pint of Hophead. Matthew stood up. It looked as though he braced himself.

"Cormoran—hi—you found it."

"You're Matthew," said Strike, holding out a hand. "Sorry I'm so late, I tried to get away earlier but I was with the sort of bloke you wouldn't want to turn your back on without permission."

Matthew returned an empty smile. He had expected Strike to be full of those kinds of comments: self-dramatizing, trying to make a mystery of what he did. By the look of him, he'd been changing a tire.

"Sit down," Robin told Strike nervously, moving along the bench so far that she was almost falling off the end. "Are you hungry? We were just talking about ordering something."

"They do reasonably decent food," said Matthew. "Thai. It's not the Mango Tree, but it's all right."

Strike smiled without warmth. He had expected Matthew to be like this: name-dropping restaurants in Belgravia to prove, after a single year in London, that he was a seasoned metropolitan.

"How did it go this afternoon?" Robin asked Strike. She thought that if Matthew only heard about the sort of things that Strike did, he would become as fascinated as she was by the process of detection and his every prejudice would fall away.

But Strike's brief description of his afternoon, omitting all identifying details of those involved, met barely concealed indifference on the part of Matthew. Strike then offered them both a drink, as they were holding empty glasses.

"You could show a bit of interest," Robin hissed at Matthew once Strike was out of earshot at the bar.

"Robin, he met a man in a shop," said Matthew. "I doubt they'll be optioning the film rights anytime soon."

Pleased with his own wit, he turned his attention to the blackboard menu on the opposite wall.

When Strike had returned with drinks, Robin insisted on battling her way up to the bar with their food order. She dreaded leaving the two men alone together, but felt that they might, somehow, find their own level without her.

Matthew's brief increase in self-satisfaction ebbed away in Robin's absence.

"You're ex-army," he found himself telling Strike, even though he had been determined not to permit Strike's life experience to dominate the conversation.

"That's right," said Strike. "SIB."

Matthew was not sure what that was.

"My father's ex-RAF," he said. "Yeah, he was in same time as Jeff Young."

"Who?"

"Welsh rugby union player? Twenty-three caps?" said Matthew.

"Right," said Strike.

"Yeah, Dad made Squadron Leader. Left in eighty-six and he's run his own property management business since. Done all right for himself. Nothing like your old man," said Matthew, a little defensively, "but all right."

Tit, thought Strike.

"What are you talking about?" Robin said anxiously, sitting back down.

"Just Dad," said Matthew.

"Poor thing," said Robin.

"Why poor thing?" snapped Matthew.

"Well—he's worried about your mum, isn't he? The mini-stroke?"

"Oh," said Matthew, "that."

Strike had met men like Matthew in the army: always officer class, but with that little pocket of insecurity just beneath the smooth surface that made them overcompensate, and sometimes overreach.

"So how are things at Lowther-French?" Robin asked Matthew, willing him to show Strike what a nice man he was, to show the real Matthew, whom she loved. "Matthew's auditing this really odd little publishing company. They're quite funny, aren't they?" she said to her fiancé.

"I wouldn't call it 'funny,' the shambles they're in," said Matthew, and he talked until their food arrived, littering his chat with references to "ninety k" and "a quarter of a mill," and every sentence was angled, like a mirror, to show him in the best possible light: his cleverness, his quick thinking, his besting of slower, stupider yet more senior colleagues, his patronage of the dullards working for the firm he was auditing.

"... trying to justify a Christmas party, when they've barely broken even in two years; it'll be more like a wake."

Matthew's confident strictures on the small firm were followed by the arrival of their food and silence. Robin, who had been hoping that Matthew would reproduce for Strike some of the kinder, more affectionate things he had found to tell her about the eccentrics at the small press, could think of nothing to say. However, Matthew's mention of a publishing party had just given Strike an idea. The detective's jaws worked more slowly. It had occurred to him that there might be an excellent opportunity to seek information on Owen Quine's whereabouts, and his capacious memory volunteered a small piece of information he had forgotten he knew.

"Got a girlfriend, Cormoran?" Matthew asked Strike directly; it was something he was keen to establish. Robin had been vague on the point.

"No," said Strike absently. "'Scuse me—won't be long, got to make a phone call."

"Yeah, no problem," said Matthew irritably, but only once Strike was once again out of earshot. "You're forty minutes late and then you piss off during dinner. We'll just sit here waiting till you deign to come back."

"*Matt!*"

Reaching the dark pavement, Strike pulled out cigarettes and his mobile phone. Lighting up, he walked away from his fellow smokers to the quiet end of the side street to stand in darkness beneath the brick arches that bore the railway line.

Culpepper answered on the third ring.

"Strike," he said. "How's it going?"

"Good. Calling to ask a favor."

"Go on," said Culpepper noncommittally.

"You've got a cousin called Nina who works for Roper Chard—"

"How the hell do you know that?"

"You told me," said Strike patiently.

"When?"

"Few months ago when I was investigating that dodgy dentist for you."

"Your fucking memory," said Culpepper, sounding less impressed than unnerved. "It's not normal. What about her?"

"Couldn't put me in touch with her, could you?" asked Strike. "Roper Chard have got an anniversary party tomorrow night and I'd like to go."

"Why?"

"I've got a case," said Strike evasively. He never shared with Culpepper details of the high-society divorces and business ruptures he was investigating, in spite of Culpepper's frequent requests to do so. "And I just gave you the scoop of your bloody career."

"Yeah, all right," said the journalist grudgingly, after a short hesitation. "I suppose I could do that for you."

"Is she single?" Strike asked.

"What, you after a shag, too?" said Culpepper, and Strike noted that he seemed amused instead of peeved at the thought of Strike trying it on with his cousin.

"No, I want to know whether it'll look suspicious if she takes me to the party."

"Oh, right. I think she's just split up with someone. I dunno. I'll text you the number. Wait till Sunday," Culpepper added with barely suppressed glee. "A tsunami of shit's about to hit Lord Porker."

"Call Nina for me first, will you?" Strike asked him. "And tell her who I am, so she understands the gig?"

Culpepper agreed to it and rang off. In no particular hurry to return to Matthew, Strike smoked his cigarette down to the butt before moving back inside.

The packed room, he thought, as he made his way across it, bowing his head to avoid hanging pots and street signs, was like Matthew: it tried too hard. The decor included an old-fashioned stove and an ancient till, multiple shopping baskets, old prints and plates: a contrived panoply of junk-shop finds.

Matthew had hoped to have finished his noodles before Strike returned, to underline the length of his absence, but had not quite managed it. Robin was looking miserable and Strike, wondering what had passed between them while he had been gone, felt sorry for her.

"Robin says you're a rugby player," he told Matthew, determined to make an effort. "Could've played county, is that right?"

They made laborious conversation for another hour: the wheels turned most easily while Matthew was able to talk about himself. Strike noticed Robin's habit of feeding Matthew lines and cues, each designed to open up an area of conversation in which he could shine.

"How long have you two been together?" he asked.

"Nine years," said Matthew, with a slight return of his former combative air.

"That long?" said Strike, surprised. "What, were you at university together?"

"School," said Robin, smiling. "Sixth form."

"Wasn't a big school," said Matthew. "She was the only girl with any brains who was fanciable. No choice."

Tosser, thought Strike.

Their way home lay together as far as Waterloo station; they walked through the darkness, continuing to make small talk, then parted at the entrance to the Tube.

"There," said Robin hopelessly, as she and Matthew walked away towards the escalator. "He's nice, isn't he?"

"Punctuality's shit," said Matthew, who could find no other charge to lay against Strike that did not sound insane. "He'll probably arrive forty minutes bloody late and ruin the service."

But it was tacit consent to Strike's attendance and, in the absence of genuine enthusiasm, Robin supposed it could have been worse.

Matthew, meanwhile, was brooding in silence on things he would have confessed to nobody. Robin had accurately described her boss's looks—the pube-like hair, the boxer's profile—but Matthew had not expected Strike to be so big. He had a couple of inches on Matthew, who enjoyed being the tallest man in his office. What was more, while he would have found it distasteful showboating if Strike had held forth about his experiences in Afghanistan and Iraq, or told them how his leg had been blown off, or how he had earned the medal that Robin seemed to find so impressive, his silence on these subjects had been almost more irritating. Strike's heroism, his action-packed life, his experiences of travel and danger had somehow hovered, spectrally, over the conversation.

Beside him on the train, Robin too sat in silence. She had not enjoyed the evening one bit. Never before had she known Matthew quite like that; or at least, never before had she *seen* him like that. It was Strike, she thought, puzzling over the matter as the train jolted them. Strike had somehow made her see Matthew through his eyes. She did not know quite how he had done it—all that questioning Matthew about rugby—some people might have thought it was polite, but Robin knew better... or was she just annoyed that he had been late, and blaming him for things that he had not intended?

And so the engaged couple sped home, united in unexpressed irritation with the man now snoring loudly as he rattled away from them on the Northern line.

11

Let me know
Wherefore I should be thus neglected.

John Webster, *The Duchess of Malfi*

"Is that Cormoran Strike?" asked a girlish upper-middle-class voice at twenty to nine the following morning.

"It is," said Strike.

"It's Nina. Nina Lascelles. Dominic gave me your number."

"Oh yeah," said Strike, who was standing bare-chested in front of the shaving mirror he usually kept beside the kitchen sink, the shower room being both dark and cramped. Wiping shaving foam from around his mouth with his forearm, he said:

"Did he tell you what it was about, Nina?"

"Yeah, you want to infiltrate Roper Chard's anniversary party."

"'Infiltrate' is a bit strong."

"But it sounds much more exciting if we say 'infiltrate.'"

"Fair enough," he said, amused. "I take it you're up for this?"

"Oooh, yes, fun. Am I allowed to guess why you want to come and spy on everyone?"

"Again, 'spy' isn't really—"

"Stop spoiling things. Am I allowed a guess?"

"Go on then," said Strike, taking a sip from his mug of tea, his eyes on the window. It was foggy again; the brief spell of sunshine extinguished.

"*Bombyx Mori*," said Nina. "Am I right? I am, aren't I? Say I'm right."

"You're right," said Strike and she gave a squeal of pleasure.

78

"I'm not even supposed to be talking about it. There's been a lockdown, emails round the company, lawyers storming in and out of Daniel's office. Where shall we meet? We should hook up somewhere first and turn up together, don't you think?"

"Yeah, definitely," said Strike. "Where's good for you?"

Even as he took a pen from the coat hanging behind the door he thought longingly of an evening at home, a good long sleep, an interlude of peace and rest before an early start on Saturday morning, tailing his brunet client's faithless husband.

"D'you know Ye Olde Cheshire Cheese?" asked Nina. "On Fleet Street? Nobody from work'll be in there, and it's walking distance to the office. I know it's corny but I love it."

They agreed to meet at seven thirty. As Strike returned to his shaving, he asked himself how likely it was that he would meet anyone who knew Quine's whereabouts at his publisher's party. *The trouble is*, Strike mentally chided the reflection in the circular mirror as the pair of them strafed stubble from their chins, *you keep acting like you're still SIB. The nation's not paying you to be thorough anymore, mate.*

But he knew no other way; it was part of a short but inflexible personal code of ethics that he had carried with him all his adult life: do the job and do it well.

Strike was intending to spend most of the day in the office, which under normal circumstances he enjoyed. He and Robin shared the paperwork; she was an intelligent and often helpful sounding board and as fascinated now with the mechanics of an investigation as she had been when she had joined him. Today, however, he headed downstairs with something bordering on reluctance and, sure enough, his seasoned antennae detected in her greeting a self-conscious edge that he feared would shortly break through into "What did you think of Matthew?"

This, Strike reflected, retiring to the inner office and shutting the door on the pretext of making phone calls, was exactly why it was a bad idea to meet your only member of staff outside working hours.

Hunger forced him to emerge a few hours later. Robin had bought sandwiches as usual, but she had not knocked on the door to let him know that they were there. This, too, seemed to point to feelings of awkwardness after the previous evening. To postpone the moment when it must be mentioned, and in the hope that if he kept off the subject long enough she might never bring it up (although he had never known the tactic to work on a woman before), Strike told her truthfully that he had just got off the phone with Mr. Gunfrey.

"Is he going to go to the police?" asked Robin.

"Er—no. Gunfrey isn't the type of bloke who goes to the police if someone's bothering him. He's nearly as bent as the bloke who wants to cut his son. He's realized he's in over his head this time, though."

"Didn't you think of recording what that gangster was paying you to do and taking it to the police yourself?" asked Robin, without thinking.

"No, Robin, because it'd be obvious where the tip-off came from and it'll put a strain on business if I've got to dodge hired killers while doing surveillance."

"But Gunfrey can't keep his son at home forever!"

"He won't have to. He's going to take the family off for a surprise holiday in the States, phone our knife-happy friend from LA and tell him he's given the matter some thought and changed his mind about interfering with his business interests. Shouldn't look too suspicious. The bloke's already done enough shitty stuff to him to warrant a cooling off. Bricks through his windscreen, threatening calls to his wife."

"S'pose I'll have to go back to Crouch End next week, say the boy never showed up and give his monkey back." Strike sighed. "Not very plausible, but I don't want them to come looking for me."

"He gave you a—?"

"Monkey—five hundred quid, Robin," said Strike. "What do they call that in Yorkshire?"

"Shockingly little to stab a teenager," said Robin forcefully and then, catching Strike off guard, "What did you think of Matthew?"

"Nice bloke," lied Strike automatically.

He refrained from elaboration. She was no fool; he had been impressed before now by her instinct for the lie, the false note. Nevertheless, he could not help hurrying them on to a different subject.

"I'm starting to think, maybe next year, if we're turning a proper profit and you've already had your pay rise, we could justify taking someone else on. I'm working flat out here, I can't keep going like this forever. How many clients have you turned down lately?"

"A couple," Robin responded coolly.

Surmising that he had been insufficiently enthusiastic about Matthew but resolute that he would not be any more hypocritical than he had already been, Strike withdrew shortly afterwards into his office and shut the door again.

However, on this occasion, Strike was only half right.

Robin had indeed felt deflated by his response. She knew that if Strike had genuinely liked Matthew he would never have been as definitive as "nice bloke." He'd have said "Yeah, he's all right," or "I s'pose you could do worse."

What had irritated and even hurt was his suggestion of bringing in another employee. Robin turned back to her computer monitor and started typing fast and furiously, banging the keys harder than usual as she made up this week's invoice for the divorcing brunet. She had thought—evidently wrongly—that she was here as more than a secretary. She had helped Strike secure the evidence that had convicted Lula Landry's killer; she had even collected some of it alone, on her own initiative. In the months since, she had several times operated way beyond the duties of a PA, accompanying Strike on surveillance jobs when it would look more natural for him to be in a couple, charming doormen and recalcitrant witnesses who instinctively took offense at Strike's bulk and surly expression, not to mention pretending to be a variety of women on the telephone that Strike, with his deep bass voice, had no hope of impersonating.

Robin had assumed that Strike was thinking along the same lines that she was: he occasionally said things like "It's good for your detective training" or "You could use a countersurveillance course." She had assumed that once the business was on a sounder footing (and she could plausibly claim to have helped make it so) she would be given the training she knew she needed. But now it seemed that these hints had been mere throwaway lines, vague pats on the head for the typist. So what was she doing here? Why had she thrown away something much better? (In her temper, Robin chose to forget how little she had wanted that human resources job, however well paid.)

Perhaps the new employee would be female, able to perform these useful jobs, and she, Robin, would become receptionist and secretary to both of them, and never leave her desk again. It was not for that that she had stayed with Strike, given up a much better salary and created a recurring source of tension in her relationship.

At five o'clock on the dot Robin stopped typing in midsentence, pulled on her trench coat and left, closing the glass door behind her with unnecessary force.

The bang woke Strike up. He had been fast asleep at his desk, his head on his arms. Checking his watch he saw that it was five and wondered who had just come into the office. Only when he opened the dividing door and saw that Robin's coat and bag were gone and her computer monitor dark did he realize that she had left without saying good-bye.

"Oh, for fuck's sake," he said impatiently.

She wasn't usually sulky; it was one of the many things he liked about her. What did it matter if he didn't like Matthew? He wasn't the one marrying him. Muttering irritably under his breath, Strike locked up and climbed the stairs to his attic room, intending to eat and change before meeting Nina Lascelles.

12

She is a woman of an excellent assurance, and an extraordinary happy wit, and tongue.

Ben Jonson, *Epicoene, or The Silent Woman*

Strike proceeded along the dark, cold Strand towards Fleet Street that evening with his hands balled deep in his pockets, walking as briskly as fatigue and an increasingly sore right leg would permit. He regretted leaving the peace and comfort of his glorified bedsit; he was not sure that anything useful would come of this evening's expedition and yet, almost against his will, he was struck anew in the frosty haze of this winter's night by the aged beauty of the old city to which he owed a divided childhood allegiance.

Every taint of the touristic was wiped away by the freezing November evening: the seventeenth-century façade of the Old Bell Tavern, with its diamond windowpanes aglow, exuded a noble antiquity; the dragon standing sentinel on top of the Temple Bar marker was silhouetted, stark and fierce, against the star-studded blackness above; and in the far distance the misty dome of St. Paul's shone like a rising moon. High on a brick wall above him as he approached his destination were names that spoke of Fleet Street's inky past—the *People's Friend*, the *Dundee Courier*—but Culpepper and his journalistic ilk had long since been driven out of their traditional home to Wapping and Canary Wharf. The law dominated the area now, the Royal Courts of Justice staring down upon the passing detective, the ultimate temple of Strike's trade.

In this forgiving and strangely sentimental mood, Strike approached the round yellow lamp across the road that marked the entrance to Ye

Olde Cheshire Cheese and headed up the narrow passageway that led to the entrance, stooping to avoid hitting his head on the low lintel.

A cramped wood-paneled entrance lined with ancient oil paintings opened onto a tiny front room. Strike ducked again, avoiding the faded wooden sign "Gentlemen only in this bar," and was greeted at once with an enthusiastic wave from a pale, petite girl whose dominant feature was a pair of large brown eyes. Huddled in a black coat beside the log fire, she was cradling an empty glass in two small white hands.

"Nina?"

"I knew it was you, Dominic described you to a T."

"Can I get you a drink?"

She asked for a white wine. Strike fetched himself a pint of Sam Smith and edged onto the uncomfortable wooden bench beside her. London accents filled the room. As though she had read his mood, Nina said:

"It's still a real pub. It's only people who never come here who think it's full of tourists. And Dickens came here, and Johnson and Yeats... I love it."

She beamed at him and he smiled back, mustering real warmth with several mouthfuls of beer inside him.

"How far's your office?"

"About a ten-minute walk," she said. "We're just off the Strand. It's a new building and there's a roof garden. It's going to be bloody freezing," she added, giving a preemptive shiver and drawing her coat more tightly around her. "But the bosses had an excuse not to hire anywhere. Times are hard in publishing."

"There's been some trouble about *Bombyx Mori*, you said?" asked Strike, getting down to business as he stretched out his prosthetic leg as far as it would go under the table.

"Trouble," she said, "is the understatement of the century. Daniel Chard's livid. You *don't* make Daniel Chard the baddie in a dirty novel. Not done. No. Bad idea. He's a strange man. They say he got sucked into the family business, but he really wanted to be an artist. Like Hitler," she added with a giggle.

The lights over the bar danced in her big eyes. She looked, Strike thought, like an alert and excited mouse.

"Hitler?" he repeated, faintly amused.

"He rants like Hitler when he's upset—we've found *that* out this week. Nobody's ever heard Daniel speak above a mumble before this. Shouting and screaming at Jerry; we could hear him through the walls."

"Have you read the book?"

She hesitated, a naughty grin playing around her mouth.

"Not officially," she said at last.

"But unofficially ... "

"I might have had a sneaky peek," she said.

"Isn't it under lock and key?"

"Well, yeah, it's in Jerry's safe."

A sly sideways glance invited Strike to join her in gentle mockery of the innocent editor.

"The trouble is, he's told everyone the combination because he keeps forgetting it and that means he can ask us to remind him. Jerry's the sweetest, straightest man in the world and I don't think it would have occurred to him that we'd have a read if we weren't supposed to."

"When did you look at it?"

"The Monday after he got it. Rumors were really picking up by then, because Christian Fisher had rung about fifty people over the weekend and read bits of the book over the phone. I've heard he scanned it and started emailing parts around, as well."

"This would have been before lawyers started getting involved?"

"Yeah. They called us all together and gave us this ridiculous speech about what would happen if we talked about the book. It was just nonsense, trying to tell us the company's reputation would suffer if the CEO's ridiculed—we're about to go public, or that's the rumor—and ultimately our jobs would be imperiled. I don't know how the lawyer kept a straight face saying it. My dad's a QC," she went on airily, "and he says Chard'll have a hard time going after any of us when so many people outside the company know."

"Is he a good CEO, Chard?" asked Strike.

"I suppose so," she said restlessly, "but he's quite mysterious and dignified so ... well, it's just funny, what Quine wrote about him."

"Which was ... ?"

"Well, in the book Chard's called Phallus Impudicus and—"

Strike choked on his pint. Nina giggled.

"He's called 'Impudent Cock'?" Strike asked, laughing, wiping his mouth on the back of his hand. Nina laughed; a surprisingly dirty cackle for one who looked like an eager schoolgirl.

"You did Latin? I gave it up, I hated it—but we all know what 'phallus' is, right? I had to look it up and *Phallus impudicus* is actually the proper name for a toadstool called stinkhorn. Apparently they smell vile and... well," she giggled some more, "they look like rotting knobs. Classic Owen: dirty names and everyone with their bits out."

"And what does Phallus Impudicus get up to?"

"Well, he walks like Daniel, talks like Daniel, looks like Daniel and he enjoys a spot of necrophilia with a handsome writer he's murdered. It's really gory and disgusting. Jerry always said Owen thinks the day wasted if he hasn't made his readers gag at least twice. Poor Jerry," she added quietly.

"Why 'poor Jerry'?" asked Strike.

"He's in the book as well."

"And what kind of phallus is he?"

Nina giggled again.

"I couldn't tell you, I didn't read the bit about Jerry. I just flicked through to find Daniel because everyone said it was so gross and funny. Jerry was only out of his office half an hour, so I didn't have much time—but we all know he's in there, because Daniel hauled Jerry in, made him meet the lawyers and add his name to all the stupid emails telling us the sky will fall in if we talk about *Bombyx Mori*. I suppose it makes Daniel feel better that Owen's attacked Jerry too. He knows everyone loves Jerry, so I expect he thinks we'll all keep our mouths shut to protect him.

"God knows why Quine's gone for Jerry, though," Nina added, her smile fading a little. "Because Jerry hasn't got an enemy in the world. Owen *is* a bastard, really," she added as a quiet afterthought, staring down at her empty wineglass.

"Want another drink?" Strike asked.

He returned to the bar. There was a stuffed gray parrot in a glass case on the wall opposite. It was the only bit of genuine whimsy he could see and he was prepared, in his mood of tolerance for this authentic bit of old London, to do it the courtesy of assuming that it had once squawked and chattered within these walls and had not been bought as a mangy accessory.

"You know Quine's gone missing?" Strike asked, once back beside Nina.

"Yeah, I heard a rumor. I'm not surprised, the fuss he's caused."

"D'you know Quine?"

"Not really. He comes into the office sometimes and tries to flirt, you know, with his stupid cloak draped round him, showing off, always trying to shock. I think he's a bit pathetic, and I've always hated his books. Jerry persuaded me to read *Hobart's Sin* and I thought it was dreadful."

"D'you know if anyone's heard from Quine lately?"

"Not that I know of," said Nina.

"And no one knows why he wrote a book that was bound to get him sued?"

"Everyone assumes he's had a major row with Daniel. He rows with everyone in the end; he's been with God knows how many publishers over the years.

"I heard Daniel only publishes Owen because he thinks it makes it look as though Owen's forgiven him for being awful to Joe North. Owen and Daniel don't really like each other, that's common knowledge."

Strike remembered the image of the beautiful blond young man hanging on Elizabeth Tassel's wall.

"How was Chard awful to North?"

"I'm a bit vague on the details," said Nina. "But I know he *was*. I know Owen swore he'd never work for Daniel, but then he ran through nearly every other publisher so he had to pretend he'd been wrong about Daniel and Daniel took him on because he thought it made him look good. That's what everyone says, anyway."

"And has Quine rowed with Jerry Waldegrave, to your knowledge?"

"No, which is what's so bizarre. Why attack Jerry? He's lovely! Although from what I've heard, you can't really—"

For the first time, as far as Strike could tell, she considered what she was about to say before proceeding a little more soberly:

"Well, you can't really tell what Owen's getting at in the bit about Jerry, and as I say, I haven't read it. But Owen's done over loads of people," Nina went on. "I heard his own wife's in there, and apparently he's been *vile* about Liz Tassel, who might be a bitch, but everyone knows she's stuck by Owen through thick and thin. Liz'll never be able to place anything with Roper Chard again; everyone's furious at her. I know she was disinvited for tonight on Daniel's orders—pretty humiliating. And there's supposed to be a party for Larry Pinkelman, one of her other authors, in a couple of weeks and they *can't* uninvite her from that—Larry's such an old sweetheart, everyone loves him—but God knows what reception she'll get if she turns up.

"Anyway," said Nina, shaking back her light brown fringe and changing the subject abruptly, "how are you and I supposed to know each other, once we get to the party? Are you my boyfriend, or what?"

"Are partners allowed at this thing?"

"Yeah, but I haven't told anyone I'm seeing you, so we can't have been going out long. We'll say we got together at a party last weekend, OK?"

Strike heard, with almost identical amounts of disquiet and gratified vanity, the enthusiasm with which she suggested a fictional tryst.

"Need a pee before we go," he said, raising himself heavily from the wooden bench as she drained her third glass.

The stairs down to the bathroom in Ye Olde Cheshire Cheese were vertiginous and the ceiling so low that he smacked his head even while stooping. As he rubbed his temple, swearing under his breath, it seemed to Strike that he had just been given a divine clout over the head, to remind him what was, and what was not, a good idea.

13

It is reported, you possess a book
Wherein you have quoted by intelligence
The names of all notorious offenders,
Lurking about the city.

John Webster, *The White Devil*

Experience had taught Strike that there was a certain type of woman to whom he was unusually attractive. Their common characteristics were intelligence and the flickering intensity of badly wired lamps. They were often attractive and usually, as his very oldest friend Dave Polworth liked to put it, "total fucking flakes." Precisely what it was about him that attracted the type, Strike had never taken the time to consider, although Polworth, a man of many pithy theories, took the view that such women ("nervy, overbred") were subconsciously looking for what he called "carthorse blood."

Strike's ex-fiancée, Charlotte, might have been said to be queen of the species. Beautiful, clever, volatile and damaged, she had returned again and again to Strike in the face of familial opposition and her friends' barely veiled disgust. He had finally put an end to sixteen years of their on-again, off-again relationship in March and she had become engaged almost immediately to the ex-boyfriend from whom Strike, so many years ago in Oxford, had won her. Barring one exceptional night since, Strike's love life had been voluntarily barren. Work had filled virtually every waking hour and he had successfully resisted advances, subtle or overt, from the likes of his glamorous brunet client, soon-to-be divorcées with time to kill and loneliness to assuage.

But there was always the dangerous urge to submit, to brave complications for a night or two of consolation, and now Nina Lascelles was hurrying along beside him in the dark Strand, taking two strides to his one, and informing him of her exact address in St. John's Wood "so it looks like you've been there." She barely came up to his shoulder and Strike had never found very small women attractive. Her torrent of chat about Roper Chard was laden with more laughter than was strictly necessary and once or twice she touched his arm to emphasize a point.

"Here we are," she said at last, as they approached a tall modern building with a revolving glass door and the words "Roper Chard" picked out in shining orange Perspex across the stonework.

A wide lobby dotted with people in evening dress faced a line of metal sliding doors. Nina pulled an invitation out of her bag and showed it to what looked like hired help in a badly fitting tuxedo, then she and Strike joined twenty others in a large mirrored lift.

"This floor's for meetings," Nina shouted up to him as they debouched into a crowded open-plan area where a band was playing to a sparsely populated dance floor. "It's usually partitioned. So—who do you want to meet?"

"Anyone who knew Quine well and might have an idea where he is."

"That's only Jerry, really ... "

They were buffeted by a fresh consignment of guests from the lift behind them and moved into the crowd. Strike thought he felt Nina grab the back of his coat, like a child, but he did not reciprocate by taking her hand or in any way reinforce the impression that they were boyfriend and girlfriend. Once or twice he heard her greet people in passing. They eventually won through to the far wall, where tables manned by white-coated waiters groaned with party food and it was possible to make conversation without shouting. Strike took a couple of dainty crab cakes and ate them, deploring their minuscule size, while Nina looked around.

"Can't see Jerry anywhere, but he's probably up on the roof, smoking. Shall we try up there? Oooh, look there—Daniel Chard, mingling with the herd!"

"Which one?"

"The bald one."

A respectful little distance had been left around the head of the company, like the flattened circle of corn that surrounds a rising helicopter, as he talked to a curvaceous young woman in a tight black dress.

Phallus Impudicus; Strike could not repress a grin of amusement, yet Chard's baldness suited him. He was younger and fitter-looking than Strike had expected and handsome in his way, with thick dark eyebrows over deep-set eyes, a hawkish nose and a thin-lipped mouth. His charcoal suit was unexceptional but his tie, which was pale mauve, was much wider than the average and bore drawings of human noses. Strike, whose dress sense had always been conventional, an instinct honed by the sergeants' mess, could not help but be intrigued by this small but forceful statement of nonconformity in a CEO, especially as it was drawing the occasional glance of surprise or amusement.

"Where's the drink?" Nina said, standing pointlessly on tiptoe.

"Over there," said Strike, who could see a bar in front of the windows that showed a view of the dark Thames. "Stay here, I'll get them. White wine?"

"Champers, if Daniel's pushed the boat out."

He took a route through the crowd so that he could, without ostentation, bring himself in close proximity to Chard, who was letting his companion do all the talking. She had that air of slight desperation of the conversationalist who knows that they are failing. The back of Chard's hand, which was clutching a glass of water, Strike noticed, was covered in shiny red eczema. Strike paused immediately behind Chard, ostensibly to allow a party of young women to pass in the opposite direction.

"... and it really was awfully funny," the girl in the black dress was saying nervously.

"Yes," said Chard, who sounded deeply bored, "it must have been."

"And was New York wonderful? I mean—not wonderful—was it useful? Fun?" asked his companion.

"Busy," said Chard and Strike, though he could not see the CEO, thought he actually yawned. "Lots of digital talk."

A portly man in a three-piece suit who appeared drunk already, though it was barely eight thirty, stopped in front of Strike and invited him, with overdone courtesy, to proceed. Strike had no choice but to accept the elaborately mimed invitation and so passed out of range of Daniel Chard's voice.

"Thanks," said Nina a few minutes later, taking her champagne from Strike. "Shall we go up to the roof garden, then?"

"Great," said Strike. He had taken champagne too, not because he liked it, but because there had been nothing else there he cared to drink. "Who's that woman Daniel Chard's talking to?"

Nina craned to see as she led Strike towards a helical metal staircase.

"Joanna Waldegrave, Jerry's daughter. She's just written her first novel. Why? Is that your type?" she asked, with a breathy little laugh.

"No," said Strike.

They climbed the mesh stairs, Strike relying heavily once more on the handrail. The icy night air scoured his lungs as they emerged onto the top of the building. Stretches of velvety lawn, tubs of flowers and young trees, benches dotted everywhere; there was even a floodlit pond where fish darted, flame-like, beneath the black lily pads. Outdoor heaters like giant steel mushrooms had been placed in groups between neat square lawns and people were huddled under them, their backs turned to the synthetic pastoral scene, looking inwards at their fellow smokers, cigarette tips glowing.

The view over the city was spectacular, velvet black and jeweled, the London Eye glowing neon blue, the Oxo Tower with its ruby windows, the Southbank Center, Big Ben and the Palace of Westminster shining golden away to the right.

"Come on," said Nina, and she boldly took Strike's hand and led him towards an all-female trio, whose breath rose in gusts of white mist even when they were not exhaling smoke.

"Hi guys," said Nina. "Anyone seen Jerry?"

"He's pissed," said a redhead baldly.

"*Oh no*," said Nina. "And he was doing so well!"

A lanky blonde glanced over her shoulder and murmured:

"He was half off his face in Arbutus last week."

"It's *Bombyx Mori*," said an irritable-looking girl with short dark hair. "And the anniversary weekend in Paris didn't come off. Fenella had another tantrum, I think. *When* is he going to leave her?"

"Is she here?" asked the blonde avidly.

"Somewhere," said the dark girl. "Aren't you going to introduce us, Nina?"

There was a flurry of introduction that left Strike none the wiser as to which of the girls was Miranda, Sarah or Emma, before the four women plunged again into a dissection of the unhappiness and drunkenness of Jerry Waldegrave.

"He should have ditched Fenella years ago," said the dark girl. "Vile woman."

"Shh!" hissed Nina and all four of them became unnaturally still as a man nearly as tall as Strike ambled up to them. His round, doughy face was partly concealed by large horn-rimmed glasses and a tangle of brown hair. A brimming glass of red wine was threatening to spill over his hand.

"Guilty silence," he noted with an amiable smile. His speech had a sonorous over-deliberation that to Strike declared a practiced drunk. "Three guesses what you're talking about: *Bombyx*—*Mori*—Quine. Hi," he added, looking at Strike and stretching out a hand: their eyes were on a level. "We haven't met, have we?"

"Jerry—Cormoran, Cormoran—Jerry," said Nina at once. "My date," she added, an aside directed more at the three women beside her than at the tall editor.

"Cameron, was it?" asked Waldegrave, cupping a hand around his ear.

"Close enough," said Strike.

"Sorry," said Waldegrave. "Deaf on one side. And have you ladies been gossiping in front of the tall dark stranger," he said, with rather ponderous humor, "in spite of Mr. Chard's very clear instructions that nobody outside the company should be made privy to our guilty secret?"

"You won't tell on us, will you, Jerry?" asked the dark girl.

"If Daniel really wanted to keep that book quiet," said the redhead impatiently, though with a swift glance over her shoulder to check that the boss was nowhere nearby, "he shouldn't be sending lawyers all over town trying to hush it up. People keep calling me, asking what's going on."

"Jerry," said the dark girl bravely, "why did you have to speak to the lawyers?"

"Because I'm in it, Sarah," said Waldegrave, with a wave of his glass that sent a slug of the contents slopping onto the manicured lawn. "In it up to my malfunctioning ears. In the book."

The women all made sounds of shock and protestation.

"What could Quine possibly say about you, when you've been so decent to him?" demanded the dark girl.

"The burden of Owen's song is that I'm gratuitously brutal to his masterpieces," said Waldegrave, and he made a scissor-like gesture with the hand not grasping the glass.

"Oh, is that all?" said the blonde, with the faintest tinge of disappointment. "Big deal. He's lucky to have a deal at all, the way he carries on."

"Starting to look like he's gone underground again," commented Waldegrave. "Not answering any calls."

"Cowardly bastard," said the redhead.

"I'm quite worried about him, actually."

"Worried?" repeated the redhead incredulously. "You can't be serious, Jerry."

"You'd be worried too, if you'd read that book," said Waldegrave, with a tiny hiccup. "I think Owen's cracking up. It reads like a suicide note."

The blonde let out a little laugh, hastily repressed when Waldegrave looked at her.

"I'm not joking. I think he's having a breakdown. The subtext, under all the usual grotesquerie, is: everyone's against me, everyone's out to get me, everyone hates me—"

"Everyone *does* hate him," interjected the blonde.

"No rational person would have imagined it could be published. And now he's disappeared."

"He's always doing that, though," said the redhead impatiently. "It's his party piece, isn't it, doing a runner? Daisy Carter at Davis-Green told me he went off in a huff twice when they were doing *The Balzac Brothers* with him."

"I'm worried about him," said Waldegrave stubbornly. He took a deep drink of wine and said, "Might've slit his wrists—"

"Owen wouldn't kill himself!" scoffed the blonde. Waldegrave

looked down at her with what Strike thought was a mixture of pity
and dislike.

"People *do* kill themselves, you know, Miranda, when they think
their whole reason for living is being taken away from them. Even
the fact that other people think their suffering is a joke isn't enough
to shake them out of it."

The blonde girl looked incredulous, then glanced around the circle
for support, but nobody came to her defense.

"Writers are different," said Waldegrave. "I've never met one
who was any good who wasn't screwy. Something bloody Liz Tassel
would do well to remember."

"She claims she didn't know what was in the book," said Nina.
"She's telling everyone she was ill and didn't read it properly—"

"I know Liz Tassel," growled Waldegrave and Strike was interested to see a flash of authentic anger in this amiable, drunken editor.
"She knew what she was bloody doing when she put that book out.
She thought it was her last chance to make some money off Owen.
Nice bit of publicity off the back of the scandal about Fancourt,
whom she's hated for years ... but now the shit's hit the fan she's
disowning her client. Bloody outrageous behavior."

"Daniel disinvited her tonight," said the dark girl. "I had to ring
her and tell her. It was horrible."

"D'you know where Owen might've gone, Jerry?" asked Nina.

Waldegrave shrugged.

"Could be anywhere, couldn't he? But I hope he's all right, wherever he is. I can't help being fond of the silly bastard, in spite of it all."

"What *is* this big Fancourt scandal that he's written about?" asked the
redhead. "I heard someone say it was something to do with a review ... "

Everyone in the group apart from Strike began to talk at once, but
Waldegrave's voice carried over the others' and the women fell silent
with the instinctive courtesy women often show to incapacitated males.

"Thought everyone knew that story," said Waldegrave on another
faint hiccup. "In a nutshell, Michael's first wife Elspeth wrote a very
bad novel. An anonymous parody of it appeared in a literary magazine. She cut the parody out, pinned it to the front of her dress and
gassed herself, *à la* Sylvia Plath."

The redhead gasped.

"She *killed* herself?"

"Yep," said Waldegrave, swigging wine again. "Writers: screwy."

"Who wrote the parody?"

"Everyone's always thought it was Owen. He denied it, but then I suppose he would, given what it led to," said Waldegrave. "Owen and Michael never spoke again after Elspeth died. But in *Bombyx Mori*, Owen finds an ingenious way of suggesting that the real author of the parody was Michael himself."

"*God*," said the redhead, awestruck.

"Speaking of Fancourt," said Waldegrave, glancing at his watch, "I'm supposed to be telling you all that there's going to be a grand announcement downstairs at nine. You girls won't want to miss it."

He ambled away. Two of the girls ground out their cigarettes and followed him. The blonde drifted off towards another group.

"Lovely, Jerry, isn't he?" Nina asked Strike, shivering in the depths of her woolen coat.

"Very magnanimous," said Strike. "Nobody else seems to think that Quine didn't know exactly what he was doing. Want to get back in the warm?"

Exhaustion was lapping at the edges of Strike's consciousness. He wanted passionately to go home, to begin the tiresome process of putting his leg to sleep (as he described it to himself), to close his eyes and attempt eight straight hours' slumber until he had to rise and place himself again in the vicinity of another unfaithful husband.

The room downstairs was more densely packed than ever. Nina stopped several times to shout and bawl into the ears of acquaintances. Strike was introduced to a squat romantic novelist who appeared dazzled by the glamour of cheap champagne and the loud band, and to Jerry Waldegrave's wife, who greeted Nina effusively and drunkenly through a lot of tangled black hair.

"She always sucks up," said Nina coldly, disengaging herself and leading Strike closer to the makeshift stage. "She comes from money and makes it clear that she married down with Jerry. Horrible snob."

"Impressed by your father the QC, is she?" asked Strike.

"Scary memory you've got," said Nina, with an admiring look.

"No, I think it's … well, I'm the Honorable Nina Lascelles really. I mean, who gives a shit? But people like Fenella do."

An underling was now angling a microphone at a wooden lectern on a stage near the bar. Roper Chard's logo, a rope knot between the two names, and "100th Anniversary" were emblazoned on a banner.

There followed a tedious ten-minute wait during which Strike responded politely and appropriately to Nina's chatter, which required a great effort, as she was so much shorter, and the room was increasingly noisy.

"Is Larry Pinkelman here?" he asked, remembering the old children's writer on Elizabeth Tassel's wall.

"Oh no, he hates parties," said Nina cheerfully.

"I thought you were throwing him one?"

"How did you know that?" she asked, startled.

"You just told me so, in the pub."

"Wow, you really pay attention, don't you? Yeah, we're doing a dinner for the reprint of his Christmas stories, but it'll be very small. He hates crowds, Larry, he's really shy."

Daniel Chard had at last reached the stage. The talk faded to a murmur and then died. Strike detected tension in the air as Chard shuffled his notes and then cleared his throat.

He must have had a great deal of practice, Strike thought, and yet his public speaking was barely competent. Chard looked up mechanically to the same spot over the crowd's head at regular intervals; he made eye contact with nobody; he was, at times, barely audible. After taking his listeners on a brief journey through the illustrious history of Roper Publishing, he made a modest detour into the antecedents of Chard Books, his grandfather's company, described their amalgamation and his own humble delight and pride, expressed in the same flat monotone as the rest, in finding himself, ten years on, as head of the global company. His small jokes were greeted with exuberant laughter fueled, Strike thought, by discomfort as much as alcohol. Strike found himself staring at the sore, boiled-looking hands. He had once known a young private in the army whose eczema had become so bad under stress that he had had to be hospitalized.

"There can be no doubt," said Chard, turning to what Strike, one of the tallest men in the room and close to the stage, could see was the last page of his speech, "that publishing is currently undergoing a period of rapid changes and fresh challenges, but one thing remains as true today as it was a century ago: content is king. While we boast the best writers in the world, Roper Chard will continue to excite, to challenge and to entertain. And it is in that context"—the approach of a climax was declared not by any excitement, but by a relaxation in Chard's manner induced by the fact that his ordeal was nearly over—"that I am honored and delighted to tell you that we have this week secured the talents of one of the finest authors in the world. Ladies and gentlemen, please welcome Michael Fancourt!"

A perceptible intake of breath rolled like a breeze across the crowd. A woman yelped excitedly. Applause broke out somewhere to the rear of the room and spread like crackling fire to the front. Strike saw a distant door open, the glimpse of an overlarge head, a sour expression, before Fancourt was swallowed by the enthusiastic employees. It was several minutes before he emerged onto the stage to shake Chard's hand.

"Oh my God," an excitedly applauding Nina kept saying. "Oh my *God*."

Jerry Waldegrave, who like Strike rose head and shoulders above the mostly female crowd, was standing almost directly opposite them on the other side of the stage. He was again holding a full glass, so could not applaud, and he raised it to his lips, unsmiling, as he watched Fancourt gesture for quiet in front of the microphone.

"Thanks, Dan," said Fancourt. "Well, I certainly never expected to find myself here," he said, and these words were greeted by a raucous outbreak of laughter, "but it feels like a homecoming. I wrote for Chard and then I wrote for Roper and they were good days. I was an angry young man"—widespread titters—"and now I'm an angry old man"—much laughter and even a small smile from Daniel Chard—"and I look forward to raging for you"—effusive laughter from Chard as well as the crowd; Strike and Waldegrave seemed to be the only two in the room not convulsed. "I'm delighted to be back and I'll do my best to—what was it, Dan?—keep Roper Chard exciting, challenging and entertaining."

A storm of applause; the two men were shaking hands amid camera flashes.

"Half a mill, I reckon," said a drunken man behind Strike, "and ten k to turn up tonight."

Fancourt descended the stage right in front of Strike. His habitually dour expression had barely varied for the photographs, but he looked happier as hands stretched out towards him. Michael Fancourt did not disdain adulation.

"*Wow*," said Nina to Strike. "Can you *believe* that?"

Fancourt's overlarge head had disappeared into the crowd. The curvaceous Joanna Waldegrave appeared, trying to make her way towards the famous author. Her father was suddenly behind her; with a drunken lurch he reached out a hand and took her upper arm none too gently.

"He's got other people to talk to, Jo, leave him."

"Mummy's made a beeline, why don't you grab *her*?"

Strike watched Joanna stalk away from her father, evidently angry. Daniel Chard had vanished too; Strike wondered whether he had slipped out of a door while the crowd was busy with Fancourt.

"Your CEO doesn't love the limelight," Strike commented to Nina.

"They say he's got a lot better," said Nina, who was still gazing towards Fancourt. "He could barely look up from his notes ten years ago. He's a good businessman, though, you know. Shrewd."

Curiosity and tiredness tussled inside Strike.

"Nina," he said, drawing his companion away from the throng pressing around Fancourt; she permitted him to lead her willingly, "where did you say the manuscript of *Bombyx Mori* is?"

"In Jerry's safe," she said. "Floor below this." She sipped champagne, her huge eyes shining. "Are you asking what I think you're asking?"

"How much trouble would you be in?"

"Loads," she said insouciantly. "But I've got my keycard on me and everyone's busy, aren't they?"

Her father, Strike thought ruthlessly, was a QC. They would be wary of how they dismissed her.

"D'you reckon we could run off a copy?"

"Let's do it," she said, throwing back the last of her drink.

The lift was empty and the floor below dark and deserted. Nina opened the door to the department with her keycard and led him confidently between blank computer monitors and deserted desks towards a large corner office. The only light came from perennially lit London beyond the windows and the occasional tiny orange light indicating a computer on standby.

Waldegrave's office was not locked but the safe, which stood behind a hinged bookcase, operated on a keypad. Nina input a four-number code. The door swung open and Strike saw an untidy stack of pages lying inside.

"That's it," she said happily.

"Keep your voice down," Strike advised her.

Strike kept watch while she ran off a copy for him at the photo-copier outside the door. The endless swish and hum was strangely soothing. Nobody came, nobody saw; fifteen minutes later, Nina was replacing the manuscript in the safe and locking it up.

"There you go."

She handed him the copy, with several strong elastic bands holding it together. As he took it she leaned in for a few seconds; a tipsy sway, an extended brush against him. He owed her something in return, but he was shatteringly tired; both the idea of going back to that flat in St. John's Wood and of taking her to his attic in Denmark Street were unappealing. Would a drink, tomorrow night perhaps, be adequate repayment? And then he remembered that tomorrow night was his birthday dinner at his sister's. Lucy had said he could bring someone.

"Want to come to a tedious dinner party tomorrow night?" he asked her.

She laughed, clearly elated.

"What'll be tedious about it?"

"Everything. You'd cheer it up. Fancy it?"

"Well—why not?" she said happily.

The invitation seemed to meet the bill; he felt the demand for some physical gesture recede. They made their way out of the dark department in an atmosphere of friendly camaraderie, the copied manuscript of *Bombyx Mori* hidden beneath Strike's overcoat. After noting down her address and phone number, he saw her safely into a taxi with a sense of relief and release.

14

There he sits a whole afternoon sometimes, reading of these same abominable, vile, (a pox on them, I cannot abide them!) rascally verses.

Ben Jonson, *Every Man in His Humour*

They marched against the war in which Strike had lost his leg the next day, thousands snaking their way through the heart of chilly London bearing placards, military families to the fore. Strike had heard through mutual army friends that the parents of Gary Topley—dead in the explosion that had cost Strike a limb—would be among the demonstrators, but it did not occur to Strike to join them. His feelings about the war could not be encapsulated in black on a square white placard. Do the job and do it well had been his creed then and now, and to march would be to imply regrets he did not have. And so he strapped on his prosthesis, dressed in his best Italian suit and headed off to Bond Street.

The treacherous husband he sought was insisting that his estranged wife, Strike's brunet client, had lost, through her own drunken carelessness, several pieces of very valuable jewelry while the couple were staying at a hotel. Strike happened to know that the husband had an appointment in Bond Street this morning, and had a hunch that some of that allegedly lost jewelry might be making a surprise reappearance.

His target entered the jeweler's while Strike examined the windows of a shop opposite. Once he had left, half an hour later, Strike took himself off for a coffee, allowed two hours to elapse, then strode inside the jeweler's and proclaimed his wife's love of emeralds, which pretense resulted, after half an hour's staged deliberation over various pieces, in the production of the very necklace that the brunet had suspected her errant husband of having pocketed. Strike bought it at once, a transaction only made possible by the fact that his client had advanced him ten thousand pounds for the purpose. Ten thousand pounds to prove her husband's deceit was as nothing to a woman who stood to receive a settlement of millions.

Strike picked up a kebab on his way home. After locking the necklace in a small safe he had installed in his office (usually used for the protection of incriminating photographs) he headed upstairs, made himself a mug of strong tea, took off the suit and put on the TV so that he could keep an eye on the build-up to the Arsenal–Spurs match. He then stretched out comfortably on his bed and started to read the manuscript he had stolen the night before.

As Elizabeth Tassel had told him, *Bombyx Mori* was a perverse *Pilgrim's Progress*, set in a folkloric no-man's-land in which the eponymous hero (a young writer of genius) set out from an island populated by inbred idiots too blind to recognize his talent on what seemed to be a largely symbolic journey towards a distant city. The richness and strangeness of the language and imagery were familiar to Strike from his perusal of *The Balzac Brothers*, but his interest in the subject matter drew him on.

The first familiar character to emerge from the densely written and frequently obscene sentences was Leonora Quine. As the brilliant young Bombyx journeyed through a landscape populated by various dangers and monsters he came across Succuba, a woman described succinctly as a "well-worn whore," who captured and tied him up and succeeded in raping him. Leonora was described to the life: thin and dowdy, with her large glasses and her flat, deadpan manner. After being systematically abused for several days, Bombyx persuaded Succuba to release him. She was so desolate at his departure that Bombyx agreed to take her along: the first example of the story's frequent strange, dream-like reversals, whereby what had been bad and frightening became good and sensible without justification or apology.

A few pages further on, Bombyx and Succuba were attacked by a creature called the Tick, which Strike recognized easily as Elizabeth Tassel: square-jawed, deep-voiced and frightening. Once again Bombyx took pity on the thing once it had finished violating him, and permitted it to join him. The Tick had an unpleasant habit of suckling from Bombyx while he slept. He started to become thin and weak.

Bombyx's gender appeared strangely mutable. Quite apart from his apparent ability to breast-feed, he was soon showing signs of pregnancy, despite continuing to pleasure a number of apparently nymphomaniac women who strayed regularly across his path.

Wading through ornate obscenity, Strike wondered how many portraits of real people he was failing to notice. The violence of Bombyx's encounters with other humans was disturbing; their perversity and cruelty left barely an orifice unviolated; it was a sadomasochistic frenzy. Yet Bombyx's essential innocence and purity were a constant theme, the simple statement of his genius apparently all the reader needed to absolve him of the crimes in which he colluded as freely as the supposed monsters around him. As he turned the pages, Strike remembered Jerry Waldegrave's opinion that Quine was mentally ill; he was starting to have some sympathy with his view ...

The match was about to start. Strike set the manuscript down, feeling as though he had been trapped for a long time inside a dark, grubby basement, away from natural light and air. Now he felt only pleasurable anticipation. He was confident Arsenal were about to win—Spurs had not managed to beat them at home in seventeen years.

And for forty-five minutes Strike lost himself in pleasure and frequent bellows of encouragement while his team went two–nil up.

At halftime, and with a feeling of reluctance, he muted the sound and returned to the bizarre world of Owen Quine's imagination.

He recognized nobody until Bombyx drew close to the city that was his destination. Here, on a bridge over the moat that surrounded the city walls, stood a large, shambling and myopic figure: the Cutter.

The Cutter sported a low cap instead of horn-rimmed glasses, and carried a wriggling, bloodstained sack over his shoulder. Bombyx accepted the Cutter's offer to lead him, Succuba and the Tick to a secret door into the city. Inured by now to sexual violence, Strike was unsurprised that the Cutter turned out to be intent on Bombyx's castration. In the ensuing fight, the bag rolled off the Cutter's back and a dwarfish female creature burst out of it. The Cutter let Bombyx, Succuba and the Tick escape while he pursued the dwarf; Bombyx and his companions managed to find a chink in the city's walls and looked back to see the Cutter drowning the little creature in the moat.

Strike had been so engrossed in his reading that he had not realized the match had restarted. He glanced up at the muted TV.

"*Fuck!*"

Two all: unbelievably Spurs had drawn level. Strike threw the manuscript aside, appalled. Arsenal's defense was crumbling before his eyes. This should have been a win. They had been set to go top of the league.

"*FUCK!*" Strike bellowed ten minutes later as a header soared past Fabiański.

Spurs had won.

He turned off the TV with several more expletives and checked his watch. There was only half an hour in which to shower and change before picking up Nina Lascelles in St. John's Wood; the round trip to Bromley was going to cost him a fortune. He contemplated the prospect of the final quarter of Quine's manuscript with distaste, feeling much sympathy for Elizabeth Tassel, who had skimmed the final passages.

He was not even sure why he was reading it, other than curiosity.

Downcast and irritable, he moved off towards the shower, wishing that he could have spent the night at home and feeling, irrationally, that if he had not allowed his attention to be distracted by the obscene, nightmarish world of *Bombyx Mori*, Arsenal might have won.

15

I tell you 'tis not modish to know relations in town.

William Congreve, *The Way of the World*

"So? What did you think of *Bombyx Mori*?" Nina asked him as they pulled away from her flat in a taxi he could ill afford. If he had not invited her, Strike would have made the journey to Bromley and back by public transport, time-consuming and inconvenient though that would have been.

"Product of a diseased mind," said Strike.

Nina laughed.

"But you haven't read any of Owen's other books; they're nearly as bad. I admit this one's got a *serious* gag factor. What about Daniel's suppurating knob?"

"I haven't got there yet. Something to look forward to."

Beneath yesterday evening's warm woolen coat she was wearing a clinging, strappy black dress, of which Strike had had an excellent view when she had invited him into her St. John's Wood flat while she collected bag and keys. She was also clutching a bottle of wine that she had seized from her kitchen when she saw that he was empty-handed. A clever, pretty girl with nice manners, but her willingness to meet him the very night following their first introduction, and that night a Saturday to boot, hinted at recklessness, or perhaps neediness.

Strike asked himself again what he thought he was playing at as they rolled away from the heart of London towards a realm of owner-occupiers, towards spacious houses crammed with coffee makers and HD televisions, towards everything that he had never owned and which his sister assumed, anxiously, must be his ultimate ambition.

It was like Lucy to throw him a birthday dinner at her own house. She was fundamentally unimaginative and, even though she often seemed more harried there than anywhere else, she rated her home's attractions highly. It was like her to insist on giving him a dinner he didn't want, but which she could not understand him not wanting. Birthdays in Lucy's world were always celebrated, never forgotten: there must be cake and candles and cards and presents; time must be marked, order preserved, traditions upheld.

As the taxi passed through the Blackwall Tunnel, speeding them below the Thames into south London, Strike recognized that the act of bringing Nina with him to the family party was a declaration of nonconformity. In spite of the conventional bottle of wine held on her lap, she was highly strung, happy to take risks and chances. She lived alone and talked books not babies; she was not, in short, Lucy's kind of woman.

Nearly an hour after he had left Denmark Street, with his wallet fifty pounds lighter, Strike helped Nina out into the dark chill of Lucy's street and led her down a path beneath the large magnolia tree that dominated the front garden. Before ringing the doorbell Strike said, with some reluctance:

"I should probably tell you: this is a birthday dinner. For me."

"Oh, you should have said! Happy—"

"It isn't today," said Strike. "No big deal."

And he rang the doorbell.

Strike's brother-in-law, Greg, let them inside. A lot of arm slapping followed, as well as an exaggerated show of pleasure at the sight of Nina. This emotion was conspicuous by its absence in Lucy, who bustled down the hall holding a spatula like a sword and wearing an apron over her party dress.

"*You didn't say you were bringing someone!*" she hissed in Strike's ear as he bent to kiss her cheek. Lucy was short, blonde and round-faced; nobody ever guessed that they were related. She was the result of another of their mother's liaisons with a well-known musician. Rick was a rhythm guitarist who, unlike Strike's father, maintained an amicable relationship with his offspring.

"I thought you asked me to bring a guest," Strike muttered to his sister as Greg ushered Nina into the sitting room.

"I asked *whether you were going to*," said Lucy angrily. "Oh God— I'll have to go and set an extra—and *poor Marguerite*—"

"Who's Marguerite?" asked Strike, but Lucy was already hurrying off towards the dining room, spatula aloft, leaving her guest of honor alone in the hall. With a sigh, Strike followed Greg and Nina into the sitting room.

"Surprise!" said a fair-haired man with a receding hairline, getting up from the sofa at which his bespectacled wife was beaming at Strike.

"Christ almighty," said Strike, advancing to shake the outstretched hand with genuine pleasure. Nick and Ilsa were two of his oldest friends and they were the only place where the two halves of his early life intersected: London and Cornwall, happily married.

"No one told me you were going to be here!"

"Yeah, well, that's the surprise, Oggy," said Nick as Strike kissed Ilsa. "D'you know Marguerite?"

"No," said Strike, "I don't."

So this was why Lucy had wanted to check whether he was bringing anyone with him; this was the sort of woman she imagined him falling for, and living with forever in a house with a magnolia tree in the front garden. Marguerite was dark, greasy skinned and morose-looking, wearing a shiny purple dress that appeared to have been bought when she was a little thinner. Strike was sure she was a divorcée. He was developing second sight on that subject.

"Hi," she said, while thin Nina in her strappy black dress chatted with Greg; the short greeting contained a world of bitterness.

So seven of them sat down to dinner. Strike had not seen much of his civilian friends since he had been invalided out of the army. His voluntarily heavy workload had blurred the boundaries between weekday and weekend, but now he realized anew how much he liked Nick and Ilsa, and how infinitely preferable it would have been if the three of them had been alone somewhere, enjoying a curry.

"How do you know Cormoran?" Nina asked them avidly.

"I was at school with him in Cornwall," said Ilsa, smiling at Strike across the table. "On and off. Came and went, didn't you, Corm?"

And the story of Strike and Lucy's fragmented childhood was trotted out over the smoked salmon, their travels with their itinerant mother and their regular returns to St. Mawes and the aunt and uncle who had acted as surrogate parents throughout their childhood and teens.

"And then Corm got taken to London by his mother again when he was, what, seventeen?" said Ilsa.

Strike could tell that Lucy was not enjoying the conversation: she hated talk about their unusual upbringing, their notorious mother.

"And he ended up at a good rough old comprehensive with me," said Nick. "Good times."

"Nick was a useful bloke to know," said Strike. "Knows London like the back of his hand; his dad's a cabbie."

"Are you a cabbie too?" Nina asked Nick, apparently exhilarated by the exoticism of Strike's friends.

"No," said Nick cheerfully, "I'm a gastroenterologist. Oggy and I had a joint eighteenth birthday party—"

"—and Corm invited his friend Dave and me up from St. Mawes for it. First time I'd ever been to London, I was so excited—" said Ilsa.

"—and that's where we met," finished Nick, grinning at his wife.

"And still no kids, all these years later?" asked Greg, smug father of three sons.

There was the tiniest pause. Strike knew that Nick and Ilsa had been trying for a child, without success, for several years.

"Not yet," said Nick. "What d'you do, Nina?"

The mention of Roper Chard brought some animation to Marguerite, who had been regarding Strike sullenly from the other end of the table, as though he were a tasty morsel placed remorselessly out of reach.

"Michael Fancourt's just moved to Roper Chard," she stated. "I saw it on his website this morning."

"Blimey, that was only made public yesterday," said Nina. The "blimey" reminded Strike of the way Dominic Culpepper called waiters "mate"; it was, he thought, for Nick's benefit, and perhaps to demonstrate to Strike that she too could mingle happily with the proletariat. (Charlotte, Strike's ex-fiancée, had never altered her vocabulary or accent, no matter where she found herself. Nor had she liked any of his friends.)

"Oh, I'm a big fan of Michael Fancourt's," said Marguerite. "*House of Hollow*'s one of my favorite novels. I adore the Russians, and there's something about Fancourt that makes me think of Dostoyevsky ... "

Lucy had told her, Strike guessed, that he had been to Oxford, that he was clever. He wished Marguerite a thousand miles away and that Lucy understood him better.

"Fancourt can't write women," said Nina dismissively. "He tries but he can't do it. His women are all temper, tits and tampons."

Nick had snorted into his wine at the sound of the unexpected word "tits"; Strike laughed at Nick laughing; Ilsa said, giggling:

"You're thirty-six, both of you. For God's sake."

"Well, I think he's marvelous," repeated Marguerite, without the flicker of a smile. She had been deprived of a potential partner, one-legged and overweight though he might be; she was not going to give up Michael Fancourt. "And incredibly attractive. Complicated and clever, I always fall for them," she sighed in an aside to Lucy, clearly referring to past calamities.

"His head's too big for his body," said Nina, cheerfully disowning her excitement of the previous evening at the sight of Fancourt, "and he's phenomenally arrogant."

"I've always thought it was so touching, what he did for that young American writer," said Marguerite as Lucy cleared the starters away and motioned to Greg to help her in the kitchen. "Finishing his novel for him—that young novelist who died of AIDS, what was his—?"

"Joe North," said Nina.

"Surprised you felt up to coming out tonight," Nick said quietly to Strike. "After what happened this afternoon."

Nick was, regrettably, a Spurs fan.

Greg, who had returned carrying a joint of lamb and had overheard Nick's words, immediately seized on them.

"Must've stung, eh, Corm? When everyone thought they had it in the bag?"

"What's this?" asked Lucy like a schoolmistress calling the class to order as she set down dishes of potatoes and vegetables. "Oh, not football, Greg, please."

So Marguerite was left in possession of the conversational ball again.

"Yes, *House of Hollow* was inspired by the house his dead friend left to Fancourt, a place where they'd been happy when young. It's terribly touching. It's really a story of regret, loss, thwarted ambition—"

"Joe North left the house jointly to Michael Fancourt and Owen Quine, actually," Nina corrected Marguerite firmly. "And they *both* wrote novels inspired by it; Michael's won the Booker—and Owen's was panned by everyone," Nina added in an aside to Strike.

"What happened to the house?" Strike asked Nina as Lucy passed him a plate of lamb.

"Oh, this was ages ago, it'll have been sold," said Nina. "They wouldn't want to co-own anything; they've hated each other for years. Ever since Elspeth Fancourt killed herself over that parody."

"You don't know where the house is?"

"He's not *there*," Nina half-whispered.

"Who's not where?" Lucy said, barely concealing her irritation. Her plans for Strike had been disrupted. She was never going to like Nina now.

"One of our writers has gone missing," Nina told her. "His wife asked Cormoran to find him."

"Successful bloke?" asked Greg.

No doubt Greg was tired of his wife worrying volubly about her brilliant but impecunious brother, with his business barely breaking even in spite of his heavy workload, but the word "successful," with everything it connoted when spoken by Greg, affected Strike like nettle rash.

"No," he said, "I don't think you'd call Quine successful."

"Who's hired you, Corm? The publisher?" asked Lucy anxiously.

"His wife," said Strike.

"She's going to be able to pay the bill, though, right?" asked Greg. "No lame ducks, Corm, that's gotta be your number one rule of business."

"Surprised you don't jot those pearls of wisdom down," Nick told Strike under his breath as Lucy offered Marguerite more of anything on the table (compensation for not taking Strike home and getting to marry him and live two streets away with a shiny new coffee maker from Lucy-and-Greg).

After dinner they retired to the beige three-piece suite in the sitting room, where presents and cards were presented. Lucy and Greg had bought him a new watch, "Because I know your last one got broken," Lucy said. Touched that she had remembered, a swell of affection temporarily blotted out Strike's irritation that she had dragged him here tonight, and nagged him about his life choices, and married Greg ... He removed the cheap but serviceable replacement he had bought himself and put Lucy's watch on instead: it was large and shiny with a metallic bracelet and looked like a duplicate of Greg's.

Nick and Ilsa had bought him "that whisky you like": Arran Single Malt, it reminded him powerfully of Charlotte, with whom he had first tasted it, but any possibility of melancholy remembrance was chased away by the abrupt appearance in the doorway of three pajamaed figures, the tallest of whom asked:

"Is there cake yet?"

Strike had never wanted children (an attitude Lucy deplored) and barely knew his nephews, whom he saw infrequently. The eldest and youngest trailed their mother out of the room to fetch his birthday cake; the middle boy, however, made a beeline for Strike and held out a homemade card.

"That's you," said Jack, pointing at the picture, "getting your medal."

"Have you got a medal?" asked Nina, smiling and wide-eyed.

"Thanks, Jack," said Strike.

"I want to be a soldier," said Jack.

"Your fault, Corm," said Greg, with what Strike could not help feeling was a certain animus. "Buying him soldier toys. Telling him about your gun."

"Two guns," Jack corrected his father. "You had two guns," he told Strike. "But you had to give them back."

"Good memory," Strike told him. "You'll go far."

Lucy appeared with the homemade cake, blazing with thirty-six candles and decorated with what looked like hundreds of Smarties. As Greg turned out the light and everyone began to sing, Strike experienced an almost overwhelming desire to leave. He would ring a cab the instant he could escape the room; in the meantime, he hoisted a smile onto his face and blew out his candles, avoiding the gaze of Marguerite, who was smoldering at him with an unnerving lack of restraint from a nearby chair. It was not his fault that he had been made to play the decorated helpmeet of abandoned women by his well-meaning friends and family.

Strike called a cab from the downstairs bathroom and announced half an hour later, with a decent show of regret, that he and Nina would have to leave; he had to be up early the next day.

Out in the crowded and noisy hall, after Strike had neatly dodged being kissed on the mouth by Marguerite, while his nephews worked off their overexcitement and a late-night sugar rush, and Greg helped Nina officiously into her coat, Nick muttered to Strike:

"I didn't think you fancied little women."

"I don't," Strike returned quietly. "She nicked something for me yesterday."

"Yeah? Well, I'd show your gratitude by letting her go on top," said Nick. "You could squash her like a beetle."

16

…let not our supper be raw, for you shall have blood enough, your belly full.

Thomas Dekker and Thomas Middleton,
The Honest Whore

Strike knew immediately upon waking the following morning that he was not in his own bed. It was too comfortable, the sheets too smooth; the daylight stippling the covers fell from the wrong side of the room and the sound of the rain pattering against the window was muffled by drawn curtains. He pushed himself up into a sitting position, squinting around at Nina's bedroom, glimpsed only briefly by lamplight the previous evening, and caught sight of his own naked torso in a mirror opposite, thick dark chest hair making a black blot against the pale blue wall behind him.

Nina was absent, but he could smell coffee. As he had anticipated, she had been enthusiastic and energetic in bed, driving away the slight melancholy that had threatened to follow him from his birthday celebrations. Now, though, he wondered how quickly he would be able to extricate himself. To linger would be to raise expectations he was not prepared to meet.

His prosthetic leg was propped against the wall beside the bed. On the point of sliding himself out of bed to reach it he drew back, because the bedroom door opened and in walked Nina, fully dressed and damp-haired, with newspapers under her arm, two mugs of coffee in one hand and a plate of croissants in the other.

"I nipped out," she said breathlessly. "God, it's horrible out there. Feel my nose, I'm frozen."

"You didn't have to do that," he said, gesturing to the croissants.

"I'm starving and there's a fabulous bakery up the road. Look at this—*News of the World*—Dom's big exclusive!"

A photograph of the disgraced peer whose hidden accounts Strike had revealed to Culpepper filled the middle of the front page, flanked on three sides by pictures of two of his lovers and of the Cayman Island documents Strike had wrested from his PA. LORD PORKER OF PAYWELL screamed the headline. Strike took the paper from Nina and skim-read the story. Culpepper had kept his word: the heartbroken PA was not mentioned anywhere.

Nina was sitting beside Strike on the bed, reading along with him, emitting faintly amused comments: "Oh God, how anyone could, look at him" and "Oh wow, that's disgusting."

"Won't do Culpepper any harm," Strike said, closing the paper when both had finished. The date at the top of the front page caught his eye: 21 November. It was his ex-fiancée's birthday.

A small, painful tug under the solar plexus and a sudden gush of vivid, unwelcome memories…a year ago, almost to the hour, he had woken up beside Charlotte in Holland Park Avenue. He remembered her long black hair, wide hazel-green eyes, a body the like of which he would never see again, never be permitted to touch…They had been happy, that morning: the bed a life raft bobbing on the turbulent sea of their endlessly recurring troubles. He had presented her with a bracelet, the purchase of which had necessitated (though she did not know it) the taking out of a loan at horrifying rates of interest…and two days later, on his own birthday, she had given him an Italian suit, and they had gone out to dinner and actually fixed on a date when they would marry at last, sixteen years after they had first met…

But the naming of a day had marked a new and dreadful phase in their relationship, as though it had damaged the precarious tension in which they were used to living. Charlotte had become steadily more volatile, more capricious. Rows and scenes, broken china, accusations of his unfaithfulness (when it had been she, as he now believed, who had been secretly meeting the man to whom she was now engaged)…

114

they had struggled on for nearly four months until, in a final, filthy explosion of recrimination and rage, everything had ended for good.

A rustle of cotton: Strike looked around, almost surprised to find himself still in Nina's bedroom. She was about to strip off her top, intending to get back into bed with him.

"I can't stay," he told her, stretching across for his prosthesis again.

"Why not?" she asked with her arms folded across her front, gripping the hem of her shirt. "Come on—it's Sunday!"

"I've got to work," he lied. "People need investigating on Sundays too."

"Oh," she said, trying to sound matter-of-fact but looking crestfallen.

He drank his coffee, keeping the conversation bright but impersonal. She watched him strap his leg on and head for the bathroom, and when he returned to dress she was curled up in a chair, munching a croissant with a slightly forlorn air.

"You're sure you don't know where this house was? The one Quine and Fancourt inherited?" he asked her as he pulled on his trousers.

"What?" she said, confused. "Oh—God, you're not going looking for that, are you? I told you, it'll have been sold years ago!"

"I might ask Quine's wife about it," said Strike.

He told her that he would call her, but briskly, so that she might understand these to be empty words, a matter of form, and left her house with a feeling of faint gratitude, but no guilt.

The rain jabbed again at his face and hands as he walked down the unfamiliar street, heading for the Tube station. Christmassy fairy lights twinkled from the window of the bakery where Nina had just bought croissants. Strike's large hunched reflection slid across the rain-spotted surface, clutching in one cold fist the plastic carrier bag which Lucy had helpfully given him to carry his cards, his birthday whisky and the box of his shiny new watch.

His thoughts slid irresistibly back to Charlotte, thirty-six but looking twenty-five, celebrating her birthday with her new fiancé. Perhaps she had received diamonds, Strike thought; she had always said she didn't care for such things, but when they had argued the glitter of all he could not give her had sometimes been flung back hard in his face . . .

Successful bloke? Greg had asked of Owen Quine, by which he meant: "Big car? Nice house? Fat bank balance?"

Strike passed the Beatles Coffee Shop with its jauntily positioned black-and-white heads of the Fab Four peering out at him, and entered the relative warmth of the station. He did not want to spend this rainy Sunday alone in his attic rooms in Denmark Street. He wanted to keep busy on the anniversary of Charlotte Campbell's birth.

Pausing to take out his mobile, he telephoned Leonora Quine.

"Hello?" she said brusquely.

"Hi, Leonora, it's Cormoran Strike here—"

"Have you found Owen?" she demanded.

"Afraid not. I'm calling because I've just heard that your husband was left a house by a friend."

"What house?"

She sounded tired and irritable. He thought of the various moneyed husbands he had come up against professionally, men who hid bachelor apartments from their wives, and wondered whether he had just given away something that Quine had been keeping from his family.

"Isn't it true? Didn't a writer called Joe North leave a house jointly to—?"

"Oh, *that*," she said. "Talgarth Road, yeah. That was thirty-odd years ago, though. What d'you wanna know about that for?"

"It's been sold, has it?"

"No," she said resentfully, "because bloody Fancourt never let us. Out of spite, it is, because *he* never uses it. It just sits there, no use to anyone, moldering away."

Strike leaned back against the wall beside the ticket machines, his eyes fixed on a circular ceiling supported by a spider's web of struts. This, he told himself again, is what comes of taking on clients when you're wrecked. He should have asked if they owned any other properties. He should have checked.

"Has anyone gone to see whether your husband's there, Mrs. Quine?"

She emitted a hoot of derision.

"He wouldn't go *there!*" she said, as though Strike were suggesting that her husband had hidden in Buckingham Palace. "He hates it, he never goes near it! Anyway, I don't think it's got furniture or nothing."

"Have you got a key?"

"I dunno. But Owen'd *never* go there! He hasn't been near it in years. It'd be an 'orrible place to stay, old and empty."

"If you could have a look for the key—"

"I can't go tearing off to Talgarth Road, I've got Orlando!" she said, predictably. "Anyway, I'm telling you, he wouldn't—"

"I'm offering to come over now," said Strike, "get the key from you, if you can find it, and go and check. Just to make sure we've looked everywhere."

"Yeah, but—it's Sunday," she said, sounding taken aback.

"I know it is. D'you think you could have a look for the key?"

"All right, then," she said after a short pause. "But," with a last burst of spirit, "he won't be there!"

Strike took the Tube, changing once, to Westbourne Park and then, collar turned up against the icy deluge, marched towards the address that Leonora had scribbled down for him at their first meeting.

It was another of those odd pockets of London where millionaires sat within a stone's throw of working-class families who had occupied their homes for forty years or more. The rain-washed scene presented an odd diorama: sleek new apartment blocks behind quiet nondescript terraces, the luxurious new and the comfortable old.

The Quines' family home was in Southern Row, a quiet backstreet of small brick houses, a short walk from a whitewashed pub called the Chilled Eskimo. Cold and wet, Strike squinted up at the sign overhead as he passed; it depicted a happy Inuit relaxing beside a fishing hole, his back to the rising sun.

The door of the Quines' house was a peeling sludge green. Everything about the frontage was dilapidated, including the gate hanging on by only one hinge. Strike thought of Quine's predilection for comfortable hotel rooms as he rang the doorbell and his opinion of the missing man fell a little further.

"You were quick," was Leonora's gruff greeting on opening the door. "Come in."

He followed her down a dim, narrow hallway. To the left, a door stood ajar onto what was clearly Owen Quine's study. It looked untidy and dirty. Drawers hung open and an old electric typewriter sat skewed on the desk. Strike could picture Quine tearing pages from it in his rage at Elizabeth Tassel.

"Any luck with the key?" Strike asked Leonora as they entered the dark, stale-smelling kitchen at the end of the hall. The appliances all looked as though they were at least thirty years old. Strike had an idea that his Aunt Joan had owned the identical dark brown microwave back in the eighties.

"Well, I found *them*," Leonora told him, gesturing towards half a dozen keys lying on the kitchen table. "I dunno whether any of them's the right one."

None of them was attached to a key ring and one of them looked too big to open anything but a church door.

"What number Talgarth Road?" Strike asked her.

"Hundred and seventy-nine."

"When were you last there?"

"Me? I never been there," she said with what seemed genuine indifference. "I wasn't int'rested. Silly thing to do."

"What was?"

"Leaving it to them." In the face of Strike's politely inquiring face she said impatiently, "That Joe North, leaving it to Owen and Michael Fancourt. He said it was for them to write in. They've never used it since. Useless."

"And you've never been there?"

"No. They got it round the time I had Orlando. I wasn't int'rested," she repeated.

"Orlando was born then?" Strike asked, surprised. He had been vaguely imagining Orlando as a hyperactive ten-year-old.

"In eighty-six, yeah," said Leonora. "But she's handicapped."

"Oh," said Strike. "I see."

"Upstairs sulking now, cos I had to tell her off," said Leonora, in one of her bursts of expansiveness. "She nicks things. She knows it's wrong but she keeps doing it. I caught her taking Edna-Next-Door's purse out of her bag when she come round yesterday. It wasn't cos of the money," she said quickly, as though he had made an accusation. "It's cos she liked the color. Edna understands cos she knows her, but not everyone does. I tell her it's wrong. She knows it's wrong."

"All right if I take these and try them, then?" Strike asked, scooping the keys into his hand.

"If y'want," said Leonora, but she added defiantly, "He won't be there."

Strike pocketed his haul, turned down Leonora's afterthought offer of tea or coffee and returned to the cold rain.

He found himself limping again as he walked towards Westbourne Park Tube station, which would mean a short journey with minimal changes. He had not taken as much care as usual in attaching his prosthesis in his haste to get out of Nina's flat, nor had he been able to apply any of those soothing products that helped protect the skin beneath it.

Eight months previously (on the very day that he had later been stabbed in his upper arm) he had taken a bad fall down some stairs. The consultant who had examined it shortly afterwards had informed him that he had done additional, though probably reparable, damage to the medial ligaments in the knee joint of his amputated leg and advised ice, rest and further investigation. But Strike had not been able to afford rest and had not wished for further tests, so he had strapped up the knee and tried to remember to elevate his leg when sitting. The pain had mostly subsided but occasionally, when he had done a lot of walking, it began to throb and swell again.

The road along which Strike was trudging curved to the right. A tall, thin, hunched figure was walking behind him, its head bowed so that only the top of a black hood was visible.

Of course, the sensible thing to do would be to go home, now, and rest his knee. It was Sunday. There was no need for him to go marching all over London in the rain.

He won't be there, said Leonora in his head.

But the alternative was returning to Denmark Street, listening to the rain hammering against the badly fitting window beside his bed under the eaves, with photo albums full of Charlotte too close, in the boxes on the landing...

Better to move, to work, to think about other people's problems...

Blinking in the rain, he glanced up at the houses he was passing and glimpsed in his peripheral vision the figure following twenty yards behind him. Though the dark coat was shapeless, Strike had the impression from the short, quick steps, that the figure was female.

Now Strike noticed something curious about the way she was walking, something unnatural. There was none of the self-preoccupation of the lone stroller on a cold wet day. Her head was not bowed in protection against the elements, nor was she maintaining a steady pace with the simple view of achieving a destination. She kept adjusting her speed in tiny but, to Strike, noticeable increments, and every few steps the hidden face beneath the hood presented itself to the chilly onslaught of the driving rain, then vanished again into shadow. She was keeping him in her sights.

What had Leonora said at their first meeting?

I think I've been followed. Tall, dark girl with round shoulders.

Strike experimented by speeding up and slowing down infinitesimally. The space between them remained constant; her hidden face flickered up and down more frequently, a pale pink blur, to check his position.

She was not experienced at following people. Strike, who was an expert, would have taken the opposite pavement, pretended to be talking on a mobile phone; concealed his focused and singular interest in the subject...

For his own amusement, he faked a sudden hesitation, as though he had been caught by a doubt as to the right direction. Caught off guard, the dark figure stopped dead, paralyzed. Strike strolled on again and after a few seconds heard her footsteps echoing on the wet pavement behind him. She was too foolish even to realize that she had been rumbled.

Westbourne Park station came into sight a little way ahead: a long, low building of golden brick. He would confront her there, ask her the time, get a good look at her face.

Turning into the station, he drew quickly to the far side of the entrance, waiting for her, out of sight.

Some thirty seconds later he glimpsed the tall, dark figure jogging towards the entrance through the glittering rain, hands still in her pockets; she was frightened that she might have missed him, that he was already on a train.

He took a swift, confident step out into the doorway to face her—
the false foot slipped on the wet tiled floor and skidded.

"*Fuck!*"

With an undignified descent into half-splits, he lost his footing and
fell; in the long, slow-motion seconds before he reached the dirty wet
floor, landing painfully on the bottle of whisky in his carrier bag, he
saw her freeze in silhouette in the entrance, then vanish like a startled
deer.

"Bollocks," he gasped, lying on the sopping tiles while people at
the ticket machines stared. He had twisted his leg again as he fell;
it felt as though he might have torn a ligament; the knee that had
been merely sore was now screaming in protest. Inwardly cursing
imperfectly mopped floors and prosthetic ankles of rigid construction,
Strike tried to get up. Nobody wanted to approach him. No doubt
they thought he was drunk—Nick and Ilsa's whisky had now escaped
the carrier bag and was rolling clunkily across the floor.

Finally a London Underground employee helped him to his
feet, muttering about there being a sign warning of the wet floor;
hadn't the gentleman seen it, wasn't it prominent enough? He
handed Strike his whisky. Humiliated, Strike muttered a thank you
and limped over to the ticket barriers, wanting only to escape the
countless staring eyes.

Safely on a southbound train he stretched out his throbbing leg
and probed his knee as best he could through his suit trousers. It felt
tender and sore, exactly as it had after he had fallen down those stairs
last spring. Furious, now, with the girl who had been following him,
he tried to make sense of what had happened.

When had she joined him? Had she been watching the Quine
place, seen him go inside? Might she (an unflattering possibility) have
mistaken Strike for Owen Quine? Kathryn Kent had certainly done
so, briefly, in the dark . . .

Strike got to his feet some minutes before changing at Hammersmith
to better prepare himself for what might be a perilous descent. By
the time he reached his destination of Barons Court, he was limping
heavily and wishing that he had a stick. He made his way out of a
ticket hall tiled in Victorian pea green, placing his feet with care on the

floor covered in grimy wet prints. Too soon he had left the dry shelter of the small jewel of a station, with its art nouveau lettering and stone pediments, and proceeded in the relentless rain towards the rumbling dual carriageway that lay close by.

To his relief and gratitude, he realized that he had emerged on that very stretch of Talgarth Road where the house he sought stood.

Though London was full of these kinds of architectural anomalies, he had never seen buildings that jarred so obviously with their surroundings. The old houses sat in a distinctive row, dark redbrick relics of a more confident and imaginative time, while traffic rumbled unforgivingly past them in both directions, for this was the main artery into London from the west.

They were ornate late-Victorian artists' studios, their lower windows leaded and latticed and oversized arched north-facing windows on their upper floors, like fragments of the vanished Crystal Palace. Wet, cold and sore though he was, Strike paused for a few seconds to look up at number 179, marveling at its distinctive architecture and wondering how much the Quines would stand to make if Fancourt ever changed his mind and agreed to sell.

He heaved himself up the white front steps. The front door was sheltered from the rain by a brick canopy richly ornamented with carved stone swags, scrolls and badges. Strike brought out the keys one by one with cold, numb fingers.

The fourth one he tried slid home without protest and turned as though it had been doing so for years. One gentle click and the front door slid open. He crossed the threshold and closed the door behind him.

A shock, like a slap in the face, like a falling bucket of water. Strike fumbled with his coat collar, dragging it up over his mouth and nose to protect them. Where he should have smelled only dust and old wood, something sharp and chemical was overwhelming him, catching in his nose and throat.

He reached automatically for a switch on the wall beside him, producing a flood of light from two bare lightbulbs hanging from the ceiling. The hallway, which was narrow and empty, was paneled in honey-colored wood. Twisted columns of the same material supported an arch halfway along its length. At first glance it was serene, gracious, well proportioned.

But with eyes narrowed Strike slowly took in the wide, burn-like stains on the original woodwork. A corrosive, acrid fluid—which was making the still, dusty air burn—had been splashed everywhere in what seemed to have been an act of wanton vandalism; it had stripped varnish from the aged floorboards, blasted the patina off the bare wood stairs ahead, even been thrown over the walls so that large patches of painted plaster were bleached and discolored.

After a few seconds of breathing through his thick serge collar, it occurred to Strike that the place was too warm for an uninhabited house. The heating had been cranked up high, which made the fierce chemical smell waft more pungently than if it had been left to disperse in the chill of a winter's day.

Paper rustled under his feet. Looking down, he saw a smattering of takeaway menus and an envelope addressed TO THE OCCUPIER/ CARETAKER. He stooped and picked it up. It was a brief, angry handwritten note from the next-door neighbor, complaining about the smell.

Strike let the note fall back onto the doormat and moved forwards into the hall, observing the scars left on every surface where the chemical substance had been thrown. To his left was a door; he opened it. The room beyond was dark and empty; it had not been tarnished with the bleach-like substance. A dilapidated kitchen, also devoid of furnishings, was the only other room on the lower floor. The deluge of chemicals had not spared it; even a stale half loaf of bread on the sideboard had been doused.

Strike headed up the stairs. Somebody had climbed or descended them, pouring the vicious, corrosive substance from a capacious container; it had spattered everywhere, even onto the landing windowsill, where the paint had bubbled and split apart.

On the first floor, Strike came to a halt. Even through the thick wool of his overcoat he could smell something else, something that the pungent industrial chemical could not mask. Sweet, putrid, rancid: the stench of decaying flesh.

He did not try either of the closed doors on the first floor. Instead, with his birthday whisky swaying stupidly in its plastic bag, he followed slowly in the footsteps of the pourer of acid, up a second flight of stained stairs from which the varnish had been burned away, the carved banisters scorched bare of their waxy shine.

The stench of decay grew stronger with every step Strike took. It reminded him of the time they stuck long sticks into the ground in Bosnia and pulled them out to sniff the ends, the one fail-safe way of finding the mass graves. He pressed his collar more tightly to his mouth as he reached the top floor, to the studio where a Victorian artist had once worked in the unchanging northern light.

Strike did not hesitate on the threshold except for the seconds it took to tug his shirt sleeve down to cover his bare hand, so that he would make no mark on the wooden door as he pushed it open. Silence but for a faint squeak of hinges, and then the desultory buzzing of flies.

He had expected death, but not this.

A carcass: trussed, stinking and rotting, empty and gutted, lying on the floor instead of hanging from a metal hook where surely it belonged. But what looked like a slaughtered pig wore human clothing.

It lay beneath the high arched beams, bathed in light from that gigantic Romanesque window, and though it was a private house and the traffic sloshed still beyond the glass, Strike felt that he stood retching in a temple, witness to sacrificial slaughter, to an act of unholy desecration.

Seven plates and seven sets of cutlery had been set around the decomposing body as though it were a gigantic joint of meat. The torso had been slit from throat to pelvis and Strike was tall enough to see, even from the threshold, the gaping black cavity that had been left behind. The intestines were gone, as though they had been eaten. Fabric and flesh had been burned away all over the corpse, heightening the vile impression that it had been cooked and feasted upon. In places the burned, decomposing cadaver was shining, almost liquid in appearance. Four hissing radiators were hastening the decay.

The rotted face lay furthest away from him, near the window. Strike squinted at it without moving, trying not to breathe. A wisp of yellowing beard clung still to the chin and a single burned-out eye socket was just visible.

And now, with all his experience of death and mutilation, Strike had to fight down the urge to vomit in the almost suffocating mingled stenches of chemical and corpse. He shifted his carrier bag up his thick forearm, drew his mobile phone out of his pocket and took photographs of the scene from as many angles as he could manage without moving further into the room. Then he backed out of the studio, allowing the door to swing shut, which did nothing to mitigate the almost solid stink, and called 999.

Slowly and carefully, determined not to slip and fall even though he was desperate to regain fresh, clean, rain-washed air, Strike proceeded back down the tarnished stairs to wait for the police in the street.

17

Best while you have it use your breath,
There is no drinking after death.

John Fletcher, The Bloody Brother

It was not the first time that Strike had visited New Scotland Yard at the insistence of the Met. His previous interview had also concerned a corpse, and it occurred to the detective, as he sat waiting in an inter-rogation room many hours later, the pain in his knee less acute after several hours of enforced inaction, that he had had sex the previous evening then too.

Alone in a room hardly bigger than the average office's stationery cupboard, his thoughts stuck like flies to the rotting obscenity he had found in the artist's studio. The horror of it had not left him. In his professional capacity he had viewed bodies that had been dragged into positions intended to suggest suicide or accident; had examined corpses bearing horrific traces of attempts to disguise the cruelty to which they had been subjected before death; he had seen men, women and children maimed and dismembered; but what he had seen at 179 Talgarth Road was something entirely new. The malignity of what had been done there had been almost orgiastic, a carefully calibrated display of sadistic showmanship. Worst to con-template was the order in which acid had been poured, the body disemboweled: had it been torture? Had Quine been alive or dead while his killer laid out place settings around him?

The huge vaulted room where Quine's body lay would now, no doubt, be swarming with men in full-body protective suits, gathering forensic evidence. Strike wished he were there with them. Inactivity after such a discovery was hateful to him. He burned with professional frustration. Shut out from the moment the police had arrived, he had been relegated to a mere blunderer who had stumbled onto the scene (and "scene," he thought suddenly, was the right word in more ways than one: the body tied up and arranged in the light from that giant church-like window ... a sacrifice to some demonic power ... seven plates, seven sets of cutlery ...)

The frosted glass window of the interrogation room blocked out everything beyond it but the color of the sky, now black. He had been in this tiny room for a long time and still the police had not finished taking his statement. It was difficult to gauge how much of their desire to prolong the interview was genuine suspicion, how much animosity. It was right, of course, that the person who discovered a murder victim should be subjected to thorough questioning, because they often knew more than they were willing to tell, and not infrequently knew every-thing. However, in solving the Lula Landry case Strike might be said to have humiliated the Met, who had so confidently pronounced her death suicide. Strike did not think he was being paranoid in thinking that the attitude of the crop-haired female detective inspector who had just left the room contained a determination to make him sweat. Nor did he think that it had been strictly necessary for quite so many of her colleagues to look in on him, some of them lingering only to stare at him, others delivering snide remarks.

If they thought they were inconveniencing him, they were wrong. He had nowhere else to be and they had fed him quite a decent meal. If they had only let him smoke, he would have been quite comfort-able. The woman who had been questioning him for an hour had told him he might go outside, accompanied, into the rain for a ciga-rette, but inertia and curiosity had kept him in his seat. His birthday whisky sat beside him in its carrier bag. He thought that if they kept him here much longer he might break it open. They had left him a plastic beaker of water.

The door behind him whispered over the dense gray carpet.

"Mystic Bob," said a voice.

Richard Anstis of the Metropolitan Police and the Territorial

Army entered the room grinning, his hair wet with rain, carrying a bundle of papers under his arm. One side of his face was heavily scarred, the skin beneath his right eye pulled taut. They had saved his sight at the field hospital in Kabul while Strike had lain unconscious, doctors working to preserve the knee of his severed leg.

"Anstis!" said Strike, taking the policeman's proffered hand. "What the——?"

"Pulled rank, mate, I'm going to handle this one," said Anstis, dropping into the seat lately vacated by the surly female detective. "You're not popular round here, you know. Lucky for you, you've got Uncle Dickie on your side, vouching for you."

He always said that Strike had saved his life, and perhaps it was true. They had been under fire on a yellow dirt road in Afghanistan. Strike himself was not sure what had made him sense the imminent explosion. The youth running from the roadside ahead with what looked like his younger brother could simply have been fleeing the gunfire. All he knew was that he had yelled at the driver of the Viking to brake, an injunction not followed—perhaps not heard— that he had reached forward, grabbed Anstis by the back of the shirt and hauled him one-handed into the back of the vehicle. Had Anstis remained where he was he would probably have suffered the fate of young Gary Topley, who had been sitting directly in front of Strike, and of whom they could find only the head and torso to bury.

"Need to run through this story one more time, mate," said Anstis, spreading out in front of him the statement that he must have taken from the female officer.

"All right if I drink?" asked Strike wearily.

Under Anstis's amused gaze, Strike retrieved the Arran single malt from the carrier bag and added two fingers to the lukewarm water in his plastic cup.

"Right: you were hired by his wife to find the dead man... we're assuming the body's this writer, this——"

"Owen Quine, yeah," supplied Strike, as Anstis squinted over his colleague's handwriting. "His wife hired me six days ago."

"And at that point he'd been missing——?"

"Ten days."

128

"But she hadn't been to the police?"

"No. He did this regularly: dropped out of sight without telling anyone where he was, then coming home again. He liked taking off for hotels without his wife."

"Why did she bring you in this time?"

"Things are difficult at home. There's a disabled daughter and money's short. He'd been away a bit longer than usual. She thought he'd gone off to a writer's retreat. She didn't know the name of the place, but I checked and he wasn't there."

"Still don't see why she called you rather than us."

"She says she called your lot in once before when he went walkabout and he was angry about it. Apparently he'd been with a girlfriend."

"I'll check that," said Anstis, making a note. "What made you go to that house?"

"I found out last night the Quines co-owned it."

A slight pause.

"His wife hadn't mentioned it?"

"No," said Strike. "Her story is that he hated the place and never went near it. She gave the impression she'd half forgotten they even owned it—"

"Is that likely?" murmured Anstis, scratching his chin. "If they're skint?"

"It's complicated," said Strike. "The other owner's Michael Fancourt—"

"I've heard of him."

"—and she says he won't let them sell. There was bad blood between Fancourt and Quine." Strike drank his whisky; it warmed throat and stomach. (Quine's stomach, his entire digestive tract, had been cut out. Where the hell was it?) "Anyway, I went along at lunchtime and there he was—or most of him was."

The whisky had made him crave a cigarette worse than ever.

"The body's a real fucking mess, from what I've heard," said Anstis. "Wanna see?"

Strike pulled his mobile phone from his pocket, brought up the photographs of the corpse and handed it across the desk.

"Holy shit," said Anstis. After a minute of silent contemplation of the rotting corpse he asked, disgusted, "What are those around him ... plates?"

"Yep," said Strike.

"That mean anything to you?"

"Nothing," said Strike.

"Any idea when he was last seen alive?"

"The last time his wife saw him was the night of the fifth. He'd just had dinner with his agent, who'd told him he couldn't publish his latest book because he's libeled Christ knows how many people, including a couple of very litigious men."

Anstis looked down at the notes left by DI Rawlins.

"You didn't tell Bridget that."

"She didn't ask. We didn't strike up much of a rapport."

"How long's this book been in the shops?"

"It isn't in the shops," said Strike, adding more whisky to his beaker. "It hasn't been published yet. I told you, he rowed with his agent because she told him he couldn't publish it."

"Have you read it?"

"Most of it."

"Did his wife give you a copy?"

"No, she says she's never read it."

"She forgot she owned a second house and she doesn't read her own husband's books," said Anstis without emphasis.

"Her story is that she reads them once they've got proper covers on," said Strike. "For what it's worth, I believe her."

"Uh-huh," said Anstis, who was now scribbling additions to Strike's statement. "How did you get a copy of the manuscript?"

"I'd prefer not to say."

"Could be a problem," said Anstis, glancing up.

"Not for me," said Strike.

"We might need to come back to that one, Bob."

Strike shrugged, then asked:

"Has his wife been told?"

"Should have been by now, yeah."

Strike had not called Leonora. The news that her husband was dead must be broken in person by somebody with the necessary training. He had done the job himself, many times, but he was out of practice; in any case, his allegiance this afternoon had been to the desecrated remains of Owen Quine, to stand watch over them until he had delivered them safely into the hands of the police.

He had not forgotten what Leonora would be going through while he was interrogated at Scotland Yard. He had imagined her opening the door to the police officer—or two of them, perhaps—the first thrill of alarm at the sight of the uniform; the hammer blow dealt to the heart by the calm, understanding, sympathetic invitation to retire indoors; the horror of the pronouncement (although they would not tell her, at least at first, about the thick purple ropes binding her husband, or the dark empty cavern that a murderer had made of his chest and belly; they would not say that his face had been burned away by acid or that somebody had laid out plates around him as though he were a giant roast . . . Strike remembered the platter of lamb that Lucy had handed around nearly twenty-four hours previously. He was not a squeamish man, but the smooth malt seemed to catch in his throat and he set down his beaker).

"How many people know what's in this book, d'you reckon?" asked Anstis slowly.

"No idea," said Strike. "Could be a lot by now. Quine's agent, Elizabeth Tassel—spelled like it sounds," he added helpfully, as Anstis scribbled, "sent it to Christian Fisher at Crossfire Publishing and he's a man who likes to gossip. Lawyers got involved to try and stop the talk."

"More and more interesting," muttered Anstis, writing fast. "You want anything else to eat, Bob?"

"I want a smoke."

"Won't be long," promised Anstis. "Who's he libeled?"

"The question is," said Strike, flexing his sore leg, "whether it's libel, or whether he's exposed the truth about people. But the characters I recognized were—give us a pen and paper," he said, because it was quicker to write than to dictate. He said the names aloud as he jotted them down: "Michael Fancourt, the writer; Daniel Chard, who's head of Quine's publisher; Kathryn Kent, Quine's girlfriend—"

"There's a girlfriend?"

131

"Yeah, they've been together over a year, apparently. I went to see her—Stafford Cripps House, part of Clement Attlee Court—and she claimed he wasn't at her flat and she hadn't seen him ... Liz Tassel, his agent; Jerry Waldegrave, his editor, and"—a fractional hesitation—"his wife."

"He's put his wife in there as well, has he?"

"Yeah," said Strike, pushing the list over the desk to Anstis. "But there are a load of other characters I wouldn't recognize. You've got a wide field if you're looking for someone he put in the book."

"Have you still got the manuscript?"

"No." Strike, expecting the question, lied easily. Let Anstis get a copy of his own, without Nina's fingerprints on it.

"Anything else you can think of that might be helpful?" Anstis asked, sitting up straight.

"Yeah," said Strike. "I don't think his wife did it."

Anstis shot Strike a quizzical look not unmixed with warmth. Strike was godfather to the son who had been born to Anstis just two days before both of them had been blown out of the Viking. Strike had met Timothy Cormoran Anstis a handful of times and had not been impressed in his favor.

"OK, Bob, sign this for us and I can give you a lift home."

Strike read through the statement carefully, took pleasure in correcting DI Rawlins's spelling in a few places, and signed.

His mobile rang as he and Anstis walked down the long corridor towards the lifts, Strike's knee protesting painfully.

"Cormoran Strike?"

"It's me, Leonora," she said, sounding almost exactly as she usually did, except that her voice was perhaps a little less flat.

Strike gestured to Anstis that he was not ready to enter the lift and drew aside from the policeman, to a dark window beneath which traffic was winding in the endless rain.

"Have the police been to see you?" he asked her.

"Yeah. I'm with them now."

"I'm very sorry, Leonora," he said.

"You all right?" she asked gruffly.

"Me?" said Strike, surprised. "I'm fine."

"They ain't giving you a hard time? They said you was being interviewed. I said to 'em, 'He only found Owen cos I asked him, what's he bin arrested for?'"

"They hadn't arrested me," said Strike. "Just needed a statement."

"But they've kept you all this time."

"How d'you know how long—?"

"I'm here," she said. "I'm downstairs in the lobby. I wanna see you, I made 'em bring me."

Astonished, with the whisky sitting on his empty stomach, he said the first thing that occurred to him.

"Who's looking after Orlando?"

"Edna," said Leonora, taking Strike's concern for her daughter as a matter of course. "When are they gonna let you go?"

"I'm on my way out now," he said.

"Who's that?" asked Anstis when Strike had rung off. "Charlotte worrying about you?"

"Christ, no," said Strike as they stepped together into the lift. He had completely forgotten that he had never told Anstis about the breakup. As a friend from the Met, Anstis was sealed off in a compartment on his own where gossip could not travel. "That's over. Ended months ago."

"Really? Tough break," said Anstis, looking genuinely sorry as the lift began to move downwards. But Strike thought that some of Anstis's disappointment was for himself. He had been one of the friends most taken with Charlotte, with her extraordinary beauty and her dirty laugh. "Bring Charlotte over" had been Anstis's frequent refrain when the two men had found themselves free of hospitals and the army, back in the city that was their home.

Strike felt an instinctive desire to shield Leonora from Anstis, but it was impossible. When the lift doors slid open there she was, thin and mousy, with her limp hair in combs, her old coat wrapped around her and an air of still wearing bedroom slippers even though her feet were clad in scuffed black shoes. She was flanked by the two uniformed officers, one female, who had evidently broken the news of Quine's death and then brought her here. Strike deduced from the guarded glances they gave Anstis that Leonora had given them reason to wonder; that her reaction to the news that her husband was dead had struck them as unusual.

Dry-faced and matter-of-fact, Leonora seemed relieved to see Strike.

"There you are," she said. "Why'd they keep you so long?"

Anstis looked at her curiously, but Strike did not introduce them.

"Shall we go over here?" he asked her, indicating a bench along the wall. As he limped off beside her he felt the three police officers draw together behind them.

"How are you?" he asked her, partly in the hope that she might exhibit some sign of distress, to assuage the curiosity of those watching.

"Dunno," she said, dropping onto the plastic seat. "I can't believe it. I never thought he'd go there, the silly sod. I s'pose some burglar got in and done it. He should've gone to a hotel like always, shouldn't he?"

They had not told her much, then. He thought that she was more shocked than she appeared, more than she knew herself. The act of coming to him seemed the disoriented action of somebody who did not know what else to do, except to turn to the person who was supposed to be helping her.

"Would you like me to take you home?" Strike asked her.

"I 'spect they'll give me a lift back," she said, with the same sense of untroubled entitlement she had brought to the statement that Elizabeth Tassel would pay Strike's bill. "I wanted to see you to check you was all right and I hadn't got you in trouble, and I wanted to ask you if you'll keep working for me."

"Keep working for you?" Strike repeated.

For a split second he wondered whether it was possible that she had not quite grasped what had happened, that she thought Quine was still out there somewhere to be found. Did her faint eccentricity of manner mask something more serious, some fundamental cognitive problem?

"They think I know something about it," said Leonora. "I can tell."

Strike hesitated on the verge of saying "I'm sure that's not true," but it would have been a lie. He was only too aware that Leonora, wife of a feckless, unfaithful husband, who had chosen not to contact the police and to allow ten days to elapse before making a show of looking for him, who had a key to the empty house where his body had been found and who would undoubtedly be able to take him by surprise, would be the first and most important suspect. Nevertheless, he asked:

"Why d'you think that?"

"I can tell," she repeated. "Way they were talking to me. And they've said they wanna look in our house, in his study."

It was routine, but he could see how she would feel this to be intrusive and ominous.

"Does Orlando know what's happened?" he asked.

"I told her but I don't think she realizes," said Leonora, and for the first time he saw tears in her eyes. "She says, 'Like Mr. Poop'—he was our cat that was run over—but I don't know if she understands, not really. You can't always tell with Orlando. I haven't told her someone killed him. Can't get my head around it."

There was a short pause in which Strike hoped, irrelevantly, that he was not giving off whisky fumes.

"Will you keep working for me?" she asked him directly. "You're better'n them, that's why I wanted you in the first place. Will you?"

"Yes," he said.

"Cos I can tell they think I had something to do with it," she repeated, standing up, "way they was talking to me."

She drew her coat more tightly around her.

"I'd better get back to Orlando. I'm glad you're all right."

She shuffled off to her escort again. The female police officer looked taken aback to be treated like a taxi driver but after a glance at Anstis acceded to Leonora's request for a lift home.

"The hell was that about?" Anstis asked him after the two women had passed out of earshot.

"She was worried you'd arrested me."

"Bit eccentric, isn't she?"

"Yeah, a bit."

"You didn't tell her anything, did you?" asked Anstis.

"No," said Strike, who resented the question. He knew better than to pass information about a crime scene to a suspect.

"You wanna be careful, Bob," said Anstis awkwardly, as they passed through the revolving doors into the rainy night. "Not to get under anyone's feet. It's murder now and you haven't got many friends round these parts, mate."

"Popularity's overrated. Listen, I'll get a cab—no," he said firmly, over Anstis's protestations, "I need to smoke before I go anywhere. Thanks, Rich, for everything."

They shook hands; Strike turned up his collar against the rain and with a wave of farewell limped off along the dark pavement. He was almost as glad to have shaken off Anstis as to take the first sweet pull on his cigarette.

18

For this I find, where jealousy is fed,
Horns in the mind are worse than on the head.

Ben Jonson, Every Man in His Humour

Strike had completely forgotten that Robin had left the office in what he categorized as a sulk on Friday afternoon. He only knew that she was the one person he wanted to talk to about what had happened, and while he usually avoided telephoning her at weekends, the circumstances felt exceptional enough to justify a text. He sent it from the taxi he found after fifteen minutes tramping wet, cold streets in the dark.

Robin was curled up at home in an armchair with *Investigative Interviewing: Psychology and Practice*, a book she had bought online. Matthew was on the sofa, speaking on the landline to his mother in Yorkshire, who was feeling unwell again. He rolled his eyes whenever Robin reminded herself to look up and smile sympathetically at his exasperation.

When her mobile vibrated, Robin glanced at it irritably; she was trying to concentrate on *Investigative Interviewing*.

Found Quine murdered. C

She let out a mingled gasp and shriek that made Matthew start. The book slipped out of her lap and fell, disregarded, to the floor. Seizing the mobile, she ran with it to the bedroom.

Matthew talked to his mother for twenty minutes more, then went and listened at the closed bedroom door. He could hear Robin asking questions and being given what seemed to be long, involved answers. Something about the timbre of her voice convinced him that it was Strike on the line. His square jaw tightened.

When Robin finally emerged from the bedroom, shocked and awestruck, she told her fiancé that Strike had found the missing man he had been hunting, and that he had been murdered. Matthew's natural curiosity tugged him one way, but his dislike of Strike, and the fact that he had dared contact Robin on a Sunday evening, pulled him another.

"Well, I'm glad something's happened to interest you tonight," he said. "I know you're bored shitless by Mum's health."

"You bloody hypocrite!" gasped Robin, winded by the injustice.

The row escalated with alarming speed. Strike's invitation to the wedding; Matthew's sneering attitude to Robin's job; what their life together was going to be; what each owed the other: Robin was horrified by how quickly the very fundamentals of their relationship were dragged out for examination and recrimination, but she did not back down. A familiar frustration and anger towards the men in her life had her in its grip—to Matthew, for failing to see why her job mattered to her so much; to Strike, for failing to recognize her potential.

(But he had called her when he had found the body...She had managed to slip in a question—"Who else have you told?"—and he had answered, without any sign that he knew what it would mean to her, "No one, only you.")

Meanwhile, Matthew was feeling extremely hard done by. He had noticed lately something that he knew he ought not to complain about, and which grated all the more for his feeling that he must lump it: before she worked for Strike, Robin had always been first to back down in a row, first to apologize, but her conciliatory nature seemed to have been warped by the stupid bloody job...

They only had one bedroom. Robin pulled spare blankets from on top of the wardrobe, grabbed clean clothes from inside it and announced her intention to sleep on the sofa. Sure that she would cave before long (the sofa was hard and uncomfortable) Matthew did not try to dissuade her.

But he had been wrong in expecting her to soften. When he woke the following morning it was to find an empty sofa and Robin gone. His anger increased exponentially. She had doubtless headed for work an hour earlier than usual, and his imagination—Matthew was not usually imaginative—showed him that big, ugly bastard opening the door of his flat, not the office below ...

19

. . . I to you will open
The book of a black sin, deep printed in me.
. . . my disease lies in my soul.

Thomas Dekker, *The Noble Spanish Soldier*

Strike had set his alarm for an early hour, with the intention of securing some peaceful, uninterrupted time without clients or telephone. He rose at once, showered and breakfasted, took great care over the fastening of the prosthesis onto a definitely swollen knee and, forty-five minutes after waking, limped into his office with the unread portion of *Bombyx Mori* under his arm. A suspicion that he had not confided to Anstis was driving him to finish the book as a matter of urgency.

After making himself a mug of strong tea he sat down at Robin's desk, where the light was best, and began to read.

Having escaped the Cutter and entered the city that had been his destination, Bombyx decided to rid himself of the companions of his long journey, Succuba and the Tick. This he did by taking them to a brothel where both appeared satisfied to work. Bombyx departed alone in search of Vainglorious, a famous writer and the man whom he hoped would be his mentor.

Halfway along a dark alleyway, Bombyx was accosted by a woman with long red hair and a demonic expression, who was taking a handful of dead rats home for supper. When she learned Bombyx's identity Harpy invited him to her house, which turned out to be a cave littered with animal skulls. Strike skim-read the sex, which took up four pages and involved Bombyx being strung up from the ceiling and whipped. Then, like the Tick, Harpy attempted to breast-feed from Bombyx, but in spite of being tied up he managed to beat her off. While his nipples leaked a dazzling supernatural light, Harpy wept and revealed her own breasts, from which leaked something dark brown and glutinous.

Strike scowled over this image. Not only was Quine's style starting to seem parodic, giving Strike a sense of sickened surfeit, the scene read like an explosion of malice, an eruption of pent-up sadism. Had Quine devoted months, perhaps years, of his life to the intention of causing as much pain and distress as possible? Was he sane? Could a man in such masterly control of his style, little though Strike liked it, be classified as mad?

He took a drink of tea, reassuringly hot and clean, and read on. Bombyx was on the point of leaving Harpy's house in disgust when another character burst in through her door: Epicoene, whom the sobbing Harpy introduced as her adopted daughter. A young girl, whose open robes revealed a penis, Epicoene insisted that she and Bombyx were twin souls, understanding, as they did, both the male and the female. She invited him to sample her hermaphrodite's body, but first to hear her sing. Apparently under the impression that she had a beautiful voice, she emitted barks like a seal until Bombyx ran from her with his ears covered.

Now Bombyx saw for the first time, high on a hill in the middle of the city, a castle of light. He climbed the steep streets towards it until hailed from a dark doorway by a male dwarf, who introduced himself as the writer Vainglorious. He had Fancourt's eyebrows, Fancourt's surly expression and sneering manner, and offered Bombyx a bed for the night, "having heard of your great talent."

To Bombyx's horror, a young woman was chained up inside the house, writing at a rolltop desk. Burning brands lay white hot in the fire, to which were attached phrases in twisted metal such as *pertinacious gudgeon* and *chrysostomatic intercourse*. Evidently expecting Bombyx to be amused, Vainglorious explained that he had set his young wife Effigy to write her own book, so that she would not bother him while he created his next masterpiece. Unfortunately, Vainglorious explained, Effigy had no talent, for which she must be punished. He removed one of the brands from the fire, at which Bombyx fled the house, pursued by Effigy's shrieks of pain.

Bombyx sped on towards the castle of light where he imagined he would find his refuge. Over the door was the name *Phallus Impudicus*, but nobody answered Bombyx's knock. He therefore skirted the castle, peering in through windows until he saw a naked bald man standing over the corpse of a golden boy whose body was covered in stab wounds, each of which emitted the same dazzling light that issued from Bombyx's own nipples. Phallus's erect penis appeared to be rotting.

"Hi."

Strike started and looked up. Robin was standing there in her trench coat, her face pink, long red-gold hair loose, tousled and gilded in the early sunlight streaming through the window. Just then, Strike found her beautiful.

"Why are you so early?" he heard himself ask.

"Wanted to know what's going on."

She stripped off her coat and Strike looked away, mentally castigating himself. Naturally she looked good, appearing unexpectedly when his mind had been full of the image of a naked bald man, displaying a diseased penis...

"D'you want another tea?"

"That'd be great, thanks," he said without lifting his eyes from the manuscript. "Give me five, I want to finish this..."

And with a feeling that he was diving again into contaminated water, he re-immersed himself in the grotesque world of *Bombyx Mori*.

As Bombyx stared through the window of the castle, transfixed by the horrible sight of Phallus Impudicus and the corpse, he found himself roughly seized by a crowd of hooded minions, dragged inside the castle and stripped naked in front of Phallus Impudicus. By this time, Bombyx's belly was enormous and he appeared ready to give birth. Phallus Impudicus gave ominous directions to his minions, which left the naive Bombyx convinced that he was to be the guest of honor at a feast.

Six of the characters that Strike had recognized—Succuba, the Tick, the Cutter, Harpy, Vainglorious and Impudicus—were now joined by Epicoene. The seven guests sat down at a large table on which stood a large jug, the contents of which were smoking, and a man-sized empty platter.

When Bombyx arrived in the hall, he found that there was no seat for him. The other guests rose, moved towards him with ropes and overpowered him. He was trussed up, placed on the platter and slit open. The mass that had been growing inside him was revealed to be a ball of supernatural light, which was ripped out and locked in a casket by Phallus Impudicus.

The contents of the smoking jug were revealed to be vitriol, which the seven attackers poured gleefully over the still-living, shrieking Bombyx. When at last he fell silent, they began to eat him.

The book ended with the guests filing out of the castle, discussing their memories of Bombyx without guilt, leaving behind them an empty hall, the still-smoking remains of the corpse on the table and the locked casket of light hanging, lamp-like, above him.

"Shit," said Strike quietly.

He looked up. Robin had placed a fresh tea beside him without his noticing. She was perched on the sofa, waiting quietly for him to finish.

"It's all in here," said Strike. "What happened to Quine. It's here."

"What d'you mean?"

"The hero of Quine's book dies exactly the way Quine died. Tied up, guts torn out, something acidic poured over him. In the book they eat him."

Robin stared at him.

"The plates. Knives and forks..."

"Exactly," said Strike.

Without thinking, he pulled his mobile out of his pocket and brought up the photos he had taken, then caught sight of her frightened expression.

"No," he said, "sorry, forgot you're not—"

"Give it to me," she said.

What had he forgotten? That she was not trained or experienced, not a policewoman or a soldier? She wanted to live up to his momentary forgetfulness. She wanted to step up, to be more than she was.

"I want to see," she lied.

He handed over the telephone with obvious misgivings.

Robin did not flinch, but as she stared at the open hole in the cadaver's chest and stomach her own insides seemed to shrink in horror. Raising her mug to her lips, she found that she did not want to drink. The worst was the angled close-up of the face, eaten away by whatever had been poured on it, blackened and with that burned-out eye socket...

The plates struck her as an obscenity. Strike had zoomed in on one of them; the place setting had been meticulously arranged.

"My God," she said numbly, handing the phone back.

"Now read this," said Strike, handing her the relevant pages.

She did so in silence. When she had finished, she looked up at him with eyes that seemed to have doubled in size.

"My *God*," she said again.

Her mobile rang. She pulled it out of the handbag on the sofa beside her and looked at it. Matthew. Still furious at him, she pressed "ignore."

"How many people," she asked Strike, "d'you think have read this book?"

"Could be a lot of them by now. Fisher emailed bits of it all over town; between him and the lawyers' letters, it's become hot property."

And a strange, random thought crossed Strike's mind as he spoke: that Quine could not have arranged better publicity if he had tried... but he could not have poured acid over himself while tied up, or cut out his own guts...

"It's been kept in a safe at Roper Chard that half the company seems to know the code for," he went on. "That's how I got hold of it."

"But don't you think the killer's likely to be someone who's *in* the—?"

Robin's mobile rang again. She glanced down at it: Matthew. Again, she pressed "ignore."

"Not necessarily," said Strike, answering her unfinished question. "But the people he's written about are going to be high on the list when the police start interviewing. Of the characters I recognize, Leonora claims not to have read it, so does Kathryn Kent—"

"Do you believe them?" asked Robin.

"I believe Leonora. Not sure about Kathryn Kent. How did the line go? 'To see thee tortur'd would give me pleasure'?"

"I can't believe a woman would have done that," said Robin at once, glancing at Strike's mobile now lying on the desk between them.

"Did you never hear about the Australian woman who skinned her lover, decapitated him, cooked his head and buttocks and tried to serve him up to his kids?"

"You're not serious."

"I'm totally serious. Look it up on the net. When women turn, they really turn," said Strike.

"He was a big man ... "

"If it was a woman he trusted? A woman he met for sex?"

"Who do we know for sure has read it?"

"Christian Fisher, Elizabeth Tassel's assistant Ralph, Tassel herself, Jerry Waldegrave, Daniel Chard—they're all characters, except Ralph and Fisher. Nina Lascelles—"

"Who are Waldegrave and Chard? Who's Nina Lascelles?"

"Quine's editor, the head of his publisher and the girl who helped me nick this," said Strike, giving the manuscript a slap.

Robin's mobile rang for the third time.

"Sorry," she said impatiently, and picked it up. "Yes?"

"Robin."

Matthew's voice sounded strangely congested. He never cried and he had never before shown himself particularly overcome by remorse at an argument.

"Yes?" she said, a little less sharply.

"Mum's had another stroke. She's—she's—"

An elevator drop in the pit of her stomach.

"Matt?"

He was crying.

"Matt?" she repeated urgently.

"'S dead," he said, like a little boy.

"I'm coming," said Robin. "Where are you? I'll come now."

Strike was watching her face. He saw tidings of death there and hoped it was nobody she loved, neither of her parents, none of her brothers ...

"All right," she was saying, already on her feet. "Stay there. I'm coming.

"It's Matt's mother," she told Strike. "She's died."

It felt utterly unreal. She could not believe it.

"They were only talking on the phone last night," she said. Remembering Matt's rolling eyes and the muffled voice she had just heard, she was overwhelmed with tenderness and sympathy. "I'm so sorry but—"

"Go," said Strike. "Tell him I'm sorry, will you?"

"Yes," said Robin, trying to fasten her handbag, her fingers grown clumsy in her agitation. She had known Mrs. Cunliffe since primary school. She slung her raincoat over her arm. The glass door flashed and closed behind her.

Strike's eyes remained fixed for a few seconds on the place where Robin had vanished. Then he looked down at his watch. It was barely nine o'clock. The brunet divorcée whose emeralds lay in his safe was due at the office in just over half an hour.

He cleared and washed the mugs, then took out the necklace he had recovered, locked up the manuscript of *Bombyx Mori* in the safe instead, refilled the kettle and checked his emails.

They'll postpone the wedding.

He did not want to feel glad about it. Pulling out his mobile, he called Anstis, who answered almost at once.

"Bob?"

"Anstis, I don't know whether you've already got this, but there's something you should know. Quine's last novel describes his murder."

"Say that again?"

Strike explained. It was clear from the brief silence after he had finished speaking that Anstis had not yet had the information.

"Bob, I need a copy of that manuscript. If I send someone over—?"

"Give me three quarters of an hour," said Strike.

He was still photocopying when his brunet client arrived.

"Where's your secretary?" were her first words, turning to him with a coquettish show of surprise, as though she was sure he had arranged for them to be alone.

"Off sick. Diarrhea and vomiting," said Strike repressively. "Shall we go through?"

20

Is Conscience a comrade for an old Soldier?

Francis Beaumont and John Fletcher, *The False One*

Late that evening Strike sat alone at his desk while the traffic rumbled through the rain outside, eating Singapore noodles with one hand and scribbling a list for himself with the other. The rest of the day's work over, he was free to turn his attention fully to the murder of Owen Quine and in his spiky, hard-to-read handwriting was jotting down those things that must be done next. Beside some of them he had jotted the letter A for Anstis, and if it had crossed Strike's mind that it might be considered arrogant or deluded of a private detective with no authority in the investigation to imagine he had the power to delegate tasks to the police officer in charge of the case, the thought did not trouble him.

Having worked with Anstis in Afghanistan, Strike did not have a particularly high opinion of the police officer's abilities. He thought Anstis competent but unimaginative, an efficient recognizer of patterns, a reliable pursuer of the obvious. Strike did not despise these traits—the obvious was usually the answer and the methodical ticking of boxes the way to prove it—but this murder was elaborate, strange, sadistic and grotesque, literary in inspiration and ruthless in execution. Was Anstis capable of comprehending the mind that had nurtured a plan of murder in the fetid soil of Quine's own imagination?

Strike's mobile rang, piercing in the silence. Only when he had put it to his ear and heard Leonora Quine did he realize that he had been hoping it would be Robin.

"How are you?" he asked.

"I've had the police here," she said, cutting through the social niceties. "They've been all through Owen's study. I didn't wanna, but Edna said I should let 'em. Can't we be left in peace after what just happened?"

"They've got grounds for a search," said Strike. "There might be something in Owen's study that'll give them a lead on his killer."

"Like what?"

"I don't know," said Strike patiently, "but I think Edna's right. It was best to let them in."

There was a silence.

"Are you still there?" he asked.

"Yeah," she said, "and now they've left it locked up so I can't get in it. And they wanna come back. I don't like them being here. Orlando don't like it. One of 'em," she sounded outraged, "asked if I wanted to move out of the house for a bit. I said, 'No, I bloody don't.' Orlando's never stayed anywhere else, she couldn't deal with it. I'm not going anywhere."

"The police haven't said they want to question you, have they?"

"No," she said. "Only asked if they can go in the study."

"Good. If they want to ask you questions—"

"I should get a lawyer, yeah. That's what Edna said."

"Would it be all right if I come and see you tomorrow morning?" he asked.

"Yeah." She sounded glad. "Come round ten, I need to go shopping first thing. Couldn't get out all day. I didn't wanna leave them in the house without me here."

Strike hung up, reflecting again that Leonora's manner was unlikely to be standing her in good stead with the police. Would Anstis see, as Strike did, that Leonora's slight obtuseness, her failure to produce what others felt was appropriate behavior, her stubborn refusal to look at what she did not wish to look at—arguably the very qualities that had enabled her to endure the ordeal of living with Quine—would have made it impossible for her to kill him? Or would her oddities, her refusal to show normal grief reactions because of an innate though perhaps unwise honesty, cause the suspicion already lying in Anstis's mundane mind to swell, obliterating other possibilities?

There was an intensity, almost a feverishness, about the way Strike returned to his scribbling, left hand still shoveling food into his mouth. Thoughts came fluently, cogently: jotting down the questions he wanted answered, locations he wanted cased, the trails he wanted followed. It was a plan of action for himself and a means of nudging Anstis in the right direction, of helping open his eyes to the fact that it was not *always* the wife when a husband was killed, even if the man had been feckless, unreliable and unfaithful.

At last Strike cast his pen down, finished the noodles in two large mouthfuls and cleared his desk. His notes he put into the cardboard folder with Owen Quine's name on the spine, having first crossed out "Missing Person" and substituted the word "Murder." He turned off the lights and was on the point of locking the glass door when he thought of something and returned to Robin's computer.

And there it was, on the BBC website. Not headline news, of course, because whatever Quine might have thought, he had not been a very famous man. It came three stories below the main news that the EU had agreed to a bailout for the Irish Republic.

The body of a man believed to be writer Owen Quine, 58, has been found in a house in Talgarth Road, London. Police have launched a murder inquiry following the discovery, which was made yesterday by a family friend.

There was no photograph of Quine in his Tyrolean cloak, nor were there details of the horrors to which the body had been subjected. But it was early days; there was time.

Upstairs in his flat, some of Strike's energy deserted him. He dropped onto his bed and rubbed his eyes wearily, then fell backwards and lay there, fully dressed, his prosthesis still attached. Thoughts he had managed to keep at bay now pressed in upon him...

Why had he not alerted the police to the fact that Quine had been missing for nearly two weeks? Why had he not suspected that Quine might be dead? He had had answers to these questions when DI

Rawlins had put them to him, reasonable answers, sane answers, but he found it much more difficult to satisfy himself.

He did not need to take out his phone to see Quine's body. The vision of that bound, decaying corpse seemed imprinted on his retinas. How much cunning, how much hatred, how much perversity had it taken to turn Quine's literary excrescence into reality? What kind of human being could bring themselves to slit a man open and pour acid over him, to gut him and lay plates around his empty corpse?

Strike could not rid himself of the unreasonable conviction that he ought somehow to have smelled the scene from afar, like the carrion bird he had trained to be. How had he—with his once-notorious instinct for the strange, the dangerous, the suspicious—not realized that the noisy, self-dramatizing, self-publicizing Quine had been gone too long, that he was too silent?

Because the silly bastard kept crying wolf ... and because I'm knackered.

He rolled over, heaved himself off the bed and headed for the bathroom, but his thoughts kept scurrying back to the body: the gaping hole in the torso, the burned-out eye sockets. The killer had moved around that monstrosity while it was still bleeding, when Quine's screams had perhaps barely stopped echoing through the great vaulted space, and gently straightened forks ... and there was another question for his list: what, if anything, had the neighbors heard of Quine's final moments?

Strike got into bed at last, covered his eyes with a large, hairy forearm and listened to his own thoughts, which were gabbling at him like a workaholic twin who would not pipe down. Forensics had already had more than twenty-four hours. They would have formed opinions, even if all tests were not yet in. He must call Anstis, find out what they were saying ...

Enough, he told his tired, hyperactive brain. *Enough.*

And by the same power of will that in the army had enabled him to fall instantly asleep on bare concrete, on rocky ground, on lumpy camp beds that squeaked rusty complaints about his bulk whenever he moved, he slid smoothly into sleep like a warship sliding out on dark water.

21

Is he then dead?
What, dead at last, quite, quite for ever dead?

William Congreve, *The Mourning Bride*

At a quarter to nine the next morning Strike made his way slowly down the metal stairs, asking himself, not for the first time, why he did not do something about getting the birdcage lift fixed. His knee was still sore and puffy after his fall, so he was allowing over an hour to get to Ladbroke Grove, because he could not afford to keep taking taxis.

A gust of icy air stung his face as he opened the door, then everything went white as a flash went off inches from his eyes. He blinked—the outlines of three men danced in front of him—he threw up his hand against another volley of flashes.

"Why didn't you inform the police that Owen Quine was missing, Mr. Strike?"

"Did you know he was dead, Mr. Strike?"

For a split second he considered retreat, slamming the door on them, but that meant being trapped and having to face them later.

"No comment," he said coolly and walked into them, refusing to alter his course by a hair's breadth, so that they were forced to step out of his path, two asking questions and one running backwards, snapping and snapping. The girl who so often joined Strike for smoking breaks in the doorway of the guitar shop was gaping at the scene through the window.

"Why didn't you tell anyone he'd been missing for more than a fortnight, Mr. Strike?"

"Why didn't you notify the police?"

Strike strode in silence, his hands in his pockets and his expression grim. They scurried along beside him, trying to make him talk, a pair of razor-beaked seagulls dive-bombing a fishing trawler.

"Trying to show them up again, Mr. Strike?"

"Get one over on the police?"

"Publicity good for business, Mr. Strike?"

He had boxed in the army. In his imagination he wheeled around and delivered a left hook to the floating rib area, so that the little shit crumpled...

"Taxi!" he shouted.

Flash, flash, flash went the camera as he got into it; thankfully the lights ahead turned green, the taxi moved smoothly away from the curb and they gave up running after a few steps.

Fuckers, Strike thought, glancing over his shoulder as the taxi rounded a corner. Some bastard at the Met must have tipped them off that he had found the body. It would not have been Anstis, who had held back the information from the official statement, but one of the embittered bastards who had not forgiven him for Lula Landry.

"You famous?" asked the cabbie, staring at him in the rearview mirror.

"No," said Strike shortly. "Drop me at Oxford Circus, will you?"

Disgruntled at such a short fare, the cabbie muttered under his breath.

Strike took out his mobile and texted Robin again.

2 journalists outside door when I left. Say you work for Crowdy.

Then he called Anstis.

"Bob."

"I've just been doorstepped. They know I found the body."

"How?"

"You're asking me?"

A pause.

"It was always going to come out, Bob, but I didn't give it to them."

"Yeah, I saw the 'family friend' line. They're trying to make out I didn't tell you lot because I wanted the publicity."

"Mate, I never—"

"Be good to have that rebutted by an official source, Rich. Mud sticks and I've got a livelihood to make here."

"I'll get it done," promised Anstis. "Listen, why don't you come over for dinner tonight? Forensics have got back with their first thoughts; be good to talk it over."

"Yeah, great," said Strike as the taxi approached Oxford Circus. "What time?"

He remained standing on the Tube train, because sitting meant having to get up again and that put more strain on his sore knee. As he was going through Royal Oak he felt his mobile buzz and saw two texts, the first from his sister Lucy.

Many Happy Returns, Stick! Xxx

He had completely forgotten that today was his birthday. He opened the second text.

Hi Cormoran, thanks for warning about journos, just met them, they're still hanging round the outside door. See you later. Rx

Grateful that the day was temporarily dry, Strike reached the Quine house just before ten. It looked just as dingy and depressing in weak sunlight as it had the last time he had visited, but with a difference: there was a police officer standing in front of it. He was a tall young copper with a pugnacious-looking chin and when he saw Strike walking towards him with the ghost of a limp, his eyebrows contracted.

"Can I ask who you are, sir?"

"Yeah, I expect so," said Strike, walking past him and ringing the doorbell. Anstis's dinner invitation notwithstanding, he was not feeling sympathetic to the police just now. "Should be just about within your capabilities."

The door opened and Strike found himself face to face with a tall, gangling girl with sallow skin, a mop of curly light brown hair, a wide mouth and an ingenuous expression. Her eyes, which were a clear, pale green, were large and set far apart. She was wearing what was either a long sweatshirt or a short dress that ended above bony knees and fluffy pink socks, and she was cradling a large plush orangutan to her flat chest. The toy ape had Velcro attachments on its paws and was hanging around her neck.

"Hullo," she said. She swayed very gently, side to side, putting weight first on one foot, then on the other.

"Hello," said Strike. "Are you Orlan—?"

"Can I have your name, please, sir?" asked the young policeman loudly.

"Yeah, all right—if I can ask why you're standing outside this house," said Strike with a smile.

"There's been press interest," said the young policeman.

"A man came," said Orlando, "and with a camera and Mum said—"

"Orlando!" called Leonora from inside the house. "What are you doing?"

She came stumping down the hall behind her daughter, gaunt and white-faced in an ancient navy blue dress with its hem hanging down.

"Oh," she said, "it's you. Come in."

As he stepped over the threshold, Strike smiled at the policeman, who glared back.

"What's your name?" Orlando asked Strike as the front door closed behind them.

"Cormoran," he said.

"That's a funny name."

"Yeah, it is," said Strike and something made him add, "I was named after a giant."

"That's funny," said Orlando, swaying.

"Go in," said Leonora curtly, pointing Strike towards the kitchen. "I need the loo. Be with you in a mo."

Strike proceeded down the narrow hallway. The door of the study was closed and, he suspected, still locked.

On reaching the kitchen he discovered to his surprise that he was not the only visitor. Jerry Waldegrave, the editor from Roper Chard, was sitting at the kitchen table, clutching a bunch of flowers in somber purples and blues, his pale face anxious. A second bunch of flowers, still in its cellophane, protruded from a sink half filled with dirty crockery. Supermarket bags of food sat unpacked on the sides.

"Hi," said Waldegrave, scrambling to his feet and blinking earnestly at Strike through his horn-rimmed glasses. Evidently he did not recognize the detective from their previous meeting on the dark roof garden because he asked, as he held out his hand, "Are you family?"

"Family friend," said Strike as they shook hands.

"Terrible thing," said Waldegrave. "Had to come and see if I could do anything. She's been in the bathroom ever since I arrived."

"Right," said Strike.

Waldegrave resumed his seat. Orlando edged crabwise into the dark kitchen, cuddling her furry orangutan. A very long minute passed while Orlando, clearly the most at ease, unabashedly stared at both of them.

"You've got nice hair," she announced at last to Jerry Waldegrave. "It's like a hairstack."

"I suppose it is," said Waldegrave and he smiled at her. She edged out again.

Another brief silence followed, during which Waldegrave fidgeted with the flowers, his eyes darting around the kitchen.

"Can't believe it," he said at last.

They heard the loud flushing of a toilet upstairs, a thumping on the stairs, and Leonora returned with Orlando at her heels.

"Sorry," she said to the two men. "I'm a bit upset."

It was obvious that she was referring to her stomach.

"Look, Leonora," said Jerry Waldegrave in an agony of awkwardness, getting to his feet, "I don't want to intrude when you've got your friend here—"

"Him? He's not a friend, he's a detective," said Leonora.

"Sorry?"

Strike remembered that Waldegrave was deaf in one ear.

"He's called a name like a giant," said Orlando.

"He's a detective," said Leonora loudly, over her daughter.

"Oh," said Waldegrave, taken aback. "I didn't—why—?"

"Cos I need one," said Leonora shortly. "The police think I done it to Owen."

There was a silence. Waldegrave's discomfort was palpable.

"My daddy died," Orlando informed the room. Her gaze was direct and eager, seeking a reaction. Strike, who felt that something was required of one of them, said:

"I know. It's very sad."

"Edna said it was sad," replied Orlando, as though she had hoped for something more original, and she slid out of the room again.

"Sit down," Leonora invited the two men. "They for me?" she added, indicating the flowers in Waldegrave's hand.

"Yes," he said, fumbling a little as he handed them over but remaining on his feet. "Look, Leonora, I don't want to take up any of your time just now, you must be so busy with—with arrangements and—"

"They won't let me have his body," said Leonora with devastating honesty, "so I can't make no arrangements yet."

"Oh, and there's a card," said Waldegrave desperately, feeling in his pockets. "Here … well, if there's anything we can do, Leonora, anything—"

"Can't see what anyone can do," said Leonora shortly, taking the envelope he proffered. She sat down at the table where Strike had already pulled up a chair, glad to take the weight off his leg.

"Well, I think I'll be off, leave you to it," said Waldegrave. "Listen, Leonora, I hate to ask at a time like this, but *Bombyx Mori* … have you got a copy here?"

"No," she said. "Owen took it with him."

"I'm so sorry, but it would help us if … could I have a look and see if any of it's been left behind?"

She peered up at him through those huge, outdated glasses.

"Police've taken anything he left," she said. "They went through the study like a dose of salts yesterday. Locked it up and taken the key—I can't even go in there myself now."

"Oh, well, if the police need … no," said Waldegrave, "fair enough. No, I'll see myself out, don't get up."

He walked up the hall and they heard the front door close behind him.

"Dunno why he came," said Leonora sullenly. "Make him feel like he's done something nice, I suppose."

She opened the card he had given her. There was a watercolor of violets on the front. Inside were many signatures.

"Being all nice now, because they feel guilty," said Leonora, throwing the card down on the Formica-topped table.

"Guilty?"

"They never appreciated him. You got to market books," she said, surprisingly. "You got to promote 'em. It's up to the publishers to give 'em a push. They wouldn't never get him on TV or anything like he needed."

Strike guessed that these were complaints she had learned from her husband.

"Leonora," he said, taking out his notebook. "Is it all right if I ask you a couple of questions?"

"I s'pose. I don't know nothing, though."

"Have you heard from anyone who spoke to Owen or saw him after he left here on the fifth?"

She shook her head.

"No friends, no family?"

"No one," she said. "D'you want a cup of tea?"

"Yeah, that'd be great," said Strike, who did not much fancy anything made in this grubby kitchen, but wanted to keep her talking.

"How well d'you know the people at Owen's publisher?" he asked over the noisy filling of the kettle.

She shrugged.

"Hardly at all. Met that Jerry when Owen done a book signing once."

"You're not friendly with anyone at Roper Chard?"

"No. Why would I be? It was Owen worked with them, not me."

"And you haven't read *Bombyx Mori*, have you?" Strike asked her casually.

"I've told you that already. I don't like reading 'em till they're published. Why's everyone keep asking me that?" she said, looking up from the plastic bag in which she had been rummaging for biscuits.

"What was the matter with the body?" she demanded suddenly. "What happened to him? They won't tell me. They took his toothbrush for DNA to identify him. Why won't they let me see him?"

He had dealt with this question before, from other wives, from distraught parents. He fell back, as so often before, on partial truth.

"He'd been lying there for a while," he said.

"How long?"

"They don't know yet."

"How was it done?"

"I don't think they know that exactly, yet."

"But they must..."

She fell silent as Orlando shuffled back into the room, clutching not just her plush orangutan but also a sheaf of brightly colored drawings.

"Where's Jerry gone?"

"Back to work," said Leonora.

"He's got nice hair. I don't like your hair," she told Strike. "It's fuzzy."

"I don't like it much, either," he said.

"He don't want to look at pictures now, Dodo," said her mother impatiently, but Orlando ignored her mother and spread her paintings out on the table for Strike to see.

"I did them."

They were recognizably flowers, fish and birds. A child's menu could be read through the back of one of them.

"They're very good," said Strike. "Leonora, d'you know if the police found any bits of *Bombyx Mori* yesterday, when they searched the study?"

"Yeah," she said, dropping tea bags into chipped mugs. "Two old typewriter ribbons; they'd fallen down the back of the desk. They come out and ask me where the rest of 'em were; I said, he took 'em when he went."

"I like Daddy's study," announced Orlando, "because he gives me paper for drawing."

"It's a tip, that study," said Leonora, switching the kettle on. "Took 'em ages to look through everything."

"Auntie Liz went in there," said Orlando.

"When?" asked Leonora, glaring at her daughter with two mugs in her hands.

"When she came and you were in the loo," said Orlando. "She walked into Daddy's study. I seen her."

"She don't have no right to go in there," said Leonora. "Was she poking around?"

"No," said Orlando. "She just walked in and then she walked out and she saw me an' she was crying."

"Yeah," said Leonora with a satisfied air. "She was tearful with me an' all. Another one feeling guilty."

"When did she come over?" Strike asked Leonora.

"First thing Monday," said Leonora. "Wanted to see if she could help. Help! She's done enough."

Strike's tea was so weak and milky it looked as though it had never known a tea bag; his preference was for a brew the color of creosote. As he took a polite, token sip, he remembered Elizabeth Tassel's avowed wish that Quine had died when her Doberman bit him.

"I like her lipstick," announced Orlando.

"You like everyone's everything today," said Leonora vaguely, sitting back down with her own mug of weak tea. "I asked her why she done it, why she told Owen he couldn't publish his book, and upset him like that."

"And what did she say?" asked Strike.

"That he's gone and put a load of real people in it," said Leonora. "I dunno why they're so upset about that. He always does it." She sipped her tea. "He's put me in loads of 'em."

Strike thought of Succuba, the "well-worn whore," and found himself despising Owen Quine.

"I wanted to ask you about Talgarth Road."

"I don't know why he went there," she said immediately. "He hated it. He wanted to sell it for years but that Fancourt wouldn't."

"Yeah, I've been wondering about that."

Orlando had slid onto the chair beside him, one bare leg twisted underneath her as she added vibrantly colored fins to a picture of a large fish with a pack of crayons she appeared to have pulled from thin air.

"How come Michael Fancourt's been able to block the sale all these years?"

"It's something to do with how it was left to 'em by that bloke Joe. Something about how it was to be used. I dunno. You'd have to ask Liz, she knows all about it."

"When was the last time Owen was there, do you know?"

"Years ago," she said. "I dunno. Years."

"I want more paper to draw," Orlando announced.

"I haven't got any more," said Leonora. "It's all in Daddy's study. Use the back of this."

She seized a circular from the cluttered work surface and pushed it across the table to Orlando, but her daughter shoved it away and left the kitchen at a languid walk, the orangutan swinging from her neck. Almost at once they heard her trying to force the door of the study.

"Orlando, *no!*" barked Leonora, jumping up and hurrying into the hall. Strike took advantage of her absence to lean back and pour away most of his milky tea into the sink; it spattered down the bouquet clinging traitorously to the cellophane.

"*No*, Dodo. You can't do that. *No*. We're not allowed—*we're not allowed, get off it—*"

A high-pitched wail and then a loud thudding proclaimed Orlando's flight upstairs. Leonora reappeared in the kitchen with a flushed face.

"I'll be paying for that all day now," she said. "She's unsettled. Don't like the police here."

She yawned nervously.

"Have you slept?" Strike asked.

"Not much. Cos I keep thinking, *Who?* Who'd do it to him? He upsets people, I know that," she said distractedly, "but that's just how he is. Temperamental. He gets angry over little things. He's always been like that, he don't mean anything by it. Who'd kill him for that?"

"Michael Fancourt must still have a key to the house," she went on, twisting her fingers together as she jumped subject. "I thought that last night when I couldn't sleep. I know Michael Fancourt don't like him, but that's ages ago. Anyway, Owen never did that thing Michael said he did. He never wrote it. But Michael Fancourt wouldn't kill Owen." She looked up at Strike with clear eyes as innocent as her daughter's. "He's rich, isn't he? Famous...he wouldn't."

Strike had always marveled at the strange sanctity conferred upon celebrities by the public, even while the newspapers denigrated, hunted or hounded them. No matter how many famous people were convicted of rape or murder, still the belief persisted, almost pagan in its intensity: not *him*. It couldn't be *him*. He's *famous*.

"And that bloody Chard," burst out Leonora, "sending Owen threatening letters. Owen never liked him. And then he signs the card and says if there's anything he can do … where's that card?"

The card with the picture of violets had vanished from the table.

"She's got it," said Leonora, flushing angrily. "She's taken it." And so loudly that it made Strike jump she bellowed "DODO!" at the ceiling.

It was the irrational anger of a person in the first raw stages of grief and, like her upset stomach, revealed just how she was suffering beneath the surly surface.

"DODO!" shouted Leonora again. "What have I told you about taking things that don't belong—?"

Orlando reappeared with startling suddenness in the kitchen, still cuddling her orangutan. She must have crept back down without them hearing, as quiet as a cat.

"You took my card!" said Leonora angrily. "What have I told you about taking things that don't belong to you? Where is it?"

"I like the flowers," said Orlando, producing the glossy but now crumpled card, which her mother snatched from her.

"It's *mine*," she told her daughter. "See," she went on, addressing Strike and pointing to the longest handwritten message, which was in precise copperplate: "'Do let me know if there is anything you need. Daniel Chard.' Bloody hypocrite."

"Daddy didn't like Dannulchar," said Orlando. "He told me."

"He's a bloody hypocrite, I know that," said Leonora, who was squinting at the other signatures.

"He give me a paintbrush," said Orlando, "after he touched me."

There was a short, pregnant silence. Leonora looked up at her. Strike had frozen with his mug halfway to his lips.

"What?"

"I didn't like him touching me."

"What are you talking about? Who touched you?"

"At Daddy's work."

"Don't talk so silly," said her mother.

"When Daddy took me and I saw—"

"He took her in a month ago or more, because I had a doctor's appointment," Leonora told Strike, flustered, on edge. "I don't know what she's on about."

"...and I saw the pictures for books that they put on, all colored," said Leonora, "an' Dannulchar did touch—"

"You don't even know who Daniel Chard is," said Leonora.

"He's got no hair," said Orlando. "And after Daddy took me to see the lady an' I gave her my best picture. She had nice hair."

"What lady? What are you talking—?"

"When Dannulchar touched me," said Orlando loudly. "He touched me and I shouted and after he gave me a paintbrush."

"You don't want to go round saying things like that," said Leonora and her strained voice cracked. "Aren't we in enough— Don't be stupid, Orlando."

Orlando grew very red in the face. Glaring at her mother, she left the kitchen. This time she slammed the door hard behind her; it did not close, but bounced open again. Strike heard her stamping up the stairs; after a few steps she started shrieking incomprehensibly.

"Now she's upset," said Leonora dully, and tears toppled out of her pale eyes. Strike reached over to the ragged kitchen roll on the side, ripped some off and pressed it into her hand. She cried silently, her thin shoulders shaking, and Strike sat in silence, drinking the dregs of his horrible tea.

"Met Owen in a pub," she mumbled unexpectedly, pushing up her glasses and blotting her wet face. "He was there for the festival. Hay-on-Wye. I'd never heard of him, but I could tell he was some-one, way he was dressed and talking."

And a faint glow of hero worship, almost extinguished by years of neglect and unhappiness, of putting up with his airs and tantrums, of trying to pay the bills and care for their daughter in this shabby little house, flickered again behind her tired eyes. Perhaps it had rekindled because her hero, like all the best heroes, was dead; perhaps it would burn forever now, like an eternal flame, and she would forget the worst and cherish the idea of him she had once loved...as long as she did not read his final manuscript, and his vile depiction of her...

"Leonora, I wanted to ask you something else," Strike said gently, "and then I'll be off. Have you had anymore dog excrement through your letter box in the last week?"

"In the last week?" she repeated thickly, still dabbing her eyes. "Yeah. Tuesday we did, I think. Or Wednesday, was it? But yeah. One more time."

"And have you seen the woman you thought was following you?"

She shook her head, blowing her nose.

"Maybe I imagined it, I dunno . . ."

"And are you all right for money?"

"Yeah," she said, blotting her eyes. "Owen had life insurance. I made him take it out, cos of Orlando. So we'll be all right. Edna's offered to lend me till it comes through."

"Then I'll be off," said Strike, pushing himself back to his feet.

She trailed him up the dingy hall, still sniffing, and before the door had closed behind him he heard her calling:

"Dodo! Dodo, come down, I didn't mean it!"

The young policeman outside stood partially blocking Strike's path. He looked angry.

"I know who you are," he said. His mobile phone was still clutched in his hand. "You're Cormoran Strike."

"No flies on you, are there?" said Strike. "Out of the way now, sonny, some of us have got proper work to do."

22

… what murderer, hell-hound, devil can this be?

Ben Jonson, *Epicoene, or The Silent Woman*

Forgetting that getting up was the difficult part when his knee was sore, Strike dropped into a corner seat on the Tube train and rang Robin.

"Hi," he said, "have those journalists gone?"

"No, they're still hanging round outside. You're on the news, did you know?"

"I saw the BBC website. I rang Anstis and asked him to help play down the stuff about me. Has he?"

He heard her fingers tapping on the keyboard.

"Yeah, he's quoted: 'DI Richard Anstis has confirmed rumors that the body was found by private investigator Cormoran Strike, who made news earlier this year when he—'"

"Never mind that bit."

"'Mr. Strike was employed by the family to find Mr. Quine, who often went away without informing anyone of his whereabouts. Mr. Strike is not under suspicion and police are satisfied with his account of the discovery of the body.'"

"Good old Dickie," said Strike. "This morning they were implying I conceal bodies to drum up business. Surprised the press are this interested in a dead fifty-eight-year-old has-been. It's not as though they know how grisly the killing was yet."

"It isn't Quine who's got them interested," Robin told him. "It's you."

The thought gave Strike no pleasure. He did not want his face in the papers or on the television. The photographs of him that had appeared in the wake of the Lula Landry case had been small (room had been required for pictures of the stunning model, preferably partially clothed); his dark, surly features did not reproduce well in smudgy newsprint and he had managed to avoid a full-face picture as he entered court to give evidence against Landry's killer. They had dredged up old photographs of him in uniform, but these had been years old, when he had been several stone lighter. Nobody had recognized him on appearance alone since his brief burst of fame and he had no wish to further endanger his anonymity.

"I don't want to run into a bunch of hacks. Not," he added wryly, as his knee throbbed, "that I could run if you paid me. Could you meet me—"

His favorite local was the Tottenham, but he did not want to expose it to the possibility of future press incursions.

"—in the Cambridge in about forty minutes?"

"No problem," she said.

Only after he had hung up did it occur to Strike, first, that he ought to have asked after the bereaved Matthew, and second, that he ought to have asked her to bring his crutches.

The nineteenth-century pub stood on Cambridge Circus. Strike found Robin upstairs on a leather banquette among brass chandeliers and gilt-framed mirrors.

"Are you all right?" she asked in concern as he limped towards her.

"Forgot I didn't tell you," he said, lowering himself gingerly into the chair opposite her with a groan. "I knackered my knee again on Sunday, trying to catch a woman who was following me."

"What woman?"

"She tailed me from Quine's house to the Tube station, where I fell over like a tit and she took off. She matches the description of a woman Leonora says has been hanging around since Quine disappeared. I could really use a drink."

"I'll get it," said Robin, "as it's your birthday. And I got you a present."

She lifted onto the table a small basket covered in cellophane, adorned with ribbon and containing Cornish food and drink: beer, cider, sweets and mustard. He felt ridiculously touched.

"You didn't have to do that..."

But she was already out of earshot, at the bar. When she returned, carrying a glass of wine and a pint of London Pride, he said, "Thanks very much."

"You're welcome. So do you think this strange woman's been watching Leonora's house?"

Strike took a long, welcome pull on his pint.

"And possibly putting dog shit through her front door, yeah," said Strike. "I can't see what she had to gain from following me, though, unless she thought I was going to lead her to Quine."

He winced as he raised the damaged leg onto a stool under the table.

"I'm supposed to be doing surveillance on Brocklehurst and Burnett's husband this week. Great bloody time to knacker my leg."

"I could follow them for you."

The excited offer was out of Robin's mouth before she knew it, but Strike gave no evidence of having heard her.

"How's Matthew doing?"

"Not great," said Robin. She could not decide whether Strike had registered her suggestion or not. "He's gone home to be with his dad and sister."

"Masham, isn't it?"

"Yes." She hesitated, then said: "We're going to have to postpone the wedding."

"Sorry."

She shrugged.

"We couldn't do it so soon...it's been a horrible shock for the family."

"Did you get on well with Matthew's mother?" Strike asked.

"Yes, of course. She was..."

But in fact, Mrs. Cunliffe had always been difficult; a hypochondriac, or so Robin had thought. She had been feeling guilty about that in the last twenty-four hours.

"...lovely," said Robin. "So how's poor Mrs. Quine doing?"

Strike described his visit to Leonora, including the brief appearance of Jerry Waldegrave and his impressions of Orlando.

"What exactly's wrong with her?" Robin asked.

"Learning difficulties they call it, don't they?"

He paused, remembering Orlando's ingenuous smile, her cuddly orangutan.

"She said something strange while I was there and it seemed to be news to her mother. She told us she went into work with her father once, and that the head of Quine's publisher touched her. Name of Daniel Chard."

He saw reflected in Robin's face the unacknowledged fear that the words had conjured back in the dingy kitchen.

"How, touched her?"

"She wasn't specific. She said, 'He touched me' and 'I don't like being touched.' And that he gave her a paintbrush after he'd done it. It might not be that," said Strike in response to Robin's loaded silence, her tense expression. "He might've accidentally knocked into her and given her something to placate her. She kept going off on one while I was there, shrieking because she didn't get what she wanted or her mum had a go at her."

Hungry, he tore open the cellophane on Robin's gift, pulled out a chocolate bar and unwrapped it while Robin sat in thoughtful silence.

"Thing is," said Strike, breaking the silence, "Quine implied in *Bombyx Mori* that Chard's gay. I think that's what he's saying, anyway."

"Hmm," said Robin, unimpressed. "And do you believe everything Quine wrote in that book?"

"Well, judging by the fact that he set lawyers on Quine, it upset Chard," said Strike, breaking off a large chunk of chocolate and putting it in his mouth. "Mind you," he continued thickly, "the Chard in *Bombyx Mori*'s a murderer, possibly a rapist and his knob's falling off, so the gay stuff might not have been what got his goat."

"It's a constant theme in Quine's work, sexual duality," said Robin and Strike stared at her, chewing, his brows raised. "I nipped into Foyles on the way to work and bought a copy of *Hobart's Sin*," she explained. "It's all about a hermaphrodite."

Strike swallowed.

"He must've had a thing about them; there's one in *Bombyx Mori* too," he said, examining the cardboard covering of his chocolate bar. "This was made in Mullion. That's down the coast from where I grew up ... How's *Hobart's Sin*—any good?"

"I wouldn't be fussed about reading past the first few pages if its author hadn't just been murdered," admitted Robin.

"Probably do wonders for his sales, getting bumped off."

"My point is," Robin pressed on doggedly, "that you can't necessarily trust Quine when it comes to other people's sex lives, because his characters all seem to sleep with anyone and anything. I looked him up on Wikipedia. One of the key features of his books is how characters keep swapping their gender or sexual orientation."

"*Bombyx Mori*'s like that," grunted Strike, helping himself to more chocolate. "This is good, want a bit?"

"I'm supposed to be on a diet," said Robin sadly. "For the wedding."

Strike did not think she needed to lose any weight at all, but said nothing as she took a piece.

"I've been thinking," said Robin diffidently, "about the killer."

"Always keen to hear from the psychologist. Go on."

"I'm *not* a psychologist," she half laughed.

She had dropped out of her psychology degree. Strike had never pressed her for an explanation, nor had she ever volunteered one. It was something they had in common, dropping out of university. He had left when his mother had died of a mysterious overdose and, perhaps because of this, he had always assumed that something traumatic had made Robin leave too.

"I've just been wondering why they tied his murder so obviously to the book. On the surface it looks like a deliberate act of revenge and malice, to show the world that Quine got what he deserved for writing it."

"Looks like that," agreed Strike, who was still hungry; he reached over to a neighboring table and plucked a menu off it. "I'm going to have steak and chips, want something?"

Robin chose a salad at random and then, to spare Strike's knee, went up to the bar to give their order.

"But on the other hand," Robin continued, sitting back down, "copycatting the last scene of the book could have seemed like a good way of concealing a different motive, couldn't it?"

She was forcing herself to speak matter-of-factly, as though they were discussing an abstract problem, but Robin had not been able to forget the pictures of Quine's body: the dark cavern of the gouged-out torso, the burned-out crevices where once had been mouth and eyes. If she thought about what had been done to Quine too much, she knew that she might not be able to eat her lunch, or that she might somehow betray her horror to Strike, who was watching her with a disconcertingly shrewd expression in his dark eyes.

"It's all right to admit what happened to him makes you want to puke," he said through a mouthful of chocolate.

"It doesn't," she lied automatically. Then, "Well, obviously—I mean, it was horrific—"

"Yeah, it was."

If he had been back with his SIB colleagues he would have been making jokes about it by now. Strike could remember many afternoons laden with pitch-black humor: it was the only way to get through certain investigations. Robin, however, was not yet ready for professionally callous self-defense and her attempt at dispassionate discussion of a man whose guts had been torn out proved it.

"Motive's a bitch, Robin. Nine times out of ten you only find out *why* when you've found out *who*. It's means and opportunity we want. Personally," he took a gulp of beer, "I think we might be looking for someone with medical knowledge."

"Medical—?"

"Or anatomical. It didn't look amateur, what they did to Quine. They could've hacked him to bits, trying to remove the intestines, but I couldn't see any false starts: one clean, confident incision."

"Yes," said Robin, struggling to maintain her objective, clinical manner. "That's true."

"Unless we're dealing with some literary maniac who just got hold of a good textbook," mused Strike. "Seems a stretch, but you don't know ... If he was tied up and drugged and they had enough nerve, they might've been able to treat it like a biology lesson ... "

Robin could not restrain herself.

"I know you always say motive's for lawyers," she said a little desperately (Strike had repeated this maxim many times since she had come to work for him), "but humor me for a moment. The killer must have felt that to murder Quine in the same way as the book was worth it for some reason that outweighed the obvious disadvantages—"

"Which were?"

"Well," said Robin, "the logistical difficulties of making it such an—an *elaborate* killing, and the fact that the pool of suspects would be confined to people who've read the book—"

"Or heard about it in detail," said Strike, "and you say 'confined,' but I'm not sure we're looking at a small number of people. Christian Fisher made it his business to spread the contents of the book as far and as wide as he could. Roper Chard's copy of the manuscript was in a safe to which half the company seems to have had access."

"But..." said Robin.

She broke off as a sullen barman came over to dump cutlery and paper napkins on their table.

"But," she resumed when he had sloped away, "Quine can't have been killed that recently, can he? I mean, I'm no expert..."

"Nor am I," said Strike, polishing off the last of the chocolate and contemplating the peanut brittle with less enthusiasm, "but I know what you mean. That body looked as though it had been there at least a week."

"Plus," said Robin, "there must have been a time lag between the murderer reading *Bombyx Mori* and actually killing Quine. There was a lot to organize. They had to get ropes and acid and crockery into an uninhabited house..."

"And unless they already knew he was planning to go to Talgarth Road, they had to track Quine down," said Strike, deciding against the peanut brittle because his steak and chips were approaching, "or lure him there."

The barman set down Strike's plate and Robin's bowl of salad, greeted their thanks with an indifferent grunt and retreated.

"So when you factor in the planning and practicalities, it doesn't seem possible that the killer can have read the book any later than two or three days after Quine went missing," said Strike, loading up his fork. "Trouble is, the further back we set the moment when the killer started plotting Quine's murder, the worse it looks for my client. All Leonora had to do was walk a few steps up her hall; the manuscript was hers for the reading as soon as Quine finished it. Come to think of it, he could've told her how he was planning to end it months ago."

Robin ate her salad without tasting it.

"And does Leonora Quine seem..." she began tentatively.

"Like the kind of woman who'd disembowel her husband? No, but the police fancy her and if you're looking for motive, she's lousy with it. He was a crap husband: unreliable, adulterous and he liked depicting her in disgusting ways in his books."

"*You* don't think she did it, do you?"

"No," Strike said, "but we're going to need a lot more than my opinion to keep her out of jail."

Robin took their empty glasses back to the bar for refills without asking; Strike felt very fond of her as she set another pint in front of him.

"We've also got to look at the possibility that somebody got the wind up that Quine was going to self-publish over the internet," said Strike, shoveling chips into his mouth, "a threat he allegedly made to a packed restaurant. That might constitute a motive for killing Quine, under the right conditions."

"You mean," said Robin slowly, "if the killer recognized something in the manuscript that they didn't want to get a wider audience?"

"Exactly. The book's pretty cryptic in parts. What if Quine had found out something serious about somebody and put a veiled reference in the book?"

"Well, that would make sense," said Robin slowly, "because I keep thinking, *Why kill him?* The fact is, nearly all of these people had more effective means of dealing with the problem of a libelous book, didn't they? They could have told Quine they wouldn't represent it or publish it, or they could have threatened him with legal action, like this Chard man. His death's going to make the situation much worse for anyone who's a character in the book, isn't it? There's already much more publicity than there would have been otherwise."

"Agreed," said Strike. "But you're assuming the killer's thinking rationally."

"This wasn't a crime of passion," retorted Robin. "They planned it. They really thought it through. They must have been ready for the consequences."

"True again," said Strike, eating chips.

"I've been having a bit of a look at *Bombyx Mori* this morning."

"After you got bored with *Hobart's Sin*?"

"Yes... well, it was there in the safe and..."

"Read the whole thing, the more the merrier," said Strike. "How far did you get?"

"I skipped around," said Robin. "I read the bit about Succuba and the Tick. It's spiteful, but it doesn't feel as though there's anything... well... *hidden* there. He's basically accusing both his wife and his agent of being parasites on him, isn't he?"

Strike nodded.

"But later on, when you get to Epi—Epi—how do you say it?"

"Epicoene? The hermaphrodite?"

"Is that a real person, do you think? What's with the singing? It doesn't feel as though it's really *singing* he's talking about, does it?"

"And why does his girlfriend Harpy live in a cave full of rats? Symbolism, or something else?"

"And the bloodstained bag over the Cutter's shoulder," said Robin, "and the dwarf he tries to drown..."

"And the brands in the fire at Vainglorious's house," said Strike, but she looked puzzled. "You haven't got that far? But Jerry Waldegrave explained that to a bunch of us at the Roper Chard party. It's about Michael Fancourt and his first—"

Strike's mobile rang. He pulled it out and saw Dominic Culpepper's name. With a small sigh, he answered.

"Strike?"

"Speaking."

"What the fuck's going on?"

Strike did not waste time pretending not to know what Culpepper was talking about.

"Can't discuss it, Culpepper. Could prejudice the police case."

"Fuck that—we've got a copper talking to us already. He says this Quine's been slaughtered exactly the way a bloke's killed in his latest book."

"Yeah? And how much are you paying the stupid bastard to shoot his mouth off and screw up the case?"

"Bloody hell, Strike, you get mixed up in a murder like this and you don't even think of ringing me?"

"I don't know what you think our relationship is about, mate," said Strike, "but as far as I'm concerned, I do jobs for you and you pay me. That's it."

"I put you in touch with Nina so you could get in that publisher's party."

"The least you could do after I handed you a load of extra stuff you'd never asked for on Parker," said Strike, spearing stray chips with his free hand. "I could've withheld that and shopped it all round the tabloids."

"If you want paying—"

"No, I don't want paying, dickhead," said Strike irritably, as Robin turned her attention tactfully to the BBC website on her own phone. "I'm not going to help screw up a murder investigation by dragging in the *News of the World*."

"I could get you ten grand if you throw in a personal interview."

"Bye, Cul—"

"Wait! Just tell me which book it is—the one where he describes the murder."

Strike pretended to hesitate.

"*The Brothers Balls ... Balzac*," he said.

Smirking, he cut the call and reached for the menu to examine the puddings. Hopefully Culpepper would spend a long afternoon wading through tortured syntax and palpated scrotums.

"Anything new?" Strike asked as Robin looked up from her phone.

"Not unless you count the *Daily Mail* saying that family friends thought Pippa Middleton would make a better marriage than Kate."

Strike frowned at her.

"I was just looking at random things while you were on the phone," said Robin, a little defensively.

"No," said Strike, "not that. I've just remembered—Pippa2011."

"I don't—" said Robin, confused, and still thinking of Pippa Middleton.

"Pippa2011—on Kathryn Kent's blog. She claimed to have heard a bit of *Bombyx Mori*."

Robin gasped and set to work on her mobile.

"It's here!" she said, a few minutes later. "'What would you say if I told you he'd read it to me'! And that was..." Robin scrolled upwards, "on October the twenty-first. October the twenty-first! She might've known the ending before Quine even disappeared."

"That's right," said Strike. "I'm having apple crumble, want anything?"

When Robin had returned from placing yet another order at the bar, Strike said:

"Anstis has asked me to dinner tonight. Says he's got some preliminary stuff in from forensics."

"Does he know it's your birthday?" asked Robin.

"Christ, no," said Strike, and he sounded so revolted by the idea that Robin laughed.

"Why would that be bad?"

"I've already had one birthday dinner," said Strike darkly. "Best present I could get from Anstis would be a time of death. The earlier they set it, the smaller the number of likely suspects: the ones who got their hands on the manuscript early. Unfortunately, that includes Leonora, but you've got this mysterious Pippa, Christian Fisher—"

"Why Fisher?"

"Means and opportunity, Robin: he had early access, he's got to go on the list. Then there's Elizabeth Tassel's assistant Ralph, Elizabeth Tassel herself and Jerry Waldegrave. Daniel Chard presumably saw it shortly after Waldegrave. Kathryn Kent denies reading it, but I'm taking that with a barrel of salt. And then there's Michael Fancourt."

Robin looked up, startled.

"How can he—?"

Strike's mobile rang again; it was Nina Lascelles. He hesitated, but the reflection that her cousin might have told her he had just spoken to Strike persuaded him to take the call.

"Hi," he said.

"Hi, Famous Person," she said. He heard an edge, inexpertly covered by breathy high spirits. "I've been too scared to call you in case you're being inundated with press calls and groupies and things."

"Not so much," said Strike. "How're things at Roper Chard?"

"Insane. Nobody's doing any work; it's all we can talk about. Was it really, honestly murder?"

"Looks like it."

"God, I can't believe it…I don't suppose you can tell me anything, though?" she asked, barely suppressing the interrogative note.

"The police won't want details getting out at this stage."

"It was to do with the book, wasn't it?" she said. "*Bombyx Mori.*"

"I couldn't say."

"And Daniel Chard's broken his leg."

"Sorry?" he said, thrown by the non sequitur.

"Just so many odd things happening," she said. She sounded keyed up, overwrought. "Jerry's all over the place. Daniel rang him up from Devon just now and was yelling at him again—half the office heard because Jerry put him on speakerphone by accident and then couldn't find the button to turn him off. He can't leave his weekend house because of his broken leg. Daniel, I mean."

"Why was he yelling at Waldegrave?"

"Security on *Bombyx*," she said. "The police have got a full copy of the manuscript from somewhere and Daniel's *not* happy about it.

"Anyway," she said, "I just thought I'd ring and say congrats—I suppose you congratulate a detective when they find a body, or don't you? Call me when you're not so busy."

She rang off before he could say anything else.

"Nina Lascelles," he said as the waiter reappeared with his apple crumble and a coffee for Robin. "The girl—"

"Who stole the manuscript for you," said Robin.

"Your memory would've been wasted in HR," said Strike, picking up his spoon.

"Are you serious about Michael Fancourt?" she asked quietly.

"Course," said Strike. "Daniel Chard must've told him what Quine had done—he wouldn't have wanted Fancourt to hear it from anyone else, would he? Fancourt's a major acquisition for them. No, I think we've got to assume that Fancourt knew, early on, what was in—"

Now Robin's mobile rang.

"Hi," said Matthew.

"Hi, how are you?" she asked anxiously.

"Not great."

Somewhere in the background, someone turned up the music: "*First day that I saw you, thought you were beautiful …*"

"Where are you?" asked Matthew sharply.

"Oh … in a pub," said Robin.

Suddenly the air seemed full of pub noises; clinking glasses, raucous laughter from the bar.

"It's Cormoran's birthday," she said anxiously. (After all, Matthew and his colleagues went to the pub on each other's birthdays …)

"That's nice," said Matthew, sounding furious. "I'll call you later."

"Matt, no—wait—"

Mouth full of apple crumble, Strike watched out of the corner of his eye as she got up and moved away to the bar without explanation, evidently trying to redial Matthew. The accountant was unhappy that his fiancée had gone out to lunch, that she was not sitting shiva for his mother.

Robin redialed and redialed. She got through at last. Strike finished both his crumble and his third pint and realized that he needed the bathroom.

His knee, which had not troubled him much while he ate, drank and talked to Robin, complained violently when he stood. By the time he got back to his seat he was sweating a little with the pain. Judging by the expression on her face, Robin was still trying to placate Matthew. When at last she hung up and rejoined him, he returned a short answer to whether or not he was all right.

"You know, I could follow the Brocklehurst girl for you," she offered again, "if your leg's too—?"

"No," snapped Strike.

He felt sore, angry with himself, irritated by Matthew and suddenly a bit nauseous. He ought not to have eaten the chocolate before having steak, chips, crumble and three pints.

"I need you to go back to the office and type up Gunfrey's last invoice. And text me if those bloody journalists are still around, because I'll go straight from here to Anstis's, if they are.

"We really need to be thinking about taking someone else on," he added under his breath.

Robin's expression hardened.

"I'll go and get typing, then," she said. She snatched up her coat and bag and left. Strike caught a glimpse of her angry expression, but an irrational vexation prevented him from calling her back.

23

For my part, I do not think she hath a soul so black
To act a deed so bloody.

John Webster, *The White Devil*

An afternoon in the pub with his leg propped up had not much reduced the swelling in Strike's knee. After buying painkillers and a cheap bottle of red on the way to the Tube, he set out for Greenwich where Anstis lived with his wife, Helen, commonly known as Helly. The journey to their house in Ashburnham Grove took him over an hour due to a delay on the Central line; he stood the whole way, keeping his weight on his left leg, regretting anew the hundred pounds he had spent on taxis to and from Lucy's house.

By the time he got off the Docklands Light Railway spots of rain were again peppering his face. He turned up his collar and limped away into the darkness for what should have been a five-minute walk, but which took him nearly fifteen.

Only as he turned the corner into the neat terraced street with its well-tended front gardens did it occur to Strike that he ought, perhaps, to have brought a gift for his godson. He felt as little enthusiasm for the social part of the evening ahead as he felt eager to discuss with Anstis the forensic information.

Strike did not like Anstis's wife. Her nosiness was barely concealed beneath a sometimes cloying warmth; it emerged from time to time like a flick knife flashing suddenly from beneath a fur coat. She gushed gratitude and solicitousness every time Strike swam into her orbit, but he could tell that she itched for details of his checkered past, for information about his rock star father, his dead, drug-taking mother, and he could well imagine that she would yearn for details of his breakup with Charlotte, whom she had always treated with an effusiveness that failed to mask dislike and suspicion.

At the party following the christening of Timothy Cormoran Anstis—which had been postponed until he was eighteen months old, because his father and his godfather had to be airlifted out of Afghanistan and discharged from their respective hospitals—Helly had insisted on making a tearful, tipsy speech about how Strike had saved her baby's daddy's life, and how much it meant to her to have him agree to be Timmy's guardian angel, too. Strike, who had not been able to think of any valid reason to refuse being the boy's godfather, had stared at the tablecloth while Helly spoke, careful not to meet Charlotte's eye in case she made him laugh. She had been wearing— he remembered it vividly—his favorite peacock blue wrap-over dress, which had clung to every inch of her perfect figure. Having a woman that beautiful on his arm, even while he was still on crutches, had acted as a counterweight to the half a leg still not yet fit for a prosthesis. It had transformed him from the Man With Only One Foot to the man who had managed—miraculously, as he knew nearly every man who came into contact with her must think—to snag a fiancée so stunning that men stopped talking in midsentence when she entered the room.

"Cormy, darling," crooned Helly when she opened the door. "Look at you, all famous . . . we thought you'd forgotten us."

Nobody else ever called him Cormy. He had never bothered to tell her he disliked it.

She treated him, without encouragement, to a tender hug that he knew was intended to suggest pity and regret for his single status. The house was warm and brightly lit after the hostile winter night outside and he was glad to see, as he extricated himself from Helly, Anstis stride into view, holding a pint of Doom Bar as a welcoming gift.

"Ritchie, let him get inside. Honestly . . ."

But Strike had accepted the pint and taken several grateful mouthfuls before he bothered to take off his coat.

Strike's three-and-a-half-year-old godson burst into the hall, making shrill engine noises. He was very like his mother, whose features, small and pretty though they were, were oddly bunched up in the middle of her face. Timothy sported Superman pajamas and was swiping at the walls with a plastic lightsaber.

"Oh, Timmy, darling, *don't*, our lovely new paintwork...He wanted to stay up and see his Uncle Cormoran. We tell him about you all the time," said Helly.

Strike contemplated the small figure without enthusiasm, detecting very little reciprocal interest from his godson. Timothy was the only child Strike knew whose birthday he had a hope of remembering, not that this had ever led Strike to buy him a present. The boy had been born two days before the Viking had exploded on that dusty road in Afghanistan, taking with it Strike's lower right leg and part of Anstis's face.

Strike had never confided in anyone how, during long hours in his hospital bed, he had wondered why it had been Anstis he had grabbed and pulled towards the back of the vehicle. He had gone over it in his mind: the strange presentiment, amounting almost to certainty, that they were about to explode, and the reaching out and seizing of Anstis, when he could equally have grabbed Sergeant Gary Topley.

Was it because Anstis had spent most of the previous day Skyping Helen within earshot of Strike, looking at the newborn son he might otherwise never have met? Was that why Strike's hand had reached without hesitation for the older man, the Territorial Army police-man, and not Red Cap Topley, engaged but childless? Strike did not know. He was not sentimental about children and he disliked the wife he had saved from widowhood. He knew himself to be merely one among millions of soldiers, dead and living, whose split-second actions, prompted by instinct as much as training, had forever altered other men's fates.

"Do you want to read Tim his bedtime story, Cormy? We've got a new book, haven't we, Timmy?"

Strike could think of little he wanted to do less, especially if it involved the hyperactive boy sitting on his lap and perhaps kicking his right knee.

Anstis led the way into the open-plan kitchen and dining area. The walls were cream, the floorboards bare, a long wooden table stood near

French windows at the end of the room, surrounded by chairs uphol-
stered in black. Strike had the vague idea that they had been a different
color when he had last been here, with Charlotte. Helly bustled in
behind them and thrust a highly colored picture book into Strike's
hands. He had no choice but to sit down on a dining-room chair, with
his godson placed firmly beside him, and to read the story of *Kyla the
Kangaroo Who Loved to Bounce,* which was (as he would not usually have
noticed) published by Roper Chard. Timothy did not appear remotely
interested in Kyla's antics and played with his lightsaber throughout.

"Bedtime Timmy, give Cormy a kiss," Helly told her son, who,
with Strike's silent blessing, merely wriggled off his chair and ran
out of the kitchen yelling protests. Helly followed. Mother and son's
raised voices grew muffled as they thumped upstairs.

"He'll wake Tilly," predicted Anstis and, sure enough, when Helly
reappeared it was with a howling one-year-old in her arms, whom
she thrust at her husband before turning to the oven.

Strike sat stolidly at the kitchen table, growing steadily hungrier,
and feeling profoundly grateful that he did not have children. It took
nearly three quarters of an hour for the Anstises to persuade Tilly
back into her bed. At last the casserole reached the table and, with it,
another pint of Doom Bar. Strike could have relaxed but for the sense
that Helly Anstis was now gearing up for the attack.

"I was so, so sorry to hear about you and Charlotte," she told him.

His mouth was full, so he mimed vague appreciation of her sympathy.

"Ritchie!" she said playfully as her husband made to pour her a
glass of wine. "I don't think so! We're expecting again," she told
Strike proudly, one hand on her stomach.

He swallowed.

"Congratulations," he said, staggered that they looked so pleased
at the prospect of another Timothy or Tilly.

Right on cue, their son reappeared and announced that he was
hungry. To Strike's disappointment, it was Anstis who left the table
to deal with him, leaving Helly staring beadily at Strike over a forkful
of *boeuf bourguignon.*

"So she's getting married on the fourth. I can't even *imagine* what
that feels like for you."

"Who's getting married?" Strike asked.

Helly looked amazed.

"Charlotte," she said.

Dimly, down the stairs, came the sound of his godson wailing.

"Charlotte's getting married on the fourth of December," said Helly, and with her realization that she was the first to give him the news came a look of burgeoning excitement; but then something in Strike's expression seemed to unnerve her.

"I ... I heard," she said, dropping her gaze to her plate as Anstis returned.

"Little bugger," he said. "I've told him I'll smack his bum for him if he gets out of bed again."

"He's just excited," said Helly, who still seemed flustered by the anger she had sensed in Strike, "because Cormy's here."

The casserole had turned to rubber and polystyrene in Strike's mouth. How could Helly Anstis know when Charlotte was getting married? The Anstises hardly moved in the same circles as her or her future husband, who (as Strike despised himself for remembering) was the son of the Fourteenth Viscount of Croy. What did Helly Anstis know about the world of private gentlemen's clubs, of Savile Row tailoring and coked-up supermodels of which the Hon. Jago Ross had been a habitué all his trust-funded life? She knew no more than Strike himself. Charlotte, to whom it was native territory, had joined Strike in a social no-man's-land when they had been together, a place where neither was comfortable with the other's social set, where two utterly disparate norms collided and everything became a struggle for common ground.

Timothy was back in the kitchen, crying hard. Both his parents stood up this time and jointly moved him back towards his bedroom while Strike, hardly aware that they had gone, was left to disappear into a fug of memories.

Charlotte had been volatile to the point that one of her stepfathers had once tried to have her committed. She lied as other women breathed; she was damaged to her core. The longest consecutive period that she and Strike had ever managed together was two years, yet as often as their trust in each other had splintered they had been drawn back together, each time (so it seemed to Strike) more fragile than they had been before, but with the longing for each other strengthening. For sixteen years Charlotte had defied the disbelief and disdain of her family and friends to return, over and over again, to a large, illegitimate and latterly disabled soldier. Strike would have advised any friend to leave and not look back, but he had come to see her like a virus in his blood that he doubted he would ever eradicate; the best he could hope for was to control its symptoms. The final breach had come eight months previously, just before he had become newsworthy through the Landry case. She had finally told an unforgivable lie, he had left her for good and she had retreated into a world where men still went grouse shooting and women had tiaras in the family vault; a world she had told him she despised (although it looked as though that had been a lie too ...).

The Anstises returned, minus Timothy but with a sobbing and hiccuping Tilly.

"Bet you're glad you haven't got any, aren't you?" said Helly gaily, sitting back down at the table with Tilly on her lap. Strike grinned humorlessly and did not contradict her.

There had been a baby: or more accurately the ghost, the promise of a baby and then, supposedly, the death of a baby. Charlotte had told him that she was pregnant, refused to consult a doctor, changed her mind about dates, then announced that all was over without a shred of proof that it had ever been real. It was a lie most men would have found impossible to forgive and for Strike it had been, as surely she must have known, the lie to end all lies and the death of that tiny amount of trust that had survived years of her mythomania.

Marrying on the fourth of December, in eleven days' time ... how could Helly Anstis know?

He was perversely grateful, now, for the whining and tantrums of the two children, which effectively disrupted conversation all through a pudding of rhubarb flan and custard. Anstis's suggestion that they take fresh beers into his study to go over the forensic report was the best Strike had heard all day. They left a slightly sulky Helly, who clearly felt that she had not had her money's worth out of Strike, to manage the now very sleepy Tilly and the unnervingly wide-awake

Timothy, who had reappeared to announce that he had spilled his drinking water all over his bed.

Anstis's study was a small, book-lined room off the hall. He offered Strike the computer chair and sat on an old futon. The curtains were not drawn; Strike could see a misty rain falling like dust motes in the light of an orange streetlamp.

"Forensics say it's as hard a job as they've ever had," Anstis began, and Strike's attention was immediately all his. "All this is unofficial, mind, we haven't got everything in yet."

"Have they been able to tell what actually killed him?"

"Blow to the head," said Anstis. "The back of his skull's been stoved in. It might not've been instantaneous, but the brain trauma alone would've killed him. They can't be sure he was dead when he was carved open, but he was almost certainly unconscious."

"Small mercies. Any idea whether he was tied up before or after he was knocked out?"

"There's some argument about that. There's a patch of skin under the ropes on one of his wrists that's bruised, which they think indicates he was tied up before he was killed, but we've no indication whether he was still conscious when the ropes were put on him. The problem is, all that bloody acid everywhere's taken away any marks on the floor that might've shown a struggle, or the body being dragged. He was a big, heavy guy—"

"Easier to handle if he was trussed up," agreed Strike, thinking of short, thin Leonora, "but it'd be good to know the angle he was hit at."

"From just above," said Anstis, "but as we don't know whether he was hit standing, sitting or kneeling..."

"I think we can be sure he was killed in that room," said Strike, following his own train of thought. "I can't see anyone being strong enough to carry a body that heavy up those stairs."

"The consensus is that he died more or less on the spot where the body was found. That's where the greatest concentration of the acid is."

"D'you know what kind of acid it was?"

"Oh, didn't I say? Hydrochloric."

Strike struggled to remember something of his chemistry lessons. "Don't they use that to galvanize steel?"

"Among other things. It's as caustic a substance as you can legally buy and it's used in a load of industrial processes. Heavy-duty cleaning agent as well. One weird thing about it is, it occurs naturally in humans. In our gastric acid."

Strike sipped his beer, considering.

"In the book, they pour vitriol on him."

"Vitriol's sulphuric acid, and hydrochloric acid derives from it. Seriously corrosive to human tissue—as you saw."

"Where the hell did the killer get that amount of the stuff?"

"Believe it or not, it looks like it was already in the house."

"Why the hell—?"

"Still haven't found anyone who can tell us. There were empty gallon containers on the kitchen floor, and dusty containers of the same description in a cupboard under the stairs, full of the stuff and unopened. They came from an industrial chemicals company in Birmingham. There were marks on the empty ones that looked as though they'd been made by gloved hands."

"Very interesting," said Strike, scratching his chin.

"We're still trying to check when and how they were bought."

"What about the blunt object that bashed his head in?"

"There's an old-fashioned doorstop in the studio—solid iron and shaped like one, with a handle: almost certainly that. It fits with the impression in his skull. That's had hydrochloric acid poured all over it like nearly everything else."

"How's time of death looking?"

"Yeah, well, that's the tricky bit. The entomologist won't commit himself, says the condition of the corpse throws out all the usual calculations. The fumes from the hydrochloric acid alone would've kept insects away for a while, so you can't date the death from infestation. No self-respecting blowfly wants to lay eggs in acid. We had a maggot or two on bits of the body that weren't doused in the stuff, but the usual infestation didn't occur.

"Meanwhile, the heating in the house had been cranked right up, so the body might've rotted a bit faster than it would ordinarily have done in this weather. But the hydrochloric acid would've tended to mess with normal decomposition. Parts of him are burned to the bone.

"The deciding factor would have been the guts, last meal and so on, but they'd been lifted clean out of the body. Looks like they left with the killer," said Anstis. "I've never heard of that being done before, have you? Pounds of raw intestine taken away."

"No," said Strike, "it's a new one on me."

"Bottom line: forensics are refusing to commit themselves to a time frame except to say he's been dead at least ten days. But I had a private word with Underhill, who's the best of them, and he told me off the record that he thinks Quine's been dead a good two weeks. He reckons, though, even when they've got everything in the evidence'll still be equivocal enough to give defending counsel a lot to play with."

"What about pharmacology?" asked Strike, his thoughts circling back to Quine's bulk, the difficulty of handling a body that big.

"Well, he might've been drugged," agreed Anstis. "We haven't had blood results back yet and we're analyzing the contents of the bottles in the kitchen as well. But"—he finished his beer and set down the glass with a flourish—"there's another way he could've made things easy for a killer. Quine liked being tied up—sex games."

"How d'you know that?"

"The girlfriend," said Anstis. "Kathryn Kent."

"You've already talked to her, have you?"

"Yep," said Anstis. "We found a taxi driver who picked up Quine at nine o'clock on the fifth, a couple of streets away from his house, and dropped him in Lillie Road."

"Right by Stafford Cripps House," said Strike. "So he went straight from Leonora to the girlfriend?"

"Well, no, he didn't. Kent was away, staying with her dying sister, and we've got corroboration—she spent the night at the hospice. She says she hasn't seen him for a month, but was surprisingly forthcoming on their sex life."

"Did you ask for details?"

"I got the impression she thought we knew more than we did. They came pouring out without much prodding."

"Suggestive," said Strike. "She told me she'd never read *Bombyx Mori*—"

"She told us that too."

"—but her character ties up and assaults the hero in the book. Maybe she wanted it on record that she ties people up for sex, not torture or murder. What about the copy of the manuscript Leonora says he took away with him? All the notes and the old typewriter ribbons? Did you find them?"

"Nope," said Anstis. "Until we find out whether he stayed somewhere else before he went to Talgarth Road, we're going to assume the killer took them. The place was empty except for a bit of food and drink in the kitchen and a camping mattress and sleeping bag in one of the bedrooms. It looks like Quine was dossing down there. Hydrochloric acid's been poured around that room too, all over Quine's bed."

"No fingerprints? Footprints? Unexplained hair, mud?"

"Nothing. We've still got people working on the place, but the acid's obliterated everything in its path. Our people are wearing masks just so the fumes don't rip their throats out."

"Anyone apart from this taxi driver admitted to seeing Quine since he disappeared?"

"Nobody's seen him entering Talgarth Road but we've got a neighbor at number 183 who swears she saw Quine *leave* it at one in the morning. Early hours of the sixth. The neighbor was letting herself in after a bonfire-night party."

"It was dark and she was two doors down, so what she actually saw was ... ?"

"Silhouette of a tall figure in a cloak, carrying a holdall."

"A holdall," repeated Strike.

"Yep," said Anstis.

"Did the cloaked figure get into a car?"

"No, it walked out of sight, but obviously a car could have been parked round the corner."

"Anyone else?"

"I've got an old geezer in Putney swearing he saw Quine on the eighth. Rang his local police station and described him accurately."

"What was Quine doing?"

"Buying books in the Bridlington Bookshop, where the bloke works."

"How convincing a witness is he?"

"Well, he's old, but he claims he can remember what Quine bought and the physical description's good. And we've got another woman who lives in the flats across the road from the crime scene who reckons she passed Michael Fancourt walking past the house, also on the morning of the eighth. You know, that author with the big head? Famous one?"

"Yeah, I do," said Strike slowly.

"Witness claims she looked back at him over her shoulder and stared, because she recognized him."

"He was just walking past?"

"So she claims."

"Anybody checked that with Fancourt yet?"

"He's in Germany, but he's said he's happy to cooperate with us when he gets back. Agent bending over backwards to be helpful."

"Any other suspicious activity around Talgarth Road? Camera footage?"

"The only camera's at the wrong angle for the house, it watches traffic—but I'm saving the best till last. We've got a different neighbor—other side, four doors down—who swears he saw a fat woman in a burqa letting herself in on the afternoon of the fourth, carrying a plastic bag from a halal takeaway. He says he noticed because the house had been empty so long. He claims she was there for an hour, then left."

"He's sure she was in Quine's house?"

"So he says."

"And she had a key?"

"That's his story."

"A burqa," repeated Strike. "Bloody hell."

"I wouldn't swear his eyesight's great; he's got very thick lenses in his glasses. He told me he didn't know of any Muslims living in the street, so it had caught his attention."

"So we've got two alleged sightings of Quine since he walked out on his wife: early hours of the sixth, and on the eighth, in Putney."

"Yeah," said Anstis, "but I wouldn't pin too much hope on either of them, Bob."

"You think he died the night he left," said Strike, more statement than question, and Anstis nodded.

"Underhill thinks so."

"No sign of the knife?"

"Nothing. The only knife in the kitchen was a very blunt, everyday one. Definitely not up to the job."

"Who do we know had a key to the place?"

"Your client," said Anstis, "obviously. Quine himself must've had one. Fancourt's got two, he's already told us that by phone. The Quines lent one to his agent when she was organizing some repairs for them; she says she gave it back. A next-door neighbor's got a key so he can let himself in if anything goes wrong with the place."

"Didn't he go in once the stink got bad?"

"One side *did* put a note through the door complaining about the smell, but the key holder left for two months in New Zealand a fortnight ago. We've spoken to him by phone. Last time he was in the house was in about May, when he took delivery of a couple of packages while some workmen were in and put them in the hall. Mrs. Quine's vague about who else might have been lent a key over the years."

"She's an odd woman, Mrs. Quine," Anstis went on smoothly, "isn't she?"

"Haven't thought about it," lied Strike.

"You know the neighbors heard her chasing him, the night he disappeared?"

"I didn't know."

"Yeah. She ran out of the house after him, screaming. The neighbors all say"—Anstis was watching Strike closely—"that she yelled 'I know where you're off to, Owen!'"

"Well, she thought she did know," Strike said with a shrug. "She thought he was going to the writer's retreat Christian Fisher told him about. Bigley Hall."

"She's refusing to move out of the house."

"She's got a mentally handicapped daughter who's never slept anywhere else. Can you imagine Leonora overpowering Quine?"

"No," said Anstis, "but we know it turned him on to be tied up, and I doubt they were married for thirty-odd years without her knowing that."

"You think they had a row, then she tracked him down and suggested a bit of bondage?"

Anstis gave the suggestion of a small, token laugh, then said:

"It doesn't look great for her, Bob. Angry wife with the key to the house, early access to the manuscript, plenty of motive if she knew about the mistress, especially if there was any question of Quine leaving her and the daughter for Kent. Only her word for it that 'I know where you're going' meant this writer's retreat and not the house on Talgarth Road."

"Sounds convincing when you put it like that," Strike said.

"But you don't think so."

"She's my client," said Strike. "I'm being paid to think of alternatives."

"Has she told you where she used to work?" asked Anstis, with the air of a man about to play his trump card. "Back in Hay-on-Wye, before they were married?"

"Go on," said Strike, not without a degree of apprehension.

"In her uncle's butcher's shop," said Anstis.

Outside the study door Strike heard Timothy Cormoran Anstis thudding down the stairs again, screaming his head off at some fresh disappointment. For the first time in their unsatisfactory acquaintance, Strike felt a real empathy for the boy.

24

All well bred persons lie—Besides, you are a woman; you must never speak what you think...

William Congreve, *Love for Love*

Strike's dreams that night, fueled by a day's consumption of Doom Bar, by talk of blood, acid and blowflies, were strange and ugly.

Charlotte was getting married and he, Strike, was running to an eerie Gothic cathedral, running on two whole, functioning legs, because he knew that she had just given birth to his child and he needed to see it, to save it. There she was, in the vast, dark empty space, alone at the altar, struggling into a blood-red gown, and somewhere out of sight, perhaps in a cold vestry, lay his baby, naked, helpless and abandoned.

"Where is it?" he asked.

"You're not seeing it. You didn't want it. Anyway, there's something wrong with it," she said.

He was afraid of what he would see if he went to find the baby. Her bridegroom was nowhere to be seen but she was ready for the wedding, in a thick scarlet veil.

"Leave it, it's horrible," she said coldly, pushing past him, walking alone away from the altar, back up the aisle towards the distant doorway. "You'd only touch it," she shouted over her shoulder. "I don't want you *touching* it. You'll see it eventually. It'll have to be announced," she added in a vanishing voice, as she became a sliver of scarlet dancing in the light of the open doors, "in the papers..."

He was suddenly awake in the morning gloom, his mouth dry and his knee throbbing ominously in spite of a night's rest.

Winter had slid in the night like a glacier over London. A hard frost had iced the outside of his attic window and the temperature inside his rooms, with their ill-fitting windows and doors and the total lack of insulation under the roof, had plummeted.

Strike got up and reached for a sweater lying on the end of his bed. When he came to fix on his prosthesis, he found that his knee was exceptionally swollen after the journey to and from Greenwich. The shower water took longer than usual to heat up; he cranked up the thermostat, fearing burst pipes and frozen gutters, subzero living quarters and an expensive plumber. After drying himself off, he unearthed his old sports bandages from the box on the landing to strap up his knee.

He knew, now, as clearly as though he had spent the night puzzling it out, how Helly Anstis knew Charlotte's wedding plans. He had been stupid not to think of it before. His subconscious had known.

Once clean, dressed and breakfasted he headed downstairs. Glancing out of the window behind his desk, he noted that the knifelike cold was keeping away the little cluster of journalists who had waited in vain for his return the previous day. Sleet pattered on the windows as he moved back to the outer office and Robin's computer. Here, in the search engine, he typed: *charlotte campbell hon jago ross wedding*.

Pitiless and prompt came the results.

Tatler, December 2010: Cover girl Charlotte Campbell on her wedding to the future Viscount of Croy...

"*Tatler*," said Strike aloud in the office.

He only knew of the magazine's existence because its society pages were full of Charlotte's friends. She had bought it, sometimes, to read ostentatiously in front of him, commenting on men she had once slept with, or whose stately homes she had partied in.

And now she was the Christmas cover girl.

Even strapped up, his knee complained at having to support him down the metal stairs and out into the sleet. There was an early morning queue at the counter of the newsagents. Calmly he scanned the shelves of magazines: soap stars on the cheap ones and film stars on the expensive; December issues almost sold out, even though they were still in November. Emma Watson in white on the cover of *Vogue* ("The Super Star Issue"), Rihanna in pink on *Marie Claire* ("The Glamour Issue") and on the cover of *Tatler*...

Pale, perfect skin, black hair blown away from high cheekbones and wide hazel-green eyes, flecked like a russet apple. Two huge diamonds dangling from her ears and a third on the hand lying lightly against her face. A dull, blunt hammer blow to the heart, absorbed without the slightest external sign. He took the magazine, the last on the shelf, paid for it and returned to Denmark Street.

It was twenty to nine. He shut himself in his office, sat down at his desk and laid the magazine down in front of him.

IN–CROY–ABLE! Former Wild Child turned future Viscountess, Charlotte Campbell.

The strap line ran across Charlotte's swanlike neck.

It was the first time he had looked at her since she had clawed his face in this very office and run from him, straight into the arms of the Honorable Jago Ross. He supposed that they must airbrush all their pictures. Her skin could not be this flawless, the whites of her eyes this pure, but they had not exaggerated anything else, not the exquisite bone structure, nor (he was sure) the size of the diamond on her finger.

Slowly he turned to the contents page and then to the article within. A double-page picture of Charlotte, very thin in a glittering silver floor-length dress, standing in the middle of a long gallery lined with tapestries; beside her, leaning on a card table and looking like a dissolute arctic fox, was Jago Ross. More photographs over the page: Charlotte sitting on an ancient four-poster, laughing with her head thrown back, the white column of her neck rising from a sheer cream blouse; Charlotte and Jago in jeans and wellington boots, walking hand in hand over the parkland in front of their future home with two Jack Russells at their heels; Charlotte windswept on the castle keep, looking over a shoulder draped in the Viscount's tartan.

Doubtless Helly Anstis had considered it four pounds ten well spent.

On 4 December this year, the seventeenth-century chapel at the Castle of Croy (NEVER "Croy Castle"—it annoys the family) will be dusted off for its first wedding in over a century. Charlotte Campbell, breathtakingly beautiful daughter of 1960s It Girl Tula Clermont and academic and broadcaster Anthony Campbell, will marry the Hon Jago Ross, heir to the castle and to his father's titles, principal of which is Viscount of Croy.

The future Viscountess is a not altogether uncontroversial addition to the Rosses of Croy, but Jago laughs at the idea that anyone in his family could be less than delighted to welcome the former wild child into his old and rather grand Scottish family.

"Actually, my mother always hoped we'd marry," he says. "We were boyfriend and girlfriend at Oxford but I suppose we were just too young... found each other again in London ... both just out of relationships ..."

Were you? thought Strike. *Were you both just out of relationships? Or were you fucking her at the same time I was, so that she didn't know which of us had fathered the baby she was worried she might be carrying? Changing the dates to cover every eventuality, keeping her options open...*

... made headlines in her youth when she went missing from Bedales for seven days, causing a national search ... admitted to rehab at the age of 25 ...

"Old news, move on, nothing to see," says Charlotte brightly. "Look, I had a lot of fun in my youth, but it's time to settle down and honestly, I can't wait."

Fun, was it? Strike asked her stunning picture. *Fun, standing on that roof and threatening to jump? Fun, calling me from that psychiatric hospital and begging me to get you out?*

Ross, fresh from a very messy divorce that has kept the gossip columns busy ... "I wish we could have settled it without the lawyers," he sighs ... "I can't wait to be a step-mummy!" trills Charlotte ...

("If I have to spend one more evening with the Anstises' bratty kids, Corm, I swear to God I'll brain one of them." And, in Lucy's suburban back garden, watching Strike's nephews playing football, "Why are these children such *shits?*" The expression on Lucy's round face when she overheard it...)

His own name, leaping off the page.

... including a surprising fling with Jonny Rokeby's eldest son Cormoran Strike, who made headlines last year...

...a surprising fling with Jonny Rokeby's eldest son...
...Jonny Rokeby's eldest...
He closed the magazine with a sudden, reflexive movement and slid it into his bin.

Sixteen years, on and off. Sixteen years of the torture, the madness and occasional ecstasy. And then—after all those times she had left him, throwing herself into the arms of other men as other women cast themselves onto railway tracks—he had walked out. In doing so, he had crossed an unforgivable Rubicon, for it had always been understood that he should stand rock-like, to be left and returned to, never flinching, never giving up. But on that night when he had confronted her with the tangle of lies she had told about the baby in her belly and she had become hysterical and furious, the mountain had moved at last: out of the door, with an ashtray flung after it.

His black eye had barely healed when she had announced her engagement to Ross. Three weeks it had taken her, because she knew only one way to respond to pain: to wound the transgressor as deeply as possible, with no thought for the consequences to herself. And he knew in his bones, no matter how arrogant his friends might tell him he was being, that the *Tatler* pictures, the dismissal of their relationship in the terms that would hurt him most (he could hear her spelling it out for the society mag: "he's *Jonny Rokeby's* son"); the Castle of Fucking Croy... all of it, *all* of it, was done with a view to hurting him, wanting him to watch and to see, to regret and to pity. She had known what Ross was; she had told Strike about the poorly disguised alcoholism and violence, passed through the blue-blooded network of gossip that had kept her informed through the years. She had laughed about her lucky escape. Laughed.

Self-immolation in a ball gown. *Watch me burn, Bluey.* The wedding was in ten days' time and if he had ever been sure of anything in his life, it was that if he called Charlotte right now and said "Run away with me," even after their filthy scenes, the hateful things she had called him, the lies and the mess and the several tons of baggage under which their relationship had finally splintered, she would say yes. Running away was her life's blood and he had been her favorite destination, freedom and safety combined; she had said it to him over and over again after fights that would have killed them both if emotional wounds could bleed: "I need you. You're my everything, you know that. You're the only place I've ever felt safe, Bluey…"

He heard the glass door onto the landing open and close, the familiar sounds of Robin arriving at work, removing her coat, filling the kettle.

Work had always been his salvation. Charlotte had hated the way he could switch, from crazy, violent scenes, from her tears and her pleas and her threats, to immerse himself totally in a case. She had never managed to stop him putting on his uniform, never prevented his return to work, never succeeded in forcing him away from an investigation. She deplored his focus, his allegiance to the army, his ability to shut her out, seeing it as a betrayal, as abandonment.

Now, on this cold winter's morning, sitting in his office with her picture in the bin beside him, Strike found himself craving orders, a case abroad, an enforced sojourn on another continent. He did not want to trail after unfaithful husbands and girlfriends, or insert himself into the petty disputes of shoddy businessmen. Only one subject had ever matched Charlotte for the fascination it exercised over him: unnatural death.

"Morning," he said, limping into the outer office, where Robin was making two mugs of tea. "We'll have to be quick with these. We're going out."

"Where?" asked Robin in surprise.

The sleet was sliding wetly down their windows. She could still feel how it had burned her face as she hurried over the slippery pavements, desperate to get inside.

"Got stuff to do on the Quine case."

It was a lie. The police had all the power; what could he do that they were not doing better? And yet he knew in his gut that Anstis lacked the nose for the strange and the warped that would be needed to find this killer.

"You've got Caroline Ingles at ten."

"Shit. Well, I'll put her off. Thing is, forensics reckon Quine died very soon after he disappeared."

He took a mouthful of hot, strong tea. He seemed more purposeful, more energized than she had seen him for a while.

"That puts the spotlight right back on the people who had early access to the manuscript. I want to find out where they all live, and whether they live alone. Then we're going to recce their houses. Find out how hard it would've been to get in and out carrying a bag of guts. Whether they might have places they could bury or burn evidence."

It was not much, but it was all he could do today, and he was desperate to do something.

"You're coming," he added. "You're always good at this stuff."

"What, being your Watson?" she said, apparently indifferent. The anger she had carried with her out of the Cambridge the previous day had not quite burned out. "We could find out about their houses online. Look at them on Google Earth."

"Yeah, good thinking," rejoined Strike. "Why case locations when you could just look at out-of-date photos?"

Stung, she said:

"I'm more than happy—"

"Good. I'll cancel Ingles. You get online and find out addresses for Christian Fisher, Elizabeth Tassel, Daniel Chard, Jerry Waldegrave and Michael Fancourt. We'll nip along to Clem Attlee Court and have another look from the point of view of hiding evidence; from what I saw in the dark there were a lot of bins and bushes… Oh, and call the Bridlington Bookshop in Putney. We can have a word with the old bloke who claims he met Quine there on the eighth."

He strode back into his office and Robin sat down at her computer. The scarf she had just hung up was dripping icily onto the floor, but she did not care. The memory of Quine's mutilated body continued to haunt her, yet she was possessed of an urge (concealed from Matthew like a dirty secret) to find out more, to find out everything.

What infuriated her was that Strike, who of all people should have understood, could not see in her what so obviously burned in him.

25

Thus 'tis when a man will be ignorantly officious, do services, and not know his why...

Ben Jonson, *Epicoene, or The Silent Woman*

They left the office in a sudden flurry of feathery snowflakes, Robin with the various addresses she had taken from an online directory on her mobile phone. Strike wanted to revisit Talgarth Road first, so Robin told him the results of her directory searches while standing in a Tube carriage that, at the tail end of the rush hour, was full but not packed. The smell of wet wool, grime and Gore-Tex filled their nostrils as they talked, holding the same pole as three miserable-looking Italian backpackers.

"The old man who works in the bookshop's on holiday," she told Strike. "Back next Monday."

"All right, we'll leave him till then. What about our suspects?"

She raised an eyebrow at the word, but said:

"Christian Fisher lives in Camden with a woman of thirty-two—a girlfriend, do you think?"

"Probably," agreed Strike. "That's inconvenient... our killer needed peace and solitude to dispose of bloodstained clothing—not to mention a good stone's worth of human intestine. I'm looking for somewhere you can get in and out of without being seen."

"Well, I looked at pictures of the place on Google Street View," said Robin with a certain defiance. "The flat's got a common entrance with three others."

"And it's miles away from Talgarth Road."

"But you don't *really* think Christian Fisher did it, do you?" asked Robin.

"Strains credulity a bit," Strike admitted. "He barely knew Quine—he's not in the book—can't see it."

They alighted at Holborn, where Robin tactfully slowed her pace to Strike's, not commenting on his limp or the way he was using his upper body to propel himself along.

"What about Elizabeth Tassel?" he asked as he walked.

"Fulham Palace Road, alone."

"Good," said Strike. "We'll go and have a look at that, see if she's got any freshly dug flower beds."

"Won't the police be doing this?" Robin asked.

Strike frowned. He was perfectly aware that he was a jackal slinking on the periphery of the case, hoping the lions might leave a scrap on a minor bone.

"Maybe," he said, "maybe not. Anstis thinks Leonora did it and he doesn't change his mind easily; I know, I worked with him on a case in Afghanistan. Speaking of Leonora," he added casually, "Anstis has found out she used to work in a butcher's."

"Oh bugger," said Robin.

Strike grinned. At times of tension, her Yorkshire accent became more pronounced: he had heard "*boogger*."

They got onto a much emptier Piccadilly line train to Barons Court; relieved, Strike fell into a seat.

"Jerry Waldegrave lives with his wife, right?" he asked Robin.

"Yes, if she's called Fenella. In Hazlitt Road, Kensington. A Joanna Waldegrave lives in the basement—"

"Their daughter," said Strike. "Budding novelist, she was at the Roper Chard party. And Daniel Chard?"

"Sussex Street, Pimlico, with a couple called Nenita and Manny Ramos—"

"Sound like servants."

"—and he's got a property in Devon as well: Tithebarn House."

"Which is presumably where he's currently laid up with his broken leg."

"And Fancourt's ex-directory," she finished, "but there's loads of biographical stuff about him online. He owns an Elizabethan place just outside Chew Magna called Endsor Court."

"Chew Magna?"

"It's in Somerset. He lives there with his third wife."

"Bit far to go today," said Strike regretfully. "No bachelor pad near Talgarth Road where he could stash guts in the freezer?"

"Not that I could find."

"So where was he staying when he went to stare at the crime scene? Or had he come up for the day for a spot of nostalgia?"

"If it really was him."

"Yeah, if it was him…and there's Kathryn Kent too. Well, we know where she lives and we know it's alone. Quine got dropped off in her vicinity on the night of the fifth, Anstis says, but she was away. Maybe Quine had forgotten she was at her sister's," Strike mused, "and maybe when he found out she wasn't home he went to Talgarth Road instead? She could have come back from the hospice to meet him there. We'll have a look round her place second."

As they moved west Strike told Robin about the different witnesses who claimed to have seen a woman in a burqa entering the building on the fourth of November and Quine himself leaving the building in the early hours of the sixth.

"But one or both of them could be mistaken or lying," he concluded.

"A woman in a burqa. You don't think," said Robin tentatively, "the neighbor might be a mad Islamophobe?"

Working for Strike had opened her eyes to the array and intensity of phobias and grudges she had never realized burned in the public's breast. The tide of publicity surrounding the solving of the Landry case had washed onto Robin's desk a number of letters that had alternately disturbed and amused her.

There had been the man who had begged Strike to turn his clearly considerable talents to an investigation of the stranglehold of "international Jewry" on the world banking system, a service for which he regretted he would not be able to pay but for which he did not doubt that Strike would receive worldwide acclaim. A young woman had written a twelve-page letter from a secure psychiatric unit, begging

Strike to help her prove that everybody in her family had been spirited away and replaced with identical impostors. An anonymous writer of unknown gender had demanded that Strike help them expose a national campaign of satanic abuse which they knew to be operating through the offices of the Citizens Advice Bureau.

"They could be loons," Strike agreed. "Nutters love murder. It does something to them. People have to listen to them, for a start."

A young woman wearing a hijab was watching them talk from an opposite seat. She had large, sweet, liquid-brown eyes.

"Assuming somebody really did enter the house on the fourth, I've got to say a burqa's a bloody good way of getting in and out without being recognized. Can you think of another way of totally concealing your face and body that wouldn't make people challenge you?"

"And they were carrying a halal takeaway?"

"Allegedly. Was his last meal halal? Is that why the killer removed the guts?"

"And this woman—"

"Could've been a man ... "

"—was seen leaving the house an hour later?"

"That's what Anstis said."

"So they weren't lying in wait for Quine?"

"No, but they could have been laying in plates," said Strike and Robin winced.

The young woman in the hijab got off at Gloucester Road.

"I doubt there'd be closed-circuit cameras in a bookshop," sighed Robin. She had become quite preoccupied with CCTV since the Landry case.

"I'd've thought Anstis would have mentioned it," agreed Strike.

They emerged at Barons Court into another squall of snow. Squinting against the feathery flakes they proceeded, under Strike's direction, up to Talgarth Road. He was feeling the need for a stick ever more strongly. On his release from hospital, Charlotte had given him an elegant antique Malacca cane that she claimed had belonged to a great-grandfather. The handsome old stick had been too short for Strike, causing him to list to the right as he walked. When she had packaged up his things to remove from her flat, the cane had not been among them.

It was clear, as they approached the house, that the forensics team was still busy in number 179. The entrance was taped up and a single police officer, arms folded tightly against the cold, stood guard outside. She turned her head as they approached. Her eyes fixed on Strike and narrowed.

"Mr. Strike," she said sharply.

A male plainclothes officer with ginger hair who had been standing in the doorway talking to somebody just inside whipped around, caught sight of Strike and descended the slippery steps at speed.

"Morning," said Strike brazenly. Robin was torn between admiration for his cheek and trepidation; she had an innate respect for the law.

"What are you doing back here, Mr. Strike?" asked the ginger-haired man suavely. His eyes wandered over Robin in a way that she found vaguely offensive. "You can't come in."

"Pity," said Strike. "We'll just have to peruse the perimeter, then."

Ignoring the pair of officers watching his every move, Strike limped past them to number 183 and proceeded through the gates and up the front steps. Robin could think of nothing to do but follow him; she did it self-consciously, aware of the eyes on her back.

"What are we doing?" she muttered as they reached the shelter of the brick canopy and were hidden from the staring police. The house seemed empty, but she was a little worried that someone might be about to open the front door.

"Gauging whether the woman who lives here could've seen a cloaked figure carrying a holdall leaving 179 at two in the morning," said Strike. "And you know what? I think she could, unless that streetlamp's out. OK, let's try the other side.

"Parky, isn't it?" Strike said to the frowning constable and her companion as he and Robin walked back past them. "Four doors down, Anstis said," he added quietly to Robin. "So that'll be 171 ... "

Again, Strike marched up the front steps, Robin walking foolishly after him.

"You know, I was wondering whether he could've mistaken the house, but 177's got that red plastic dustbin in front. Burqa would've walked up the steps right behind it, which would've made it easy to tell—"

The front door opened.

"Can I help you?" said a well-spoken man in thick-lensed glasses.

As Strike began to apologize for coming to the wrong house, the ginger-haired officer shouted something incomprehensible from the pavement outside 179. When nobody responded, he climbed over the plastic tape blocking entrance to the property and began to jog towards them.

"That man," he shouted absurdly, pointing at Strike, "is not a policeman!"

"He didn't say he was," replied the spectacled man in meek surprise.

"Well, I think we're done here," Strike told Robin.

"Aren't you worried," Robin asked him as they walked back towards the Tube station, a little amused but mostly eager to leave the scene, "what your friend Anstis is going to say about you skulking around the crime scene like this?"

"Doubt he'll be happy," Strike said, looking around for CCTV cameras, "but keeping Anstis happy isn't in my job description."

"It was decent of him to share the forensic stuff with you," Robin said.

"He did that to try and warn me off the case. He thinks everything points to Leonora. Trouble is, at the moment, everything does."

The road was packed with traffic, which was watched by a single camera as far as Strike could see, but there were many side roads leading off it down which a person wearing Owen Quine's Tyrolean cloak, or a burqa, might slide out of sight without anyone being the wiser as to their identity.

Strike bought two takeaway coffees in the Metro Café that stood in the station building, then they passed back through the pea-green ticket hall and set off for West Brompton.

"What you've got to remember," said Strike as they stood at Earl's Court waiting to change trains, Robin noticing how Strike kept all his weight on his good leg, "is that Quine disappeared on the fifth. Bonfire night."

"God, of course!" said Robin.

"Flashes and bangs," said Strike, gulping coffee fast so as to empty his cup before they had to get on; he did not trust himself to balance coffee and himself on the wet, icy floors. "Rockets going off in every direction, drawing everyone's attention. No big surprise that nobody saw a figure in a cloak entering the building that night."

"You mean Quine?"

"Not necessarily."

Robin pondered this for a while.

"Do you think the man in the bookshop's lying about Quine going in there on the eighth?"

"I don't know," said Strike. "Too early to say, isn't it?"

But that, he realized, was what he believed. The sudden activity around a deserted house on the fourth and fifth was strongly suggestive.

"Funny, the things people notice," said Robin as they climbed the red-and-green stairs at West Brompton, Strike now grimacing every time he put down his right leg. "Memory's an odd thing, isn't—"

Strike's knee suddenly felt red hot and he slumped against the railings along the bridge over the tracks. A suited man behind him swore impatiently at finding a sudden, sizable impediment in his path and Robin walked on a few paces, still talking, before realizing that Strike was no longer beside her. She hurried back to find him pale, sweating and obliging commuters to take a detour around him as he stood slumped against the railings.

"Felt something go," he said through gritted teeth, "in my knee. Shit … *shit!*"

"We'll get a taxi."

"Never get one in this weather."

"Then let's get back on the train and go back to the office."

"No, I want—"

He had never felt his dearth of resources more keenly than at this moment, standing on the iron lattice bridge beneath the arched glass ceiling where snow was settling. In the old days there had always been a car for him to drive. He could have summoned witnesses to him. He had been Special Investigation Branch, in charge, in control.

"If you want to do this, we need a taxi," Robin said firmly. "It's a long walk up Lillie Road from here. Haven't—"

She hesitated. They never mentioned Strike's disability except obliquely.

"Haven't you got a stick or something?"

"Wish I had," he said through numb lips. What was the point in pretending? He was dreading having to walk even to the end of the bridge.

"We can get one," said Robin. "Chemists sometimes sell them. We'll find one."

And then, after another momentary hesitation, she said:

"Lean on me."

"I'm too heavy."

"To balance. Use me like a stick. Do it," she said firmly.

He put his arm around her shoulders and they made their way slowly over the bridge and paused beside the exit. The snow had temporarily passed, but the cold was, if anything, worse than it had been.

"Why aren't there seats anywhere?" asked Robin, glaring around.

"Welcome to my world," said Strike, who had withdrawn his arm from around her shoulders the instant they had stopped.

"What d'you think's happened?" Robin asked, looking down at his right leg.

"I dunno. It was all puffed up this morning. I probably shouldn't have put the prosthesis on, but I hate using crutches."

"Well, you can't go traipsing up Lillie Road in the snow like this. We'll get a cab and you can go back to the office—"

"No. I want to do something," he said angrily. "Anstis is convinced it's Leonora. It isn't."

Everything was pared down to the essential when you were in this degree of pain.

"All right," said Robin. "We'll split up and you can go in a cab. OK? *OK?*" she said insistently.

"All right," he said, defeated. "You go up to Clem Attlee Court."

"What am I looking for?"

"Cameras. Hiding places for clothing and intestines. Kent can't have kept them in her flat if she took them; they'd stink. Take pictures on your phone—anything that seems useful ... "

It seemed pathetically little to him as he said it, but he had to do something. For some reason, he kept remembering Orlando, with her wide, vacant smile and her cuddly orangutan.

"And then?" asked Robin.

"Sussex Street," said Strike after a few seconds' thought. "Same thing. And then give me a ring and we'll meet up. You'd better give me the numbers of Tassel's and Waldegrave's houses."

She gave him a piece of paper.

"I'll get you a taxi."

Before he could thank her she had marched away onto the cold street.

26

I must look to my footing:
In such slippery ice-pavements men had need
To be frost-nail'd well, they may break their necks
    else...

John Webster, *The Duchess of Malfi*

It was fortunate that Strike still had the five hundred pounds in cash in his wallet that had been given him to cut up a teenage boy. He told the taxi driver to take him to Fulham Palace Road, home of Elizabeth Tassel, took note of the route as he traveled and would have arrived at her house in a mere four minutes had he not spotted a Boots. He asked the driver to pull up and wait, and reemerged from the chemists shortly afterwards, walking much more easily with the aid of an adjustable stick.

He estimated that a fit woman might make the journey on foot in less than half an hour. Elizabeth Tassel lived further from the murder scene than Kathryn Kent but Strike, who knew the area reasonably well, was sure that she could have made her way through most residential backstreets while avoiding the attention of cameras, and that she might have avoided detection even with a car.

Her home looked drab and dingy on this bleak winter's day. Another redbrick Victorian house, but with none of the grandeur or whimsy of Talgarth Road, it stood on a corner, fronted by a dank garden overshadowed by overgrown laburnum bushes. Sleet fell again as Strike stood peering over the garden gate, trying to keep his cigarette alight by cupping it in his hand. There were gardens front and back, both well shielded from the public view by the dark bushes quivering with the weight of the icy downpour. The upper windows of the house looked out over the Fulham Palace Road Cemetery, a depressing view one month from midwinter, with bare trees reaching bony arms silhouetted into a white sky, old tombstones marching into the distance.

Could he imagine Elizabeth Tassel in her smart black suit, with her scarlet lipstick and her undisguised fury at Owen Quine, returning here under cover of darkness, stained with blood and acid, carrying a bag full of intestines?

The cold was nipping viciously at Strike's neck and fingers. He ground out the stub of his cigarette and asked the taxi driver, who had watched with curiosity tinged with suspicion as he scrutinized Elizabeth Tassel's house, to take him to Hazlitt Road in Kensington. Slumped in the backseat he gulped down painkillers with a bottle of water that he had bought in Boots.

The cab was stuffy and smelled of stale tobacco, ingrained dirt and ancient leather. The windscreen wipers swished like muffled metronomes, rhythmically clearing the blurry view of broad, busy Hammersmith Road, where small office blocks and short rows of terraced houses sat side by side. Strike looked out at Nazareth House Care Home: more red brick, church-like and serene, but with security gates and a lodge keeping a firm separation between those cared for and those who were not.

Blythe House came into view through the misty windows, a grand palace-like structure with white cupolas, looking like a large pinkish cake in the gray sleet. Strike had a vague notion that it was used as a store for one of the big museums these days. The taxi turned right into Hazlitt Road.

"What number?" asked the driver.

"I'll get out here," said Strike, who did not wish to descend directly in front of the house, and had not forgotten that he still had to pay back the money he was squandering. Leaning heavily on the stick and grateful for its rubber-coated end, which gripped the slippery pavement well, he paid the driver and walked along the street to take a closer look at the Waldegrave residence.

These were real town houses, four stories high including the basements, golden brick with classical white pediments, carved wreaths beneath the upper windows and wrought-iron balustrades. Most of them had been converted into flats. There were no front gardens, only steps descending to the basements.

A faintly ramshackle flavor had permeated the street, a gentle middle-class dottiness that expressed itself in the random collections of potted plants on one balcony, a bicycle on another and, on a third, limp, wet and possibly soon-to-be-frozen washing forgotten in the sleet.

The house that Waldegrave shared with his wife was one of the very few that had not been converted into flats. As he stared up at it, Strike wondered how much a top editor earned and remembered Nina's statement that Waldegrave's wife "came from money." The Waldegraves' first-floor balcony (he had to cross the street to see it clearly) sported two sodden deck chairs printed with the covers of old Penguin paperbacks, flanking a tiny iron table of the kind found in Parisian bistros.

He lit another cigarette and recrossed the road to peer down at the basement flat where Waldegrave's daughter lived, considering as he did so whether Quine might have discussed the contents of *Bombyx Mori* with his editor before delivering the manuscript. Could he have confided to Waldegrave how he envisaged the final scene of *Bombyx Mori*? And could that amiable man in horn-rimmed glasses have nodded enthusiastically and helped hone the scene in all its ludicrous gore, knowing that he would one day enact it?

There were black bin bags heaped around the front door of the basement flat. It looked as though Joanna Waldegrave had been having a comprehensive clear-out. Strike turned his back and contemplated the fifty windows, at a conservative estimate, that overlooked the Waldegrave family's two front doors. Waldegrave would have had to have been very lucky not to be seen coming and going out of this heavily overlooked house.

But the trouble was, Strike reflected gloomily, that even if Jerry Waldegrave had been spotted sneaking into his house at two in the morning with a suspicious, bulging bag under his arm, a jury might take some persuading that Owen Quine had not been alive and well at the time. There was too much doubt about the time of death. The murderer had now had as long as nineteen days in which to dispose of evidence, a long and useful period.

Where could Owen Quine's guts have gone? What, Strike asked himself, did you do with pounds and pounds of freshly severed human intestine and stomach? Bury them? Dump them in a river? Throw them in a communal bin? They would surely not burn well…

The front door of the Waldegraves' house opened and a woman with black hair and heavy frown lines walked down the three front steps. She was wearing a short scarlet coat and looked angry.

"I've been watching you out of the window," she called to Strike as she approached and he recognized Waldegrave's wife, Fenella. "What do you think you're doing? Why are you so interested in my house?"

"I'm waiting for the agent," Strike lied at once, showing no sign of embarrassment. "This is the basement flat for rent, right?"

"Oh," she said, taken aback. "No—that's three down," she said, pointing.

He could tell that she teetered on the verge of an apology but decided not to bother. Instead she clattered past him on patent stilettos ill suited to the snowy conditions towards a Volvo parked a short way away. Her black hair revealed gray roots and their brief proximity had brought with it a whiff of bad breath stained with alcohol. Mindful that she could see him in her rearview mirror, he hobbled in the direction she had indicated, waited until she had pulled away— very narrowly missing the Citroën in front of her—then walked carefully to the end of the road and down a side street, where he was able to peer over a wall into a long row of small private back gardens.

There was nothing of note in the Waldegraves' except an old shed. The lawn was scuffed and scrubby and a set of rustic furniture sat sadly at its far end with a look of having been abandoned long ago. Staring at the untidy plot, Strike reflected gloomily on the possibility of lockups, allotments and garages he might not know about.

With an inward groan at the thought of the long, cold, wet walk ahead, he debated his options. He was nearest to Kensington Olympia, but it only opened the District line he needed at weekends. As an overground station, Hammersmith would be easier to navigate than Barons Court, so he decided on the longer journey.

He had just passed into Blythe Road, wincing with every step on his right leg, when his mobile rang: Anstis.

"What are you playing at, Bob?"

"Meaning?" asked Strike, limping along, a stabbing in his knee.

"You've been hanging around the crime scene."

"Went back for a look. Public right of way. Nothing actionable."

"You were trying to interview a neighbor—"

"He wasn't supposed to open his front door," said Strike. "I didn't say a word about Quine."

"Look, Strike—"

The detective noticed the reversion to his actual name without regret. He had never been fond of the nickname Anstis had given him.

"I told you, you've got to keep out of our way."

"Can't, Anstis," said Strike matter-of-factly. "I've got a client—"

"Forget your client," said Anstis. "She's looking more and more like a killer with every bit of information we get. My advice is, cut your losses because you're making yourself a lot of enemies. I warned you—"

"You did," said Strike. "You couldn't have been clearer. Nobody's going to be able to blame you, Anstis."

"I'm not warning you off because I'm trying to cover my arse," snapped Anstis.

Strike kept walking in silence, the mobile pressed awkwardly to his ear. After a short pause Anstis said:

"We've got the pharmacological report back. Small amount of blood alcohol, nothing else."

"OK."

"And we're sending dogs out to Mucking Marshes this afternoon. Trying to keep ahead of the weather. They say there's heavy snow on the way."

Mucking Marshes, Strike knew, was the UK's biggest landfill site; it serviced London, the municipal and commercial waste of which was floated down the Thames in ugly barges.

"You think the guts were dumped in a dustbin, do you?"

"A skip. There's a house renovation going on round the corner from Talgarth Road; they had two parked out front until the eighth. In this cold the guts might not have attracted flies. We've checked and that's where everything the builders take away ends up: Mucking Marshes."

"Well, good luck with that," said Strike.

"I'm trying to save you time and energy, mate."

"Yeah. Very grateful."

And after insincere thanks for Anstis's hospitality of the previous evening Strike rang off. He then paused, leaning against a wall, the better to dial a new number. A tiny Asian woman with a pushchair, whom he had not heard walking behind him, had to swerve to avoid him, but unlike the man on the West Brompton bridge she did not swear at him. The walking stick, like a burqa, conferred protective status; she gave him a small smile as she passed.

Leonora Quine answered within three rings.

"Bloody police are back," was her greeting.

"What do they want?"

"They're asking to look all over the house and garden now," she said. "Do I have to let 'em?"

Strike hesitated.

"I think it's sensible to let them do whatever they want. Listen, Leonora," he felt no compunction about reverting to a military peremptoriness, "have you got a lawyer?"

"No, why? I ain't under arrest. Not yet."

"I think you need one."

There was a pause.

"D'you know any good ones?" she asked.

"Yes," said Strike. "Call Ilsa Herbert. I'll send you her number now."

"Orlando don't like the police poking—"

"I'm going to text you this number, and I want you to call Ilsa immediately. All right? *Immediately*."

"All right," she said grumpily.

He rang off, found his old school friend's number on his mobile and sent it to Leonora. He then called Ilsa and explained, with apologies, what he had just done.

"I don't know why you're saying sorry," she said cheerfully. "We love people who are in trouble with the police, it's our bread and butter."

"She might qualify for legal aid."

"Hardly anyone does these days," said Ilsa. "Let's just hope she's poor enough."

Strike's hands were numb and he was very hungry. He slid the mobile back into his coat pocket and limped on to Hammersmith Road. There on the opposite pavement was a snug-looking pub, black painted, the round metal sign depicting a galleon in full sail. He headed straight for it, noting how much more patient waiting drivers were when you were using a stick.

Two pubs in two days...but the weather was bad and his knee excruciating; Strike could not muster any guilt. The Albion's interior was as cozy as its exterior suggested. Long and narrow, an open fire burned at the far end; there was an upper gallery with a balustrade and much polished wood. Beneath a black iron spiral staircase to the first floor were two amps and a microphone stand. Black-and-white photographs of celebrated musicians were hung along one cream wall.

The seats by the fire were taken. Strike bought himself a pint, picked up a bar menu and headed to the tall table surrounded by bar stools next to the window onto the street. As he sat down he noticed, sandwiched between pictures of Duke Ellington and Robert Plant, his own long-haired father, sweaty post-performance, apparently sharing a joke with the bass player whom he had once, according to Strike's mother, tried to strangle.

("Jonny was never good on speed," Leda had confided to her uncomprehending nine-year-old son.)

His mobile rang again. With his eyes on his father's picture, he answered.

"Hi," said Robin. "I'm back at the office. Where are you?"

"The Albion on Hammersmith Road."

"You've had an odd call. I found the message when I got back."

"Go on."

"It's Daniel Chard," said Robin. "He wants to meet you."

Frowning, Strike turned his eyes away from his father's leather jumpsuit to gaze down the pub at the flickering fire. "Daniel Chard wants to meet me? How does Daniel Chard even know I exist?"

"For God's sake, you found the body! It's been all over the news."

"Oh yeah—there's that. Did he say why?"

"He says he's got a proposition."

213

A vivid mental image of a naked, bald man with an erect, suppurating penis flashed in Strike's mind like a projector slide and was instantly dismissed.

"I thought he was holed up in Devon because he'd broken his leg."

"He is. He wonders whether you'd mind traveling down to see him."

"Oh, does he?"

Strike pondered the suggestion, thinking of his workload, the meetings he had during the rest of the week. Finally, he said:

"I could do it Friday if I put off Burnett. What the hell does he want? I'll need to hire a car. An automatic," he added, his leg throbbing painfully under the table. "Could you do that for me?"

"No problem," said Robin. He could hear her scribbling.

"I've got a lot to tell you," he said. "D'you want to join me for lunch? They've got a decent menu. Shouldn't take you more than twenty minutes if you grab a cab."

"Two days running? We can't keep getting taxis and buying lunch out," said Robin, even though she sounded pleased at the idea.

"That's OK. Burnett loves spending her ex's money. I'll charge it to her account."

Strike hung up, decided on a steak and ale pie and limped to the bar to order.

When he resumed his seat his eyes drifted absently back to his father in skin-tight leathers, with his hair plastered around his narrow, laughing face.

The Wife knows about me and pretends not to ... she won't let him go even if it's the best thing for everyone ...

I know where you're off to, Owen!

Strike's gaze slid along the row of black-and-white megastars on the wall facing him.

Am I deluded? he asked John Lennon silently, who looked down at him through round glasses, sardonic, pinch-nosed.

Why did he not believe, even in the face of what he had to admit were suggestive signs to the contrary, that Leonora had murdered her husband? Why did he remain convinced that she had come to his office not as a cover but because she was genuinely angry that Quine

214

had run away like a sulky child? He would have sworn on oath that it had never crossed her mind that her husband might be dead...Lost in thought, he had finished his pint before he knew it.

"Hi," said Robin.

"That was quick!" said Strike, surprised to see her.

"Not really," said Robin. "Traffic's quite heavy. Shall I order?"

Male heads turned to look at her as she walked to the bar, but Strike did not notice. He was still thinking about Leonora Quine, thin, plain, graying, hunted.

When Robin returned with another pint for Strike and a tomato juice for herself she showed him the photographs that she had taken on her phone that morning of Daniel Chard's town residence. It was a white stucco villa complete with balustrade, its gleaming black front door flanked by columns.

"It's got an odd little courtyard, sheltered from the street," said Robin, showing Strike a picture. Shrubs stood in big-bellied Grecian urns. "I suppose Chard could have dumped the guts into one of those," she said flippantly. "Pulled out the tree and buried them in the earth."

"Can't imagine Chard doing anything so energetic or dirty, but that's the way to keep thinking," said Strike, remembering the publisher's immaculate suit and flamboyant tie. "How about Clem Attlee Court—as full of hiding places as I remember?"

"Loads of them," said Robin, showing him a fresh set of pictures. "Communal bins, bushes, all sorts. The only thing is, I just can't imagine being able to do it unseen, or that somebody wouldn't notice them fairly quickly. There are people around all the time and everywhere you go you're being overlooked by about a hundred windows. You might manage it in the middle of the night, but there are cameras too.

"But I did notice something else. Well...it's just an idea."

"Go on."

"There's a medical center right in front of the building. Might they not sometimes dispose of—"

"Human waste!" said Strike, lowering his pint. "Bloody hell, that's a thought."

"Should I get onto it, then?" asked Robin, trying to conceal the pleasure and pride she felt at Strike's look of admiration. "Try and find out how and when—?"

"Definitely!" said Strike. "That's a much better lead than Anstis's. He thinks," he explained, answering her look of inquiry, "the guts were dumped in a skip close by Talgarth Road, that the killer just carried them round the corner and chucked them in."

"Well, they could have," began Robin, but Strike frowned exactly the way Matthew did if ever she mentioned an idea or a belief of Strike's.

"This killing was planned to the hilt. We're not dealing with a murderer who'd just have dumped a holdall full of human guts round the corner from the corpse."

They sat in silence while Robin reflected wryly that Strike's dislike of Anstis's theories might be due to innate competitiveness more than any objective evaluation. Robin knew something about male pride; quite apart from Matthew, she had three brothers.

"So what were Elizabeth Tassel's and Jerry Waldegrave's places like?"

Strike told her about Waldegrave's wife thinking he had been watching her house.

"Very shirty about it."

"Odd," said Robin. "If I saw somebody staring at our place I wouldn't leap to the conclusion that they were—you know—*watching* it."

"She's a drinker like her husband," said Strike. "I could smell it on her. Meanwhile, Elizabeth Tassel's place is as good a murderer's hideout as I've ever seen."

"What d'you mean?" asked Robin, half amused, half apprehensive.

"Very private, barely overlooked."

"Well, I still don't think—"

"—it's a woman. You said."

Strike drank his beer in silence for a minute or two, considering a course of action that he knew would irritate Anstis more than any other. He had no right to interrogate suspects. He had been told to keep out of the way of the police.

Picking up his mobile, he contemplated it for a moment, then called Roper Chard and asked to speak to Jerry Waldegrave.

"Anstis told you not to get under their feet!" Robin said, alarmed.

"Yeah," said Strike, the line silent in his ear, "advice he's just repeated, but I haven't told you half what's been going on. Tell you in—"

"Hello?" said Jerry Waldegrave on the end of the line.

"Mr. Waldegrave," said Strike and introduced himself, though he had already given his name to Waldegrave's assistant. "We met briefly yesterday morning, at Mrs. Quine's."

"Yes, of course," said Waldegrave. He sounded politely puzzled.

"As I think Mrs. Quine told you, she's hired me because she's worried that the police suspect her."

"I'm sure that can't be true," said Waldegrave at once.

"That they suspect her, or that she killed her husband?"

"Well—both," said Waldegrave.

"Wives usually come in for close scrutiny when a husband dies," said Strike.

"I'm sure they do, but I can't... well, I can't believe any of it, actually," said Waldegrave. "The whole thing's incredible and horrible."

"Yeah," said Strike. "I was wondering whether we could meet so I could ask you a few questions? I'm happy," said the detective, with a glance at Robin, "to come to your house—after work—whatever suits."

Waldegrave did not answer immediately.

"Naturally I'll do anything to help Leonora, but what do you imagine I can tell you?"

"I'm interested in *Bombyx Mori*," said Strike. "Mr. Quine put a lot of unflattering portraits in the book."

"Yeah," said Waldegrave. "He did."

Strike wondered whether Waldegrave had been interviewed by the police yet; whether he had already been asked to explain the contents of bloody sacks, the symbolism of a drowned dwarf.

"All right," said Waldegrave. "I don't mind meeting you. My diary's quite full this week. Could you make... let's see... lunch on Monday?"

"Great," said Strike, reflecting sourly that this would mean him footing the bill, and that he would have preferred to see inside Waldegrave's house. "Where?"

"I'd rather stick close to the office; I've got a full afternoon. Would you mind Simpson's-in-the-Strand?"

Strike thought it an odd choice but agreed, his eyes on Robin's. "One o'clock? I'll get my secretary to book it. See you then."

"He's going to meet you?" said Robin as soon as Strike had hung up.

"Yeah," said Strike. "Fishy."

She shook her head, half laughing.

"He didn't seem particularly keen, from all I could hear. And don't you think the fact that he's agreed to meet at all looks like he's got a clear conscience?"

"No," said Strike. "I've told you this before; plenty of people hang around the likes of me to gauge how the investigation's going. They can't leave well enough alone, they feel compelled to keep explaining themselves.

"Need a pee ... hang on ... got more to tell you ... "

Robin sipped her tomato juice while Strike hobbled away using the new stick.

Another flurry of snow passed the window, swiftly dispersing. Robin looked up at the black-and-white photographs opposite and recognized, with a slight shock, Jonny Rokeby, Strike's father. Other than the fact that both were over six feet tall, they did not resemble each other in the slightest; it had taken a DNA test to prove paternity. Strike was listed as one of the rock star's progeny on Rokeby's Wikipedia entry. They had met, so Strike had told Robin, twice. After staring for a while at Rokeby's very tight and revealing leather trousers, Robin forced herself to gaze out of the window again, afraid of Strike catching her staring at his father's groin.

Their food arrived as Strike returned to the table.

"The police are searching the whole of Leonora's house now," Strike announced, picking up his knife and fork.

"Why?" asked Robin, fork suspended in midair.

"Why d'you think? Looking for bloody clothing. Checking the garden for freshly dug holes full of her husband's innards. I've put her on to a lawyer. They haven't got enough to arrest her yet, but they're determined to find something."

"You genuinely don't think she did it?"

"No, I don't."

Strike had cleared his plate before he spoke again.

"I'd love to talk to Fancourt. I want to know why he joined Roper Chard when Quine was there and he was supposed to hate him. They'd have been bound to meet."

"You think Fancourt killed Quine so he wouldn't have to meet him at office parties?"

"Good one," said Strike wryly.

He drained his pint glass, picked up his mobile yet again, dialed Directory Inquiries and shortly afterwards was put through to the Elizabeth Tassel Literary Agency.

Her assistant, Ralph, answered. When Strike gave his name, the young man sounded both fearful and excited.

"Oh, I don't know ... I'll ask. Putting you on hold."

But he appeared to be less than adept with the telephone system, because after a loud click the line remained open. Strike could hear a distant Ralph informing his boss that Strike was on the telephone and her loud, impatient retort.

"What the bloody hell does he want now?"

"He didn't say."

Heavy footsteps, the sound of the receiver being snatched off the desk.

"Hello?"

"Elizabeth," said Strike pleasantly. "It's me, Cormoran Strike."

"Yes, Ralph's just told me. What is it?"

"I was wondering if we could meet. I'm still working for Leonora Quine. She's convinced that the police suspect her of her husband's murder."

"And what do you want to talk to me for? *I* can't tell you whether she did or not."

Strike could imagine the shocked faces of Ralph and Sally, listening in the smelly old office.

"I've got a few more questions about Quine."

"Oh, for God's sake," growled Elizabeth. "Well, I suppose I could do lunch tomorrow if it suits. Otherwise I'm busy until—"

"Tomorrow would be great," said Strike. "But it doesn't have to be lunch, I could—?"

"Lunch suits me."

"Great," said Strike at once.

"Pescatori, Charlotte Street," she said. "Twelve thirty unless you hear differently."

She rang off.

"They love their bloody lunches, book people," Strike said. "Is it too much of a stretch to think they don't want me at home in case I spot Quine's guts in the freezer?"

Robin's smile faded.

"You know, you could lose a friend over this," she said, pulling on her coat. "Ringing people up and asking to question them."

Strike grunted.

"Don't you care?" she asked, as they left the warmth for biting cold, snowflakes burning their faces.

"I've got plenty more friends," said Strike, truthfully, without bombast.

"We should have a beer every lunchtime," he added, leaning heavily on his stick as they headed off towards the Tube, their heads bowed against the white blur. "Breaks up the working day."

Robin, who had adjusted her stride to his, smiled. She had enjoyed today more than almost any since she had started work for Strike, but Matthew, still in Yorkshire, helping plan his mother's funeral, must not know about the second trip to a pub in two days.

27

That I should trust a man, whom I had known betray his friend!

William Congreve, *The Double-Dealer*

An immense carpet of snow was rolling down over Britain. The morning news showed the northeast of England already buried in powdery whiteness, cars stranded like so many hapless sheep, headlamps feebly glinting. London waited its turn beneath an increasingly ominous sky and Strike, glancing at the weather map on his TV as he dressed, wondered whether his drive to Devon the next day would be possible, whether the M5 would even be navigable. Determined though he was to meet the incapacitated Daniel Chard, whose invitation struck him as highly peculiar, he dreaded driving even an automatic with his leg in this condition.

The dogs would still be out on Mucking Marshes. He imagined them as he attached the prosthesis, his knee puffier and more painful than ever; their sensitive, quivering noses probing the freshest patches of landfill under these threatening gunmetal clouds, beneath circling seagulls. They might already have started, given the limited daylight, dragging their handlers through the frozen garbage, searching for Owen Quine's guts. Strike had worked alongside sniffer dogs. Their wriggling rumps and wagging tails always added an incongruously cheerful note to searches.

He was disconcerted by how painful it was to walk downstairs. Of course, in an ideal world he would have spent the previous day with an ice pack pressed to the end of his stump, his leg elevated, not tramping all over London because he needed to stop himself thinking about Charlotte and her wedding, soon to take place in the restored chapel of the Castle of Croy...not Croy Castle, *because it annoys the fucking family*. Nine days to go...

The telephone rang on Robin's desk as he unlocked the glass door. Wincing, he hurried to get it. The suspicious lover and boss of Miss Brocklehurst wished to inform Strike that his PA was at home in his bed with a bad cold, so he was not to be charged for surveillance until she was up and about again. Strike had barely replaced the receiver when it rang again. Another client, Caroline Ingles, announced in a voice throbbing with emotion that she and her errant husband had reconciled. Strike was offering insincere congratulations when Robin arrived, pink-faced with cold.

"It's getting worse out there," she said when he had hung up. "Who was that?"

"Caroline Ingles. She's made up with Rupert."

"*What?*" said Robin, stunned. "After all those lap-dancers?"

"They're going to work on their marriage for the sake of the kids."

Robin made a little snort of disbelief.

"Snow looks bad up in Yorkshire," Strike commented. "If you want to take tomorrow off and leave early—?"

"No," said Robin, "I've booked myself on the Friday-night sleeper, I should be fine. If we've lost Ingles, I could call one of the waiting-list clients—?"

"Not yet," said Strike, slumping down on the sofa and unable to stop his hand sliding to his swollen knee as it protested painfully.

"Is it still sore?" Robin asked diffidently, pretending she had not seen him wince.

"Yeah," said Strike. "But that's not why I don't want to take on another client," he added sharply.

"I know," said Robin, who had her back to him, switching on the kettle. "You want to concentrate on the Quine case."

Strike was not sure whether her tone was reproachful.

"She'll pay me," he said shortly. "Quine had life insurance, she made him take it out. So there's money there now."

Robin heard his defensiveness and did not like it. Strike was making the assumption that her priority was money. Hadn't she proved that it was not when she had turned down much better paid jobs to work for him? Hadn't he noticed the willingness with which she was trying to help him prove that Leonora Quine had not killed her husband?

She set a mug of tea, a glass of water and paracetamol down beside him.

"Thanks," he said, through gritted teeth, irritated by the painkillers even though he intended to take a double dose.

"I'll book a taxi to take you to Pescatori at twelve, shall I?"

"It's only round the corner," he said.

"You know, there's pride, and then there's stupidity," said Robin, with one of the first flashes of real temper he had ever seen in her.

"Fine," he said, eyebrows raised. "I'll take a bloody taxi."

And in truth, he was glad of it three hours later as he limped, leaning heavily on the cheap stick, which was now warping from his weight, to the taxi waiting at the end of Denmark Street. He knew now that he ought not to have put on the prosthesis at all. Getting out of the cab a few minutes later in Charlotte Street was tricky, the taxi driver impatient. Strike reached the noisy warmth of Pescatori with relief.

Elizabeth was not yet there but had booked under her name. Strike was shown to a table for two beside a pebble-set and whitewashed wall. Rustic wooden beams crisscrossed the ceiling; a rowing boat was suspended over the bar. Across the opposite wall were jaunty orange leather booths. From force of habit, Strike ordered a pint, enjoying the light, bright Mediterranean charm of his surroundings, watching the snow drifting past the windows.

The agent arrived not long afterwards. He tried to stand as she approached the table but fell back down again quickly. Elizabeth did not seem to notice.

She looked as though she had lost weight since he had last seen her; the well-cut black suit, the scarlet lipstick and the steel-gray bob did not lend her dash today, but looked like a badly chosen disguise. Her face was yellowish and seemed to sag.

"How are you?" he asked.

"How do you think I am?" she croaked rudely. "What?" she snapped at a hovering waiter. "Oh. Water. Still."

She picked up her menu with an air of having given away too much and Strike could tell that any expression of pity or concern would be unwelcome.

"Just soup," she told the waiter when he returned for their order.

"I appreciate you seeing me again," Strike said when the waiter had departed.

"Well, God knows Leonora needs all the help she can get," said Elizabeth.

"Why do you say that?"

Elizabeth narrowed her eyes at him.

"Don't pretend to be stupid. She told me she insisted on being brought to Scotland Yard to see you, right after she got the news about Owen."

"Yeah, she did."

"And how did she think that would look? The police probably expected her to collapse in a heap and all sh-she wants to do is see her detective friend."

She suppressed a cough with difficulty.

"I don't think Leonora gives any thought to the impression she makes on other people," said Strike.

"N-no, well, you're right there. She's never been the brightest."

Strike wondered what impression Elizabeth Tassel thought she made on the world; whether she realized how little she was liked. She allowed the cough that she had been trying to suppress free expression and he waited for the loud, seal-like barks to pass before asking:

"You think she should have faked some grief?"

"I don't say it's fake," snapped Elizabeth. "I'm sure she is upset in her own limited way. I'm just saying it wouldn't hurt to play the grieving widow a bit more. It's what people expect."

"I suppose you've talked to the police?"

"Of course. We've been through the row in the River Café, over and over the reason I didn't read the damn book properly. And they wanted to know my movements after I last saw Owen. Specifically, the three days after I saw him."

She glared interrogatively at Strike, whose expression remained impassive.

"I take it they think he died within three days of our argument?"

"I've no idea," lied Strike. "What did you tell them about your movements?"

"That I went straight home after Owen stormed out on me, got up at six next morning, took a taxi to Paddington and went to stay with Dorcus."

"One of your writers, I think you said?"

"Yes, Dorcus Pengelly, she—"

Elizabeth noticed Strike's small grin and, for the first time in their acquaintance, her face relaxed into a fleeting smile.

"It's her real name, if you can believe it, not a pseudonym. She writes pornography dressed up as historical romance. Owen was very sniffy about her books, but he'd have killed for her sales. They go," said Elizabeth, "like hotcakes."

"When did you get back from Dorcus's?"

"Late Monday afternoon. It was supposed to be a nice long weekend, but *nice*," said Elizabeth tensely, "thanks to *Bombyx Mori*, it was *not*.

"I live alone," she continued. "I can't *prove* I went home, that I didn't murder Owen as soon as I got back to London. I certainly *felt* like doing it..."

She drank more water and continued:

"The police were mostly interested in the book. They seem to think it's given a lot of people a motive."

It was her first overt attempt to get information out of him.

"It looked like a lot of people at first," said Strike, "but if they've got the time of death right and Quine died within three days of your row in the River Café, the number of suspects will be fairly limited."

"How so?" asked Elizabeth sharply, and he was reminded of one of his most scathing tutors at Oxford, who used this two-word question like a giant needle to puncture ill-founded theorizing.

"Can't give you that information, I'm afraid," Strike replied pleasantly. "Mustn't prejudice the police case."

Her pallid skin, across the small table, was large-pored and coarse-grained, the olive-dark eyes watchful.

"They asked me," she said, "to whom I had shown the manuscript during the few days I had it before sending it to Jerry and Christian—

answer: nobody. And they asked me with whom Owen discusses his manuscripts while he's writing them. I don't know why that was," she said, her black eyes still fixed on Strike's. "Do they think somebody egged him on?"

"I don't know," Strike lied again. "*Does* he discuss the books he's working on?"

"He might have confided bits in Jerry Waldegrave. He barely deigned to tell me his titles."

"Really? He never asked your advice? Did you say you'd studied English at Oxford—?"

"I took a first," she said angrily, "but that counted for less than nothing with Owen, who incidentally was thrown off his course at Loughborough or some such place, and never got a degree at all. Yes, and Michael once kindly told Owen that I'd been 'lamentably derivative' as a writer back when we were students, and Owen never forgot it." The memory of the old slight had given a purple tinge to her yellowish skin. "Owen shared Michael's prejudice about women in literature. Neither of them minded women *praising* their work, of c-course—" She coughed into her napkin and emerged red-faced and angry. "Owen was a bigger glutton for praise than any author I've ever met, and they are most of them insatiable."

Their food arrived: tomato and basil soup for Elizabeth and cod and chips for Strike.

"You told me when we last met," said Strike, having swallowed his first large mouthful, "that there came a point when you had to choose between Fancourt and Quine. Why *did* you choose Quine?"

She was blowing on a spoonful of soup and seemed to give her answer serious consideration before speaking.

"I felt—at that time—that he was more sinned against than sinning."

"Did this have something to do with the parody somebody wrote of Fancourt's wife's novel?"

"'Somebody' didn't write it," she said quietly. "Owen did."

"Do you know that for sure?"

"He showed it to me before he sent it to the magazine. I'm afraid," Elizabeth met Strike's gaze with cold defiance, "it made me laugh.

It was painfully accurate and very funny. Owen was always a good literary mimic."

"But then Fancourt's wife killed herself."

"Which was a tragedy, of course," said Elizabeth, without notice-able emotion, "although nobody could have reasonably expected it. Frankly, anybody who's going to kill themselves because of a bad review has no business writing a novel in the first place. But natu-rally enough, Michael was livid with Owen and I think the more so because Owen got cold feet and denied authorship once he heard about Elspeth's suicide. It was, perhaps, a surprisingly cowardly atti-tude for a man who liked to be thought of as fearless and lawless.

"Michael wanted me to drop Owen as a client. I refused. Michael hasn't spoken to me since."

"Was Quine making more money for you than Fancourt at the time?" Strike asked.

"Good God, no," she said. "It wasn't to my *pecuniary* advantage to stick with Owen."

"Then why—?"

"I've just told you," she said impatiently. "I believe in freedom of speech, up to and including upsetting people. Anyway, days after Elspeth killed herself, Leonora gave birth to premature twins. Something went badly wrong at the birth; the boy died and Orlando is... I take it you've met her by now?"

As he nodded, Strike's dream of the other night came back to him suddenly: the baby that Charlotte had given birth to, but that she would not let him see...

"Brain damaged," Elizabeth went on. "So Owen was going through his own personal tragedy at the time, and unlike Michael, he hadn't b-brought any of it on h-himself—"

Coughing again, she caught Strike's look of faint surprise and made an impatient staying gesture with her hand, indicating that she would explain when the fit had passed. Finally, after another sip of water, she croaked:

"Michael only encouraged Elspeth to write to keep her out of his hair while he worked. They had nothing in common. He married her because he's terminally touchy about being lower middle class. She was an earl's daughter who thought marrying Michael would mean nonstop literary parties and sparkling, intellectual chat. She didn't realize she'd be alone most of the time while Michael worked. She was," said Elizabeth with disdain, "a woman of few resources.

"But she got excited at the idea of being a writer. Have you any idea," said the agent harshly, "how many people think they can write? You cannot imagine the crap I am sent, day in, day out. Elspeth's novel would have been rejected out of hand under normal circumstances, it was so pretentious and silly, but they weren't normal circumstances. Having encouraged her to produce the damn thing, Michael didn't have the balls to tell her it was awful. He gave it to his publisher and they took it to keep Michael happy. It had been out a week when the parody appeared."

"Quine implies in *Bombyx Mori* that Fancourt really wrote the parody," said Strike.

"I know he does—and *I* wouldn't want to provoke Michael Fancourt," she added in an apparent aside that begged to be heard.

"What do you mean?"

There was a short pause in which he could almost see Elizabeth deciding what to tell him.

"I met Michael," she said slowly, "in a tutorial group studying Jacobean revenge tragedies. Let's just say it was his natural milieu. He adores those writers; their sadism and their lust for vengeance ... rape and cannibalism, poisoned skeletons dressed up as women ... sadistic retribution is Michael's obsession."

She glanced up at Strike, who was watching her.

"What?" she said curtly.

When, he wondered, were the details of Quine's murder going to explode across the newspapers? The dam must already be straining, with Culpepper on the case.

"Did Fancourt take sadistic retribution when you chose Quine over him?"

She looked down at the bowl of red liquid and pushed it abruptly away from her.

"We were close friends, very close, but he's never said a word to me from the day that I refused to sack Owen. He did his best to warn other writers away from my agency, said I was a woman of no honor or principle.

"But I hold one principle sacred and he knew it," she said firmly. "Owen hadn't done anything, in writing that parody, that Michael hadn't done a hundred times to other writers. Of course I regretted the aftermath deeply, but it was one of the times—the few times— when I felt that Owen was morally in the clear."

"Must've hurt, though," Strike said. "You'd known Fancourt longer than Quine."

"We've been enemies longer than we've been friends, now."

It was not, Strike noted, a proper answer.

"You mustn't think…Owen wasn't always—he wasn't *all* bad," Elizabeth said restlessly. "You know, he was obsessed with virility, in life and in his work. Sometimes it was a metaphor for creative genius, but at other times it's seen as the bar to artistic fulfillment. The plot of *Hobart's Sin* turns on Hobart, who's both male and female, having to choose between parenthood and abandoning his aspirations as a writer: aborting his baby, or abandoning his brainchild.

"But when it came to fatherhood in real life—you understand, Orlando wasn't…you wouldn't have chosen your child to…to… but he loved her and she loved him."

"Except for the times he walked out on the family to consort with mistresses or fritter away money in hotel rooms," suggested Strike.

"All right, he wouldn't have won Father of the Year," snapped Elizabeth, "but there was love there."

A silence fell over the table and Strike decided not to break it. He was sure that Elizabeth Tassel had agreed to this meeting, as she had requested the last, for reasons of her own and he was keen to hear them. He therefore ate his fish and waited.

"The police have asked me," she said finally, when his plate was almost clear, "whether Owen was blackmailing me in some way."

"Really?" said Strike.

The restaurant clattered and chattered around them, and outside the snow fell thicker than ever. Here again was the familiar phenomenon of which he had spoken to Robin: the suspect who wished to re-explain, worried that they had not made a good enough job of it on their first attempt.

"They've taken note of the large dollops of money passing from my account to Owen's over the years," said Elizabeth.

Strike said nothing; her ready payment of Quine's hotel bills had struck him as out of character in their previous meeting.

"What do they think anyone could blackmail me for?" she asked him with a twist to her scarlet mouth. "My professional life has been scrupulously honest. I have no private life to speak of. I'm the very definition of a blameless spinster, aren't I?"

Strike, who judged it impossible to answer such a question, however rhetorical, without giving offense, said nothing.

"It started when Orlando was born," Elizabeth said. "Owen had managed to get through all the money he'd ever made and Leonora was in intensive care for two weeks after the birth, and Michael Fancourt was screaming to anybody who'd listen that Owen had murdered his wife.

"Owen was a pariah. Neither he nor Leonora had any family. I lent him money, as a friend, to get baby things. Then I advanced him money for a mortgage on a bigger house. Then there was money for specialists to look at Orlando when it was clear that she wasn't developing quite as she should, and therapists to help her. Before I knew it, I was the family's personal bank. Every time royalties came in Owen would make a big fuss about repaying me, and sometimes I'd get a few thousand back.

"At heart," said the agent, the words tumbling out of her, "Owen was an overgrown child, which could make him unbearable or charming. Irresponsible, impulsive, egotistical, amazingly lacking in conscience, but he could also be fun, enthusiastic and engaging. There was a pathos, a funny fragility about him, however badly he behaved, that made people feel protective. Jerry Waldegrave felt it. Women felt it. *I* felt it. And the truth is that I kept on hoping, even believing, that one day he'd produce another *Hobart's Sin*. There was always something, in every bloody awful book he's written, something that meant you couldn't completely write him off."

A waiter came over to take away their plates. Elizabeth waved away his solicitous inquiry as to whether there had been something wrong with her soup and asked for a coffee. Strike accepted the offer of the dessert menu.

"Orlando's sweet, though," Elizabeth added gruffly. "Orlando's very sweet."

"Yeah ... she seemed to think," said Strike, watching her closely, "that she saw you going into Quine's study the other day, while Leonora was in the bathroom."

He did not think that she had expected the question, nor did she seem to like it.

"She saw that, did she?"

She sipped water, hesitated, then said:

"I'd challenge anyone depicted in *Bombyx Mori*, given the chance of seeing what other nasty jottings Owen might have left lying around, not to take the opportunity of having a look."

"Did you find anything?"

"No," she said, "because the place was a tip. I could see immediately that it would take far too long to search and," she raised her chin defiantly, "to be absolutely frank, I didn't want to leave fingerprints. So I left as quickly as I walked in. It was the—possibly ignoble— impulse of a moment."

She seemed to have said everything she had come to say. Strike ordered an apple and strawberry crumble and took the initiative.

"Daniel Chard wants to see me," he told her. Her olive-dark eyes widened in surprise.

"Why?"

"I don't know. Unless the snow's too bad, I'm going down to visit him in Devon tomorrow. I'd like to know, before I meet him, why he's portrayed as the murderer of a young blond man in *Bombyx Mori*."

"I'm not providing a key to that filthy book for you," retorted Elizabeth with a return of all her former aggression and suspicion. "No. Not doing it."

"That's a shame," said Strike, "because people are talking."

"Am I likely to compound my own egregious mistake in sending the damn thing out into the world by gossiping about it?"

"I'm discreet," Strike assured her. "Nobody needs to know where I got my information."

But she merely glared at him, cold and impassive.

"What about Kathryn Kent?"

"What about her?"

"Why is the cave of her lair in *Bombyx Mori* full of rat skulls?"

Elizabeth said nothing.

"I know Kathryn Kent's Harpy, I've met her," said Strike patiently. "All you're doing by explaining is saving me some time. I suppose you want to find out who killed Quine?"

"So bloody transparent," she said witheringly. "Does that usually work on people?"

"Yeah," he said matter-of-factly, "it does."

She frowned, then said abruptly and not altogether to his surprise:

"Well, after all, I don't owe Kathryn Kent any loyalty. If you must know, Owen was making a fairly crude reference to the fact that she works at an animal-testing facility. They do disgusting things there to rats, dogs and monkeys. I heard all about it at one of the parties Owen brought her to. There she was, falling out of her dress and trying to impress me," said Elizabeth, with contempt. "I've seen her work. She makes Dorcus Pengelly look like Iris Murdoch. Typical of the dross—the dross—"

Strike managed several mouthfuls of his crumble while she coughed hard into her napkin.

"—the *dross* the internet has given us," she finished, her eyes watering. "And almost worse, she seemed to expect me to be on her side against the scruffy students who'd attacked their laboratories. I'm a vet's daughter: I grew up with animals and I like them much better than I like people. I found Kathryn Kent a horrible person."

"Any idea who Harpy's daughter Epicoene's supposed to be?" asked Strike.

"No," said Elizabeth.

"Or the dwarf in the Cutter's bag?"

"I'm not explaining any more of the wretched book!"

"Do you know if Quine knew a woman called Pippa?"

"I never met a Pippa. But he taught creative writing courses; middle-aged women trying to find their *raison d'être*. That's where he picked up Kathryn Kent."

She sipped her coffee and glanced at her watch.

"What can you tell me about Joe North?" Strike asked.

She glanced at him suspiciously.

"Why?"

"Curious," said Strike.

He did not know why she chose to answer; perhaps because North was long dead, or because of that streak of sentimentality he had first divined back in her cluttered office.

"He was from California," she said. "He'd come over to London to find his English roots. He was gay, a few years younger than Michael, Owen and me, and writing a very frank first novel about the life he'd led in San Francisco.

"Michael introduced him to me. Michael thought his stuff was first class, and it was, but he wasn't a fast writer. He was partying hard, and also, which none of us knew for a couple of years, he was HIV-positive and not looking after himself. There came a point when he developed full-blown AIDS." Elizabeth cleared her throat. "Well, you'll remember how much hysteria there was about HIV when it first emerged."

Strike was inured to people thinking that he was at least ten years older than he was. In fact, he had heard from his mother (never one to guard her tongue in deference to a child's sensibilities) about the killer disease that was stalking those who fucked freely and shared needles.

"Joe fell apart physically and all the people who'd wanted to know him when he was promising, clever and beautiful melted away, except—to do them credit—" said Elizabeth grudgingly, "Michael and Owen. They rallied round Joe, but he died with his novel unfinished.

"Michael was ill and couldn't go to Joe's funeral, but Owen was a pallbearer. In gratitude for the way they'd looked after him, Joe left the pair of them that rather lovely house, where they'd once partied and sat up all night discussing books. I was there for a few of those evenings. They were ... happy times," said Elizabeth.

"How much did they use the house after North died?"

"I can't answer for Michael, but I'd doubt he's been there since he fell out with Owen, which was not long after Joe's funeral," said

Elizabeth with a shrug. "Owen never went there because he was terrified of running into Michael. The terms of Joe's will were peculiar:
I think they call it a restrictive covenant. Joe stipulated that the house
was to be preserved as an artists' refuge. That's how Michael's managed to block the sale all these years; the Quines have never managed
to find another artist, or artists, to sell to. A sculptor rented it for a
while, but that didn't work out. Of course, Michael's always been as
picky as possible about tenants to stop Owen benefiting financially,
and he can afford lawyers to enforce his whims."

"What happened to North's unfinished book?" asked Strike.

"Oh, Michael abandoned work on his own novel and finished
Joe's posthumously. It's called *Towards the Mark* and Harold Weaver
published it: it's a cult classic, never been out of print."

She checked her watch again.

"I need to go," she said. "I've got a meeting at two thirty. My
coat, please," she called to a passing waiter.

"Somebody told me," said Strike, who remembered perfectly well
that it had been Anstis, "that you supervised work on Talgarth Road
a while back?"

"Yes," she said indifferently, "just one more of the unusual jobs
Quine's agent ended up doing for him. It was a matter of coordinat-
ing repairs, putting in workmen. I sent Michael a bill for half and he
paid up through his lawyers."

"You had a key?"

"Which I passed to the foreman," she said coldly, "then returned
to the Quines."

"You didn't go and see the work yourself?"

"Of course I did; I needed to check it had been done. I think I
visited twice."

"Was hydrochloric acid used in any of the renovation, do you know?"

"The police asked me about hydrochloric acid," she said. "Why?"

"I can't say."

She glowered. He doubted that people often refused Elizabeth
Tassel information.

"Well, I can only tell you what I told the police: it was probably
left there by Todd Harkness."

"Who?"

"The sculptor I told you about who rented the studio space. Owen found him and Fancourt's lawyers couldn't find a reason to object. What nobody realized was that Harkness worked mainly in rusted metal and used some very corrosive chemicals. He did a lot of damage in the studio before being asked to leave. Fancourt's side did *that* cleanup operation and sent *us* the bill."

The waiter had brought her coat, to which a few dog hairs clung. Strike could hear a faint whistle from her laboring chest as she stood up. With a peremptory shake of the hand, Elizabeth Tassel left.

Strike took another taxi back to the office with the vague intention of being conciliatory to Robin; somehow they had rubbed each other up the wrong way that morning and he was not quite sure how it had happened. However, by the time he had finally reached the outer office he was sweating with the pain in his knee and Robin's first words drove all thought of propitiation from his mind.

"The car hire company just called. They haven't got an automatic, but they can give you—"

"It's got to be an automatic!" snapped Strike, dropping onto the sofa in an eruption of leathery flatulence that irritated him still further. "I can't bloody drive a manual in this state! Have you rung—?"

"Of course I've tried other places," said Robin coldly. "I've tried everywhere. Nobody can give you an automatic tomorrow. The weather forecast's atrocious, anyway. I think you'd do better to—"

"I'm going to interview Chard," said Strike.

Pain and fear were making him angry: fear that he would have to give up the prosthesis and resort to crutches again, his trouser leg pinned up, staring eyes, pity. He hated hard plastic chairs in disinfected corridors; hated his voluminous notes being unearthed and pored over, murmurs about changes to his prosthesis, advice from calm medical men to rest, to mollycoddle his leg as though it were a sick child he had to carry everywhere with him. In his dreams he was not one-legged; in his dreams he was whole.

Chard's invitation had been an unlooked-for gift; he intended to seize it. There were many things he wanted to ask Quine's publisher.

The invitation itself was glaringly strange. He wanted to hear Chard's reason for dragging him to Devon.

"Did you hear me?" asked Robin.

"What?"

"I said, 'I could drive you.'"

"No, you can't," said Strike ungraciously.

"Why not?"

"You've got to be in Yorkshire."

"I've got to be at King's Cross tomorrow night at eleven."

"The snow's going to be terrible."

"We'll set out early. Or," said Robin with a shrug, "you can cancel Chard. But the forecast for next week's awful too."

It was difficult to reverse from ingratitude to the opposite with Robin's steely gray-blue eyes upon him.

"All right," he said stiffly. "Thanks."

"Then I need to go and pick up the car," said Robin.

"Right," said Strike through gritted teeth.

Owen Quine had not thought women had any place in literature: he, Strike, had a secret prejudice, too—but what choice did he have, with his knee screaming for mercy and no automatic car for hire?

28

... that (of all other) was the most fatal and dangerous exploit that ever I was ranged in, since I first bore arms before the face of the enemy ...

Ben Jonson, *Every Man in His Humour*

At five o'clock the following morning, a muffled and gloved Robin boarded one of the first Tube trains of the day, her hair glistening with snowflakes, a small backpack over her shoulder and carrying a weekend bag into which she had packed the black dress, coat and shoes that she would need for Mrs. Cunliffe's funeral. She did not dare count on getting back home after the round trip to Devon, but intended to go straight to King's Cross once she had returned the car to the hire company.

Sitting on the almost empty train she consulted her own feelings about the day ahead and found them mixed. Excitement was her dominant emotion, because she was convinced that Strike had some excellent reason for interviewing Chard that could not wait. Robin had learned to trust her boss's judgment and his hunches; it was one of the things that so irritated Matthew.

Matthew... Robin's black-gloved fingers tightened on the handle of the bag beside her. She kept lying to Matthew. Robin was a truthful person and never, in the nine years that they had been together, had she lied, or not until recently. Some had been lies of omission. Matthew had asked her on the telephone on Wednesday night what she had done at work that day and she had given him a brief and heavily edited version of her activities, omitting her trip with Strike to the house where Quine had been murdered, lunch at the Albion

237

and, of course, the walk across the bridge at West Brompton station with Strike's heavy arm over her shoulder.

But there had been outright lies too. Just last night he had asked her, like Strike, whether she oughtn't take the day off, get an earlier train.

"I tried," she had said, the lie sliding easily from her lips before she considered it. "They're all full. It's the weather, isn't it? I suppose people are taking the train instead of risking it in their cars. I'll just have to stick with the sleeper."

What else could I say? thought Robin as the dark windows reflected her own tense face back at her. *He'd have gone ballistic.*

The truth was that she wanted to go to Devon; she wanted to help Strike; she wanted to get out from behind her computer, however much quiet satisfaction her competent administration of the business gave her, and investigate. Was that wrong? Matthew thought so. It wasn't what he'd counted on. He had wanted her to go with the advertising agency, into human resources, at nearly twice the salary. London was so expensive. Matthew wanted a bigger flat. He was, she supposed, carrying her...

Then there was Strike. A familiar frustration, a tight knot in her stomach: *we'll have to get someone else in.* Constant mentions of this prospective partner, who was assuming mythical substance in Robin's mind: a short-haired, shrew-faced woman like the police officer who had stood guard outside the crime scene in Talgarth Road. She would be competent and trained in all the ways that Robin was not, and unencumbered (for the very first time, in this half empty, brightly lit Tube carriage, with the world dark outside and her ears full of rumble and clatter, she said it openly to herself) by a fiancé like Matthew.

But Matthew was the axis of her life, the fixed center. She loved him; she had always loved him. He had stuck with her through the worst time in her life, when many young men would have left. She wanted to marry him and she was going to marry him. It was just that they had never had fundamental disagreements before, never. Something about her job, her decision to stay with Strike, about Strike himself, had introduced a rogue element into their relationship, something threatening and new...

The Toyota Land Cruiser that Robin had hired had been parked overnight in the Q-Park in Chinatown, one of the nearest car parks to Denmark Street, where there was no parking at all. Slipping and sliding in her flattest smart shoes, the weekend bag swinging from her right hand, Robin hurried through the darkness to the multistory, refusing to think anymore about Matthew, or what he would think or say if he could see her, heading off for six hours alone in the car with Strike. After placing her bag in the boot, Robin sat back in the driver's seat, set up the sat nav, adjusted the heating and left the engine running to warm up the icy interior.

Strike was a little late, which was unlike him. Robin whiled away the wait by acquainting herself fully with the controls. She loved cars, had always loved driving. By the age of ten she had been able to drive the tractor on her uncle's farm as long as someone helped her release the handbrake. Unlike Matthew, she had passed her test the first time. She had learned not to tease him about this.

Movement glimpsed in her rearview mirror made her look up. A dark-suited Strike was making his way laboriously towards the car on crutches, his right trouser leg pinned up.

Robin felt a sick, swooping feeling in the pit of her stomach—not because of the amputated leg, which she had seen before, and in much more troubling circumstances, but because it was the first time that she had known Strike forsake the prosthesis in public.

She got out of the car, then wished she hadn't when she caught his scowl.

"Good thinking, getting a four-by-four," he said, silently warning her not to talk about his leg.

"Yeah, I thought we'd better in this weather," said Robin.

He moved around to the passenger seat. Robin knew she must not offer help; she could feel an exclusion zone around him as though he were telepathically rejecting all offers of assistance or sympathy, but she was worried that he would not be able to get inside unaided. Strike threw his crutches onto the backseat and stood for a moment precariously balanced; then, with a show of upper body strength that she had never seen before, pulled himself smoothly into the car.

Robin jumped back in hastily, closed her door, put her seatbelt on and reversed out of the parking space. Strike's preemptive rejection of her concern sat like a wall between them and to her sympathy was added a twist of resentment that he would not let her in to that tiny degree. When had she ever fussed over him or tried to mother him? The most she had ever done was pass him paracetamol...

Strike knew himself to be unreasonable, but the awareness merely increased his irritation. On waking it had been obvious that to try to force the prosthesis onto his leg, when the knee was hot, swollen and extremely painful, would be an act of idiocy. He had been forced to descend the metal stairs on his backside, like a small child. Traversing Charing Cross Road on ice and crutches had earned him the stares of those few early-morning pedestrians who were braving the subzero darkness. He had never wanted to return to this state but here he was, all because of a temporary forgetfulness that he was not, like the dream Strike, whole.

At least, Strike noted with relief, Robin could drive. His sister, Lucy, was distractible and unreliable behind the wheel. Charlotte had always driven her Lexus in a manner that caused Strike physical pain: speeding through red lights, turning up one-way streets, smoking and chatting on her mobile, narrowly missing cyclists and the opening doors of parked cars... Ever since the Viking had blown up around him on that yellow dirt road, Strike had found it difficult to be driven by anyone except a professional.

After a long silence, Robin said:

"There's coffee in the backpack."

"What?"

"In the backpack—a flask. I didn't think we should stop unless we really have to. And there are biscuits."

The windscreen wipers were carving their way through flecks of snow.

"You're a bloody marvel," said Strike, his reserve crumbling. He had not had breakfast: trying and failing to attach his false leg, finding a pin for his suit trousers, digging out his crutches and getting himself downstairs had taken twice the time he had allowed. And in spite of herself, Robin gave a small smile.

Strike poured himself coffee and ate several bits of shortbread, his appreciation of Robin's deft handling of the strange car increasing as his hunger decreased.

240

"What does Matthew drive?" he asked as they sped over the Boston Manor viaduct.

"Nothing," said Robin. "We haven't got a car in London."

"Yeah, no need," said Strike, privately reflecting that if he ever gave Robin the salary she deserved they might be able to afford one.

"So what are you planning to ask Daniel Chard?" Robin asked.

"Plenty," said Strike, brushing crumbs off his dark jacket. "First off, whether he'd fallen out with Quine and, if so, what about. I can't fathom why Quine—total dickhead though he clearly was—decided to attack the man who had his livelihood in his hands and who had the money to sue him into oblivion."

Strike munched shortbread for a while, swallowed, then added:

"Unless Jerry Waldegrave's right and Quine was having a genuine breakdown when he wrote it and lashed out at anyone he thought he could blame for his lousy sales."

Robin, who had finished reading *Bombyx Mori* while Strike had been having lunch with Elizabeth Tassel the previous day, said:

"Isn't the writing too coherent for somebody having a breakdown?"

"The syntax might be sound, but I don't think you'd find many people who'd disagree that the content's bloody insane."

"His other writing's very like it."

"None of his other stuff's as crazy as *Bombyx Mori*," said Strike. "*Hobart's Sin* and *The Balzac Brothers* both had plots."

"This has got a plot."

"Has it? Or is Bombyx's little walking tour just a convenient way of stringing together a load of attacks on different people?"

The snow fell thick and fast as they passed the exit to Heathrow, talking about the novel's various grotesqueries, laughing a little over its ludicrous jumps of logic, its absurdities. The trees on either side of the motorway looked as though they had been dusted with tons of icing sugar.

"Maybe Quine was born four hundred years too late," said Strike, still eating shortbread. "Elizabeth Tassel told me there's a Jacobean revenge play featuring a poisoned skeleton disguised as a woman. Presumably someone shags it and dies. Not a million miles away from Phallus Impudicus getting ready to—"

"Don't," said Robin, with a half laugh and a shudder.

But Strike had not broken off because of her protest, or because of any sense of repugnance. Something had flickered deep in his subconscious as he spoke. Somebody had told him...someone had said...but the memory was gone in a flash of tantalizing silver, like a minnow vanishing in pondweed.

"A poisoned skeleton," Strike muttered, trying to capture the elusive memory, but it was gone.

"And I finished *Hobart's Sin* last night as well," said Robin, overtaking a dawdling Prius.

"You're a sucker for punishment," said Strike, reaching for a sixth biscuit. "I didn't think you were enjoying it."

"I wasn't, and it didn't improve. It's all about—"

"A hermaphrodite who's pregnant and gets an abortion because a kid would interfere with his literary ambitions," said Strike.

"You've read it!"

"No, Elizabeth Tassel told me."

"There's a bloody sack in it," said Robin.

Strike looked sideways at her pale profile, serious as she watched the road ahead, her eyes flicking to the rearview mirror.

"What's inside?"

"The aborted baby," said Robin. "It's horrible."

Strike digested this information as they passed the turning to Maidenhead.

"Strange," he said at last.

"Grotesque," said Robin.

"No, it's strange," insisted Strike. "Quine was repeating himself. That's the second thing from *Hobart's Sin* he put in *Bombyx Mori*. Two hermaphrodites, two bloody sacks. Why?"

"Well," said Robin, "they aren't *exactly* the same. In *Bombyx Mori* the bloody sack doesn't belong to the hermaphrodite and it hasn't got an aborted baby in it...maybe he'd reached the end of his invention," she said. "Maybe *Bombyx Mori* was like a—a final bonfire of all his ideas."

"The funeral pyre for his career is what it was."

Strike sat deep in thought while the scenery beyond the window became steadily more rural. Breaks in the trees showed wide fields of snow, white upon white beneath a pearly gray sky, and still the snow came thick and fast at the car.

"You know," Strike said at last, "I think there are two alternatives here. Either Quine genuinely was having a breakdown, had lost touch with what he was doing and believed *Bombyx Mori* was a masterpiece—or he meant to cause as much trouble as possible, and the duplications are there for a reason."

"What reason?"

"It's a key," said Strike. "By cross-referencing his other books, he was helping people understand what he was getting at in *Bombyx Mori*. He was trying to tell without being had up for libel."

Robin did not take her eyes off the snowy motorway, but inclined her face towards him, frowning.

"You think it was all totally deliberate? You think he wanted to cause all this trouble?"

"When you stop and think about it," said Strike, "it's not a bad business plan for an egotistical, thick-skinned man who's hardly selling any books. Kick off as much trouble as you can, get the book gossiped about all over London, threats of legal action, loads of people upset, veiled revelations about a famous writer...and then disappear where the writs can't find you and, before anyone can stop you, put it out as an ebook."

"But he was furious when Elizabeth Tassel told him she wouldn't publish it."

"Was he?" said Strike thoughtfully, "Or was he faking? Did he keep badgering her to read it because he was getting ready to stage a nice big public row? He sounds like a massive exhibitionist. Perhaps it was all part of his promotional plan. He didn't think Roper Chard got his books enough publicity—I had that from Leonora."

"So you think he'd already planned to storm out of the restaurant when he met Elizabeth Tassel?"

"Could be," said Strike.

"And to go to Talgarth Road?"

"Maybe."

The sun had risen fully now, so that the frosted treetops sparkled.

"And he got what he wanted, didn't he?" said Strike, squinting

243

as a thousand specks of ice glittered over the windscreen. "Couldn't have arranged better publicity for his book if he'd tried. Just a pity he didn't live to see himself on the BBC news.

"Oh, bollocks," he added under his breath.

"What's the matter?"

"I've finished all the biscuits … sorry," said Strike, contrite.

"That's all right," Robin said, amused. "I had breakfast."

"I didn't," Strike confided.

His antipathy to discussing his leg had been dissolved by warm coffee, by their discussion and by her practical thoughts for his comfort.

"Couldn't get the bloody prosthesis on. My knee's swollen to hell: I'm going to have to see someone. Took me ages to get sorted."

She had guessed as much, but appreciated the confidence.

They passed a golf course, its flags protruding from acres of soft whiteness, and water-filled gravel pits now sheets of burnished pewter in the winter light. As they approached Swindon Strike's phone rang. Checking the number (he half expected a repeat call from Nina Lascelles) he saw that it was Ilsa, his old schoolfriend. He also saw, with misgivings, that he had missed a call from Leonora Quine at six thirty, when he must have been struggling down Charing Cross Road on his crutches.

"Ilsa, hi. What's going on?"

"Quite a lot, actually," she said. She sounded tinny and distant; he could tell that she was in her car.

"Did Leonora Quine call you on Wednesday?"

"Yep, we met that afternoon," she said. "And I've just spoken to her again. She told me she tried to speak to you this morning and couldn't get you."

"Yeah, I had an early start, must've missed her."

"I've got her permission to tell—"

"What's happened?"

"They've taken her in for questioning. I'm on my way to the station now."

"Shit," said Strike. "*Shit*. What have they got?"

"She told me they found photographs in her and Quine's bedroom. Apparently he liked being tied up and he liked being photographed once restrained," said Ilsa with mordant matter-of-factness. "She told me all this as though she was talking about the gardening."

He could hear faint sounds of heavy traffic back in central London. Here on the motorway the loudest sounds were the swish of the windscreen wipers, the steady purr of the powerful engine and the occasional whoosh of the reckless, overtaking in the swirling snow.

"You'd think she'd have the sense to get rid of the pictures," said Strike.

"I'll pretend I didn't hear that suggestion about destroying evidence," said Ilsa mock-sternly.

"Those pictures aren't bloody evidence," said Strike. "Christ almighty, *of course* they had a kinky sex life, those two—how else was Leonora going to keep hold of a man like Quine? Anstis's mind's too clean, that's the problem; he thinks everything except the missionary position is evidence of bloody criminal tendencies."

"What do you know about the investigating officer's sexual habits?" Ilsa asked, amused.

"He's the bloke I pulled to the back of the vehicle in Afghanistan," muttered Strike.

"*Oh,*" said Ilsa.

"And he's determined to fit up Leonora. If that's all they've got, dirty photos—"

"It isn't. Did you know the Quines have got a lockup?"

Strike listened, tense, suddenly worried. Could he have been wrong, completely wrong—?

"Well, did you?" asked Ilsa.

"What've they found?" asked Strike, no longer flippant. "Not the guts?"

"*What* did you just say? It sounded like 'not the guts'!"

"What've they found?" Strike corrected himself.

"I don't know, but I expect I'll find out when I get there."

"She's not under arrest?"

"Just in for questioning, but they're sure it's her, I can tell, and I don't think she realizes how serious things are getting. When she rang me, all she could talk about was her daughter being left with the neighbor, her daughter being upset—"

"The daughter's twenty-four and she's got learning difficulties."

"Oh," said Ilsa. "Sad... Listen, I'm nearly there, I'll have to go."

"Keep me posted."

"Don't expect anything soon. I've got a feeling we're going to be a while."

"*Shit*," Strike said again as he hung up.

"What's happened?"

An enormous tanker had pulled out of the slow lane to overtake a Honda Civic with a Baby On Board sign in its rear window. Strike watched its gargantuan silver bullet of a body swaying at speed on the icy road and noted with unspoken approval that Robin slowed down, leaving more braking room.

"The police have taken Leonora in for questioning."

Robin gasped.

"They've found photos of Quine tied up in their bedroom and something else in a lockup, but Ilsa doesn't know what—"

It had happened to Strike before. The instantaneous shift from calm to calamity. The slowing of time. Every sense suddenly wire-taut and screaming.

The tanker was jackknifing.

He heard himself bellow "BRAKE!" because that was what he had done last time to try to stave off death—

But Robin slammed her foot on the accelerator. The car roared forward. There was no room to pass. The lorry hit the icy road on its side and spun; the Civic hit it, flipped over and skidded on its roof towards the side of the road; a Golf and a Mercedes had slammed into each other and were locked together, speeding towards the truck of the tanker—

They were hurtling towards the ditch at the side of the road. Robin missed the overturned Civic by an inch. Strike grabbed hold of the door handle as the Land Cruiser hit the rough ground at speed—they were going to plow into the ditch and maybe overturn—the tail end of the tanker was swinging lethally towards them, but they were traveling so fast that she missed that by a whisker—a massive jolt, Strike's head hit the roof of the car, and they had swerved back onto the icy tarmac on the other side of the pileup, unscathed.

"Holy fucking—"

She was braking at last, in total control, pulling up on the hard shoulder, and her face was as white as the snow spattering the windscreen.

"There was a kid in that Civic."

And before he could say another word she had gone, slamming the door behind her.

He leaned over the back of his seat, trying to grab his crutches. Never had he felt his disability more acutely. He had just managed to pull the crutches into the seat with him when he heard sirens. Squinting through the snowy rear window, he spotted the distant flicker of blue light. The police were there already. He was a one-legged liability. He threw the crutches back down, swearing.

Robin returned to the car ten minutes later.

"It's OK," she panted. "The little boy's all right, he was in a car seat. The lorry driver's covered in blood but he's conscious—"

"Are you OK?"

She was trembling a little, but smiled at the question.

"Yeah, I'm fine. I was just scared I was going to see a dead child."

"Right then," said Strike, taking a deep breath. "Where the *fuck* did you learn to drive like that?"

"Oh, I did a couple of advanced driving courses," said Robin with a shrug, pushing her wet hair out of her eyes.

Strike stared at her.

"When was this?"

"Not long after I dropped out of university. I was…I was going through a bad time and I wasn't going out much. It was my dad's idea. I've always loved cars.

"It was just something to do," she said, putting on her seatbelt and turning on the ignition. "Sometimes when I'm home, I go up to the farm to practice. My uncle's got a field he lets me drive in."

Strike was still staring at her.

"Are you sure you don't want to wait a bit before we—?"

"No, I've given them my name and address. We should get going."

She shifted gear and pulled smoothly out onto the motorway. Strike could not look away from her calm profile; her eyes were again fixed on the road, her hands confident and relaxed on the wheel.

"I've seen worse steering than that from defensive drivers in the army," he told her. "The ones who drive generals, who're trained to make a getaway under fire." He glanced back at the tangle of over-turned vehicles now blocking the road. "I still don't know how you got us out of that."

The near-crash had not brought Robin close to tears, but at these words of praise and appreciation she suddenly thought she might cry, let herself down. With a great effort of will she compressed her emotion into a little laugh and said:

"You realize that if I'd braked, we'd have skidded right into the tanker?"

"Yeah," said Strike, and he laughed too. "Dunno why I said that," he lied.

29

There is a path vpon your left hand side,
That leadeth from a guiltie conscience
Vnto a forrest of distrust and feare,—

Thomas Kyd, *The Spanish Tragedie*

In spite of their near-crash, Strike and Robin entered the Devonshire town of Tiverton shortly after twelve. Robin followed the sat nav's instructions past quiet country houses topped with thick layers of glittering white, over a neat little bridge spanning a river the color of flint and past a sixteenth-century church of unexpected grandeur to the far side of the town, where a pair of electric gates were discreetly set back from the road.

A handsome young Filipino man wearing what appeared to be deck shoes and an overlarge coat was attempting to prize these open manually. When he caught sight of the Land Cruiser he mimed to Robin to wind down her window.

"Frozen," he told her succinctly. "Wait a moment, please."

They sat for five minutes until at last he had succeeded in unfreezing the gates and had dug a clearing in the steadily falling snow to allow the gates to swing open.

"Do you want a lift back to the house?" Robin asked him.

He climbed into the backseat beside Strike's crutches.

"You friends of Mr. Chard?"

"He's expecting us," said Strike evasively.

Up a long and winding private driveway they went, the Land Cruiser making easy work of the heaped, crunchy overnight fall. The shiny dark green leaves of the rhododendrons lining the path had refused to bear their load of snow, so that the approach was all black and white: walls of dense foliage crowding in on the pale, powdery drive. Tiny spots of light had started popping in front of Robin's eyes. It had been a very long time since breakfast and, of course, Strike had eaten all the biscuits.

Her feeling of seasickness and a slight sense of unreality persisted as she got down out of the Toyota and looked up at Tithebarn House, which stood beside a dark patch of wood that pressed close to one side of the house. The massive oblong structure in front of them had been converted by an adventurous architect: half of the roof had been replaced by sheet glass; the other seemed to be covered in solar panels. Looking up at the place where the structure became transparent and skeletal against the bright, light gray sky made Robin feel even giddier. It reminded her of the ghastly picture on Strike's phone, the vaulted space of glass and light in which Quine's mutilated body had lain.

"Are you all right?" said Strike, concerned. She looked very pale.

"Fine," said Robin, who wanted to maintain her heroic status in his eyes. Taking deep lungfuls of the frosty air, she followed Strike, surprisingly nimble on his crutches, up the gravel path towards the entrance. Their young passenger had disappeared without another word to them.

Daniel Chard opened the front door himself. He was wearing a mandarin-collared, smock-like shirt in chartreuse silk and loose linen trousers. Like Strike, he was on crutches, his left foot and calf encased in a thick surgical boot and strapping. Chard looked down at Strike's dangling, empty trouser leg and for several painful seconds did not seem able to look away.

"And you thought you had problems," said Strike, holding out his hand.

The small joke fell flat. Chard did not smile. The aura of awkwardness, of otherness, that had surrounded him at his firm's party clung to him still. He shook Strike's hand without looking him in the eye and his welcoming words were:

"I've been expecting you to cancel all morning."

"No, we made it," said Strike unnecessarily. "This is my assistant, Robin, who's driven me down. I hope—"

"No, she can't sit outside in the snow," said Chard, though without noticeable warmth. "Come in."

He backed away on his crutches to let them move over the threshold onto highly polished floorboards the color of honey.

"Would you mind removing your shoes?"

A stocky, middle-aged Filipina woman with her black hair in a bun emerged from a pair of swing doors set into the brick wall on their right. She was clothed entirely in black and holding two white linen bags into which Strike and Robin were evidently expected to put their footwear. Robin handed hers over; it made her feel strangely vulnerable to feel the boards beneath her soles. Strike merely stood there on his single foot.

"Oh," said Chard, staring again. "No, I suppose… Mr. Strike had better keep his shoe on, Nenita."

The woman retired wordlessly into the kitchen.

Somehow, the interior of Tithebarn House increased Robin's unpleasant sensation of vertigo. No walls divided its vast interior. The first floor, which was reached by a steel and glass spiral staircase, was suspended on thick metal cables from the high ceiling. Chard's huge double bed, which seemed to be of black leather, was visible, high above them, with what looked like a huge crucifix of barbed wire hanging over it on the brick wall. Robin dropped her gaze hastily, feeling sicker than ever.

Most of the furniture on the lower level comprised cubes of white or black leather. Vertical steel radiators were interspersed with artfully simple bookshelves of more wood and metal. The dominant feature of the under-furnished room was a life-size white marble sculpture of an angel, perched on a rock and partially dissected to expose half of her skull, a portion of her guts and a slice of the bone in her leg. Her breast, Robin saw, unable to tear her eyes away, was revealed as a mound of fat globules sitting on a circle of muscle that resembled the gills of a mushroom.

Ludicrous to feel sick when the dissected body was made of cold, pure stone, mere insentient albescence, nothing like the rotting carcass preserved on Strike's mobile… *don't think about that*… she ought to have made Strike leave at least one biscuit… sweat had broken out on her upper lip, her scalp…

"You all right, Robin?" asked Strike sharply. She knew she must have changed color from the look on the two men's faces, and to her fear that she might pass out was added embarrassment that she was being a liability to Strike.

"Sorry," she said through numb lips. "Long journey...if I could have a glass of water..."

"Er—very well," said Chard, as though water were in short supply. "Nenita?"

The woman in black reappeared.

"The young lady needs a glass of water," said Chard.

Nenita gestured to Robin to follow her. Robin heard the publisher's crutches making a gentle *thump, thump* behind her on the wooden floor as she entered the kitchen. She had a brief impression of steel surfaces and whitewashed walls, and the young man to whom she had given a lift prodding at a large saucepan, then found herself sitting on a low stool.

Robin had assumed that Chard had followed to see that she was all right, but as Nenita pressed a cold glass into her hand she heard him speak somewhere above her.

"Thanks for fixing the gates, Manny."

The young man did not reply. Robin heard the clunk of Chard's crutches recede and the swinging of the kitchen doors.

"That's my fault," Strike told Chard, when the publisher rejoined him. He felt truly guilty. "I ate all the food she brought for the journey."

"Nenita can give her something," said Chard. "Shall we sit down?"

Strike followed him past the marble angel, which was reflected mistily in the warm wood below, and they headed on their four crutches to the end of the room, where a black iron woodburner made a pool of welcome warmth.

"Great place," said Strike, lowering himself onto one of the larger cubes of black leather and laying his crutches beside him. The compliment was insincere; his preference was for utilitarian comfort and Chard's house seemed to him to be all surface and show.

"Yes, I worked closely with the architects," said Chard, with a small flicker of enthusiasm. "There's a studio"—he pointed through another discreet pair of doors—"and a pool."

He too sat down, stretching out the leg that ended in the thick, strapped boot in front of him.

"How did it happen?" Strike asked, nodding towards the broken leg.

Chard pointed with the end of his crutch at the metal and glass spiral staircase.

"Painful," said Strike, eyeing the drop.

"The crack echoed all through the space," said Chard, with an odd relish. "I hadn't realized one can actually *hear* it happening."

"Would you like a tea or coffee?"

"Tea would be great."

Strike saw Chard place his uninjured foot on a small brass plate beside his seat. Slight pressure, and Manny emerged again from the kitchen.

"Tea, please, Manny," said Chard with a warmth conspicuously absent in his usual manner. The young man disappeared again, sullen as ever.

"Is that St. Michael's Mount?" Strike asked, pointing to a small picture hanging near the woodburner. It was a naive painting on what seemed to be board.

"An Alfred Wallis," said Chard, with another minor glow of enthusiasm. "The simplicity of the forms ... primitive and naive. My father knew him. Wallis only took up painting seriously in his seventies. You know Cornwall?"

"I grew up there," said Strike.

But Chard was more interested in talking about Alfred Wallis. He mentioned again that the artist had only found his true *métier* late in life and embarked on an exposition of the artist's works. Strike's total lack of interest in the subject went unnoticed. Chard was not fond of eye contact. The publisher's eyes slid from the painting to spots around the large brick interior, seeming to glance at Strike only incidentally.

"You're just back from New York, aren't you?" asked Strike when Chard drew breath.

"A three-day conference, yes," said Chard and the flare of enthusiasm faded. He gave the impression of repeating stock phrases as he said, "Challenging times. The arrival of electronic reading devices has been a game changer. Do you read?" he asked Strike, point-blank.

"Sometimes," said Strike. There was a battered James Ellroy in his flat that he had been intending to finish for four weeks, but most nights he was too tired to focus. His favorite book lay in one of the unpacked boxes of possessions on the landing; it was twenty years old and he had not opened it for a long time.

"We need readers," muttered Daniel Chard. "More readers. Fewer writers."

Strike suppressed the urge to retort, *Well, you've got rid of one of them, at least.*

Manny reappeared bearing a clear perspex tray on legs, which he set down in front of his employer. Chard leaned forward to pour the tea into tall white porcelain mugs. His leather furniture, Strike noted, did not emit the irritating sounds his own office sofa did, but then, it had probably cost ten times as much. The backs of Chard's hands were as raw and painful-looking as they had been at the company party, and in the clear overhead lighting set into the underside of the hanging first floor he looked older than he had at a distance; sixty, perhaps, yet the dark, deep-set eyes, the hawkish nose and the thin mouth were handsome still in their severity.

"He's forgotten the milk," said Chard, scrutinizing the tray. "Do you take milk?"

"Yeah," said Strike.

Chard sighed, but instead of pressing the brass plate on the floor he struggled back onto his one sound foot and his crutches, and swung off towards the kitchen, leaving Strike staring thoughtfully after him.

Those who worked with him found Daniel Chard peculiar, although Nina had described him as shrewd. His uncontrolled rages about *Bombyx Mori* had sounded to Strike like the reaction of an over-sensitive man of questionable judgment. He remembered the slight sense of embarrassment emanating from the crowd as Chard mumbled his speech at the anniversary party. An odd man, hard to read...

Strike's eyes drifted upwards. Snow was falling gently onto the clear roof high above the marble angel. The glass must be heated in some way, to prevent the snow settling, Strike concluded. And the memory of Quine, eviscerated and trussed, burned and rotting beneath a great vaulted window, returned to him. Like Robin, he suddenly found the high glass ceiling of Tithebarn House unpleasantly reminiscent.

Chard reemerged from the kitchen and swung back across the floor on his crutches, a small jug of milk held precariously in his hand.

"You'll be wondering why I asked you to come here," said Chard finally, when he had sat back down and each of them held his tea at last. Strike arranged his features to look receptive.

"I need somebody I can trust," said Chard without waiting for Strike's answer. "Someone outside the company."

One darting glance at Strike and he fixed his eyes safely on his Alfred Wallis again.

"I think," said Chard, "I may be the only person who's realized that Owen Quine did not work alone. He had an accomplice."

"An accomplice?" Strike repeated at last, as Chard seemed to expect a response.

"Yes," said Chard fervently. "Oh yes. You see, the style of *Bombyx Mori* is Owen's, but somebody else was in on it. Someone helped him."

Chard's sallow skin had flushed. He gripped and fondled the handle of one of the crutches beside him.

"The police will be interested, I think, if this can be proven?" said Chard, managing to look Strike full in the face. "If Owen was murdered because of what was written in *Bombyx Mori*, wouldn't an accomplice be culpable?"

"Culpable?" repeated Strike. "You think this accomplice persuaded Quine to insert material in the book in the hope that a third party would retaliate murderously?"

"I ... well, I'm not sure," said Chard, frowning. "He might not have expected that to happen, precisely—but he certainly intended to wreak havoc."

His knuckles were whitening as they tightened on the handle of his crutch.

"What makes you think Quine had help?" asked Strike.

"Owen couldn't have known some of the things that are insinuated in *Bombyx Mori* unless he'd been fed information," said Chard, now staring at the side of his stone angel.

"I think the police's main interest in an accomplice," said Strike slowly, "would be because he or she might have a lead on the killer."

It was the truth, but it was also a way of reminding Chard that a man had died in grotesque circumstances. The identity of the murderer did not seem of pressing interest to Chard.

"Do you think so?" asked Chard with a faint frown.

"Yeah," said Strike, "I do. And they'd be interested in an accomplice if they were able to shed light on some of the more oblique passages in the book. One of the theories the police are bound to be following is that someone killed Quine to stop him revealing something that he had hinted at in *Bombyx Mori*."

Daniel Chard was staring at Strike with an arrested expression.

"Yes. I hadn't ... Yes."

To Strike's surprise, the publisher pulled himself up on his crutches and began to move a few paces backwards and forwards, swinging on his crutches in a parodic version of those first tentative physiotherapy exercises Strike had been given, years previously, at Selly Oak Hospital. Strike saw now that he was a fit man, that biceps rippled beneath the silk sleeves.

"The killer, then—" Chard began, and then "What?" he snapped suddenly, staring over Strike's shoulder.

Robin had reemerged from the kitchen, a much healthier color.

"I'm sorry," she said, pausing, unnerved.

"This is confidential," said Chard. "No, I'm sorry. Could you return to the kitchen, please?"

"I—all right," said Robin, taken aback and, Strike could tell, offended. She threw him a look, expecting him to say something, but he was silent.

When the swing doors had closed behind Robin, Chard said angrily:

"Now I've lost my train of thought. Entirely lost—"

"You were saying something about the killer."

"Yes. Yes," said Chard manically, resuming his backwards and forwards motion, swinging on his crutches. "The killer, then, if they knew about the accomplice, might want to target him too? And perhaps that's occurred to him," said Chard, more to himself than to Strike, his eyes on his expensive floorboards. "Perhaps that accounts ... Yes."

The small window in the wall nearest Strike showed only the dark face of the wood close by the house; white flecks falling dreamily against the black.

"Disloyalty," said Chard suddenly, "cuts at me like nothing else."

He stopped his agitated thumping up and down and turned to face the detective.

"If," he said, "I told you who I suspect to have helped Owen, and asked you to bring me proof, would you feel obliged to pass that information to the police?"

It was a delicate question, thought Strike, running a hand absently over his chin, imperfectly shaved in the haste of leaving that morning.

"If you're asking me to establish the truth of your suspicions…" said Strike slowly.

"Yes," said Chard. "Yes, I am. I would like to be sure."

"Then no, I don't think I'd need to tell the police what I'm up to. But if I uncovered the fact that there was an accomplice and it looked like they might have killed Quine—or knew who had done it—I'd obviously consider myself duty-bound to inform the police."

Chard lowered himself back onto one of the large leather cubes, dropping his crutches with a clatter on the floor.

"Damn," he said, his displeasure echoing off the many hard surfaces around them as he leaned over to check that he had not dented the varnished wood.

"You know I've also been engaged by Quine's wife to try and find out who killed him?" Strike asked.

"I had heard something of the sort," said Chard, still examining his teak floorboards for damage. "That won't interfere with this line of inquiry, though?"

His self-absorption was remarkable, Strike thought. He remembered Chard's copperplate writing on the card with the painting of violets: *Do let me know if there is anything you need.* Perhaps his secretary had dictated it to him.

"Would you like to tell me who the alleged collaborator is?" asked Strike.

"This is extremely painful," mumbled Chard, his eyes flitting from Alfred Wallis to the stone angel and up to the spiral stairs.

Strike said nothing.

"It's Jerry Waldegrave," said Chard, glancing at Strike and away again. "And I'll tell you why I suspect—how I know.

"His behavior has been strange for weeks. I first noticed it when he telephoned me about *Bombyx Mori*, to tell me what Quine had done. There was no embarrassment, no apology."

"Would you have expected Waldegrave to apologize for something Quine had written?"

The question seemed to surprise Chard.

"Well—Owen was one of Jerry's authors, so yes, I would have expected some regret that Owen had depicted me in that—in that way."

And Strike's unruly imagination again showed him the naked Phallus Impudicus standing over the body of a dead young man emitting supernatural light.

"Are you and Waldegrave on bad terms?" he asked.

"I've shown Jerry Waldegrave a lot of forbearance, a considerable forbearance," said Chard, ignoring the direct question. "I kept him on full pay while he went to a treatment facility a year ago. Perhaps he feels hard done by," said Chard, "but I've been on his side, yes, on occasions when many another man, a more prudent man, might have remained neutral. Jerry's personal misfortunes are not of my making. There is resentment. Yes, I would say that there is definite resentment, however unjustified."

"Resentment about what?" asked Strike.

"Jerry isn't fond of Michael Fancourt," mumbled Chard, his eyes on the flames in the woodburner. "Michael had a—a flirtation, a long time ago, with Fenella, Jerry's wife. And as it happens, I actually *warned Michael off*, because of my friendship with Jerry. Yes!" said Chard, nodding, deeply impressed by the memory of his own actions. "I told Michael it was unkind and unwise, even in his state of... because Michael had lost his first wife, you see, not very long before.

"Michael didn't appreciate my unsolicited advice. He took offense; he took off for a different publisher. The board was very unhappy," said Chard. "It's taken us twenty-odd years to lure Michael back.

"But after all this time," Chard said, his bald pate merely one more reflective surface among the glass, polished wood and steel, "Jerry can hardly expect his personal animosities to govern company policy. Ever since Michael agreed to come back to Roper Chard, Jerry has made it his business to—to undermine me, subtly, in a hundred little ways.

"What I believe happened is this," said Chard, glancing from time to time at Strike, as though to gauge his reaction. "Jerry took Owen into his confidence about Michael's deal, which we were trying to keep under wraps. Owen had, of course, been an enemy of Fancourt's for a quarter of a century. Owen and Jerry decided to concoct this . . . this dreadful book, in which Michael and I are subjected to—to disgusting calumnies as a way of drawing attention away from Michael's arrival and as an act of revenge on both of us, on the company, on anyone else they cared to denigrate.

"And, most tellingly," said Chard, his voice echoing now through the empty space, "after I told Jerry, explicitly, to make sure the manuscript was locked safely away he allowed it to be read widely by anyone who cared to do so, and having made sure it's being gossiped about all over London, he resigns and leaves me looking—"

"When did Waldegrave resign?" asked Strike.

"The day before yesterday," said Chard, before plunging on: "and he was extremely reluctant to join me in legal action against Quine. That in itself shows—"

"Perhaps he thought bringing in lawyers would draw more attention to the book?" Strike suggested. "Waldegrave's in *Bombyx Mori* himself, isn't he?"

"*That!*" said Chard and sniggered. It was the first sign of humor Strike had seen in him and the effect was unpleasant. "You don't want to take everything at face value, Mr. Strike. Owen never knew about *that*."

"About what?"

"The Cutter character is Jerry's own work—I realized it on a third reading," said Chard. "Very, very clever: it looks like an attack on Jerry himself, but it's really a way of causing Fenella pain. They are still married, you see, but very unhappily. *Very* unhappily.

"Yes, I saw it all, on rereading," said Chard. The spotlights in the hanging ceiling made rippled reflections on his skull as he nodded.

"Owen didn't write the Cutter. He barely knows Fenella. He didn't know about that old business."

"So what exactly are the bloody sack and the dwarf supposed to—?"

"Get it out of Jerry," said Chard. "Make him tell you. Why should I help him spread slander around?"

"I've been wondering," Strike said, obediently dropping that line of inquiry, "why Michael Fancourt agreed to come to Roper Chard when Quine was working for you, given that they were on such bad terms?"

There was a short pause.

"We were under no legal obligation to publish Owen's next book," said Chard. "We had a first-look option. That was all."

"So you think Jerry Waldegrave told Quine that he was about to be dropped, to keep Fancourt happy?"

"Yes," said Chard, staring at his own fingernails. "I do. Also, I had offended Owen the last time I saw him, so the news that I might be about to drop him no doubt swept away any last vestige of loyalty he might once have felt towards me, because I took him on when every other publisher in Britain had given up on—"

"How did you offend him?"

"Oh, it was when he last came into the office. He brought his daughter with him."

"Orlando?"

"Named, he told me, for the eponymous protagonist of the novel by Virginia Woolf." Chard hesitated, his eyes flickering to Strike and then back to his nails. "She's—not quite right, his daughter."

"Really?" said Strike. "In what way?"

"Mentally," mumbled Chard. "I was visiting the art department when they came in. Owen told me he was showing her around—something he had no business doing, but Owen always made himself at home ... great sense of entitlement and self-importance, always ...

"His daughter grabbed at a mock-up cover—grubby hands—I seized her wrist to stop her ruining it—" He mimed the action in midair; with the remembrance of this act of near desecration came a look of distaste. "It was instinctive, you know, a desire to protect the image, but it upset her very much. There was a scene. Very embarrassing and uncomfortable," mumbled Chard, who seemed to suffer again in retrospect. "She became almost hysterical. Owen was furious. That, no doubt, was my crime. That, and bringing Michael Fancourt back to Roper Chard."

"Who," Strike asked, "would you think had most reason to be upset at their depiction in *Bombyx Mori*?"

"I really don't know," said Chard. After a short pause he said, "Well, I doubt Elizabeth Tassel was delighted to see herself portrayed as parasitic, after all the years of shepherding Owen out of parties to stop him making a drunken fool of himself, but I'm afraid," said Chard coldly, "I haven't got much sympathy for Elizabeth. She allowed that book to go out unread. Criminal carelessness."

"Did you contact Fancourt after you'd read the manuscript?" asked Strike.

"He had to know what Quine had done," said Chard. "Better by far that he heard it from me. He was just home from receiving the Prix Prévost in Paris. I did not make that call with relish."

"How did he react?"

"Michael's resilient," muttered Chard. "He told me not to worry, said that Owen had done himself more harm than he had done us. Michael rather enjoys his enmities. He was perfectly calm."

"Did you tell him what Quine had said, or implied, about him in the book?"

"Of course," said Chard. "I couldn't let him hear it from anyone else."

"And he didn't seem upset?"

"He said, 'The last word will be mine, Daniel. The last word will be mine.'"

"What did you understand by that?"

"Oh, well, Michael's a famous assassin," said Chard, with a small smile. "He can flay anyone alive in five well-chosen—when I say 'assassin,'" said Chard, suddenly and comically anxious, "naturally, I'm talking in literary—"

"Of course," Strike reassured him. "Did you ask Fancourt to join you in legal action against Quine?"

"Michael despises the courts as a means of redress in such matters."

"You knew the late Joseph North, didn't you?" asked Strike conversationally.

The muscles in Chard's face tightened: a mask beneath the darkening skin.

"A very—that was a very long time ago."

"North was a friend of Quine's, wasn't he?"

"I turned down Joe North's novel," said Chard. His thin mouth was working. "*That's all I did.* Half a dozen other publishers did the same. It was a mistake, commercially speaking. It had some success, posthumously. Of course," he added dismissively, "I think Michael largely rewrote it."

"Quine resented you turning his friend's book down?"

"Yes, he did. He made a lot of noise about it."

"But he came to Roper Chard anyway?"

"There was nothing personal in my turning down Joe North's book," said Chard, with heightened color. "Owen came to understand that, eventually."

There was another uncomfortable pause.

"So ... when you're hired to find a—a criminal of this type," said Chard, changing subject with palpable effort, "do you work with the police on that, or—?"

"Oh yeah," said Strike, with a wry remembrance of the animosity he had recently encountered from the force, but delighted that Chard had played so conveniently into his hands. "I've got great contacts at the Met. *Your* movements don't seem to be giving them any cause for concern," he said, with faint emphasis on the personal pronoun.

The provocative, slippery phrasing had its full effect.

"The police have looked into *my* movements?"

Chard spoke like a frightened boy, unable to muster even a pretense of self-protective sangfroid.

"Well, you know, everyone depicted in *Bombyx Mori* was bound to come in for scrutiny from the police," said Strike casually, sipping his tea, "and everything you people did after the fifth, when Quine walked out on his wife, taking the book with him, will be of interest to them."

And to Strike's great satisfaction, Chard began at once to review his own movements aloud, apparently for his own reassurance.

"Well, I didn't know anything about the book at all until the seventh," he said, staring at his bound-up foot again. "I was down here when Jerry called me ... I headed straight back up to London—Manny drove me. I spent the night at home, Manny and Nenita can confirm that ... on the Monday I met with my lawyers at the office, talked to Jerry ... I was at a dinner party that night—close friends in Notting Hill—and again Manny drove me home ... I turned in early on Tuesday because on Wednesday morning I was going to New York. I was there until the thirteenth ... home all day the fourteenth ... on the fifteenth ... "

Chard's mumbling deteriorated into silence. Perhaps he had realized that there was not the slightest need for him to explain himself to Strike. The darting look he gave the detective was suddenly cagey. Chard had wanted to buy an ally; Strike could tell that he had suddenly awoken to the double-edged nature of such a relationship. Strike was not worried. He had gained more from the interview than he had expected; to be unhired now would cost him only money.

Manny came padding back across the floor.

"You want lunch?" he asked Chard curtly.

"In five minutes," Chard said, with a smile. "I must say good-bye to Mr. Strike first."

Manny stalked away on rubber-soled shoes.

"He's sulking," Chard told Strike, with an uncomfortable half-laugh. "They don't like it down here. They prefer London."

He retrieved his crutches from the floor and pushed himself back up into a standing position. Strike, with more effort, imitated him.

"And how is—er—Mrs. Quine?" Chard said, with an air of belatedly ticking off the proprieties as they swung, like strange three-legged animals, back towards the front door. "Big redheaded woman, yes?"

"No," said Strike. "Thin. Graying hair."

"Oh," said Chard, without much interest. "I met someone else."

Strike paused beside the swing doors that led to the kitchen. Chard halted too, looking aggrieved.

"I'm afraid I need to get on, Mr. Strike—"

"So do I," said Strike pleasantly, "but I don't think my assistant would thank me for leaving her behind."

Chard had evidently forgotten the existence of Robin, whom he had so peremptorily dismissed.

"Oh, yes, of course—Manny! Nenita!"

"She's in the bathroom," said the stocky woman, emerging from the kitchen holding the linen bag containing Robin's shoes.

The wait passed in a faintly uncomfortable silence. At last Robin appeared, her expression stony, and slipped her feet back into her shoes.

The cold air bit their warm faces as the front door swung open while Strike shook hands with Chard. Robin moved directly to the car and climbed into the driver's seat without speaking to anyone.

Manny reappeared in his thick coat.

"I'll come down with you," he told Strike. "To check the gates."

"They can buzz the house if they're stuck, Manny," said Chard, but the young man paid no attention, clambering into the car as before.

The three of them rode in silence back down the black-and-white drive, through the falling snow. Manny pressed the remote control he had brought with him and the gates slid open without difficulty.

"Thanks," said Strike, turning to look at him in the backseat. "'Fraid you've got a cold walk back."

Manny sniffed, got out of the car and slammed the door. Robin had just shifted into first gear when Manny appeared at Strike's window. She applied the brake.

"Yeah?" said Strike, winding the window down.

"I didn't push him," said Manny fiercely.

"Sorry?"

"Down the stairs," said Manny. "I didn't push him. He's lying."

Strike and Robin stared at him.

"You believe me?"

"Yeah," said Strike.

"OK then," said Manny, nodding at them. "OK."

He turned and walked, slipping a little in his rubber-soled shoes, back up to the house.

30

... as an earnest of friendship and confidence, I'll acquaint you with a design that I have. To tell truth, and speak openly one to another ...

William Congreve, *Love for Love*

At Strike's insistence, they stopped for lunch at the Burger King at Tiverton Services.

"You need to eat something before we go up the road."

Robin accompanied him inside with barely a word, making no reference even to Manny's recent, startling assertion. Her cold and slightly martyred air did not entirely surprise Strike, but he was impatient with it. She queued for their burgers, because he could not manage both tray and crutches, and when she had set down the loaded tray at the small Formica table he said, trying to defuse the tension:

"Look, I know you expected me to tell Chard off for treating you like staff."

"I didn't," Robin contradicted him automatically. (Hearing him say it aloud made her feel petulant, childish.)

"Have it your own way," said Strike with an irritable shrug, taking a large bite of his first burger.

They ate in disgruntled silence for a minute or two, until Robin's innate honesty reasserted itself.

"All right, I did, a bit," she said.

Mellowed by greasy food and touched by her admission, Strike said:

"I was getting good stuff out of him, Robin. You don't start picking arguments with interviewees when they're in full flow."

265

"Sorry for my amateurishness," she said, stung all over again.

"Oh, for Christ's sake," he said. "Who's calling you—?"

"What were you intending, when you took me on?" she demanded suddenly, letting her unwrapped burger fall back onto the tray.

The latent resentment of weeks had suddenly burst its bounds. She did not care what she heard; she wanted the truth. Was she a typist and a receptionist, or was she something more? Had she stayed with Strike, and helped him climb out of penury, merely to be shunted aside like domestic staff?

"Intending?" repeated Strike, staring at her. "What d'you mean, intend—?"

"I thought you meant me to be—I thought I was going to get some—some training," said Robin, pink-cheeked and unnaturally bright-eyed. "You've mentioned it a couple of times, but then lately you've been talking about getting someone else in. I took a pay cut," she said tremulously. "I turned down better-paid jobs. I thought you meant me to be—"

Her anger, so long suppressed, was bringing her to the verge of tears, but she was determined not to give in to them. The fictional partner whom she had been imagining for Strike would never cry; not that no-nonsense ex-policewoman, tough and unemotional through every crisis...

"I thought you meant me to be—I didn't think I was just going to answer the phone."

"You don't just answer the phone," said Strike, who had just finished his first burger and was watching her struggle with her anger from beneath his heavy brows. "You've been casing murder suspects' houses with me this week. You just saved both our lives on the motorway."

But Robin was not to be deflected.

"What were you expecting me to do when you kept me on?"

"I don't know that I had any particular plan," Strike said slowly and untruthfully. "I didn't know you were this serious about the job—looking for training—"

"*How could I not be serious?*" demanded Robin loudly.

A family of four in the corner of the tiny restaurant was staring at them. Robin paid them no attention. She was suddenly livid.

The long cold journey, Strike eating all the food, his surprise that she could drive properly, her relegation to the kitchen with Chard's servants and now this—

"You give me half—*half*—what that human resources job would have paid! Why do you think I stayed? I helped you. I helped you solve the Lula Landry—"

"OK," said Strike, holding up a large, hairy-backed hand. "OK, here it is. But don't blame me if you don't like what you're about to hear."

She stared at him, flushed, straight-backed on her plastic chair, her food untouched.

"I *did* take you on thinking I could train you up. I didn't have any money for courses, but I thought you could learn on the job until I could afford it."

Refusing to feel mollified until she heard what was coming next, Robin said nothing.

"You've got a lot of aptitude for the job," said Strike, "but you're getting married to someone who hates you doing it."

Robin opened her mouth and closed it again. A sensation of having been unexpectedly winded had robbed her of the power of speech.

"You leave on the dot every day—"

"I do not!" said Robin, furious. "In case you hadn't noticed, I turned down a day off to be here now, driving you all the way to Devon—"

"Because he's away," said Strike. "Because he won't know."

The feeling of having been winded intensified. How could Strike know that she had lied to Matthew, if not in fact, then by omission?

"Even if that—whether that's true or not," she said unsteadily, "it's up to me what I do with my—it's not up to Matthew what career I have."

"I was with Charlotte sixteen years, on and off," said Strike, picking up his second burger. "Mostly off. She hated my job. It's what kept breaking us up—one of the things that kept breaking us up," he corrected himself, scrupulously honest. "She couldn't understand a vocation. Some people can't; at best, work's about status and paychecks for them, it hasn't got value in itself."

He began unwrapping the burger while Robin glared at him.

"I need a partner who can share the long hours," said Strike. "Someone who's OK with weekend work. I don't blame Matthew for worrying about you—"

"He doesn't."

The words were out of her mouth before Robin could consider them. In her blanket desire to refute everything that Strike was saying she had let an unpalatable truth escape her. The fact was that Matthew had very little imagination. He had not seen Strike covered in blood after the killer of Lula Landry had stabbed him. Even her description of Owen Quine lying trussed and disemboweled seemed to have been blurred for him by the thick miasma of jealousy through which he heard everything connected to Strike. His antipathy for her job owed nothing to protectiveness and she had never admitted as much to herself before.

"It can be dangerous, what I do," said Strike through another huge bite of burger, as though he had not heard her.

"I've been useful to you," said Robin, her voice thicker than his, though her mouth was empty.

"I know you have. I wouldn't be where I am now if I hadn't had you," said Strike. "Nobody was ever more grateful than me for a temping agency's mistake. You've been incredible, I couldn't have—don't bloody cry, that family's gawping enough already."

"I don't give a monkey's," said Robin into a handful of paper napkins and Strike laughed.

"If it's what you want," he told the top of her red-gold head, "you can go on a surveillance course when I've got the money. But if you're my partner-in-training, there'll be times that I'm going to have to ask you to do stuff that Matthew might not like. That's all I'm saying. You're the one who's going to have to work it out."

"And I will," said Robin, fighting to contain the urge to bawl. "That's what I want. That's why I stayed."

"Then cheer the fuck up and eat your burger."

Robin found it hard to eat with the huge lump in her throat. She felt shaken but elated. She had not been mistaken: Strike had seen in her what he possessed himself. They were not people who worked merely for the paycheck...

"So, tell me about Daniel Chard," she said.

He did so while the nosy family of four gathered up their things and left, still throwing covert glances at the couple they could not quite work out (had it been a lovers' tiff? A family row? How had it been so speedily resolved?).

"Paranoid, bit eccentric, self-obsessed," concluded Strike five minutes later, "but there might be something in it. Jerry Waldegrave could've collaborated with Quine. On the other hand, he might've resigned because he'd had enough of Chard, who I don't think would be an easy bloke to work for."

"D'you want a coffee?"

Robin glanced at her watch. The snow was still falling; she feared delays on the motorway that would prevent her catching the train to Yorkshire, but after their conversation she was determined to demonstrate her commitment to the job, so she agreed to one. In any case, there were things she wished to say to Strike while she was still sitting opposite him. It would not be nearly as satisfying to tell him while in the driver's seat, where she could not watch his reaction.

"I found out a bit about Chard myself," she said when she had returned with two cups and an apple pie for Strike.

"Servants' gossip?"

"No," said Robin. "They barely said a word to me while I was in the kitchen. They both seemed in foul moods."

"According to Chard, they don't like it in Devon. Prefer London. Are they brother and sister?"

"Mother and son, I think," said Robin. "He called her Mamu."

"Anyway, I asked to go to the bathroom and the staff loo's just next to an artist's studio. Daniel Chard knows a lot about anatomy," said Robin. "There are prints of Leonardo da Vinci's anatomical drawings all over the walls and an anatomical model in one corner. Creepy—wax. And on the easel," she said, "was a very detailed drawing of Manny the Manservant. Lying on the ground, in the nude."

Strike put down his coffee.

"Those are very interesting pieces of information," he said slowly.

"I thought you'd like them," said Robin, with a demure smile.

"Shines an interesting side-light on Manny's assurance that he didn't push his boss down the stairs."

"They really didn't like you being there," said Robin, "but that might have been my fault. I said you were a private detective, but Nenita—her English isn't as good as Manny's—didn't understand, so I said you were a kind of policeman."

"Leading them to assume that Chard had invited me over to complain about Manny's violence towards him."

"Did Chard mention it?"

"Not a word," said Strike. "Much more concerned about Waldegrave's alleged treachery."

After visits to the bathroom they returned to the cold, where they had to screw up their eyes against oncoming snow as they traversed the car park. A light frosting had already settled over the top of the Toyota.

"You're going to make it to King's Cross, right?" said Strike, checking his watch.

"Unless we hit trouble on the motorway," said Robin, surreptitiously touching the wood trim on the door's interior.

They had just reached the M4, where there were weather warnings on every sign and where the speed limit had been reduced to sixty, when Strike's mobile rang.

"Ilsa? What's going on?"

"Hi, Corm. Well, it could be worse. They haven't arrested her, but that was some intense questioning."

Strike turned the mobile onto speakerphone for Robin's benefit and together they listened, similar frowns of concentration on their faces as the car moved through a vortex of swirling snow, rushing the windscreen.

"They definitely think it's her," said Ilsa.

"Based on what?"

"Opportunity," said Ilsa, "and her manner. She really doesn't help herself. Very grumpy at being questioned and kept talking about you, which put their backs up. She said you'll find out who really did it."

"Bloody hell," said Strike, exasperated. "And what was in the lockup?"

"Oh yeah, that. It was a burned, bloodstained rag in among a pile of junk."

"Big effing deal," said Strike. "Could've been there years."

"Forensics will find out, but I agree, it's not much to go on seeing as they haven't even found the guts yet."

"You know about the guts?"

"Everyone knows about the guts now, Corm. It's been on the news."

Strike and Robin exchanged fleeting looks.

"When?"

"Lunchtime. I think the police knew it was about to break and brought her in to see if they could squeeze anything out of her before it all became common knowledge."

"It's one of their lot who's leaked it," said Strike angrily.

"That's a big accusation."

"I had it from the journalist who was paying the copper to talk."

"Know some interesting people, don't you?"

"Comes with the territory. Thanks for letting me know, Ilsa."

"No problem. Try and keep her out of jail, Corm. I quite like her."

"Who is that?" Robin asked as Ilsa hung up.

"Old school friend from Cornwall; lawyer. She married one of my London mates," said Strike. "I put Leonora onto her because—shit."

They had rounded a bend to find a huge tailback ahead of them. Robin applied the brake and they drew up behind a Peugeot.

"*Shit*," repeated Strike, with a glance at Robin's set profile.

"Another accident," said Robin. "I can see flashing lights."

Her imagination showed her Matthew's face if she had to telephone him and say that she was not coming, that she had missed the sleeper. His mother's funeral . . . *who misses a funeral?* She should have been there already, at Matt's father's house, helping with arrangements, taking some of the strain. Her weekend bag ought already to have been sitting in her old bedroom at home, her funeral clothes pressed and hanging in her old wardrobe, everything ready for the short walk to the church the following morning. They were burying Mrs. Cunliffe, her future mother-in-law, but she had chosen to drive off into the snow with Strike, and now they were gridlocked, two hundred miles from the church where Matthew's mother would be laid to rest.

He'll never forgive me. He'll never forgive me if I miss the funeral because I did this . . .

Why did she have to have been presented with such a choice,

today of all days? Why did the weather have to be so bad? Robin's stomach churned with anxiety and the traffic did not move.

Strike said nothing, but turned on the radio. The sound of Take That filled the car, singing about there being progress now, where once there was none. The music grated on Robin's nerves, but she said nothing.

The line of traffic moved forward a few feet.

Oh, please God, let me get to King's Cross on time, prayed Robin inside her head.

For three quarters of an hour they crawled through the snow, the afternoon light fading fast around them. What had seemed a vast ocean of time until the departure of the night train was starting to feel to Robin like a rapidly draining pool in which she might shortly be sitting alone, marooned.

Now they could see the crash ahead of them; the police, the lights, a mangled Polo.

"You'll make it," said Strike, speaking for the first time since he had turned on the radio as they waited their turn to be waved forwards by the traffic cop. "It'll be tight, but you'll make it."

Robin did not answer. She knew it was all her fault, not his: he had offered her the day off. It was she who had been insistent on coming with him to Devon, she who had lied to Matthew about the availability of train seats today. She ought to have stood all the way from London to Harrogate rather than miss Mrs. Cunliffe's funeral. Strike had been with Charlotte sixteen years, on and off, and the job had broken them. She did not want to lose Matthew. Why had she done this; why had she offered to drive Strike?

The traffic was dense and slow. By five o'clock they were traveling in thick rush-hour traffic outside Reading and crawled to a halt again. Strike turned up the news when it came on the radio. Robin tried to care what they would say about Quine's murder, but her heart was in Yorkshire now, as though it had leapfrogged the traffic and all the implacable, snowy miles between her and home.

"Police have confirmed today that murdered author Owen Quine, whose body was discovered six days ago in a house in Barons Court, London, was murdered in the same way as the hero of his last, unpublished book. No arrest has yet been made in the case.

"Detective Inspector Richard Anstis, who is in charge of the investigation, spoke to reporters earlier this afternoon."

Anstis, Strike noted, sounded stilted and tense. This was not the way he would have chosen to release the information.

"We're interested in hearing from everyone who had access to the manuscript of Mr. Quine's last novel—"

"Can you tell us exactly how Mr. Quine was killed, Detective Inspector?" asked an eager male voice.

"We're waiting for a full forensic report," said Anstis, and he was cut across by a female reporter.

"Can you confirm that parts of Mr. Quine's body were removed by the killer?"

"Part of Mr. Quine's intestines were taken away from the scene," said Anstis. "We're pursuing several leads, but we would appeal to the public for any information. This was an appalling crime and we believe the perpetrator to be extremely dangerous."

"Not again," said Robin desperately and Strike looked up to see a wall of red lights ahead. "Not another accident..."

Strike slapped off the radio, unwound his window and stuck his head out into the whirling snow.

"No," he shouted to her. "Someone stuck at the side of the road... in a drift... we'll be moving again in a minute," he reassured her.

But it took another forty minutes for them to clear the obstruction. All three lanes were packed and they resumed their journey at little more than a crawl.

"I'm not going to make it," said Robin, her mouth dry, as they finally reached the edge of London. It was twenty past ten.

"You are," said Strike. "Turn that bloody thing off," he said, thumping the sat nav into silence, "*and don't take that exit—*"

"But I've got to drop you—"

"Forget me, you don't need to drop me—next left—"

"I can't go down there, it's one way!"

"Left!" he bellowed, tugging the wheel.

"Don't do that, it's danger—"

"D'you want to miss this bloody funeral? Put your foot down! First right—"

"Where are we?"

"I know what I'm doing," said Strike, squinting through the snow. "Straight on ... my mate Nick's dad's a cabbie, he taught me some stuff—right again—ignore the bloody No Entry sign, who's coming out of there on a night like this? Straight on and left at the lights!"

"I can't just leave you at King's Cross!" she said, obeying his instructions blindly. "You can't drive it, what are you going to do with it?"

"Sod the car, I'll think of something—up here, take the second right—"

At five to eleven the towers of St. Pancras appeared to Robin like a vision of heaven through the snow.

"Pull over, get out and run," said Strike. "Call me if you make it. I'll be here if you don't."

"*Thank you.*"

And she had gone, sprinting over the snow with her weekend bag dangling from her hand. Strike watched her vanish into the darkness, imagined her skidding a little on the slippery floor of the station, not falling, looking wildly around for the platform ... She had left the car, on his instructions, at the curb on a double line. If she made the train he was stranded in a hire car he couldn't drive and which would certainly be towed.

The golden hands on the St. Pancras clock moved inexorably towards eleven o'clock. Strike saw the train doors slamming shut in his mind's eye, Robin sprinting up the platform, red-gold hair flying ...

One minute past. He fixed his eyes on the station entrance and waited.

She did not reappear. Still he waited. Five minutes past. Six minutes past.

His mobile rang.

"Did you make it?"

"By the skin of my teeth ... it was just about to leave ... Cormoran, thank you, thank you so much ... "

"No problem," he said, looking around at the dark icy ground, the deepening snow. "Have a good journey. I'd better sort myself out. Good luck for tomorrow."

"*Thank you!*" she called as he hung up.

He had owed her, Strike thought, reaching for his crutches, but that did not make the prospect of a journey across snowy London on one leg, or a hefty fine for abandoning a hire car in the middle of town, much more appealing.

31

Danger, the spur of all great minds.

George Chapman, *The Revenge of Bussy d'Ambois*

Daniel Chard would not have liked the tiny rented attic flat in Denmark Street, Strike thought, unless he could have found primitive charm in the lines of the old toaster or desk lamp, but there was much to say for it if you happened to be a man with one leg. His knee was still not ready to accept a prosthesis on Saturday morning, but surfaces were within grabbing reach; distances could be covered in short hops; there was food in the fridge, hot water and cigarettes. Strike felt a genuine fondness for the place today, with the window steamy with condensation and blurry snow visible on the sill beyond.

After breakfast he lay on his bed, smoking, a mug of dark brown tea beside him on the box that served as a bedside table, glowering not with bad temper but concentration.

Six days and nothing.

No sign of the intestines that had vanished from Quine's body, nor of any forensic evidence that would have pegged the potential killer (for he knew that a rogue hair or print would surely have prevented yesterday's fruitless interrogation of Leonora). No appeals for further sightings of the concealed figure who had entered the building shortly before Quine had died (did the police think it a figment of the thick-lensed neighbor's imagination?). No murder weapon, no incriminating footage of unexpected visitors to Talgarth Road, no suspicious ramblers noticing freshly turned earth, no mound of rotting guts revealed,

276

wrapped in a black burqa, no sign of Quine's holdall containing his notes for *Bombyx Mori*. Nothing.

Six days. He had caught killers in six hours, though admittedly those had been slapdash crimes of rage and desperation, where fountains of clues had gushed with the blood and the panicking or incompetent culprits had splattered everyone in their vicinity with their lies.

Quine's killing was different, stranger and more sinister.

As Strike raised his mug to his lips he saw the body again as clearly as though he had viewed the photograph on his mobile. It was a theater piece, a stage set.

In spite of his strictures to Robin, Strike could not help asking himself: why had it been done? Revenge? Madness? Concealment (of what?)? Forensic evidence obliterated by the hydrochloric acid, time of death obscured, entrance and departure of the crime scene achieved without detection. *Planned meticulously. Every detail thought out. Six days and not a single lead* ... Strike did not believe Anstis's claim to have several. Of course, his old friend was no longer sharing information, not after the tense warnings to Strike to butt out, to keep away.

Strike brushed ash absently off the front of his old sweater and lit a fresh cigarette from the stub of his old one.

We believe the perpetrator to be extremely dangerous, Anstis had said to the reporters, a statement, in Strike's view, that was both painfully obvious and strangely misleading.

And a memory came to him: the memory of the great adventure of Dave Polworth's eighteenth birthday.

Polworth was Strike's very oldest friend; they had known each other since nursery. Through childhood and adolescence Strike had moved away from Cornwall regularly and then returned, the friendship picking up again wherever Strike's mother and her whims had last interrupted it.

Dave had an uncle who had left for Australia in his teens and was now a multimillionaire. He had invited his nephew to come and stay for his eighteenth birthday, and to bring a mate.

Across the world the two teenagers had flown; it had been the best adventure of their young lives. They had stayed in Uncle Kevin's massive beachside house, all glass and shining wood, with a bar in the sitting room; diamond sea spray in a blinding sun and enormous pink prawns on a barbecue skewer; the accents, the beer, more beer, the sort of butterscotch-limbed blondes you never saw in Cornwall and then, on Dave's actual birthday, the shark.

"They're only dangerous if they're provoked," said Uncle Kevin, who liked his scuba diving. "No touching, lads, all right? No arsing around."

But for Dave Polworth, who loved the sea, who surfed, fished and sailed at home, arsing around was a way of life.

A killer born, with its flat dead eyes and its ranks of stiletto teeth, but Strike had witnessed the blacktip's lazy indifference as they swam over it, awed by its sleek beauty. It would have been content to glide away through the azure gloom, he knew that, but Dave was determined to touch.

He had the scar still: the shark had torn away a tidy chunk of his forearm and he had only partial feeling in his right thumb. It had not affected his ability to do his job: Dave was a civil engineer in Bristol now, and they called him "Chum" in the Victory Inn where he and Strike still met to drink Doom Bar on their visits home. Stubborn, reckless, a thrillseeker to his core, Polworth still scubadived in his free time, though he left the basking sharks of the Atlantic well alone.

There was a fine crack on the ceiling over Strike's bed. He did not think he had ever noticed it before. His eyes followed it as he remembered the shadow on a seabed and a sudden cloud of black blood; the thrashing of Dave's body in a silent scream.

The killer of Owen Quine was like that blacktip, he thought. There were no frenzied, indiscriminate predators among the suspects in this case. None of them had a known history of violence. There was not, as so often when bodies turned up, a trail of past misdemeanors leading to the door of a suspect, no bloodstained past dragging behind any of them like a bag of offal for hungry hounds. This killer was a rarer, stranger beast: the one who concealed its true nature until sufficiently disturbed. Owen Quine, like Dave Polworth, had recklessly taunted a murderer-in-waiting and unleashed horror upon himself.

Strike had heard the glib assertion many times, that everyone had it in them to kill, but he knew this to be a lie. There were undoubtedly those to whom killing was easy and pleasurable: he had met a few such. Millions had been successfully trained to end others' lives; he, Strike, was one of them. Humans killed opportunistically, for advantage and in defense, discovering in themselves the capacity for bloodshed when no alternative seemed possible; but there were also people who had drawn up short, even under the most intense pressure, unable to press their advantage, to seize the opportunity, to break the final and greatest taboo.

Strike did not underestimate what it had taken to bind, batter and slice open Owen Quine. The person who had done it had achieved their goal without detection, successfully disposed of the evidence and appeared not to be exhibiting sufficient distress or guilt to alert anyone. All of this argued a dangerous personality, a *highly* dangerous personality—if disturbed. While they believed themselves to be undetected and unsuspected, there was no danger to anybody around them. But if touched again...touched, perhaps, in the place where Owen Quine had managed to touch them...

"Fuck," murmured Strike, dropping his cigarette hastily into the ashtray beside him; it had burned down to his fingers without him noticing.

So what was he to do next? If the trail away from the crime was practically nonexistent, Strike thought, he must pursue the trail *towards* the crime. If the aftermath of Quine's death was unnaturally devoid of clues, it was time to look at his last few days of life.

Strike picked up his mobile and sighed deeply, looking at it. Was there, he asked himself, any other way of getting at the first piece of information he sought? He ran through his extensive list of acquaintances in his head, discarding options as quickly as they occurred. Finally, and without much enthusiasm, he concluded that his original choice was most likely to bring him the goods: his half-brother Alexander.

They shared a famous father, but had never lived under the same roof. Al was nine years younger than Strike and was Jonny Rokeby's legitimate son, which meant that there was virtually no point of coincidence in their lives. Al had been privately educated in Switzerland and he might be anywhere right now: in Rokeby's LA residence; on a rapper's yacht; even a white Australian beach, for Rokeby's third wife was from Sydney.

And yet of his half-siblings on his father's side, Al had shown himself more willing than any of the others to forge a relationship with his older brother. Strike remembered Al visiting him in hospital after his leg had been blown off; an awkward encounter, but touching in retrospect.

Al had brought with him to Selly Oak an offer from Rokeby that could have been made by mail: financial help in starting Strike's detective business. Al had announced the offer with pride, considering it evidence of his father's altruism. Strike had been sure that it was no such thing. He suspected that Rokeby or his advisers had been nervous about the one-legged, decorated veteran selling his story. The offer of a gift was supposed to stop his mouth.

Strike had turned down his father's largesse and then been refused by every single bank to which he applied for a loan. He had called Al back with immense reluctance, refusing to take the money as a gift, turning down a proffered meeting with his father but asking whether he could have a loan. This had evidently caused offense. Rokeby's lawyer had subsequently pursued Strike for his monthly payments with all the zeal of the most rapacious bank.

Had Strike not chosen to keep Robin on his payroll, the loan would already have been cleared. He was determined to repay it before Christmas, determined not to be beholden to Jonny Rokeby, which was why he had taken on a workload that had lately seen him working eight or nine hours, seven days a week. None of this made the prospect of calling his younger brother for a favor any more comfortable. Strike could understand Al's loyalty to a father whom he clearly loved, but any mention between them of Rokeby was necessarily charged.

Al's number rang several times and finally went to voice mail. As relieved as he was disappointed, Strike left a brief message asking Al to call him and hung up.

Lighting his third cigarette since breakfast, Strike reverted to his contemplation of the crack in the ceiling. The trail towards the crime... so much depended on when the killer had seen the manuscript, had recognized its potential as a blueprint for murder...

And, once again, he flicked through the suspects as though they were a hand of cards he had been dealt, examining their potentialities.

Elizabeth Tassel, who made no secret of the rage and pain *Bombyx*

Mori had caused her. Kathryn Kent, who claimed not to have read it at all. The still unknown Pippa2011, to whom Quine had read parts of the book back in October. Jerry Waldegrave, who had had the manuscript on the fifth, but might, if Chard was to be believed, have known what was in there way before. Daniel Chard, who claimed that he had not seen it until the seventh, and Michael Fancourt, who had heard about the book from Chard. Yes, there were sundry others, peeking and peering and giggling at the most salacious parts of the book, emailed all over London by Christian Fisher, but Strike found it very hard to work up even the vaguest of cases against Fisher, young Ralph in Tassel's office, or Nina Lascelles, none of whom were featured in *Bombyx Mori* nor had really known Quine.

He needed, Strike thought, to get closer, close enough to ruffle the people whose lives had already been mocked and distorted by Owen Quine. With only a little more enthusiasm than he had brought to the task of calling Al, he scrolled through his contact list and called Nina Lascelles.

It was a brief call. She was delighted. Of course he could come over tonight. She'd cook.

Strike could think of no other way to probe for further details of Jerry Waldegrave's private life or for Michael Fancourt's reputation as a literary assassin, but he did not look forward to the painful process of reattaching his prosthesis, not to mention the effort it would require to detach himself again, tomorrow morning, from Nina Lascelles's hopeful clutches. However, he had Arsenal versus Aston Villa to watch before he needed to leave; painkillers, cigarettes, bacon and bread.

Preoccupied with his own comfort, a mixture of football and murder on his mind, it did not occur to Strike to glance down into the snowy street where shoppers, undeterred by the freezing weather, were gliding in and out of the music stores, the instrument makers and the cafés. Had he done so, he might have seen the willowy, hooded figure in the black coat leaning against the wall between numbers six and eight, staring up at his flat. Good though his eyesight was, however, he would have been unlikely to spot the Stanley knife being turned rhythmically between long, fine fingers.

32

Rise my good angel,
Whose holy tunes beat from me that evil spirit
Which jogs mine elbow...

　　　　　　Thomas Dekker, *The Noble Spanish Soldier*

Even with snow chains on its tires the old family Land Rover driven
by Robin's mother had had a hard job of it between York station and
Masham. The wipers made fan-shaped windows, swiftly obliterated,
onto roads familiar to Robin since childhood, now transformed by
the worst winter she had seen in many years. The snow was relentless and the journey, which should have taken an hour, lasted nearly
three. There had been moments when Robin had thought she might
yet miss the funeral. At least she had been able to speak to Matthew
on her mobile, explaining that she was close. He had told her that
several others were still miles away, that he was afraid his aunt from
Cambridge might not make it at all.

At home Robin had dodged the slobbering welcome of their old
chocolate Labrador and hurtled upstairs to her room, pulling on the
black dress and coat without bothering to iron them, laddering her
first pair of tights in her haste, then running back downstairs to the
hall where her parents and brothers were waiting for her.

They walked together through the swirling snow beneath black
umbrellas, up the gentle hill Robin had climbed every day of her
primary school years and across the wide square that was the ancient
heart of her tiny hometown, their backs to the giant chimney of the
local brewery. The Saturday market had been canceled. Deep channels

had been made in the snow by those few brave souls who had crossed the square that morning, footprints converging near the church where Robin could see a crowd of black-coated mourners. The roofs of the pale gold Georgian houses lining the square wore mantels of bright, frozen icing, and still the snow kept coming. A rising sea of white was steadily burying the large square tombstones in the cemetery.

Robin shivered as the family edged towards the doors of St. Mary the Virgin, past the remnant of a ninth-century round-shafted cross that had a curiously pagan appearance, and then, at last, she saw Matthew, standing in the porch with his father and sister, pale and heart-stoppingly handsome in his black suit. As Robin watched, trying to catch his eye over the queue, a young woman reached up and embraced him. Robin recognized Sarah Shadlock, Matthew's old friend from university. Her greeting was a little more lascivious, perhaps, than was appropriate in the circumstances, but Robin's guilt about having come within ten seconds of missing the overnight train, about not having seen Matthew in nearly a week, made her feel she had no right to resent it.

"Robin," he said urgently when he saw her and he forgot to shake three people's hands as he held out his arms to her. As they hugged she felt tears prickle beneath her eyelids. This was real life, after all, Matthew and home…

"Go and sit at the front," he told her and she obeyed, leaving her family at the back of the church to sit in the front pew with Matthew's brother-in-law, who was dandling his baby daughter on his knee and greeted Robin with a morose nod.

It was a beautiful old church and Robin knew it well from the Christmas, Easter and harvest services she had attended all her life with her primary school and family. Her eyes traveled slowly from familiar object to familiar object. High above her over the chancel arch was a painting by Sir Joshua Reynolds (or, at the very least, the *school* of Joshua Reynolds) and she fixed upon it, trying to compose her mind. A misty, mystical image, the boy-angel contemplating the distant vision of a cross emitting golden rays… Who had really done it, she wondered, Reynolds or some studio acolyte? And then she felt guilty that she was indulging her perennial curiosity instead of feeling sad about Mrs. Cunliffe…

She had thought that she would be marrying here in a few weeks' time. Her wedding dress was hanging ready in the spare room's wardrobe, but instead, here was Mrs. Cunliffe's coffin coming up the aisle, shining black with silver handles, Owen Quine still in the morgue... no shiny coffin for his disemboweled body yet, rotted and burned...

Don't think about that, she told herself sternly as Matthew sat down beside her, the length of his leg warm against hers.

The last twenty-four hours had been so packed with incident that it was hard for Robin to believe she was here, at home. She and Strike might have been in hospital, they had come close to slamming head first into that overturned lorry... the driver covered in blood... Mrs. Cunliffe was probably unscathed in her silk-lined box... *Don't think about that...*

It was as though her eyes were being stripped of a comfortable soft focus. Maybe seeing things like bound and disemboweled bodies did something to you, changed the way you saw the world.

She knelt a little late for prayer, the cross-stitched hassock rough beneath her freezing knees. *Poor Mrs. Cunliffe...* except that Matthew's mother had never much liked her. *Be kind*, Robin implored herself, even though it was true. Mrs. Cunliffe had not liked the idea of Matthew being tied to the same girlfriend for so long. She had mentioned, within Robin's hearing, how good it was for young men to play the field, sow their wild oats... The way in which Robin had left university had tainted her, she knew, in Mrs. Cunliffe's eyes.

The statue of Sir Marmaduke Wyvill was facing Robin from mere feet away. As she stood for the hymn he seemed to be staring at her in his Jacobean dress, life-sized and horizontal on his marble shelf, propped up on his elbow to face the congregation. His wife lay beneath him in an identical pose. They were oddly real in their irreverent poses, cushions beneath their elbows to keep their marble bones comfortable, and above them, in the spandrels, allegorical figures of death and mortality. *Till death do us part...* and her thoughts drifted again: she and Matthew, tied together forever until they died... *no, not tied... don't think tied... What's wrong with you?* She was exhausted. The train had been overheated and jerky. She had woken on the hour, afraid that it would get stuck in the snow.

Matthew reached for her hand and squeezed her fingers.

The burial took place as quickly as decency allowed, the snow falling thick around them. There was no lingering at the graveside; Robin was not the only one perceptibly shivering.

Everyone went back to the Cunliffes' big brick house and milled around in the welcome warmth. Mr. Cunliffe, who was always a little louder than the occasion warranted, kept filling glasses and greeting people as though it were a party.

"I've missed you," Matthew said. "It's been horrible without you."

"Me too," said Robin. "I wish I could have been here."

Lying again.

"Auntie Sue's staying tonight," said Matthew. "I thought I could maybe come over to your place, be good to get away for a bit. It's been full on this week..."

"Great, yes," said Robin, squeezing his hand, grateful that she would not have to stay at the Cunliffes'. She found Matthew's sister hard work and Mr. Cunliffe overbearing.

But you could have put up with it for a night, she told herself sternly. It felt like an undeserved escape.

And so they returned to the Ellacotts' house, a short walk from the square. Matthew liked her family; he was glad to change out of his suit into jeans, to help her mother lay the kitchen table for dinner. Mrs. Ellacott, an ample woman with Robin's red-gold hair tucked up in an untidy bun, treated him with gentle kindness; she was a woman of many interests and enthusiasms, currently doing an Open University degree in English Literature.

"How're the studies going, Linda?" Matthew asked as he lifted the heavy casserole dish out of the oven for her.

"We're doing Webster, *The Duchess of Malfi*: 'And I am grown mad with 't.'"

"Difficult, is it?" asked Matthew.

"That's a quotation, love. Oh," she dropped the serving spoons onto the side with a clatter, "that reminds me—I bet I've missed it—"

She crossed the kitchen and snatched up a copy of the *Radio Times*, always present in their house.

"No, it's on at nine. There's an interview with Michael Fancourt I want to watch."

"Michael Fancourt?" said Robin, looking round. "Why?"

"He's very influenced by all those Revenge Tragedians," said her mother. "I'm hoping he'll explain the appeal."

"Seen this?" said Robin's youngest brother, Jonathan, fresh back from the corner shop with the extra milk requested by his mother. "It's on the front page, Rob. That writer with his guts ripped out—"

"Jon!" said Mrs. Ellacott sharply.

Robin knew that her mother was not reprimanding her son out of any suspicion that Matthew would not appreciate mention of her job, but because of a more general aversion to discussing sudden death in the aftermath of the burial.

"What?" said Jonathan, oblivious to the proprieties, shoving the *Daily Express* under Robin's nose.

Quine had made the front page now that the press knew what had been done to him.

HORROR AUTHOR WROTE OWN MURDER.

Horror author, Robin thought, *he was hardly that... but it makes a good headline.*

"Is your boss gonna solve it, d'you reckon?" Jonathan asked her, thumbing through the paper. "Show up the Met again?"

She began to read the account over Jonathan's shoulder, but caught Matthew's eye and moved away.

A buzzing issued from Robin's handbag, discarded in a sagging chair in the corner of the flagged kitchen, as they ate their meal of stew and baked potatoes. She ignored it. Only when they had finished eating and Matthew was dutifully helping her mother clear the table did Robin wander to her bag to check her messages. To her great surprise she saw a missed call from Strike. With a surreptitious glance at Matthew, who was busily stacking plates in the dishwasher, she called voice mail while the others chatted.

You have one new message. Received today at seven twenty p.m.

The crackle of an open line, but no speech.

Then a thud. A yell in the distance from Strike:

"No you don't, you fucking—"

A bellow of pain.

Silence. The crackle of the open line. Indeterminate crunching, dragging sounds. Loud panting, a scraping noise, the line dead.

Robin stood aghast, the phone pressed against her ear.

"What's the matter?" asked her father, glasses halfway down his nose as he paused on the way to the dresser, knives and forks in his hand.

"I think—I think my boss has—has had an accident—"

She pressed Strike's number with shaking fingers. The call went straight to voice mail. Matthew was standing in the middle of the kitchen watching her, his displeasure undisguised.

33

Hard fate when women are compell'd to woo!

Thomas Dekker and Thomas Middleton,
The Honest Whore

Strike did not hear Robin calling because, unbeknownst to him, his mobile had been knocked onto silent when it had hit the ground fifteen minutes previously. Nor was he aware that his thumb had hit Robin's number as the phone slipped through his fingers.

He had only just left his building when it happened. The door onto the street had swung shut behind him and he had had two seconds, with his mobile in his hand (waiting for a ring-back from the cab he had reluctantly ordered) when the tall figure in the black coat had come running at him through the darkness. A blur of pale skin beneath a hood and a scarf, her arm outstretched, inexpert but determined, with the knife pointing directly at him in a wavering clutch.

Bracing himself to meet her he had almost slipped again but, slamming his hand to the door, he steadied himself and the mobile fell. Shocked and furious with her, whoever she was, for the damage her pursuit had already done to his knee, he bellowed—she checked for a split second, then came at him once more.

As he swung his stick at the hand in which he had already seen the Stanley knife his knee twisted again. He let out a roar of pain and she leapt back, as though she had stabbed him without knowing it, and then, for the second time, she had panicked and taken flight, sprinting away through the snow leaving a furious and frustrated Strike unable

288

to give chase, and with no choice but to scrabble around in the snow for his phone.

Fuck this leg!

When Robin called him he was sitting in a crawling taxi, sweating with pain. It was small consolation that the tiny triangular blade he had seen glinting in his pursuer's hand had not pierced him. His knee, to which he had felt obliged to fit the prosthesis before setting out for Nina's, was excruciating once more and he was burning with rage at his inability to give chase to his mad stalker. He had never hit a woman, never knowingly hurt one, but the sight of the knife coming at him through the dark had rendered such scruples void. To the consternation of the taxi driver, who was watching his large, furious-looking passenger in the rearview mirror, Strike kept twisting in his seat in case he saw her walking along the busy Saturday-night pavements, round-shouldered in her black coat, her knife concealed in her pocket.

The cab was gliding beneath the Christmas lights of Oxford Street, large, fragile parcels of silver wrapped with golden bows, and Strike fought his ruffled temper as they traveled, feeling no pleasure at the thought of his imminent dinner date. Again and again Robin called him, but he could not feel the mobile vibrating because it was deep in his coat pocket, which lay beside him on the seat.

"Hi," said Nina with a forced smile when she opened the door to her flat half an hour after the agreed time.

"Sorry I'm late," said Strike, limping over the threshold. "I had an accident leaving the house. My leg."

He had not brought her anything, he realized, standing there in his overcoat. He should have brought wine or chocolates and he felt her notice it as her big eyes roved over him; she had good manners herself and he felt, suddenly, a little shabby.

"And I've forgotten the wine I bought you," he lied. "This is crap. Chuck me out."

As she laughed, though unwillingly, Strike felt the phone vibrate in his pocket and automatically pulled it out.

Robin. He could not think why she wanted him on a Saturday.

"Sorry," he told Nina, "gotta take this—urgent, it's my assistant—"

Her smile slipped. She turned and walked out of the hall, leaving him there in his coat.

"Robin?"

"Are you all right? What happened?"

"How did you—?"

"I've got a voice mail that sounds like a recording of you being attacked!"

"Christ, did I call you? Must've been when I dropped the phone. Yeah, that's exactly what it was—"

Five minutes later, having told Robin what had happened, he hung up his coat and followed his nose to the sitting room, where Nina had laid a table for two. The room was lamplit; she had tidied, put fresh flowers around the place. A strong smell of burnt garlic hung in the air.

"Sorry," he repeated as she returned carrying a dish. "Wish I had a nine-to-five job sometimes."

"Help yourself to wine," she said coolly.

The situation was deeply familiar. How often had he sat opposite a woman who was irritated by his lateness, his divided attention, his casualness? But here, at least, it was being played out in a minor key. If he had been late for dinner with Charlotte and taken a call from another woman as soon as he had arrived he might have expected a face full of wine and flying crockery. That thought made him feel more kindly towards Nina.

"Detectives make shit dates," he told her as he sat down.

"I wouldn't say 'shit,'" she replied, softening. "I don't suppose it's the sort of job you can leave behind."

She was watching him with her huge mouse-like eyes.

"I had a nightmare about you last night," she said.

"Getting off to a flying start, aren't we?" said Strike, and she laughed.

"Well, not really about you. We were together looking for Owen Quine's intestinal tract."

She took a big swig of wine, gazing at him.

"Did we find it?" Strike asked, trying to keep things light.

"Yes."

"Where? I'll take any leads at this point."

"In Jerry Waldegrave's bottom desk drawer," said Nina and he thought he saw her repress a shudder. "It was horrible, actually. Blood and guts when I opened it ... and you hit Jerry. It woke me up, it was so real."

She drank more wine, not touching her food. Strike, who had already taken several hearty mouthfuls (far too much garlic, but he was hungry), felt he was being insufficiently sympathetic. He swallowed hastily and said:

"Sounds creepy."

"It's because of what was on the news yesterday," she said, watching him. "Nobody realized, nobody knew he'd—he'd been killed like that. Like *Bombyx Mori*. You didn't tell me," she said, and a whiff of accusation reached him through the garlic fumes.

"I couldn't," said Strike. "It's up to the police to release that kind of information."

"It's on the front page of the *Daily Express* today. He'd have liked that, Owen. Being a headline. But I wish I hadn't read it," she said, with a furtive look at him.

He had met these qualms before. Some people recoiled once they realized what he had seen, or done, or touched. It was as though he carried the smell of death on him. There were always women who were attracted by the soldier, the policeman: they experienced a vicarious thrill, a voluptuous appreciation at the violence a man might have seen or perpetrated. Other women were repelled. Nina, he suspected, had been one of the former, but now that the reality of cruelty, sadism and sickness had been forced on her she was discovering that she might, after all, belong in the second camp.

"It wasn't fun at work yesterday," she said. "Not after we heard that. Everyone was ... It's just, if he was killed that way, if the killer copied the book ... It limits the possible suspects, doesn't it? Nobody's laughing about *Bombyx Mori* anymore, I can tell you that. It's like one of Michael Fancourt's old plots, back when the critics said he was too grisly ... And Jerry's resigned."

"I heard."

"I don't know why," she said restlessly. "He's been at Roper Chard ages. He's not being himself at all. Angry all the time, and he's usually so lovely. And he's drinking again. A lot."

She was still not eating.

"Was he close to Quine?" Strike asked.

"I think he was closer than he thought he was," said Nina slowly. "They'd worked together quite a long time. Owen drove him mad—Owen drove everyone mad—but Jerry's really upset, I can tell."

"I can't imagine Quine enjoying being edited."

"I think he was tricky sometimes," said Nina, "but Jerry won't hear a word against Owen now. He's obsessed by his breakdown theory. You heard him at the party, he thinks Owen was mentally ill and *Bombyx Mori* wasn't really his fault. And he's still *raging* against Elizabeth Tassel for letting the book out. She came in the other day to talk about one of her other authors—"

"Dorcus Pengelly?" Strike asked, and Nina gave a little gasp of laughter.

"You don't read that crap! Heaving bosoms and shipwrecks?"

"The name stuck in my mind," said Strike, grinning. "Go on about Waldegrave."

"He saw Liz coming and slammed his office door as she walked past. You've seen it, it's glass and he nearly broke it. Really unnecessary and obvious, it made everyone jump out of their skins. She looks ghastly," added Nina. "Liz Tassel. Awful. If she'd been on form, she'd have stormed into Jerry's office and told him not to be so bloody rude—"

"Would she?"

"Are you crazy? Liz Tassel's temper is legendary."

Nina glanced at her watch.

"Michael Fancourt's being interviewed on the telly this evening; I'm recording it," she said, refilling both their glasses. She still had not touched her food.

"Wouldn't mind watching that," said Strike.

She threw him an oddly calculating look and Strike guessed that she was trying to assess how much his presence was due to a desire to pick her brains, how much designs on her slim, boyish body.

His mobile rang again. For several seconds he weighed the offense he might cause if he answered it, versus the possibility that it might herald something more useful than Nina's opinions about Jerry Waldegrave.

"Sorry," he said and pulled it out of his pocket. It was his brother Al.

"Corm!" said the voice over a noisy line. "Great to hear from you, bruv!"

"Hi," said Strike repressively. "How are you?"

"Great! I'm in New York, only just got your message. What d'you need?"

He knew that Strike would only call if he wanted something, but unlike Nina, Al did not seem to resent the fact.

"Wondering if you fancied dinner this Friday," said Strike, "but if you're in New York—"

"I'm coming back Wednesday, that'd be cool. Want me to book somewhere?"

"Yeah," said Strike. "It's got to be the River Café."

"I'll get on it," said Al without asking why: perhaps he assumed that Strike merely had a yen for good Italian. "Text you the time, yeah? Look forward to it!"

Strike hung up, the first syllable of an apology already on his lips, but Nina had left for the kitchen. The atmosphere had undoubtedly curdled.

34

O Lord! what have I said? my unlucky tongue!

William Congreve, *Love for Love*

"Love is a mirage," said Michael Fancourt on the television screen. "A mirage, a chimera, a delusion."

Robin was sitting between Matthew and her mother on the faded, sagging sofa. The chocolate Labrador lay on the floor in front of the fire, his tail thumping lazily on the rug in his sleep. Robin felt drowsy after two nights of very little sleep and days of unexpected stresses and emotion, but she was trying hard to concentrate on Michael Fancourt. Beside her Mrs. Ellacott, who had expressed the optimistic hope that Fancourt might let drop some bons mots that would help with her essay on Webster, had a notebook and pen on her lap.

"Surely," began the interviewer, but Fancourt talked over him.

"We don't love each other; we love the *idea* we have of each other. Very few humans understand this or can bear to contemplate it. They have blind faith in their own powers of creation. All love, ultimately, is self-love."

Mr. Ellacott was asleep, his head back in the armchair closest to the fire and the dog. Gently he snored, with his spectacles halfway down his nose. All three of Robin's brothers had slid discreetly from the house. It was Saturday night and their mates were waiting in the Bay Horse on the square. Jon had come home from university for the funeral but did not feel he owed it to his sister's fiancé to forgo a few pints of Black Sheep with his brothers, sitting at the dimpled copper tables by the open fire.

Robin suspected that Matthew had wanted to join them but that he had felt it would be unseemly. Now he was stuck watching a literary program he would never have tolerated at home. He would have turned over without asking her, taking it for granted that she could not possibly be interested in what this sour-looking, sententious man was saying. It was not easy to like Michael Fancourt, thought Robin. The curve of both his lip and his eyebrows implied an ingrained sense of superiority. The presenter, who was well known, seemed a little nervous.

"And that is the theme of your new——?"

"One of the themes, yes. Rather than castigating himself for his foolishness when the hero realizes that he has simply imagined his wife into being, he seeks to punish the flesh-and-blood woman whom he believes has duped him. His desire for revenge drives the plot."

"Aha," said Robin's mother softly, picking up her pen.

"Many of us—most, perhaps," said the interviewer, "consider love a purifying ideal, a source of selflessness rather than——"

"A self-justifying lie," said Fancourt. "We are mammals who need sex, need companionship, who seek the protective enclave of the family for reasons of survival and reproduction. We select a so-called loved one for the most primitive reasons—my hero's preference for a pear-shaped woman is self-explanatory, I think. The loved one laughs or smells like the parent who gave one youthful succor and all else is projected, all else is invented——"

"Friendship——" began the interviewer a little desperately.

"If I could have brought myself to have sex with any of my male friends, I would have had a happier and more productive life," said Fancourt. "Unfortunately, I'm programmed to desire the female form, however fruitlessly. And so I tell myself that one woman is more fascinating, more attuned to my needs and desires, than another. I am a complex, highly evolved and imaginative creature who feels compelled to justify a choice made on the crudest grounds. This is the truth that we've buried under a thousand years of courtly bullshit."

Robin wondered what on earth Fancourt's wife (for she seemed to remember that he was married) would make of this interview. Beside her, Mrs. Ellacott had written a few words on her notepad.

"He's not talking about revenge," Robin muttered.

Her mother showed her the notepad. She had written: *What a shit he is.* Robin giggled.

Beside her, Matthew leaned over to the *Daily Express* that Jonathan had left abandoned on a chair. He turned past the front three pages, where Strike's name appeared several times in the text alongside Owen Quine's, and began to read a piece on how a high street chain of stores had banned Cliff Richard's Christmas songs.

"You've been criticized," said the interviewer bravely, "for your depiction of women, most particularly—"

"I can hear the critics' cockroach-like scurrying for their pens as we speak," said Fancourt, his lip curling in what passed for a smile. "I can think of little that interests me less than what critics say about me or my work."

Matthew turned a page of the paper. Robin glanced sideways at a picture of an overturned tanker, an upside-down Honda Civic and a mangled Mercedes.

"That's the crash we were nearly in!"

"What?" said Matthew.

She had said it without thinking. Robin's brain froze.

"That happened on the M4," Matthew said, half laughing at her for thinking she could have been involved, that she could not recognize a motorway when she saw one.

"Oh—oh yes," said Robin, pretending to peer more closely at the text beneath the picture.

But he was frowning now, catching up.

"*Were* you nearly in a car crash yesterday?"

He was speaking quietly, trying not to disturb Mrs. Ellacott, who was following Fancourt's interview. Hesitation was fatal. Choose.

"Yes, I was. I didn't want to worry you."

He stared at her. On Robin's other side she could feel her mother making more notes.

"This one?" he said, pointing at the picture, and she nodded. "Why were you on the M4?"

"I had to drive Cormoran to an interview."

"I'm thinking of women," said the interviewer, "your views on women—"

"Where the hell was the interview?"

"Devon," said Robin.

"*Devon?*"

"He's buggered his leg again. He couldn't have got there by himself."

"You drove him to *Devon?*"

"Yes, Matt, I drove him to—"

"So that's why you didn't come up yesterday? So you could—"

"Matt, of course not."

He flung down the paper, pulled himself up and strode from the room.

Robin felt sick. She looked around at the door, which he had not slammed, but closed firmly enough to make her father stir and mutter in his sleep and the Labrador wake up.

"Leave him," advised her mother, her eyes still on the screen.

Robin swung round, desperate.

"Cormoran had to get to Devon and he couldn't drive with only one leg—"

"There's no need to defend yourself to *me*," said Mrs. Ellacott.

"But now he thinks I lied about not being able to get home yesterday."

"*Did* you?" her mother asked, her eyes still fixed beadily upon Michael Fancourt. "Get *down*, Rowntree, I can't see over you."

"Well, I could've come if I'd got a first-class ticket," Robin admitted as the Labrador yawned, stretched and resettled himself on the hearthrug. "But I'd already paid for the sleeper."

"Matt's always going on about how much more money you would have made if you'd taken that HR job," said her mother, her eyes on the TV screen. "I'd have thought he'd appreciate you saving the pennies. Now shush, I want to hear about revenge."

The interviewer was trying to formulate a question.

"But where women are concerned, you haven't always—contemporary *mores*, so-called political correctness—I'm thinking particularly of your assertion that female writers—"

"This *again*?" said Fancourt, slapping his knees with his hands (the interviewer perceptibly jumped). "I said that the greatest female writers, with almost no exceptions, have been childless. A fact. And I have said that women generally, by virtue of their desire to mother, are incapable of the necessarily single-minded focus anyone must bring to the creation of literature, *true* literature. I don't retract a word. That is a *fact*."

Robin was twisting her engagement ring on her finger, torn between her desire to follow Matt and persuade him she had done nothing wrong and anger that any such persuasion should be required. The demands of *his* job came first, always; she had never known him to apologize for late hours, for jobs that took him to the far side of London and brought him home at eight o'clock at night...

"I was going to say," the interviewer hurried on, with an ingratiating smile, "that this book might give those critics pause. I thought the central female character was treated with great understanding, with real empathy. Of course"—he glanced down at his notes and up again; Robin could feel his nerves—"parallels are bound to be drawn—in dealing with the suicide of a young woman, I expect you're braced—you must be expecting—"

"That stupid people will assume that I have written an autobiographical account of my first wife's suicide?"

"Well, it's bound to be seen as—it's bound to raise questions—"

"Then let me say this," said Fancourt, and paused.

They were sitting in front of a long window looking out onto a sunny, windswept lawn. Robin wondered fleetingly when the program had been filmed—before the snows had come, clearly—but Matthew dominated her thoughts. She ought to go and find him, yet somehow she remained on the sofa.

"When Eff—Ellie died," began Fancourt, "when she died—"

The close-up felt painfully intrusive. The tiny lines at the corners of his eyes deepened as he closed them; a square hand flew to conceal his face.

Michael Fancourt appeared to be crying.

"So much for love being a mirage and a chimera," sighed Mrs.

Ellacott as she tossed down her pen. "This is no good. I wanted blood and guts, Michael. *Blood and guts.*"

Unable to stand inaction any longer, Robin got up and headed for the sitting-room door. These were not normal circumstances. Matthew's mother had been buried that day. It behooved her to apologize, to make amends.

35

We are all liable to mistakes, sir; if you own it to be so,
there needs no farther apology.

William Congreve, *The Old Bachelor*

The Sunday broadsheets next day strove to find a dignified balance
between an objective assessment of Owen Quine's life and work and
the macabre, Gothic nature of his death.

"A minor literary figure, occasionally interesting, tipping latterly
into self-parody, eclipsed by his contemporaries but continuing to
blaze his own outmoded trail," said the *Sunday Times* in a front-page
column that led to a promise of much more excitement within: *A
sadist's blueprint: see pages 10–11* and, beside a thumbnail photograph
of Kenneth Halliwell: *Books and Bookmen: literary killers p. 3 Culture.*

"Rumors about the unpublished book that allegedly inspired his
murder are now spreading beyond London's literary circles," the
Observer assured its readers. "Were it not for the dictates of good taste,
Roper Chard would have an instant bestseller on its hands."

KINKY WRITER DISEMBOWELED IN SEX GAME, declared the *Sunday
People*.

Strike had bought every paper on his way home from Nina
Lascelles's, difficult though it was to manage them all and his stick
over snowy pavements. It occurred to him as he struggled towards
Denmark Street that he was unwisely encumbered, should his
would-be assailant of the previous evening reappear, but she was
nowhere to be seen.

Later that evening he worked his way through the news stories while eating chips, lying on his bed with his prosthetic leg mercifully removed once more.

Viewing the facts through the press's distorting lens was stimulating to his imagination. At last, having finished Culpepper's piece in the *News of the World* ("Sources close to the story confirm that Quine liked to be tied up by his wife, who denies that she knew the kinky writer had gone to stay in their second home"), Strike slid the papers off his bed, reached for the notebook he kept by his bed and scribbled himself a list of reminders for the following day. He did not add Anstis's initial to any of the tasks or questions, but *bookshop man* and *MF when filmed?* were both followed by a capital R. He then texted Robin, reminding her to keep her eyes peeled for a tall woman in a black coat the following morning and not to enter Denmark Street if she was there.

Robin saw nobody answering that description on her short journey from the Tube and arrived at the office at nine o'clock next morning to find Strike sitting at her desk and using her computer.

"Morning. No nutters outside?"

"No one," said Robin, hanging up her coat.

"How's Matthew?"

"Fine," lied Robin.

The aftermath of their row about her decision to drive Strike to Devon clung to her like fumes. The argument had simmered and erupted repeatedly all through their car journey back to Clapham; her eyes were still puffy from crying and lack of sleep.

"Tough for him," muttered Strike, still frowning at the monitor. "His mother's funeral."

"Mm," said Robin, moving to fill the kettle and feeling annoyed that Strike chose to empathize with Matthew today, exactly when she would have welcomed an assurance that he was an unreasonable prick.

"What are you looking at?" she asked, setting a mug of tea at Strike's elbow, for which he gave her muttered thanks.

"Trying to find out when Michael Fancourt's interview was filmed," he said. "He was on telly on Saturday night."

"I watched that," said Robin.

"Me too," said Strike.

"Arrogant prat," said Robin, sitting down on the mock-leather sofa, which for some reason did not emit farting noises when she did it. Perhaps, Strike thought, it was his weight.

"Notice anything funny when he was talking about his late wife?" Strike asked.

"The crocodile tears were a bit much," said Robin, "seeing how he'd just been explaining how love's an illusion and all that rubbish."

Strike glanced at her again. She had the kind of fair, delicate complexion that suffered from excess emotion; the swollen eyes told their own story. Some of her animosity towards Michael Fancourt, he guessed, might be displaced from another and perhaps more deserving target.

"Thought he was faking, did you?" Strike asked. "Me too."

He glanced at his watch.

"I've got Caroline Ingles arriving in half an hour."

"I thought she and her husband had reconciled?"

"Old news. She wants to see me, something about a text she found on his phone over the weekend. So," said Strike, heaving himself up from the desk, "I need you to keep trying to find out when that interview was filmed, while I go and look over the case notes so I look like I can remember what the hell she's on about. Then I've got lunch with Quine's editor."

"And I've got some news about what the doctor's surgery outside Kathryn Kent's flat does with medical waste," said Robin.

"Go on," said Strike.

"A specialist company collects it every Tuesday. I contacted them," said Robin and Strike could tell by her sigh that the line of inquiry was about to fizzle out, "and they didn't notice anything odd or unusual about the bags they collected the Tuesday after the murder. I suppose," she said, "it was a bit unrealistic, thinking they wouldn't notice a bag of human intestines. They told me it's usually just swabs and needles, and they're all sealed up in special bags."

"Had to check it out, though," said Strike bracingly. "That's good detective work—cross off all the possibilities. Anyway, there's something else I need doing, if you can face the snow."

"I'd love to get out," said Robin, brightening at once. "What is it?"

"That man in the bookshop in Putney who reckons he saw Quine on the eighth," said Strike. "He should be back off his holidays."

"No problem," said Robin.

She had not had an opportunity over the weekend to discuss with Matthew the fact that Strike wished to give her investigative training. It would have been the wrong time before the funeral, and after their row on Saturday night would have seemed provocative, even inflammatory. Today she yearned to get out onto the streets, to investigate, to probe, and to go home and tell Matthew matter-of-factly what she had done. He wanted honesty, she would give him honesty.

Caroline Ingles, who was a worn-out blonde, spent over an hour in Strike's office that morning. When finally she had departed, looking tear-stained but determined, Robin had news for Strike.

"That interview with Fancourt was filmed on the seventh of November," she said. "I phoned the BBC. Took ages, but got there in the end."

"The seventh," repeated Strike. "That was a Sunday. Where was it filmed?"

"A film crew went down to his house in Chew Magna," said Robin. "What did you notice on the interview that's making you this interested?"

"Watch it again," said Strike. "See if you can get it on YouTube. Surprised you didn't spot it at the time."

Stung, she remembered Matthew beside her, interrogating her about the crash on the M4.

"I'm going to change for Simpson's," said Strike. "We'll lock up and leave together, shall we?"

They parted forty minutes later at the Tube, Robin heading for the Bridlington Bookshop in Putney, Strike for the restaurant on the Strand, to which he intended to walk.

"Spent way too much on taxis lately," he told Robin gruffly, unwilling to tell her how much it had cost him to take care of the Toyota Land Cruiser with which he had been stranded on Friday night. "Plenty of time."

She watched him for a few seconds as he walked away from her,

leaning heavily on his stick and limping badly. An observant childhood spent in the company of three brothers had given Robin an
unusual and accurate insight into the frequently contrary reaction of
males to female concern, but she wondered how much longer Strike
could force his knee to support him before he found himself incapacitated for longer than a few days.

It was almost lunchtime and the two women opposite Robin
on the train to Waterloo were chatting loudly, carrier bags full of
Christmas shopping between their knees. The floor of the Tube was
wet and dirty and the air full, again, of damp cloth and stale bodies.
Robin spent most of her journey trying without success to view clips
of Michael Fancourt's interview on her mobile phone.

The Bridlington Bookshop stood on a main road in Putney, its
old-fashioned paned windows crammed from top to bottom with
a mixture of new and secondhand books, all stacked horizontally.
A bell tinkled as Robin crossed the threshold into a pleasant, mil-
dewed atmosphere. A couple of ladders stood propped against shelves
crammed with more horizontally piled books reaching all the way to
the ceiling. Hanging bulbs lit the space, dangling so low that Strike
would have banged his head.

"Good morning!" said an elderly gentleman in an overlarge tweed
jacket, emerging with almost audible creaks from an office with a
dimpled glass door. As he approached, Robin caught a strong whiff
of body odor.

She had already planned her simple line of inquiry and asked at
once whether he had any Owen Quine in stock.

"Ah! Ah!" he said knowingly. "I needn't ask, I think, why the
sudden interest!"

A self-important man in the common fashion of the unworldly
and cloistered, he embarked without invitation into a lecture on
Quine's style and declining readability as he led her into the depths
of the shop. He appeared convinced, after two seconds' acquaintance,
that Robin could only be asking for a copy of one of Quine's books
because he had recently been murdered. While this was of course the
truth, it irritated Robin.

"Have you got *The Balzac Brothers*?" she asked.

"You know better than to ask for *Bombyx Mori*, then," he said, shifting a ladder with doddery hands. "Three young journalists I've had in here, asking for it."

"Why are journalists coming here?" asked Robin innocently as he began to climb the ladder, revealing an inch of mustard-colored sock above his old brogues.

"Mr. Quine shopped here shortly before he died," said the old man, now peering at spines some six feet above Robin. "*Balzac Brothers, Balzac Brothers* ... should be here ... dear, dear, I'm sure I've got a copy ... "

"He actually came in here, to your shop?" asked Robin.

"Oh yes. I recognized him instantly. I was a great admirer of Joseph North and they once appeared on the same bill at the Hay Festival."

He was coming down the ladder now, feet trembling with every step. Robin was scared he might fall.

"I'll check the computer," he said, breathing heavily. "I'm sure I've got a *Balzac Brothers* here."

Robin followed him, reflecting that if the last time the old man had set eyes on Owen Quine had been in the mid-eighties, his reliability in identifying the writer again might be questionable.

"I don't suppose you could miss him," she said. "I've seen pictures of him. Very distinctive-looking in his Tyrolean cloak."

"His eyes are different colors," said the old man, now gazing at the monitor of an early Macintosh Classic that must, Robin thought, be twenty years old: beige, boxy, big chunky keys like cubes of toffee. "You see it close up. One hazel, one blue. I think the policeman was impressed by my powers of observation and recall. I was in intelligence during the war."

He turned upon her with a self-satisfied smile.

"I was right, we *do* have a copy—secondhand. This way."

He shuffled towards an untidy bin full of books.

"That's a very important bit of information for the police," said Robin, following him.

"Yes, indeed," he said complacently. "Time of death. Yes, I could assure them that he was alive, still, on the eighth."

"I don't suppose you could remember what he came in here for," said Robin with a small laugh. "I'd love to know what he read."

"Oh yes, I remember," said her companion at once. "He bought three novels: Jonathan Franzen's *Freedom*, Joshua Ferris's *The Unnamed* and ... and I forget the third ... told me he was going away for a break and wanted reading matter. We discussed the digital phenomenon—he more tolerant of reading devices than I ... *somewhere* in here," he muttered, raking in the bin. Robin joined the search halfheartedly.

"The eighth," she repeated. "How could you be so sure it was the eighth?"

For the days, she thought, must blend quite seamlessly into each other in this dim atmosphere of mildew.

"It was a Monday," he said. "A pleasant interlude, discussing Joseph North, of whom he had very fond memories."

Robin was still none the wiser as to why he believed this particular Monday to have been the eighth, but before she could inquire further he had pulled an ancient paperback from the depths of the bin with a triumphant cry.

"There we are. There we are. I *knew* I had it."

"I can never remember dates," Robin lied as they returned to the till with their trophy. "I don't suppose you've got any Joseph North, while I'm here?"

"There was only one," said the old man. "*Towards the Mark.* Now, I know we've got that, one of my personal favorites ... "

And he headed, once more, for the ladder.

"I confuse days all the time," Robin soldiered on bravely as the mustard-colored socks were revealed again.

"Many people do," he said smugly, "but I am an adept at reconstructive deduction, ha ha. I remembered that it was a Monday, because always on a Monday I buy fresh milk and I had just returned from doing so when Mr. Quine arrived at the shop."

She waited while he scanned the shelves above her head.

"I explained to the police that I was able to date the particular Monday precisely because that evening I went to my friend Charles's house, as I do most Mondays, but I distinctly remembered telling him about Owen Quine arriving in my bookshop *and* discussing the five Anglican bishops who had defected to Rome that day. Charles is a lay preacher in the Anglican Church. He felt it deeply."

"I see," said Robin, who was making a mental note to check the date of such a defection. The old man had found North's book and was slowly descending the ladder.

"Yes, and I remember," he said, with a spurt of enthusiasm, "Charles showed me some remarkable pictures of a sinkhole that appeared overnight in Schmalkalden, Germany. I was stationed near Schmalkalden during the war. Yes... that evening, I remember, my friend interrupted me telling him about Quine visiting the shop—his interest in writers is negligible—'Weren't you in Schmalkalden?' he said"—the frail, knobbly hands were busy at the till now—"and he told me a huge crater had appeared... extraordinary pictures in the paper next day...

"Memory is a wonderful thing," he said complacently, handing Robin a brown paper bag containing her two books and receiving her ten-pound note in exchange.

"I remember that sinkhole," said Robin, which was another lie. She took her mobile out of her pocket and pressed a few buttons while he conscientiously counted change. "Yes, here it is... Schmalkalden... how amazing, that huge hole appearing out of nowhere.

"But that happened," she said, looking up at him, "on the first of November, not the eighth."

He blinked.

"No, it was the eighth," he said, with all the conviction a profound dislike of being mistaken could muster.

"But see here," said Robin, showing him the tiny screen; he pushed his glasses up his forehead to stare at it. "You definitely remember discussing Owen Quine's visit and the sinkhole in the same conversation?"

"Some mistake," he muttered, and whether he referred to the *Guardian* website, himself or Robin was unclear. He thrust her phone back at her.

"You don't remem—?"

"Is that all?" he said loudly, flustered. "Then good day to you, good day."

And Robin, recognizing the stubbornness of an offended old egoist, took her leave to the tinkling of the bell.

36

Mr. Scandal, I shall be very glad to confer with you about these things which he has uttered—his sayings are very mysterious and hieroglyphical.

William Congreve, *Love for Love*

Strike had thought that Simpson's-in-the-Strand was an odd place for Jerry Waldegrave to want to meet for lunch and his curiosity increased as he approached the imposing stone façade, with its revolving wooden doors, its brass plaques and hanging lantern. Chess motifs decorated the tiled surround of the entrance. He had never set foot there, aged London institution though it was. He had assumed it to be the home of well-heeled businessmen and out-of-towners treating themselves.

Yet Strike felt at home as soon as he set foot inside the lobby. Once an eighteenth-century gentleman's chess club, Simpson's spoke to Strike in an old and familiar language, of hierarchy, order and stately decorum. Here were the dark, sludgy clubland colors that men choose without reference to their womenfolk: thick marble columns and solid leather armchairs that would support a drunken dandy and, glimpsed beyond double doors, past the coat-check girl, a restaurant full of dark wood paneling. He might have been back in one of the sergeants' messes he had frequented during his military career. All that was needed to make the place feel truly familiar were regimental colors and a portrait of the Queen.

Solid wood-backed chairs, snowy tablecloths, silver salvers on which enormous joints of beef reposed; as Strike sat down at a table for two beside the wall he found himself wondering what Robin would make of the place, whether she would be amused or irritated by its ostentatious traditionalism.

He had been seated for ten minutes before Waldegrave appeared, peering myopically around the dining room. Strike raised a hand and Waldegrave made his way with a shambling walk towards their table.

"Hello, hello. Nice to see you again."

His light brown hair was as messy as ever and his crumpled jacket had a smear of toothpaste on the lapel. A faint gust of vinous fumes reached Strike across the small table.

"Good of you to see me," said Strike.

"Not at all. Want to help. Hope you don't mind coming here. I chose it," said Waldegrave, "because we won't run into anyone I know. My father brought me here once, years ago. Don't think they've changed a thing."

Waldegrave's round eyes, framed by his horn-rimmed glasses, traveled over the heavily molded plasterwork at the top of the dark wood paneling. It was stained ocher, as though tarnished by long years of cigarette smoke.

"Get enough of your coworkers during office hours, do you?" Strike asked.

"Nothing wrong with them," said Jerry Waldegrave, pushing his glasses up his nose and waving at a waiter, "but the atmosphere's poisonous just now. Glass of red, please," he told the young man who had answered his wave. "I don't care, anything."

But the waiter, on whose front a small knight chess piece was embroidered, answered repressively:

"I'll send over the wine waiter, sir," and retreated.

"See the clock over the doors as you come in here?" Waldegrave asked Strike, pushing his glasses up his nose again. "They say it stopped when the first woman came in here in 1984. Little in-joke. And on the menu, it says 'bill of fare.' They wouldn't use 'menu,' you see, because it was French. My father loved that stuff. I'd just got into Oxford, that's why he brought me here. He hated foreign food."

Strike could feel Waldegrave's nervousness. He was used to having that effect on people. Now was not the moment to ask whether Waldegrave had helped Quine write the blueprint for his murder.

"What did you do at Oxford?"

"English," said Waldegrave with a sigh. "My father was putting a brave face on it; he wanted me to do medicine."

The fingers of Waldegrave's right hand played an arpeggio on the tablecloth.

"Things tense at the office, are they?" asked Strike.

"You could say that," replied Waldegrave, looking around again for the wine waiter. "It's sinking in, now we know how Owen was killed. People erasing emails like idiots, pretending they never looked at the book, don't know how it ends. It's not so funny now."

"Was it funny before?" asked Strike.

"Well ... yeah, it was, when people thought Owen had just done a runner. People love seeing the powerful ridiculed, don't they? They aren't popular men, either of them, Fancourt and Chard."

The wine waiter arrived and handed the list to Waldegrave.

"I'll get a bottle, shall I?" said Waldegrave, scanning it. "I take it this is on you?"

"Yeah," said Strike, not without trepidation.

Waldegrave ordered a bottle of Château Lezongars, which Strike saw with profound misgiving cost nearly fifty quid, though there were bottles on the list that cost nearly two hundred.

"So," said Waldegrave with sudden bravado, as the wine waiter retreated, "any leads yet? Know who did it?"

"Not yet," said Strike.

An uncomfortable beat followed. Waldegrave pushed his glasses up his sweaty nose.

"Sorry," he muttered. "Crass—defense mechanism. It's—I can't believe it. I can't believe it happened."

"No one ever can," said Strike.

On a rush of confidence, Waldegrave said:

"I can't shake this mad bloody idea that Owen did it to himself. That he staged it."

"Really?" said Strike, watching Waldegrave closely.

"I know he can't have done, I know that." The editor's hands were playing a deft scale on the edge of the table now. "It's so—so *theatrical*, how he was—how he was killed. So—so grotesque. And...

the awful thing ... best publicity any author ever got his book. God, Owen loved publicity. Poor Owen. He once told me—this isn't a joke—he once told me in all seriousness that he liked to get his girl-friend to interview him. Said it clarified his thought processes. I said, 'What do you use as a mic?' taking the mickey, you know, and you know what the silly sod said? 'Biros mostly. Whatever's around.'"

Waldegrave burst into panting chuckles that sounded very like sobs.

"Poor bastard," he said. "Poor silly bastard. Lost it completely at the end, didn't he? Well, I hope Elizabeth Tassel's happy. Winding him up."

Their original waiter returned with a notebook.

"What are you having?" the editor asked Strike, focusing short-sightedly on his bill of fare.

"The beef," said Strike, who had had time to watch it being carved from the silver salver on a trolley that circulated the tables. He had not had Yorkshire pudding in years; not, in fact, since the last time he had gone back to St. Mawes to see his aunt and uncle.

Waldegrave ordered Dover sole, then craned his neck again to see whether the wine waiter was returning. When he caught sight of the man approaching with the bottle he noticeably relaxed, sinking more comfortably into his chair. His glass filled, he drank several mouthfuls before sighing like a man who had received urgent medical treatment.

"You were saying Elizabeth Tassel wound Quine up," Strike said.

"Eh?" said Waldegrave, cupping his right hand around his ear.

Strike remembered his one-sided deafness. The restaurant was indeed filling up, becoming noisier. He repeated his question more loudly.

"Oh yeah," said Waldegrave. "Yeah, about Fancourt. The pair of them liked brooding on the wrongs Fancourt did them."

"What wrongs?" asked Strike, and Waldegrave swigged more wine.

"Fancourt's been badmouthing them both for years." Waldegrave scratched his chest absentmindedly through his creased shirt and drank more wine. "Owen, because of that parody of his dead wife's novel; Liz, because she stuck by Owen—mind you, nobody's ever blamed Fancourt for leaving Liz Tassel. The woman's a bitch. Down to about two clients now. Twisted. Probably spends her evenings working out how much she lost: fifteen percent of Fancourt's royalties is big money. Booker dinners, film premieres…instead she gets Quine interviewing himself with a biro and burnt sausages in Dorcus Pengelly's back garden."

"How do you know there were burnt sausages?" asked Strike.

"Dorcus told me," said Waldegrave, who had already finished his first glass of wine and was pouring a second. "She wanted to know why Liz wasn't at the firm's anniversary party. When I told her about *Bombyx Mori*, Dorcus assured me Liz was a lovely woman. *Lovely*. Couldn't have known what was in Owen's book. Never have hurt anyone's feelings—wouldn't hurt a bloody fly—ha!"

"You disagree?"

"Bloody right I disagree. I've met people who got their start in Liz Tassel's office. They talk like kidnap victims who've been ransomed. Bully. Scary temper."

"You think she put Quine up to writing the book?"

"Well, not directly," said Waldegrave. "But you take a deluded writer who was convinced he wasn't a bestseller because people were jealous of him or not doing their jobs right and lock him in with Liz, who's always angry, bitter as sin, banging on about Fancourt doing them both down, and is it a surprise he gets wound up to fever pitch?"

"She couldn't even be bothered to read his book properly. If he hadn't died, I'd say she got what she deserved. Silly mad bastard didn't just do over Fancourt, did he? Went after her as well, ha ha! Went after bloody Daniel, went after me, went after ev'ryone. *Ev'ryone*."

In the manner of other alcoholics Strike had known, Jerry Waldegrave had crossed the line into drunkenness with two glasses of wine. His movements were suddenly clumsier, his manner more flamboyant.

"D'you think Elizabeth Tassel egged Quine on to attack Fancourt?"

"Not a doubt of it," said Waldegrave. "Not a doubt."

"But when I met her, Elizabeth Tassel said that what Quine wrote about Fancourt was a lie," Strike told Waldegrave.

"Eh?" said Waldegrave again, cupping his ear.

"She told me," said Strike loudly, "that what Quine writes in *Bombyx Mori* about Fancourt is false. That Fancourt didn't write the parody that made his wife kill herself—that Quine wrote it."

"I'm not talking about *that*," said Waldegrave, shaking his head as though Strike were being obtuse. "I don't mean—forget it. Forget it."

He was more than halfway down the bottle already; the alcohol had induced a degree of confidence. Strike held back, knowing that to push would only induce the granite stubbornness of the drunk. Better to let him drift where he wanted to go, keeping one light hand on the tiller.

"Owen liked me," Waldegrave told Strike. "Oh yeah. I knew how to handle him. Stoke that man's vanity and you could get him to do anything you wanted. Half an hour's praise before you asked him to change anything in a manuscript. 'Nother half hour's praise before you asked him to make another change. Only way.

"He didn't really wanna hurt me. Wasn't thinking straight, silly bastard. Wanted to get back on the telly. Thought ev'ryone was against him. Didn't realize he was playing with fire. Mentally ill."

Waldegrave slumped in his seat and the back of his head collided with that of a large overdressed woman sitting behind him. "Sorry! Sorry!"

While she glared over her shoulder he pulled in his chair, causing the cutlery to rattle on the tablecloth.

"So what," Strike asked, "was the Cutter all about?"

"Huh?" said Waldegrave.

This time, Strike felt sure that the cupped ear was a pose.

"The Cutter—"

"Cutter: editor—obvious," said Waldegrave.

"And the bloody sack and the dwarf you try and drown?"

"Symbolic," said Waldegrave, with an airy wave of the hand that nearly upset his wineglass. "Some idea of his I stifled, some bit of lovingly crafted prose I wanted to kill off. Hurt his feelings."

Strike, who had heard a thousand rehearsed answers, found the response too pat, too fluent, too fast.

"Just that?"

"Well," said Waldegrave, with a gasp of a laugh, "I've never drowned a dwarf, if that's what you're implying."

Drunks were always tricky interviewees. Back in the SIB, intoxicated suspects or witnesses had been a rarity. He remembered the alcoholic major whose twelve-year-old daughter had disclosed sexual abuse at her school in Germany. When Strike had arrived at the family house the major had taken a swing at him with a broken bottle. Strike had laid him out. But here in the civilian world, with the wine waiter hovering, this drunken, mild-mannered editor could choose to walk away and there would be nothing Strike could do about it. He could only hope for a chance to double back to the subject of the Cutter, to keep Waldegrave in his seat, to keep him talking.

The trolley now wended its stately way to Strike's side. A rib of Scottish beef was carved with ceremony while Waldegrave was presented with Dover sole.

No taxis for three months, Strike told himself sternly, salivating as his plate was heaped with Yorkshire puddings, potatoes and parsnips. The trolley trundled away again. Waldegrave, who was now two-thirds of the way down his bottle of wine, contemplated his fish as though he was not quite sure how it had ended up in front of him, and put a small potato in his mouth with his fingers.

"Did Quine discuss what he was writing with you, before he handed in his manuscripts?" asked Strike.

"Never," said Waldegrave. "The only thing he ever told me about *Bombyx Mori* was that the silkworm was a metaphor for the writer, who has to go through agonies to get at the good stuff. That was it."

"He never asked for your advice or input?"

"No, no, Owen always thought he knew best."

"Is that usual?"

"Writers vary," said Waldegrave. "But Owen was always up the secretive end of the scale. He liked the big reveal, you know. Appealed to his sense of drama."

"Police will have asked you about your movements after you got the book, I suppose," said Strike casually.

"Yeah, been through all that," said Waldegrave indifferently. He was attempting, without much success, to prize spines out of the Dover sole he had recklessly asked to be left on the bone. "Got the manuscript on Friday, didn't look at it until the Sunday—"

"You were meant to be away, weren't you?"

"Paris," said Waldegrave. "Anniversary weekend. Di'n't happen."

"Something came up?"

Waldegrave emptied the last of the wine into his glass. Several drops of the dark liquid fell onto the white tablecloth and spread.

"Had a row, a bloody awful row, on the way to Heathrow. Turned round, went back home."

"Rough," said Strike.

"On the rocks for years," said Waldegrave, abandoning his unequal struggle with the sole and throwing down his knife and fork with a clatter that made nearby diners look round. "JoJo's grown up. No point anymore. Splitting up."

"I'm sorry to hear that," said Strike.

Waldegrave shrugged lugubriously and took more wine. The lenses of his horn-rimmed glasses were covered in fingerprints and his shirt collar was grubby and frayed. He had the look, thought Strike, who was experienced in such matters, of a man who has slept in his clothes.

"You went straight home after the row, did you?"

"'S a big house. No need to see each other if we don't want to."

The drops of wine were spreading like crimson blossoms on the snowy tablecloth.

"Black spot, that's what this reminds me of," said Waldegrave. "*Treasure Island*, y'know...black spot. Suspicion on everyone who read that bloody book. Ev'ryone looking sideways at ev'ryone else. Ev'ryone who knows the ending's suspect. Police in my bloody office, ev'ryone staring...

"I read it on Sunday," he said, lurching back to Strike's question, "'n I told Liz Tassel what I thought of her—and life went on. Owen not answering his phone. Thought he was probably having a breakdown—had my own bloody problems. Daniel Chard going berserk...

"Fuck him. Resigned. Had enough. Accusations. No more. Being bloody bawled out in front of the whole office. No more."

"Accusations?" asked Strike.

His interview technique was starting to feel like the dexterous flicking of Subbuteo football figures; the wobbling interviewee directed by the right, light touch. (Strike had had an Arsenal set in the seventies; he had played Dave Polworth's custom-painted Plymouth Argyles, both boys lying belly-down on Dave's mum's hearthrug.)

"Dan thinks I gossiped about him to Owen. Bloody idiot. Thinks the world doesn't know … been gossip for years. Didn't have to tell Owen. Ev'ryone knows."

"That Chard's gay?"

"Gay, who cares … repressed. Not sure Dan even *knows* he's gay. But he likes pretty young men, likes painting 'em in the nude. Common knowledge."

"Did he offer to paint you?" asked Strike.

"Christ, no," said Waldegrave. "Joe North told me, years ago. Ah!"

He had caught the wine waiter's eye.

"'Nother glass of this, please."

Strike was only grateful he had not asked for a bottle.

"I'm sorry, sir, we don't do that by the—"

"Anything, then. Red. Anything.

"Years ago, this was," Waldegrave went on, picking up where he had left off. "Dan wanted Joe to pose for him; Joe told him to piss off. Common knowledge, f'years."

He leaned back, ramming the large woman behind him again, who unfortunately was now eating soup. Strike watched her angry dining companion summon a passing waiter to complain. The waiter bent down to Waldegrave and said apologetically, yet with firmness:

"Would you mind pulling in your chair, sir? The lady behind you—"

"Sorry, sorry."

Waldegrave tugged himself nearer Strike, placed his elbows on the table, pushed his tangled hair out of his eyes and said loudly:

"Head up his bloody arse."

"Who?" asked Strike, finishing with regret the best meal he had had in a long time.

"Dan. Handed the bloody company on a plate … rolling in it all his life … let him live in the country and paint his houseboy if that's what he wants … had enough of it. Start my own … start my own bloody company."

Waldegrave's mobile phone rang. It took him a while to locate it. He peered over his glasses at the caller's number before answering.

"What's up, JoJo?"

316

Busy though the restaurant was, Strike heard the response: shrill, distant screaming down the line. Waldegrave looked horrified.

"JoJo? Are you—?"

But then the doughy, amiable face became tauter than Strike could have believed. Veins stood out on Waldegrave's neck and his mouth stretched in an ugly snarl.

"Fuck you!" he said, and his voice carried loudly to all the surrounding tables so that fifty heads jerked upwards, conversations stalled. "*Do not call me on JoJo's number!* No, you drunken fucking—you heard me—I drink because I'm fucking married to *you*, that's why!"

The overweight woman behind Waldegrave looked around, outraged. Waiters were glaring; one had so far forgotten himself as to have paused with a Yorkshire pudding halfway to a Japanese businessman's plate. The decorous gentleman's club had doubtless seen other drunken brawls, but they could not fail to shock among the dark wood panels, the glass chandeliers and the bills of fare, where everything was stolidly British, calm and staid.

"Well, *whose fucking fault's that?*" shouted Waldegrave.

He staggered to his feet, ramming his unfortunate neighbor yet again, but this time there was no remonstrance from her companion. The restaurant had fallen silent. Waldegrave was weaving his way out of it, a bottle and a third to the bad, swearing into his mobile, and Strike, stranded at the table, was amused to find in himself some of the disapproval felt in the mess for the man who cannot hold his drink.

"Bill, please," said Strike to the nearest gaping waiter. He was disappointed that he had not gotten to sample the spotted dick, which he had noted on the bill of fare, but he must catch Waldegrave if he could.

While the diners muttered and watched him out of the corners of their eyes, Strike paid, pulled himself up from the table and, leaning on his stick, followed in Waldegrave's ungainly footsteps. From the outraged expression of the maître d' and the sound of Waldegrave still yelling just outside the door, Strike suspected that Waldegrave had taken some persuasion to leave the premises.

He found the editor propped up against the cold wall to the left of the doors. Snow was falling thickly all around them; the pavements were crunchy with it, passersby muffled to the ears. The backdrop of solid grandeur removed, Waldegrave no longer looked like a vaguely scruffy academic. Drunk, grubby and crumpled, swearing into a phone disguised by his large hand, he might have been a mentally ill down-and-out.

"... *not my fucking fault, you stupid bitch!* Did I write the fucking thing? Did I? ... you'd better fucking talk to her then, hadn't you? ... If you don't, I will ... Don't you threaten me, you ugly fucking slut ... if you'd kept your legs closed ... *you fucking heard me—*"

Waldegrave saw Strike. He stood gaping for a few seconds then cut the call. The mobile slipped through his fumbling fingers and landed on the snowy pavement.

"Bollocks," said Jerry Waldegrave.

The wolf had turned back into the sheep. He groped with bare fingers for the phone in the slush around his feet and his glasses fell off. Strike picked them up for him.

"Thanks. Thanks. Sorry about that. Sorry ... "

Strike saw tears on Waldegrave's puffy cheeks as the editor rammed his glasses back on. Stuffing the cracked phone into his pocket, he turned an expression of despair upon the detective.

"'S ruined my fucking life," he said. "That book. 'N I thought Owen ... one thing he held sacred. Father daughter. One thing ... "

With another dismissive gesture, Waldegrave turned and walked away, weaving badly, thoroughly drunk. He had had, the detective guessed, at least a bottle before they met. There was no point following him.

Watching Waldegrave disappear into the swirling snow, past the Christmas shoppers scrambling, laden, along the slushy pavements, Strike remembered a hand closing ungently on an upper arm, a stern man's voice, an angrier young woman's. "*Mummy's made a beeline, why don't you grab her?*"

Turning up his coat collar Strike thought he knew, now, what the meaning was: of a dwarf in a bloody bag, of the horns under the Cutter's cap and, cruelest of all, the attempted drowning.

37

...when I am provok'd to fury, I cannot incorporate with patience and reason.

William Congreve, *The Double-Dealer*

Strike set out for his office beneath a sky of dirty silver, his feet moving with difficulty through the rapidly accumulating snow, which was still falling fast. Though he had touched nothing but water, he felt a little drunk on good rich food, which gave him the false sense of well-being that Waldegrave had probably passed sometime midmorning, drinking in his office. The walk between Simpson's-in-the-Strand and his drafty little office on Denmark Street would take a fit and unimpaired adult perhaps a quarter of an hour. Strike's knee remained sore and overworked, but he had just spent more than his entire week's food budget on a single meal. Lighting a cigarette, he limped away through the knife-sharp cold, head bowed against the snow, wondering what Robin had found out at the Bridlington Bookshop.

As he walked past the fluted columns of the Lyceum Theatre, Strike pondered the fact that Daniel Chard was convinced that Jerry Waldegrave had helped Quine write his book, whereas Waldegrave thought that Elizabeth Tassel had played upon his sense of grievance until it had erupted into print. Were these, he wondered, simple cases of displaced anger? Having been balked of the true culprit by Quine's gruesome death, were Chard and Waldegrave seeking living scapegoats on whom to vent their frustrated fury? Or were they right to detect, in *Bombyx Mori*, a foreign influence?

The scarlet façade of the Coach and Horses in Wellington Street constituted a powerful temptation as he approached it, the stick doing heavy duty now, and his knee complaining: warmth, beer and a comfortable chair ... but a third lunchtime visit to the pub in a week ... not a habit he ought to develop ... Jerry Waldegrave was an object lesson in where such behavior might lead ...

He could not resist an envious glance through the window as he passed, towards lights gleaming on brass beer pumps and convivial men with slacker consciences than his own—

He saw her out of the corner of his eye. Tall and stooping in her black coat, hands in her pockets, scurrying along the slushy pavements behind him: his stalker and would-be attacker of Saturday night.

Strike's pace did not falter, nor did he turn to look at her. He was not playing games this time; there would be no stopping to test her amateurish stalking style, no letting her know that he had spotted her. On he walked without looking over his shoulder, and only a man or woman similarly expert in countersurveillance would have noticed his casual glances into helpfully positioned windows and reflective brass door plates; only they could have spotted the hyperalertness disguised as inattentiveness.

Most killers were slapdash amateurs; that was how they were caught. To persist after their encounter on Saturday night argued high-caliber recklessness and it was on this that Strike was counting as he continued up Wellington Street, outwardly oblivious to the woman following him with a knife in her pocket. As he crossed Russell Street she had dodged out of sight, faking entrance to the Marquess of Anglesey, but soon reappeared, dodging in and out of the square pillars of an office block and lurking in a doorway to allow him to pull ahead.

Strike could barely feel his knee now. He had become six foot three of highly concentrated potential. This time she had no advantage; she would not be taking him by surprise. If she had a plan at all, he guessed that it was to profit from any available opportunity. It was up to him to present her with an opportunity she dare not let pass, and to make sure she did not succeed.

Past the Royal Opera House with its classical portico, its columns and statues; in Endell Street she entered an old red telephone box, gathering her nerve, no doubt, double-checking that he was not aware of her. Strike walked on, his pace unchanging, his eyes on the street ahead. She took confidence and emerged again onto the crowded pavement, following him through harried passersby with carrier bags swinging from their hands, drawing closer to him as the street narrowed, flitting in and out of doorways.

As he drew nearer to the office he made his decision, turning left off Denmark Street into Flitcroft Street, which led to Denmark Place, where a dark passage, plastered with fliers for bands, led back to his office.

Would she dare?

As he entered the alleyway, his footsteps echoing a little off the dank walls, he slowed imperceptibly. Then he heard her coming— running at him.

Wheeling around on his sound left leg he flung out his walking stick—there was a shriek of pain as her arm met it—the Stanley knife was knocked out of her hand, hit the stone wall, rebounded and narrowly missed Strike's eye—he had her now in a ferocious grip that made her scream.

He was afraid that some hero would come to her aid, but no one appeared, and now speed was essential—she was stronger than he had expected and struggling ferociously, trying to kick him in the balls and claw his face. With a further economical twist of his body he had her in a headlock, her feet skidding and scrambling on the damp alley floor.

As she writhed in his arms, trying to bite him, he stooped to pick up the knife, pulling her down with him so that she almost lost her footing, then, abandoning the walking stick, which he could not carry while managing her, he dragged her out onto Denmark Street.

He was fast, and she so winded by the struggle that she had no breath to yell. The short cold street was empty of shoppers and no passersby on Charing Cross Road noticed anything amiss as he forced her the short distance to the black street door.

"Need in, Robin! Quickly!" he shouted on the intercom, slamming his way through the outer door as soon as Robin had buzzed it open. Up the metal steps he dragged her, his right knee now protesting violently, and she started shrieking, the screams echoing around the stairwell. Strike saw movement behind the glass door of the dour and eccentric graphic designer who worked in the office beneath his.

"Just messing around!" he bellowed at the door, heaving his pursuer upstairs.

"Cormoran? What's—oh my *God!*" said Robin, staring down from the landing. "You can't—what are you playing at? Let her go!"

"She's just—tried—to bloody—knife me again," panted Strike, and with a gigantic final effort he forced his pursuer over the threshold. "Lock the door!" he shouted at Robin, who had hurried in behind them and obeyed.

Strike threw the woman onto the mock-leather sofa. The hood fell back to reveal a long pale face with large brown eyes and thick dark wavy hair that fell to her shoulders. Her fingers terminated in pointed crimson nails. She looked barely twenty.

"You bastard! *You bastard!*"

She tried to get up, but Strike was standing over her looking murderous, so she thought better of it, slumping back onto the sofa and massaging her white neck, which bore dark pink scratch marks where he had seized her.

"Want to tell me why you're trying to knife me?" Strike asked.

"Fuck you!"

"That's original," said Strike. "Robin, call the police—"

"Noooo!" howled the woman in black like a baying dog. "He hurt me," she gasped to Robin, tugging down her top with abandoned wretchedness to reveal the marks on the strong white neck. "He dragged me, he pulled me—"

Robin looked to Strike, her hand on the receiver.

"Why have you been following me?" Strike said, panting as he stood over her, his tone threatening.

She cowered into the squeaking cushions yet Robin, whose fingers had not left the phone, detected a note of relish in the woman's fear, a whisper of voluptuousness in the way she twisted away from him.

"Last chance," growled Strike. "*Why—?*"

"What's happening up there?" came a querulous inquiry from the landing below.

Robin's eyes met Strike's. She hurried to the door, unlocked it and slid out onto the landing while Strike stood guard over his captive, his jaw set and one fist clenched. He saw the idea of screaming for help pass behind the big dark eyes, purple-shadowed like pansies, and fade away. Shaking, she began to cry, but her teeth were bared and he thought there was more rage than misery in her tears.

"All OK, Mr. Crowdy," Robin called. "Just messing around. Sorry we were so loud."

Robin returned to the office and locked the door behind her again. The woman was rigid on the sofa, tears tumbling down her face, her talon-like nails gripping the edge of the seat.

"Fuck this," Strike said. "You don't want to talk—I'm calling the police."

Apparently she believed him. He had taken barely two steps towards the phone when she sobbed:

"I wanted to stop you."

"Stop me doing what?" said Strike.

"Like you don't know!"

"Don't play fucking games with me!" Strike shouted, bending towards her with two large fists clenched. He could feel his damaged knee only too acutely now. It was her fault he had taken the fall that had damaged the ligaments all over again.

"Cormoran," said Robin firmly, sliding between them and forcing him to take a pace backwards. "Listen," she told the girl. "Listen to me. Tell him why you're doing this and maybe he won't call—"

"You've gotta be fucking joking," said Strike. "Twice she's tried to stab—"

"—maybe he won't call the police," said Robin loudly, undeterred.

The woman jumped up and tried to make a break for it towards the door.

"No you don't," said Strike, hobbling fast around Robin, catching his assailant round the waist and throwing her none too gently back onto the sofa. "*Who are you?*"

"You've hurt me now!" she shouted. "You've really hurt me—my ribs—I'll get you for assault, you bastard—"

"I'll call you Pippa, then, shall I?" said Strike.

A shuddering gasp and a malevolent stare.

"You—you—fuck—"

"Yeah, yeah, fuck me," said Strike irritably. "*Your name.*"

Her chest was heaving under the heavy overcoat.

"How will you know if I'm telling the truth, even if I tell you?" she panted, with a further show of defiance.

"I'll keep you here till I've checked," said Strike.

"Kidnap!" she shouted, her voice as rough and loud as a docker's.

"Citizen's arrest," said Strike. "You tried to fucking knife me. Now, for the last bloody time—"

"Pippa Midgley," she spat.

"Finally. Have you got ID?"

With another mutinous obscenity she slid a hand into her pocket and drew out a bus pass, which she threw to him.

"This says Phillip Midgley."

"No shit."

Watching the implication hit Strike, Robin felt a sudden urge, in spite of the tension in the room, to laugh.

"Epicoene," said Pippa Midgley furiously. "Didn't you get it? Too subtle for you, *dickhead?*"

Strike looked up at her. The Adam's apple on her scratched, marked throat was still prominent. She had buried her hands in her pockets again.

"I'll be Pippa on all my documents next year," she said.

"Pippa," Strike repeated. "You're the author of 'I'll turn the handle on the fucking rack for you,' are you?"

"*Oh*," said Robin, on a long drawn-out sigh of comprehension.

"*Oooooh*, you're so *clever*, Mr. Butch," said Pippa in spiteful imitation.

"D'you know Kathryn Kent personally, or are you just cyber-friends?"

"Why? Is knowing Kath Kent a crime now?"

"How did you know Owen Quine?"

"I don't want to talk about that bastard," she said, her chest heaving. "What he's done to me...what he's done...pretending...he lied...lying fucking bastard..."

Fresh tears splattered down her cheeks and she dissolved into hysterics. Her scarlet-tipped hands clawed at her hair, her feet drummed on the floor, she rocked backwards and forwards, wailing. Strike watched her with distaste and after thirty seconds said:

"Will you *shut the fuck*—"

But Robin quelled him with a glance, tore a handful of tissues out of the box on her desk and pushed them into Pippa's hand.

"T-t-ta—"

"Would you like a tea or coffee, Pippa?" asked Robin kindly.

"Co…fee…pl…"

"She's just tried to bloody knife me, Robin!"

"Well, she didn't manage it, did she?" commented Robin, busy with the kettle.

"Ineptitude," said Strike incredulously, "is no fucking defense under the law!"

He rounded on Pippa again, who had followed this exchange with her mouth agape.

"Why have you been following me? What are you trying to stop me doing? And I'm warning you—just because Robin here's buying the sob stuff—"

"You're working for *her!*" yelled Pippa. "That twisted bitch, his widow! She's got his money now, hasn't she—we know what you've been hired to do, we're not fucking stupid!"

"Who's 'we'?" demanded Strike, but Pippa's dark eyes slid again towards the door. "I swear to God," said Strike, whose much-tried knee was now throbbing in a way that made him want to grind his teeth, "if you go for that door one more fucking time I'm calling the police and I'll testify and be glad to watch you go down for attempted murder. And it won't be fun for you inside, Pippa," he added. "Not pre-op."

"Cormoran!" said Robin sharply.

"Stating facts," said Strike.

Pippa had shrunk back onto the sofa and was staring at Strike in unfeigned terror.

"Coffee," said Robin firmly, emerging from behind the desk and pressing the mug into one of the long-taloned hands. "Just tell him what all this is about, for God's sake, Pippa. *Tell him.*"

Unstable and aggressive though Pippa seemed, Robin could not help pitying the girl, who appeared to have given almost no thought to the possible consequences of lunging at a private detective with a blade. Robin could only assume that she possessed in extreme form the trait that afflicted her own younger brother Martin, who was notorious in their family for the lack of foresight and love of danger that had resulted in more trips to casualty than the rest of his siblings combined.

"We know she hired you to frame us," croaked Pippa.

"Who," growled Strike, "is '*she*' and who is '*us*'?"

"Leonora Quine!" said Pippa. "We know what she's like and we know what she's capable of! She hates us, me and Kath, she'd do anything to get us. She murdered Owen and she's trying to pin it on us! You can look like that all you want!" she shouted at Strike, whose heavy eyebrows had risen halfway to his thick hairline. "She's a crazy bitch, she's jealous as hell—she couldn't stand him seeing us and now she's got you poking around trying to get stuff to use against us!"

"I don't know whether you believe this paranoid bollocks—"

"We know what's going on!" shouted Pippa.

"*Shut up*. Nobody except the killer knew Quine was dead when you started stalking me. You followed me the day I found the body and I know you were following Leonora for a week before that. Why?" And when she did not answer, he repeated: "Last chance: why did you follow me from Leonora's?"

"I thought you might lead me to where he was," said Pippa.

"Why did you want to know where he was?"

"So I could fucking kill him!" yelled Pippa, and Robin was confirmed in her impression that Pippa shared Martin's almost total lack of self-preservation.

"And why did you want to kill him?" asked Strike, as though she had said nothing out of the ordinary.

"Because of what he did to us in that horrible fucking book! You know—you've read it—Epicoene—that bastard, that bastard—"

"Bloody calm down! So you'd read *Bombyx Mori* by then?"

"Yeah, of course I had—"

"And that's when you started putting shit through Quine's letter box?"

"Shit for a shit!" she shouted.

"Witty. When did you read the book?"

"Kath read the bits about us on the phone and then I went round and—"

"When did she read you the bits on the phone?"

"W-when she came home and found it lying on her doormat. Whole manuscript. She could hardly get the door open. He'd fed it through her door with a note," said Pippa Midgley. "She showed me."

"What did the note say?"

"It said 'Payback time for both of us. Hope you're happy! Owen.'"

"'Payback time for both of us'?" repeated Strike, frowning. "D'you know what that meant?"

"Kath wouldn't tell me but I know she understood. She was d-devastated," said Pippa, her chest heaving. "She's a—she's a wonderful person. You don't know her. She's been like a m-mother to me. We met on his writing course and we were like—we became like—" She caught up her breath and whimpered: "He was a bastard. He lied to us about what he was writing, he lied about—about everything—"

She began to cry again, wailing and sobbing, and Robin, worried about Mr. Crowdy, said gently:

"Pippa, just tell us what he lied about. Cormoran only wants the truth, he's not trying to frame anyone..."

She did not know whether Pippa had heard or believed her; perhaps she simply wanted to relieve her overwrought feelings, but she took a great shuddering breath and out spilled a torrent of words:

"He said I was like his second daughter, he *said* that to me; I told him *everything*, he knew my mum threw me out and *everything*. And I showed him m-m-my book about my life and he w-was so k-kind and interested and he said he'd help me get it p-published and he t-told us both, me and Kath, that we were in his n-new novel and he said I w-was a 'b-beautiful lost soul'—*that's what he said to me*," gasped Pippa, her mobile mouth working, "and he p-pretended to read a bit out to me one day, over the phone, and it was—it was lovely and then I r-read it and he'd—he'd written *that*...Kath was in b-bits... the cave...Harpy and Epicoene..."

"So Kathryn came home and found it all over the doormat, did she?" said Strike. "Came home from where—work?"

"From s-sitting in the hospice with her dying sister."

327

"And that was *when?*" said Strike for the third time.

"Who cares when it—?"

"*I fucking care!*"

"Was it the ninth?" Robin asked. She had brought up Kathryn Kent's blog on her computer, the screen angled away from the sofa where Pippa was sitting. "Could it have been Tuesday the ninth, Pippa? The Tuesday after bonfire night?"

"It was...yeah, I think it was!" said Pippa, apparently awestruck by Robin's lucky guess. "Yeah, Kath went away on bonfire night because Angela was so ill—"

"How d'you know it was bonfire night?" Strike asked.

"Because Owen told Kath he c-couldn't see her that night, because he had to do fireworks with his daughter," said Pippa. "And Kath was really upset, because he was supposed to be leaving! He'd promised her, he'd promised at *long bloody last* he'd leave his bitch of a wife, and then he says he's got to play sparklers with the reta—"

She drew up short, but Strike finished for her.

"With the retard?"

"It's just a joke," muttered Pippa, shamefaced, showing more regret about her use of the word than she had about trying to stab Strike. "Just between me and Kath: his daughter was always the excuse why Owen couldn't leave and be with Kath..."

"What did Kathryn do that night, instead of seeing Quine?" asked Strike.

"I went over to hers. Then she got the call that her sister Angela was a lot worse and she left. Angela had cancer. It had gone everywhere."

"Where was Angela?"

"In the hospice in Clapham."

"How did Kathryn get there?"

"Why's that matter?"

"Just answer the bloody question, will you?"

"I don't know—Tube, I s'pose. And she stayed with Angela for three days, sleeping on a mattress on the floor by her bed because they thought Angela was going to die any moment, but Angela kept hanging on so Kath had to go home for clean clothes and that's when she found the manuscript all over the doormat."

"Why are you sure she came home on the Tuesday?" Robin asked and Strike, who had been about to ask the same thing, looked at her in surprise. He did not know about the old man in the bookshop and the German sinkhole.

"Because on Tuesday nights I work on a helpline," said Pippa, "and I was there when Kath called me in f-floods, because she'd put the manuscript in order, and read what he'd written about us—"

"Well, this is all very interesting," said Strike, "because Kathryn Kent told the police that she'd never read *Bombyx Mori*."

Pippa's horrified expression might, under other circumstances, have been amusing.

"You fucking tricked me!"

"Yeah, you're a really tough nut to crack," said Strike. "Don't even *think* about it," he added, standing over her as she tried to get up.

"He was a—a shit!" shouted Pippa seething with impotent rage. "He was a user! Pretending to be interested in our work and using us all along, that l-lying b-bastard . . . I thought he understood what my life's been about—we used to talk for hours about it and he encouraged me with my life story—he t-told me he was going to help me get a publishing deal—"

Strike felt a sudden weariness wash over him. What was this mania to appear in print?

"—and he was just trying to keep me sweet, telling him all my most private thoughts and feelings, and Kath—what he did to Kath—you *don't understand*—I'm glad his bitch wife killed him! If she hadn't—"

"Why," demanded Strike, "d'you keep saying his wife killed Quine?"

"Because Kath's got proof!"

A short pause.

"What proof?" asked Strike.

"Wouldn't you like to know!" shouted Pippa with a cackle of hysterical laughter. "Never you mind!"

"If she's got proof, why hasn't she taken it to the police?"

"Out of compassion!" shouted Pippa. "Something *you* wouldn't—"

"Why," came a plaintive voice from outside the glass door, "is there still all this *shouting?*"

"Oh bloody hell," said Strike as the fuzzy outline of Mr. Crowdy from downstairs pressed close to the glass.

Robin moved to unlock the door.

"Very sorry, Mr. Crow—"

Pippa was off the sofa in an instant. Strike made a grab for her but his knee buckled agonizingly as he lunged. Knocking Mr. Crowdy aside she was gone, clattering down the stairs.

"Leave her!" Strike said to Robin, who looked braced to give chase. "Least I've got her knife."

"Knife?" yelped Mr. Crowdy and it took them fifteen minutes to persuade him not to contact the landlord (for the publicity following the Lula Landry case had unnerved the graphic designer, who lived in dread that another murderer might come seeking Strike and perhaps wander by mistake into the wrong office).

"Jesus H. Christ," said Strike when they had at last persuaded Crowdy to leave. He slumped down on the sofa; Robin took her computer chair and they looked at each other for a few seconds before starting to laugh.

"Decent good cop, bad cop routine we had going there," said Strike.

"I wasn't faking," said Robin, "I really did feel a bit sorry for her."

"I noticed. What about me, getting attacked?"

"Did she *really* want to stab you, or was it play-acting?" asked Robin sceptically.

"She might've liked the idea of it more than the reality," acknowledged Strike. "Trouble is, you're just as dead if you're knifed by a self-dramatizing twat as by a professional. And what she thought she'd gain by stabbing me—"

"Mother love," said Robin quietly.

Strike stared at her.

"Her own mother's disowned her," said Robin, "and she's going through a really traumatic time, I expect, taking hormones and God knows what else she's got to do before she has the operation. She thought she had a new family, didn't she? She thought Quine and Kathryn Kent were her new parents. She told us Quine said she was a second daughter to him and he put her in the book as Kathryn

Kent's daughter. But in *Bombyx Mori* he revealed her to the world as half male, half female. He also suggested that, beneath all the filial affection, she wanted to sleep with him.

"Her new father," said Robin, "had let her down very badly. But her new mother was still good and loving, and she'd been betrayed as well, so Pippa set out to get even for both of them."

She could not stop herself grinning at Strike's looked of stunned admiration.

"Why the hell did you give up that psychology degree?"

"Long story," said Robin, looking away towards the computer monitor. "She's not very old... twenty, d'you think?"

"Looked about that," agreed Strike. "Pity we never got round to asking her about her movements in the days after Quine disappeared."

"She didn't do it," said Robin with certainty, looking back at him.

"Yeah, you're probably right," sighed Strike, "if only because shoving dog shit through his letter box might've felt a bit anticlimactic after carving out his guts."

"And she doesn't seem very strong on planning or efficiency, does she?"

"An understatement," he agreed.

"Are you going to call the police about her?"

"I don't know. Maybe. But shit," he said, thumping himself on the forehead, "we didn't even find out why she was bloody singing in the book!"

"I think I might know," said Robin after a short burst of typing and reading the results on her computer monitor. "Singing to soften the voice... vocal exercises for transgendered people."

"Was that all?" asked Strike in disbelief.

"What are you saying—that she was wrong to take offense?" said Robin. "Come on—he was jeering at something really personal in a public—"

"That's not what I meant," said Strike.

He frowned out of the window, thinking. The snow was falling thick and fast.

After a while he said:

"What happened at the Bridlington Bookshop?"

"God, yes, I nearly forgot!"

She told him all about the assistant and his confusion between the first and the eighth of November.

"Stupid old sod," said Strike.

"That's a bit mean," said Robin.

"Cocky, wasn't he? Mondays are always the same, goes to his friend Charles every Monday..."

"But how do we know whether it was the Anglican bishop night or the sinkhole night?"

"You say he claims Charles interrupted him with the sinkhole story while he was telling him about Quine coming into the shop?"

"That's what he said."

"Then it's odds on Quine was in the shop on the first, not the eighth. He remembers those two bits of information as connected. Silly bugger's got confused. He *wanted* to have seen Quine after he'd disappeared, he wanted to be able to help establish time of death, so he was subconsciously looking for reasons to think it was the Monday in the time frame for the murder, not an irrelevant Monday a whole week before anyone was interested in Quine's movements."

"There's still something odd, though, isn't there, about what he claims Quine said to him?" asked Robin.

"Yeah, there is," said Strike. "Buying reading matter because he was going away for a break ... so he was already planning to go away, four days before he rowed with Elizabeth Tassel? Was he already planning to go to Talgarth Road, after all those years he was supposed to have hated and avoided the place?"

"Are you going to tell Anstis about this?" Robin asked.

Strike gave a wry snort of laughter.

"No, I'm not going to tell Anstis. We've got no real proof Quine was in there on the first instead of the eighth. Anyway, Anstis and I aren't on the best terms just now."

There was another long pause, and then Strike startled Robin by saying:

"I've got to talk to Michael Fancourt."

"Why?" she asked.

"A lot of reasons," said Strike. "Things Waldegrave said to me over lunch. Can you get on to his agent or whatever contact you can find for him?"

"Yes," said Robin, making a note for herself. "You know, I watched that interview back just now and I still couldn't—"

"Look at it again," said Strike. "Pay attention. *Think.*"

He lapsed into silence again, glaring now at the ceiling. Not wishing to break his train of thought, Robin merely set to work on the computer to discover who represented Michael Fancourt.

Finally Strike spoke over the tapping of her keyboard.

"What does Kathryn Kent think she's got on Leonora?"

"Maybe nothing," said Robin, concentrating on the results she had uncovered.

"And she's withholding it 'out of compassion'..."

Robin said nothing. She was perusing the website of Fancourt's literary agency for a contact number.

"Let's hope that was just more hysterical bullshit," said Strike.

But he was worried.

38

That in so little paper
Should lie th' undoing...

John Webster, *The White Devil*

Miss Brocklehurst, the possibly unfaithful PA, was still claiming to be incapacitated by her cold. Her lover, Strike's client, found this excessive and the detective was inclined to agree with him. Seven o'clock the following morning found Strike stationed in a shadowy recess opposite Miss Brocklehurst's Battersea flat, wrapped up in coat, scarf and gloves, yawning widely as the cold penetrated his extremities and enjoying the second of three Egg McMuffins he had picked up from McDonald's on his way.

There had been a severe weather warning for the whole of the south-east. Thick dark blue snow already lay over the entire street and the first tentative flakes of the day were drifting down from a starless sky as he waited, moving his toes from time to time to check that he could still feel them. One by one the occupants left for work, slipping and sliding off towards the station or clambering into cars whose exhausts sounded particularly loud in the muffled quiet. Three Christmas trees sparkled at Strike from living-room windows, though December would only start the following day, tangerine, emerald and neon blue lights winking garishly as he leaned against the wall, his eyes on the windows of Miss Brocklehurst's flat, laying bets with himself as to whether she would leave the house at all in this weather. His knee was still killing him, but the snow had slowed the rest of the world to a pace that matched his own. He had never seen Miss

Brocklehurst in heels lower than four inches. In these conditions, she might well be more incapacitated than he was.

In the last week the search for Quine's killer had started to eclipse all his other cases, but it was important to keep up with them unless he wanted to lose business. Miss Brocklehurst's lover was a rich man who was likely to put plenty more jobs Strike's way if he liked the detective's work. The businessman had a predilection for youthful blonds, a succession of whom (as he had freely confessed to Strike at their first meeting) had taken large amounts of money and sundry expensive gifts from him only to leave or betray him. As he showed no sign of developing better judgment of character, Strike anticipated many more lucrative hours spent tailing future Miss Brocklehursts. Perhaps it was the betrayal that thrilled his client, reflected Strike, his breath rising in clouds through the icy air; he had known other such men. It was a taste that found its fullest expression in those who became infatuated with hookers.

At ten to nine the curtains gave a small twitch. Faster than might have been expected from his attitude of casual relaxation, Strike raised the night-vision camera he had been concealing at his side.

Miss Brocklehurst stood briefly exposed to the dim snowy street in bra and pants, though her cosmetically enhanced breasts had no need of support. Behind her in the darkness of the bedroom walked a paunchy, bare-chested man who briefly cupped one breast, earning himself a giggled reproof. Both turned away into the bedroom.

Strike lowered his camera and checked his handiwork. The most incriminating image he had managed to capture showed the clear outline of a man's hand and arm, Miss Brocklehurst's face half turned in a laugh, but her embracer's face was in shadow. Strike suspected that he might be about to leave for work, so he stowed the camera in an inside pocket, ready to give slow and cumbersome chase, and set to work on his third McMuffin.

Sure enough, at five to nine Miss Brocklehurst's front door opened and the lover emerged; he resembled her boss in nothing except age and a moneyed appearance. A sleek leather messenger bag was slung diagonally across his chest, large enough for a clean shirt and a tooth-brush. Strike had seen these so frequently of late that he had come to think of them as Adulterer's Overnight Bags. The couple enjoyed a French kiss on the doorstep curtailed by the icy cold and the fact that Miss Brocklehurst was wearing less than two ounces of fabric. Then she retreated indoors and Paunchy set off towards Clapham Junction, already speaking on his mobile phone, doubtless explaining that he would be late due to the snow. Strike allowed him twenty yards' head start then emerged from his hiding place, leaning on the stick that Robin had kindly retrieved from Denmark Place the preceding afternoon.

It was easy surveillance, as Paunchy was oblivious to anything but his telephone conversation. They walked down the gentle incline of Lavender Hill together, twenty yards apart, the snow falling steadily again. Paunchy slipped several times in his handmade shoes. When they reached the station it was easy for Strike to follow him, still gabbling, into the same carriage and, under pretext of reading texts, to take pictures of him on his own mobile.

As he did so, a genuine text arrived from Robin.

Michael Fancourt's agent just called me back—MF says he'd be delighted to meet you! He's in Germany but will be back on 6th. Suggests Groucho Club whatever time suits? Rx

It was quite extraordinary, Strike thought, as the train rattled into Waterloo, how much the people who had read *Bombyx Mori* wanted to talk to him. When before had suspects jumped so eagerly at the chance to sit face to face with a detective? And what did famous Michael Fancourt hope to gain from an interview with the private detective who had found Owen Quine's body?

Strike got out of the train behind Paunchy, following him through the crowds across the wet, slippery tiles of Waterloo station, beneath the ceiling of cream girders and glass that reminded Strike of Tithebarn House. Out again into the cold, with Paunchy still oblivious and gabbling into his mobile, Strike followed him along slushy, treacherous pavements edged with clods of mucky snow, between square office blocks comprised of glass and concrete, in and out of the swarm of financial workers bustling along, ant-like, in their drab coats, until at last Paunchy turned into the car park of one of the biggest office blocks and headed for what was obviously his own car. Apparently he had felt it wiser to leave the BMW at the office than to park outside Miss Brocklehurst's flat. As Strike watched, lurking behind a convenient Range Rover, he felt the mobile in his pocket vibrate but ignored it, unwilling to draw attention to himself. Paunchy had a named parking space. After collecting a few items from his boot he headed into the building, leaving Strike free to amble over to the wall where the directors' names were written and take a photograph of Paunchy's full name and title for his client's better information.

Strike then headed back to the office. Once on the Tube he examined his phone and saw that his missed call was from his oldest friend, the shark-mangled Dave Polworth.

Polworth had the ancient habit of calling Strike "Diddy." Most people assumed this was an ironic reference to his size (all through primary school, Strike had been the biggest boy of the year and usually of the year above), but in fact it derived from the endless comings and goings from school that were due to his mother's peripatetic lifestyle. These had once, long ago, resulted in a small, shrill Dave Polworth telling Strike he was like a didicoy, the Cornish word for gypsy.

Strike returned the call as soon as he got off the Tube and they were still talking twenty minutes later when he entered his office. Robin looked up and began to speak, but seeing that Strike was on the phone merely smiled and turned back to her monitor.

"Coming home for Christmas?" Polworth asked Strike as he moved through to the inner office and closed his door.

"Maybe," said Strike.

"Few pints in the Victory?" Polworth urged him. "Shag Gwenifer Arscott again?"

"I never," said Strike (it was a joke of long standing), "shagged Gwenifer Arscott."

"Well, have another bash, Diddy, you might strike gold this time. Time someone took her cherry. And speaking of girls neither of us ever shagged ... "

The conversation degenerated into a series of salacious and very funny vignettes from Polworth about the antics of the mutual friends they had both left behind in St. Mawes. Strike was laughing so much he ignored the "call waiting" signal and did not bother to check who it was.

"Haven't got back with Milady Berserko, have you, boy?" Dave asked, this being the name he usually used for Charlotte.

"Nope," said Strike. "She's getting married in...four days," he calculated.

"Yeah, well, you be on the watch, Diddy, for signs of her galloping back over the horizon. Wouldn't be surprised if she bolts. Breathe a sigh of relief if it comes off, mate."

"Yeah," said Strike. "Right."

"That's a deal then, yeah?" said Polworth. "Home for Christmas? Beers in the Victory?"

"Yeah, why not," said Strike.

After a few more ribald exchanges Dave returned to his work and Strike, still grinning, checked his phone and saw that he had missed a call from Leonora Quine.

He wandered back into the outer office while dialing his voice mail.

"I've watched Michael Fancourt's documentary again," said Robin excitedly, "and I've realized what you—"

Strike raised a hand to quiet her as Leonora's ordinarily deadpan voice spoke in his ear, sounding agitated and disoriented.

"Cormoran, I've been bloody arrested. I don't know why— nobody's telling me nothing—they've got me at the station. They're waiting for a lawyer or something. I dunno what to do—Orlando's with Edna, I don't—anyway, that's where I am..."

A few seconds of silence and the message ended.

"Shit!" said Strike, so loudly that Robin jumped. "SHIT!"

"What's the matter?"

"They've arrested Leonora—why's she calling me, not Ilsa? *Shit*..."

He punched in Ilsa Herbert's number and waited.

"Hi Corm—"

"They've arrested Leonora Quine."

"*What?*" cried Ilsa. "*Why?* Not that bloody old rag in the lockup?"

"They might have something else."

(*Kath's got proof...*)

"Where is she, Corm?"

338

"Police station … it'll be Kilburn, that's nearest."

"Christ almighty, why didn't she call me?"

"Fuck knows. She said something about them finding her a lawyer—"

"Nobody's contacted me—God above, doesn't she *think?* Why didn't she give them my name? I'm going now, Corm, I'll dump this lot on someone else. I'm owed a favor…"

He could hear a series of thunks, distant voices, Ilsa's rapid footsteps.

"Call me when you know what's going on," he said.

"It might be a while."

"I don't care. Call me."

She hung up. Strike turned to face Robin, who looked appalled.

"Oh no," she breathed.

"I'm calling Anstis," said Strike, jabbing again at his phone.

But his old friend was in no mood to dispense favors.

"I warned you, Bob, I warned you this was coming. She did it, mate."

"What've you got?" Strike demanded.

"Can't tell you that, Bob, sorry."

"Did you get it from Kathryn Kent?"

"Can't say, mate."

Barely deigning to return Anstis's conventional good wishes, Strike hung up.

"Dickhead!" he said. "Bloody *dickhead!*"

Leonora was now in a place where he could not reach her. Strike was worried about how her grudging manner and the animosity to the police would appear to interlocutors. He could almost hear her complaining that Orlando was alone, demanding to know when she would be able to return to her daughter, indignant that the police had meddled with the daily grind of her miserable existence. He was afraid of her lack of self-preservation; he wanted Ilsa there, fast, before Leonora uttered innocently self-incriminating comments about her husband's general neglect and his girlfriends, before she could state again her almost incredible and suspicious claim that she knew nothing about her husband's books before they had proper covers on, before she attempted to explain why she had temporarily forgotten that they owned a second house where her husband's remains had lain decaying for weeks.

Five o'clock in the afternoon came and went without news from Ilsa. Looking out at the darkening sky and the snow, Strike insisted Robin go home.

"But you'll ring me when you hear?" she begged him, pulling on her coat and wrapping a thick woolen scarf around her neck.

"Yeah, of course," said Strike.

But not until six thirty did Ilsa call him back.

"Couldn't be worse," were her first words. She sounded tired and stressed. "They've got proof of purchase, on the Quines' joint credit card, of protective overalls, wellington boots, gloves and ropes. They were bought online and paid for with their Visa. Oh—and a burqa."

"You're fucking kidding me."

"I'm not. I know you think she's innocent—"

"Yeah, I do," said Strike, conveying a clear warning not to bother trying to persuade him otherwise.

"All right," said Ilsa wearily, "have it your own way, but I'll tell you this: she's not helping herself. She's being aggressive as hell, insisting Quine must have bought the stuff himself. A burqa, for God's sake...The ropes bought on the card are identical to the ones that were found tying the corpse. They asked her why Quine would want a burqa or plastic overalls of a strength to resist chemical spills, and all she said was: 'I don't bloody know, do I?' Every other sentence, she kept asking when she could go home to her daughter; she just doesn't get it. The stuff was bought six months ago and sent to Talgarth Road—it couldn't look more premeditated unless they'd found a plan in her handwriting. She's denying she knew how Quine was going to end his book, but your guy Anstis—"

"There in person, was he?"

"Yeah, doing the interrogation. He kept asking whether she really expected them to believe that Quine never talked about what he was writing. Then she says, 'I don't pay much attention.' 'So he *does* talk about his plots?' On and on it went, trying to wear her down, and in the end she says, 'Well, he said something about the silkworm being boiled.' That was all Anstis needed to be convinced she's been lying all along and she knew the whole plot. Oh, and they've found disturbed earth in their back garden."

"And I'll lay you odds they'll find a dead cat called Mr. Poop," snarled Strike.

"That won't stop Anstis," predicted Ilsa. "He's absolutely sure it's her, Corm. They've got the right to keep her until eleven a.m. tomorrow and I'm sure they're going to charge her."

"They haven't got enough," said Strike fiercely. "Where's the DNA evidence? Where are the witnesses?"

"That's the problem, Corm, there aren't any and that credit card bill's pretty damning. Look, I'm on your side," said Ilsa patiently. "You want my honest opinion? Anstis is taking a punt, hoping it's going to work out. I think he's feeling the pressure from all the press interest. And to be frank, he's feeling agitated about you slinking around the case and wants to take the initiative."

Strike groaned.

"Where did they get a six-month-old Visa bill? Has it taken them this long to go through the stuff they took out of his study?"

"No," said Ilsa. "It's on the back of one of his daughter's pictures. Apparently the daughter gave it to a friend of his months ago, and this friend went to the police with it early this morning, claiming they'd only just looked at the back and realized what was on there. What did you just say?"

"Nothing," Strike sighed.

"It sounded like 'Tashkent.'"

"Not that far off. I'll let you go, Ilsa... thanks for everything."

Strike sat for a few seconds in frustrated silence.

"Bollocks," he said softly to his dark office.

He knew how this had happened. Pippa Midgley, in her paranoia and her hysteria, convinced that Strike had been hired by Leonora to pin the murder on somebody else, had run from his office straight to Kathryn Kent. Pippa had confessed that she had blown Kathryn's pretense never to have read *Bombyx Mori* and urged her to use the evidence she had against Leonora. And so Kathryn Kent had ripped down her lover's daughter's picture (Strike imagined it stuck, with a magnet, to the fridge) and hurried off to the police station.

"*Bollocks*," he repeated, more loudly, and dialed Robin's number.

39

I am so well acquainted with despair,
I know not how to hope ...

Thomas Dekker and Thomas Middleton,
The Honest Whore

As her lawyer had predicted, Leonora Quine was charged with the murder of her husband at eleven o'clock the following morning. Alerted by phone, Strike and Robin watched the news spread online where, minute by minute, the story proliferated like multiplying bacteria. By half past eleven the *Sun* website had a full article on Leonora headed ROSE WEST LOOKALIKE WHO TRAINED AT THE BUTCHER'S.

The journalists had been busily collecting evidence of Quine's poor record as a husband. His frequent disappearances were linked to liaisons with other women, the sexual themes of his work dissected and embellished. Kathryn Kent had been located, doorstepped, photographed and categorized as "Quine's curvy red-headed mistress, a writer of erotic fiction."

Shortly before midday, Ilsa called Strike again.

"She's going to be up in court tomorrow."

"Where?"

"Wood Green, eleven o'clock. Straight from there to Holloway, I expect."

Strike had once lived with his mother and Lucy in a house a mere three minutes away from the closed women's prison that served north London.

"I want to see her."

"You can try, but I can't imagine the police will want you near her and I've got to tell you, Corm, as her lawyer, it might not look—"

"Ilsa, I'm the only chance she's got now."

"Thanks for the vote of confidence," she said drily.

"You know what I mean."

He heard her sigh.

"I'm thinking of you too. Do you really want to put the police's backs—?"

"How is she?" interrupted Strike.

"Not good," said Ilsa. "The separation from Orlando's killing her."

The afternoon was punctuated with calls from journalists and people who had known Quine, both groups equally desperate for inside information. Elizabeth Tassel's voice was so deep and rough on the phone that Robin thought her a man.

"Where's Orlando?" the agent demanded of Strike when he came to the phone, as though he had been delegated charge of all members of the Quine family. "Who's got her?"

"She's with a neighbor, I think," he said, listening to her wheeze down the line.

"My God, what a mess," rasped the agent. "Leonora … the worm turning after all these years … it's incredible … "

Nina Lascelles's reaction was, not altogether to Strike's surprise, poorly disguised relief. Murder had receded to its rightful place on the hazy edge of the possible. Its shadow no longer touched her; the killer was nobody she knew.

"His wife *does* look a bit like Rose West, doesn't she?" she asked Strike on the phone and he knew that she was staring at the *Sun*'s website. "Except with long hair."

She seemed to be commiserating with him. He had not solved the case. The police had beaten him to it.

"Listen, I'm having a few people over on Friday, fancy coming?"

"Can't, sorry," said Strike. "I'm having dinner with my brother."

He could tell that she thought he was lying. There had been an almost imperceptible hesitation before he had said "my brother," which might well have suggested a pause for rapid thought. Strike could not remember ever describing Al as his brother before. He rarely discussed his half-siblings on his father's side.

Before she left the office that evening Robin set a mug of tea in front of him as he sat poring over the Quine file. She could almost feel the anger that Strike was doing his best to hide, and suspected that it was directed at himself quite as much as at Anstis.

"It's not over," she said, winding her scarf around her neck as she prepared to depart. "We'll prove it wasn't her."

She had once before used the plural pronoun when Strike's faith in himself had been at a low ebb. He appreciated the moral support, but a feeling of impotence was swamping his thought processes. Strike hated paddling on the periphery of the case, forced to watch as others dived for clues, leads and information.

He sat up late with the Quine file that night, reviewing the notes he had made of interviews, examining again the photographs he had printed off his phone. The mangled body of Owen Quine seemed to signal to him in the silence as corpses often did, exhaling mute appeals for justice and pity. Sometimes the murdered carried messages from their killers like signs forced into their stiff dead hands. Strike stared for a long time at the burned and gaping chest cavity, the ropes tight around ankles and wrists, the carcass trussed and gutted like a turkey, but try as he might, he could glean nothing from the pictures that he did not already know. Eventually he turned off all the lights and headed upstairs to bed.

It was a bittersweet relief to have to spend Thursday morning at the offices of his brunet client's exorbitantly expensive divorce lawyers in Lincoln's Inn Fields. Strike was glad to have something to while away time that could not be spent investigating Quine's murder, but he still felt that he had been lured to the meeting under false pretenses. The flirtatious divorcée had given him to understand that her lawyer wanted to hear from Strike in person how he had collected the copious evidence of her husband's duplicity. He sat beside her at a highly polished mahogany table with room for twelve while she referred constantly to "what Cormoran managed to find out" and "as Cormoran witnessed, didn't you?," occasionally touching his wrist. It did not take Strike long to deduce from her suave lawyer's barely concealed irritation that it had not been his idea to have Strike in attendance. Nevertheless, as might have been expected when the hourly fee ran to over five hundred pounds, he showed no disposition to hurry matters along.

On a trip to the bathroom Strike checked his phone and saw, in tiny thumbnail pictures, Leonora being led in and out of Wood Green Crown Court. She had been charged and driven away in a police van. There had been plenty of press photographers but no members of the public baying for her blood; she was not supposed to have murdered anyone that the public much cared about.

A text from Robin arrived just as he was about to reenter the conference room:

Could get you in to see Leonora at 6 this evening?

Great, he texted back.

"I thought," said his flirtatious client, once he had sat back down, "that Cormoran might be rather impressive on the witness stand."

Strike had already shown her lawyer the meticulous notes and photographs he had compiled, detailing Mr. Burnett's every covert transaction, the attempted sale of the apartment and the palming of the emerald necklace included. To Mrs. Burnett's evident disappointment, neither man saw any reason for Strike to attend court in person given the quality of his records. Indeed, the lawyer could barely conceal his resentment of the reliance she seemed to place upon the detective. No doubt he thought this wealthy divorcée's discreet caresses and batted eyelashes might be better directed towards him, in his bespoke pinstripe suit, with his distinguished salt-and-pepper hair, instead of a man who looked like a limping prize fighter.

Relieved to quit the rarefied atmosphere, Strike caught the Tube back to his office, glad to take off his suit in his flat, happy to think that he would soon be rid of that particular case and in possession of the fat check that had been the only reason he had taken it. He was free now to focus on that thin, gray-haired fifty-year-old woman in Holloway who was touted as WRITER'S MOUSY WIFE EXPERT WITH CLEAVER on page two of the *Evening Standard* he had picked up on the journey.

"Was her lawyer happy?" Robin asked when he reappeared in the office.

"Reasonably," said Strike, staring at the miniature tinsel Christmas tree she had placed on her tidy desk. It was decorated with tiny baubles and LED lights.

"Why?" he asked succinctly.

"Christmas," said Robin, with a faint grin but without apology. "I was going to put it up yesterday, but after Leonora was charged I didn't feel very festive. Anyway, I've got you an appointment to see her at six. You'll need to take photo ID——"

"Good work, thanks."

"——and I got you sandwiches and I thought you might like to see this," she said. "Michael Fancourt's given an interview about Quine."

She passed him a pack of cheese and pickle sandwiches and a copy of *The Times*, folded to the correct page. Strike lowered himself onto the farting leather sofa and ate while reading the article, which was adorned with a split photograph. On the left-hand side was a picture of Fancourt standing in front of an Elizabethan country house. Photographed from below, his head looked less out of proportion than usual. On the right-hand side was Quine, eccentric and wild-eyed in his feather-trimmed trilby, addressing a sparse audience in what seemed to be a small marquee.

The writer of the piece made much of the fact that Fancourt and Quine had once known each other well, had even been considered equivalent talents.

Few now remember Quine's breakout work, *Hobart's Sin*, although Fancourt touts it still as a fine example of what he calls Quine's magical-brutalism. For all Fancourt's reputation of a man who nurses his grudges, he brings a surprising generosity to our discussion of Quine's oeuvre.

"Always interesting and often underrated," he says. "I suspect that he will be treated more kindly by future critics than our contemporaries."

This unexpected generosity is the more surprising when one considers that 25 years ago Fancourt's first wife, Elspeth Kerr, killed herself after reading a cruel parody of her first novel. The spoof was widely attributed to Fancourt's close friend and fellow literary rebel: the late Owen Quine.

"One mellows almost without realizing it—a compensation of age,

because anger is exhausting. I unburdened myself of many of the feelings about Ellie's death in my last novel, which should not be read as
autobiographical, although ... "

Strike skimmed the next two paragraphs, which appeared to be
promoting Fancourt's next book, and resumed reading at the point
where the word "violence" jumped out at him.

It is difficult to reconcile the tweed-jacketed Fancourt in front of me
with the one-time self-described literary punk who drew both plaudits
and criticism for the inventive and gratuitous violence of his early work.

"If Mr. Graham Greene was correct," wrote critic Harvey Bird of
Fancourt's first novel, "and the writer needs a chip of ice in his heart, then
Michael Fancourt surely has what it takes in abundance. Reading the rape
scene in *Bellafront* one starts to imagine that this young man's innards
must be glacial. In fact, there are two ways of looking at *Bellafront*,
which is undoubtedly accomplished and original. The first possibility is
that Mr. Fancourt has written an unusually mature first novel, in which he
has resisted the neophyte tendency to insert himself into the (anti-)heroic
role. We may wince at its grotesqueries or its morality, but nobody could
deny the power or artistry of the prose. The second, more disturbing, possibility is that Mr. Fancourt does not possess much of an organ in which
to place a chip of ice and his singularly inhuman tale corresponds to his
own inner landscape. Time—and further work—will tell."

Fancourt hailed originally from Slough, the only son of an unwed
nurse. His mother still lives in the house in which he grew up.

"She's happy there," he says. "She has an enviable capacity for enjoying the familiar."

His own home is a long way from a terraced house in Slough. Our
conversation takes place in a long drawing room crammed with Meissen
knick-knacks and Aubusson rugs, its windows overlooking the extensive
grounds of Endsor Court.

"This is all my wife's choice," says Fancourt dismissively. "My taste
in art is very different and confined to the grounds." A large trench to the
side of the building is being prepared for the concrete foundation to support a sculpture in rusted metal representing the Fury Tisiphone, which

he describes with a laugh as an "impulse buy ... the avenger of murder, you know ... a very powerful piece. My wife loathes it."

And somehow we find ourselves back where the interview began: at the macabre fate of Owen Quine.

"I haven't yet processed Owen's murder," says Fancourt quietly. "Like most writers, I tend to find out what I feel on a subject by writing about it. It is how we interpret the world, how we make sense of it."

Does this mean that we can expect a fictionalized account of Quine's killing?

"I can hear the accusations of bad taste and exploitation already," smiles Fancourt. "I dare say the themes of lost friendship, of a last chance to talk, to explain and make amends may make an appearance in due course, but Owen's murder has already been treated fictionally — by himself."

He is one of the few to have read the notorious manuscript that appears to have formed the blueprint of the murder.

"I read it the very day that Quine's body was discovered. My publisher was very keen for me to see it — I'm portrayed in it, you see." He seems genuinely indifferent about his inclusion, however insulting the portrait may have been. "I wasn't interested in calling in lawyers. I deplore censorship."

What did he think of the book, in literary terms?

"It's what Nabokov called a maniac's masterpiece," he replies, smiling. "There may be a case for publishing it in due course, who knows?"

He can't, surely, be serious?

"But why shouldn't it be published?" demands Fancourt. "Art is supposed to provoke: by that standard alone, *Bombyx Mori* has more than fulfilled its remit. Yes, why not?" asks the literary punk, ensconced in his Elizabethan manor.

"With an introduction by Michael Fancourt?" I suggest.

"Stranger things have happened," replies Michael Fancourt, with a grin. "Much stranger."

"Christ almighty," muttered Strike, throwing *The Times* back onto Robin's desk and narrowly missing the Christmas tree.

"Did you see he only claims to have read *Bombyx Mori* the day you found Quine?"

"Yeah," said Strike.

"He's lying," said Robin.

"We *think* he's lying," Strike corrected her.

Holding fast to his resolution not to waste any more money on taxis, but with the snow still falling, Strike took the number 29 bus through the darkening afternoon. It ran north, taking Strike on a twenty-minute journey through recently gritted roads. A haggard woman got on at Hampstead Road, accompanied by a small, grizzling boy. Some sixth sense told Strike that the three of them were headed in the same direction and, sure enough, both he and the woman stood to get out in Camden Road, alongside the bare flank of HMP Holloway.

"You're gonna see Mummy," she told her charge, whom Strike guessed to be her grandson, though she looked around forty.

Surrounded by bare-limbed trees and grass verges covered in thick snow, the jail might have been a redbrick university faculty but for authoritarian signs in government-issue blue and white, and the sixteen-foot-high doors set into the wall so that prison vans might pass. Strike joined the trickle of visitors, several of them with children who strained to make marks in the untouched snow heaped beside the paths. The line shuffled together past the terracotta walls with their cement frets, past the hanging baskets now balls of snow in the freezing December air. The majority of his fellow visitors were women; Strike was unique among the men not merely for his size but for the fact that he did not look as though life had pummeled him into a quiescent stupor. A heavily tattooed youth in sagging jeans walking ahead of him staggered a little with every step. Strike had seen neurological damage back in Selly Oak, but guessed that this kind had not been sustained under mortar fire.

The stout female prison officer whose job it was to check IDs examined his driver's license, then stared up at him.

"I know who you are," she said, with a piercing look.

Strike wondered whether Anstis had asked to be tipped off if he went to see Leonora. It seemed probable.

He had arrived deliberately early, so as not to waste a minute of his allotted time with his client. This foresight permitted him a coffee in the visitors' center, which was run by a children's charity. The room was bright and almost cheerful, and many of the kids greeted the trucks and teddies as old friends. Strike's haggard companion from the bus watched, gaunt and impassive, as the boy with her played with an Action Man around Strike's large feet, treating him like a massive piece of sculpture (*Tisiphone, the avenger of murder*...).

He was called through to the visitors' hall at six on the dot. Footsteps echoed off the shiny floors. The walls were of concrete blocks but bright murals painted by the prisoners did their best to soften the cavernous space, which echoed with the clang of metal and keys and the murmur of talk. The plastic seats were fixed either side of a small, low central table, similarly immovable, so as to minimize contact between prisoner and visitor, and prevent the passing of contraband. A toddler wailed. Warders stood around the walls, watching. Strike, who had only ever dealt with male prisoners, felt a repugnance for the place unusual in him. The kids staring at gaunt mothers, the subtle signs of mental illness in the fiddling and twitching of bitten fingers, drowsy, over-medicated women curled in their plastic seats were quite unlike the male detention facilities with which he was familiar.

Leonora sat waiting, tiny and fragile, pathetically glad to see him. She was wearing her own clothes, a loose sweatshirt and trousers in which she looked shrunken.

"Orlando's been in," she said. Her eyes were bright red; he could tell that she had been crying for a long time. "Didn't want to leave me. They dragged her out. Wouldn't let me calm her down."

Where she would have shown defiance and anger he could hear the beginnings of institutionalized hopelessness. Forty-eight hours had taught her that she had lost all control and power.

"Leonora, we need to talk about that credit card statement."

"I never had that card," she said, her white lips trembling. "Owen always kept it, I never had it except sometimes if I needed to go to the supermarket. He always gave me cash."

Strike remembered that she had come to him in the first place because money was running out.

"I left all our finances up to Owen, that's how he liked it, but he was careless, he never used to check his bills nor his bank statements, used to just sling 'em in his office. I used to say to him, 'You wanna check those, someone could be diddling you,' but he never cared. He'd give anything to Orlando to draw on, that's why it had her picture—"

"Never mind the picture. Somebody other than you or Owen must have had access to that credit card. We're going to run through a few people, OK?"

"All right," she mumbled, cowed.

"Elizabeth Tassel supervised work on the house in Talgarth Road, right? How was that paid for? Did she have a copy of your credit card?"

"No," said Leonora.

"Are you sure?"

"Yeah, I'm sure, cos we offered it to her and she said it was easier just to take it out of Owen's next royalties cos he was due some any time. He sells well in Finland, I dunno why, but they like his—"

"You can't think of *any* time where Elizabeth Tassel did something for the house and had the Visa card?"

"No," she said, shaking her head, "never."

"OK," said Strike, "can you remember—and take your time— any occasion when Owen paid for something with his credit card at Roper Chard?"

And to his astonishment she said, "Not at Roper Chard exactly, but yeah.

"They were all there. I was there, too. It was ... I dunno ... two years ago? Maybe less ... a big dinner for publishers, it was, at the Dorchester. They put me and Owen at a table with all the junior people. Daniel Chard and Jerry Waldegrave were nowhere near us. Anyway, there was a silent auction, you know, when you write down your bid for—"

"Yeah, I know how they work," said Strike, trying to contain his impatience.

"It was for some writers' charity, when they try and get writers outta prison. And Owen bid on a weekend in this country house hotel and he won it and he had to give his credit card details at the dinner. Some of the young girls from the publishers were there all tarted up, taking payment. He gave the girl his card. I remember that because he was pissed," she said, with a shadow of her former sullenness, "an' he paid eight hundred quid for it. Showin' off. Tryin' to make out he earned money like the others."

"He handed his credit card over to a girl from the publishers," repeated Strike. "Did she take the details at the table or—?"

"She couldn't make her little machine work," said Leonora. "She took it away and brought it back."

"Anyone else there you recognized?"

"Michael Fancourt was there with his publisher," she said, "on the other side of the room. That was before he moved to Roper Chard."

"Did he and Owen speak?"

"Not likely," she said.

"Right, what about—?" he said, and hesitated. They had never before acknowledged the existence of Kathryn Kent.

"His girlfriend coulda got at it any time, couldn't she?" said Leonora, as though she had read his mind.

"You knew about her?" he asked, matter-of-fact.

"Police said something," replied Leonora, her expression bleak. "There's always been someone. Way he was. Picking them up at his writing classes. I used to give him right tellings-off. When they said he was—when they said he was—he was tied up—"

She had started to cry again.

"I knew it must've been a woman what done it. He liked that. Got him going."

"You didn't know about Kathryn Kent before the police mentioned her?"

"I saw her name on a text on his phone one time but he said it was nothing. Said she was just one of his students. Like he always said. Told me he'd never leave us, me and Orlando."

She wiped her eyes under her outdated glasses with the back of a thin, trembling hand.

"But you never saw Kathryn Kent until she came to the door to say that her sister had died?"

"Was that her, was it?" asked Leonora, sniffing and dabbing at her eyes with her cuff. "Fat, i'n't she? Well, she could've got his credit card details any time, couldn't she? Taken it out of his wallet while he was sleeping."

It was going to be difficult to find and question Kathryn Kent, Strike knew. He was sure she would have absconded from her flat to avoid the attentions of the press.

"The things the murderer bought on the card," he said, changing tack, "were ordered online. You haven't got a computer at home, have you?"

"Owen never liked 'em, he preferred his old type—"

"Have you ever ordered shopping over the internet?"

"Yeah," she replied, and his heart sank a little. He had been hoping that Leonora might be that almost mythical beast: a computer virgin.

"Where did you do that?"

"Edna's, she let me borrow hers to order Orlando an art set for her birthday so I didn't have to go into town," said Leonora.

Doubtless the police would soon be confiscating and ripping apart the kind-hearted Edna's computer.

A woman with a shaved head and a tattooed lip at the next table began shouting at a warder, who had warned her to stay in her seat. Leonora cowered away from the prisoner as she erupted into obscenities and the officer approached.

"Leonora, there's one last thing," said Strike loudly, as the shouting at the next table reached a crescendo. "Did Owen say anything to you about meaning to go away, to take a break, before he walked out on the fifth?"

"No," she said, "'F course not."

The prisoner at the next table had been persuaded to quieten down. Her visitor, a woman similarly tattooed and only slightly less aggressive-looking, gave the prison officer the finger as she walked away.

"You can't think of anything Owen said or did that might've suggested he was planning to go away for a while?" Strike persisted as Leonora watched their neighbors with anxious, owl-like eyes.

"What?" she said distractedly. "No—he never tells—told me— always just went...If he knew he was going, why wouldn't he say good-bye?"

She began to cry, one thin hand over her mouth.

"What's going to happen to Dodo if they keep me in prison?" she asked him through her sobs. "Edna can't have her forever. She can't handle her. She went an' left Cheeky Monkey behind an' Dodo had done some pictures for me," and after a disconcerted moment or two

Strike decided that she must be talking about the plush orangutan that Orlando had been cradling on his visit to their house. "If they make me stay here—"

"I'm going to get you out," said Strike with more confidence than he felt; but what harm would it do to give her something to hold on to, something to get her through the next twenty-four hours?

Their time was up. He left the hall without looking back, wondering what it was about Leonora, faded and grumpy, fifty years old with a brain-damaged daughter and a hopeless life, that had inspired in him this fierce determination, this fury...

Because she didn't do it, came the simple answer. *Because she's innocent.*

In the last eight months a stream of clients had pushed open the engraved glass door bearing his name and the reasons they had sought him had been uncannily similar. They had come because they wanted a spy, a weapon, a means of redressing some balance in their favor or of divesting themselves of inconvenient connections. They came because they sought an advantage, because they felt they were owed retribution or compensation. Because overwhelmingly, they wanted more money.

But Leonora had come to him because she wanted her husband to come home. It had been a simple wish born of weariness and of love, if not for the errant Quine then for the daughter who missed him. For the purity of her desire, Strike felt he owed her the best he could give.

The cold air outside the prison tasted different. It had been a long time since Strike had been in an environment where following orders was the backbone of daily life. He could feel his freedom as he walked, leaning heavily on the stick, back towards the bus stop.

At the back of the bus, three drunken young women wearing headbands from which reindeer antlers protruded were singing:

"They say it's unrealistic,
But I believe in you Saint Nick..."

Bloody Christmas, thought Strike, thinking irritably of the presents he would be expected to buy for his nephews and godchildren, none of whose ages he could ever remember.

The bus groaned on through the slush and the snow. Lights of every color gleamed blurrily at Strike through the steamed-up bus window. Scowling, with his mind on injustice and murder, he effortlessly and silently repelled anyone who might have considered sitting in the seat beside him.

40

Be glad thou art unnam'd; 'tis not worth the owning.

Francis Beaumont and John Fletcher, *The False One*

Sleet, rain and snow pelted the office windows in turn the following day. Miss Brocklehurst's boss turned up at the office around midday to view confirmation of her infidelity. Shortly after Strike had bidden him farewell, Caroline Ingles arrived. She was harried, on her way to pick up her children from school, but determined to give Strike the card for the newly opened Golden Lace Gentleman's Club and Bar that she had found in her husband's wallet. Mr. Ingles's promise to stay well away from lap-dancers, call girls and strippers had been a requirement of their reconciliation. Strike agreed to stake out Golden Lace to see whether Mr. Ingles had again succumbed to temptation. By the time Caroline Ingles had left, Strike was very ready for the pack of sandwiches waiting for him on Robin's desk, but he had taken barely a mouthful when his phone rang.

Aware that their professional relationship was coming to a close, his brunet client was throwing caution to the winds and inviting Strike out to dinner. Strike thought he could see Robin smiling as she ate her sandwich, determinedly facing her monitor. He tried to decline with politeness, at first pleading his heavy workload and finally telling her that he was in a relationship.

"You never told me that," she said, suddenly cold.

"I like to keep my private and professional lives separate," he said.

She hung up halfway through his polite farewell.

"Maybe you should have gone out with her," said Robin innocently. "Just to make sure she'll pay her bill."

"She'll bloody pay," growled Strike, making up for lost time by cramming half a sandwich into his mouth. The phone buzzed. He groaned and looked down to see who had texted him.

His stomach contracted.

"Leonora?" asked Robin, who had seen his face fall.

Strike shook his head, his mouth full of sandwich.

The message comprised three words:

It was yours.

He had not changed his number since he had split up with Charlotte. Too much hassle, when a hundred professional contacts had it. This was the first time she had used it in eight months.

Strike remembered Dave Polworth's warning:

You be on the watch, Diddy, for signs of her galloping back over the horizon. Wouldn't be surprised if she bolts.

Today was the third, he reminded himself. She was supposed to be getting married tomorrow.

For the first time since he had owned a mobile phone, Strike wished it had the facility to reveal a caller's location. Had she sent this from the Castle of Fucking Croy, in an interlude between checking the canapés and the flowers in the chapel? Or was she standing on the corner of Denmark Street, watching his office like Pippa Midgley? Running away from a grand, well-publicized wedding like this would be Charlotte's crowning achievement, the very apex of her career of mayhem and disruption.

Strike put the mobile back into his pocket and started on his second sandwich. Deducing that she was not about to discover what had made Strike's expression turn stony, Robin screwed up her empty crisp packet, dropped it in the bin and said:

"You're meeting your brother tonight, aren't you?"

"What?"

"Aren't you meeting your brother—?"

"Oh yeah," said Strike. "Yeah."

"At the River Café?"

"Yeah."

It was yours.

"Why?" asked Robin.

Mine. The hell it was. If it even existed.

"What?" said Strike, vaguely aware that Robin had asked him something.

"Are you OK?"

"Yeah, I'm fine," he said, pulling himself together. "What did you ask me?"

"Why are you going to the River Café?"

"Oh. Well," said Strike, reaching for his own packet of crisps, "it's a long shot, but I want to speak to anyone who witnessed Quine and Tassel's row. I'm trying to get a handle on whether he staged it, whether he was planning his disappearance all along."

"You're hoping to find a member of staff who was there that night?" said Robin, clearly dubious.

"Which is why I'm taking Al," said Strike. "He knows every waiter in every smart restaurant in London. All my father's kids do."

When he had finished lunch he took a coffee into his office and closed the door. Sleet was again spattering his window. He could not resist glancing down into the frozen street, half-expecting (hoping?) to see her there, long black hair whipping around her perfect, pale face, staring up at him, imploring him with her flecked green-hazel eyes ... but there was nobody in the street except strangers swaddled against the relentless weather.

He was crazy on every count. She was in Scotland and it was much, much better so.

Later, when Robin had gone home, he put on the Italian suit that Charlotte had bought him over a year ago, when they had dined at this very restaurant to celebrate his thirty-fifth birthday. After pulling on his overcoat he locked his flat door and set out for the Tube in the subzero cold, still leaning on his stick.

Christmas assailed him from every window he passed; spangled lights, mounds of new objects, of toys and gadgets, fake snow on glass and sundry pre-Christmas sale signs adding a mournful note in the depths of the recession. More pre-Christmas revelers on the Friday-night Tube: girls in ludicrously tiny glittering dresses risking hypothermia for a fumble with the boy from Packaging. Strike felt weary and low.

The walk from Hammersmith was longer than he had remembered. As he proceeded down Fulham Palace Road he realized how close he was to Elizabeth Tassel's house. Presumably she had suggested the restaurant, a long way from the Quines' place in Ladbroke Grove, precisely because of its convenience to her.

After ten minutes Strike turned right and headed through the darkness towards Thames Wharf, through empty echoing streets, his breath rising in a smoky cloud. The riverside garden that in summer would be full of diners at white tableclothed chairs was buried under thick snow. The Thames glinted darkly beyond the pale carpet, iron-cold and menacing. Strike turned into the converted brick storage facility and was at once subsumed in light, warmth and noise.

There, just inside the door, leaning against the bar with his elbow on its shiny steel surface, was Al, deep in friendly conversation with the barman.

He was barely five foot ten, which was short for one of Rokeby's children, and carrying a little too much weight. His mouse-brown hair was slicked back; he had his mother's narrow jaw but he had inherited the weak divergent squint that added an attractive strangeness to Rokeby's handsome face and marked Al inescapably as his father's son.

Catching sight of Strike, Al let out a roar of welcome, bounced forwards and hugged him. Strike barely responded, being hampered by his stick and the coat he was trying to remove. Al fell back, looking sheepish.

"How are you, bruv?"

In spite of the comic Anglicism, his accent was a strange mid-Atlantic hybrid that testified to years spent between Europe and America.

"Not bad," said Strike, "you?"

"Yeah, not bad," echoed Al. "Not bad. Could be worse."

He gave a kind of exaggerated Gallic shrug. Al had been educated at Le Rosey, the international boarding school in Switzerland, and his body language still bore traces of the Continental manners he had met there. Something else underlay the response, however, something that Strike felt every time they met: Al's guilt, his defensiveness, a preparedness to meet accusations of having had a soft and easy life compared to his older brother.

"What're you having?" Al asked. "Beer? Fancy a Peroni?"

They sat side by side at the crammed bar, facing glass shelves of bottles, waiting for their table. Looking down the long, packed restaurant, with its industrial steel ceiling in stylized waves, its cerulean carpet and the wood-burning oven at the end like a giant beehive, Strike spotted a celebrated sculptor, a famous female architect and at least one well-known actor.

"Heard about you and Charlotte," Al said. "Shame."

Strike wondered whether Al knew somebody who knew her. He ran with a jet-set crowd that might well stretch to the future Viscount of Croy.

"Yeah, well," said Strike with a shrug. "For the best."

(He and Charlotte had sat here, in this wonderful restaurant by the river, and enjoyed their very last happy evening together. It had taken four months for the relationship to unravel and implode, four months of exhausting aggression and misery … *it was yours*.)

A good-looking young woman whom Al greeted by name showed them to their table; an equally attractive young man handed them menus. Strike waited for Al to order wine and for the staff to depart before explaining why they were there.

"Four weeks ago tonight," he told Al, "a writer called Owen Quine had a row with his agent in here. By all accounts the whole restaurant saw it. He stormed out and shortly afterwards—probably within days and maybe even that night—"

"—he was murdered," said Al, who had listened to Strike with his mouth open. "I saw it in the paper. You found the body."

His tone conveyed a yearning for details that Strike chose to ignore.

"There might be nothing to find out here, but I—"

"His wife did it, though," said Al, puzzled. "They've got her."

"His wife didn't do it," said Strike, turning his attention to the paper menu. He had noticed before now that Al, who had grown up surrounded by innumerable inaccurate press stories about his father and his family, never seemed to extend his healthy mistrust of British journalism to any other topic.

(It had had two campuses, Al's school: lessons by Lake Geneva in the summer months and then up to Gstaad for the winter; afternoons spent skiing and skating. Al had grown up breathing exorbitantly priced mountain air, cushioned by the companionship of other celebrity children. The distant snarling of the tabloids had been a mere background murmur in his life … this, at least, was how Strike interpreted the little that Al had told him of his youth.)

"The wife didn't do it?" said Al when Strike looked up again.

"No."

"Whoa. You gonna pull another Lula Landry?" asked Al, with a wide grin that added charm to his off-kilter stare.

"That's the idea," said Strike.

"You want me to sound out the staff?" asked Al.

"Exactly," said Strike.

He was amused and touched by how delighted Al seemed to be at being given the chance to render him service.

"No problem. No problem. Try and get someone decent for you. Where's Loulou gone? She's a smart cookie."

After they had ordered, Al strolled to the bathroom to see whether he could spot the smart Loulou. Strike sat alone, drinking Tignanello ordered by Al, watching the white-coated chefs working in the open kitchen. They were young, skilled and efficient. Flames darted, knives flickered, heavy iron pans moved hither and thither.

He's not stupid, Strike thought of his brother, watching Al meander back towards the table, leading a dark girl in a white apron. *He's just …*

"This is Loulou," said Al, sitting back down. "She was here that night."

"You remember the argument?" Strike asked her, focusing at once on the girl who was too busy to sit but stood smiling vaguely at him.

"Oh yeah," she said. "It was really loud. Brought the place to a standstill."

"Can you remember what the man looked like?" Strike said, keen to establish that she had witnessed the right row.

"Fat bloke wearing a hat, yeah," she said. "Yelling at a woman with gray hair. Yeah, they had a real bust-up. Sorry, I'm going to have to—"

And she was gone, to take another table's order.

"We'll grab her on the way back," Al reassured Strike. "Eddie sends his best, by the way. Wishes he could've been here."

"How's he doing?" asked Strike, feigning interest. Where Al had shown himself keen to forge a friendship, his younger brother, Eddie, seemed indifferent. He was twenty-four and the lead singer in his own band. Strike had never listened to any of their music.

"He's great," said Al.

Silence fell between them. Their starters arrived and they ate without talking. Strike knew that Al had achieved excellent grades in his International Baccalaureate. One evening in a military tent in Afghanistan, Strike had seen a photograph online of eighteen-year-old Al in a cream blazer with a crest on the pocket, long hair swept sideways and gleaming gold in the bright Geneva sun. Rokeby had had his arm around Al, beaming with paternal pride. The picture had been newsworthy because Rokeby had never been photographed in a suit and tie before.

"Hello, Al," said a familiar voice.

And, to Strike's astonishment, there stood Daniel Chard on crutches, his bald head reflecting the subtle spots shining from the industrial waves above them. Wearing a dark red open-necked shirt and a gray suit, the publisher looked stylish among this more bohemian crowd.

"Oh," said Al, and Strike could tell that he was struggling to place Chard, "er—hi—"

"Dan Chard," said the publisher. "We met when I was speaking to your father about his autobiography?"

"Oh—oh yeah!" said Al, standing up and shaking hands. "This is my brother Cormoran."

If Strike had been surprised to see Chard approach Al, it was nothing to the shock that registered on Chard's face at the sight of Strike.

"Your—your brother?"

"Half-brother," said Strike, inwardly amused by Chard's evident bewilderment. How could the hireling detective be related to the playboy prince?

The effort it had cost Chard to approach the son of a potentially lucrative subject seemed to have left him with nothing to spare for a three-way awkward silence.

"Leg feeling better?" Strike asked.

"Oh, yes," said Chard. "Much. Well, I'll … I'll leave you to your dinner."

He moved away, swinging deftly between tables, and resumed his seat where Strike could no longer watch him. Strike and Al sat back down, Strike reflecting on how very small London was once you reached a certain altitude; once you had left behind those who could not easily secure tables at the best restaurants and clubs.

"Couldn't remember who he was," said Al with a sheepish grin.

"He's thinking of writing his autobiography, is he?" Strike asked.

He never referred to Rokeby as Dad, but tried to remember not to call him Rokeby in front of Al.

"Yeah," said Al. "They're offering him big money. I dunno whether he's going to go with that bloke or one of the others. It'll probably be ghosted."

Strike wondered fleetingly how Rokeby might treat his eldest son's accidental conception and disputed birth in such a book. Perhaps, he thought, Rokeby would skip any mention of it. That would certainly be Strike's preference.

"He'd still like to meet you, you know," said Al, with an air of having screwed himself up to say it. "He's really proud … he read everything about the Landry case."

"Yeah?" said Strike, looking around the restaurant for Loulou, the waitress who remembered Quine.

"Yeah," said Al.

"So what did he do, interview publishers?" Strike asked. He thought of Kathryn Kent, of Quine himself, the one unable to find a publisher, the other dropped; and the aging rock star able to take his pick.

"Yeah, kind of," said Al. "I dunno if he's going to do it or not. I think that Chard guy was recommended to him."

"Who by?"

"Michael Fancourt," said Al, wiping his plate of risotto clean with a piece of bread.

"Rokeby knows Fancourt?" asked Strike, forgetting his resolution.

"Yeah," said Al, with a slight frown; then: "Let's face it, Dad knows everyone."

It reminded Strike of the way Elizabeth Tassel had said "I thought everyone knew" why she no longer represented Fancourt, but there was a difference. To Al, "everyone" meant the "someones": the rich, the famous, the influential. The poor saps who bought his father's music were nobodies, just as Strike had been nobody until he had burst into prominence for catching a killer.

"When did Fancourt recommend Roper Chard to—when did he recommend Chard?" asked Strike.

"Dunno—few months ago?" said Al vaguely. "He told Dad he'd just moved there himself. Half a million advance."

"Nice," said Strike.

"Told Dad to watch the news, that there'd be a buzz about the place once he moved."

Loulou the waitress had moved back into view. Al hailed her again; she approached with a harried expression.

"Give me ten," she said, "and I'll be able to talk. Just give me ten."

While Strike finished his pork, Al asked about his work. Strike was surprised by the genuineness of Al's interest.

"D'you miss the army?" Al asked.

"Sometimes," admitted Strike. "What are you up to these days?"

He felt a vague guilt at not having asked already. Now that he came to think about it, he was not clear how, or whether, Al had ever earned his living.

"Might be going into business with a friend," said Al.

Not working, then, thought Strike.

"Bespoke services … leisure opportunities," muttered Al.

"Great," said Strike.

"Will be if it comes to anything," said Al.

A pause. Strike looked around for Loulou, the whole point of being here, but she was out of sight, busy as Al had probably never been busy in his life.

"You've got credibility, at least," said Al.

"Hmn?" said Strike.

"Made it on your own, haven't you?" said Al.

"What?"

Strike realized that there was a one-sided crisis happening at the table. Al was looking at him with a mixture of mingled defiance and envy.

"Yeah, well," said Strike, shrugging his large shoulders.

He could not think of any more meaningful response that would not sound superior or aggrieved, nor did he wish to encourage Al in what seemed to be an attempt to have a more personal conversation than they had ever managed.

"You're the only one of us who doesn't use it," said Al. "Don't suppose it would've helped in the army, anyway, would it?"

Futile to pretend not to know what "it" was.

"S'pose not," said Strike (and indeed, on the rare occasions that his parentage had attracted the attention of fellow soldiers he had met nothing but incredulity, especially given how little he looked like Rokeby).

But he thought wryly of his flat on this ice-cold winter night: two and a half cluttered rooms, ill-fitting windowpanes. Al would be spending tonight in Mayfair, in their father's staffed house. It might be salutary to show his brother the reality of independence before he romanticized it too much...

"S'pose you think this is self-pitying bloody whinging?" demanded Al.

Strike had seen Al's graduation photograph online a bare hour after interviewing an inconsolable nineteen-year-old private who had accidentally shot his best friend in the chest and neck with a machine gun.

"Everyone's entitled to whinge," said Strike.

Al looked as though he might take offense, then, reluctantly, grinned.

Loulou was suddenly beside them, clutching a glass of water and deftly removing her apron with one hand before she sat down with them.

"OK, I've got five minutes," she said to Strike without preamble. "Al says you want to know about that jerk of a writer?"

365

"Yeah," said Strike, focusing at once. "What makes you say he was a jerk?"

"He loved it," she said, sipping her water.

"Loved—?"

"Causing a scene. He was yelling and swearing, but it was for show, you could tell. He wanted everyone to hear him, he wanted an audience. He wasn't a good actor."

"Can you remember what he said?" asked Strike, pulling out a notebook. Al was watching excitedly.

"There was loads of it. He called the woman a bitch, said she'd lied to him, that he'd put the book out himself and screw her. But he was enjoying himself," she said. "It was fake fury."

"And what about Eliz—the woman?"

"Oh, she was bloody furious," said Loulou cheerfully. "*She* wasn't pretending. The more he ponced about waving his arms and shouting at her, the redder she got—shaking with anger, she could hardly contain herself. She said something about 'roping in that stupid bloody woman' and I think it was around then that he stormed out, parking her with the bill, everyone staring at her—she looked mortified. I felt awful for her."

"Did she try and follow him?"

"No, she paid and then went into the loo for a bit. I wondered whether she was crying, actually. Then she left."

"That's very helpful," said Strike. "You can't remember anything else they said to each other?"

"Yeah," said Loulou calmly, "he shouted, 'All because of Fancourt and his limp fucking dick.'"

Strike and Al stared at her.

"'All because of Fancourt and his limp fucking dick'?" repeated Strike.

"Yeah," said Loulou. "That was the bit that made the restaurant go quiet—"

"You can see why it would," commented Al, with a snigger.

"She tried to shout him down, she was absolutely incensed, but he wasn't having any of it. He was loving the attention. Lapping it up.

"Look, I've got to get going," said Loulou, "sorry." She stood up and re-tied her apron. "See you, Al."

She did not know Strike's name, but smiled at him as she bustled away again.

Daniel Chard was leaving; his bald head had reappeared over the crowd, accompanied by a group of similarly aged and elegant people, all of them walking out together, talking, nodding to each other. Strike watched them go with his mind elsewhere. He did not notice the removal of his empty plate.

All because of Fancourt and his limp fucking dick ...

Odd.

I can't shake this mad bloody idea that Owen did it to himself. That he staged it ...

"You all right, bruv?" asked Al.

A note with a kiss: *Payback time for both of us ...*

"Yeah," said Strike.

Load of gore and arcane symbolism ... stoke that man's vanity and you could get him to do anything you wanted ... two hermaphrodites, two bloody bags ... A beautiful lost soul, that's what he said to me ... the silkworm was a metaphor for the writer, who has to go through agonies to get at the good stuff ...

Like the turning lid that finds its thread, a multitude of disconnected facts revolved in Strike's mind and slid suddenly into place, incontrovertibly correct, unassailably right. He turned his theory around and around: it was perfect, snug and solid.

The problem was that he could not yet see how to prove it.

41

Think'st thou my thoughts are lunacies of love?
No, they are brands firèd in Pluto's forge…

Robert Greene, Orlando Furioso

Strike rose early next morning after a night of broken sleep, tired, frustrated and edgy. He checked his phone for messages before showering and after dressing, then went downstairs into his empty office, irritated that Robin was not there on a Saturday and feeling the absence, unreasonably, as a mark of her lack of commitment. She would have been a useful sounding board this morning; he would have liked company after his revelation of the previous evening. He considered phoning her, but it would be infinitely more satisfying to tell her face to face rather than doing it over the telephone, particularly if Matthew were listening in.

Strike made himself tea but let it grow cold while he pored over the Quine file.

The sense of his impotence ballooned in the silence. He kept checking his mobile.

He wanted to do something, but he was completely stymied by lack of official status, having no authority to make searches of private property or to enforce the cooperation of witnesses. There was nothing he could do until his interview with Michael Fancourt on Monday, unless… Ought he to call Anstis and lay his theory before him? Strike frowned, running thick fingers through his dense hair, imagining Anstis's patronizing response. There was literally not a shred of evidence. All was conjecture—*but I'm right*, thought Strike with easy arrogance, *and he's screwed up.* Anstis had neither the wit nor the imagination to appreciate a theory that explained every oddity in the killing, but which would seem to him incredible compared to the easy solution, riddled with inconsistencies and unanswered questions though the case against Leonora was.

Explain, Strike demanded of an imaginary Anstis, *why a woman smart enough to spirit away his guts without trace would have been dumb enough to order ropes and a burqa on her own credit card. Explain why a mother with no relatives, whose sole preoccupation in life is the well-being of her daughter, would risk a life sentence. Explain why, after years of accommodating Quine's infidelity and sexual quirks to keep their family together, she suddenly decided to kill him?*

But to the last question Anstis might just have a reasonable answer: that Quine had been on the verge of leaving his wife for Kathryn Kent. The author's life had been well insured: perhaps Leonora would have decided that financial security as a widow would be preferable to an uncertain hand-to-mouth existence while her feckless ex squandered money on his second wife. A jury would buy that version of events, especially if Kathryn Kent took the stand and confirmed that Quine had promised to marry her.

Strike was afraid that he had blown his chance with Kathryn Kent, turning up unexpectedly on her doorstep as he had—in retrospect a clumsy, inept move. He had scared her, looming out of the darkness on her balcony, making it only too easy for Pippa Midgley to paint him as Leonora's sinister stooge. He ought to have proceeded with finesse, eased himself into her confidence the way he had done with Lord Parker's PA, so that he could extract confessions like teeth under the influence of concerned sympathy, instead of jack-booting to her door like a bailiff.

He checked his mobile again. No messages. He glanced at his watch. It was barely half past nine. Against his will, he felt his attention tugging to be free of the place where he wanted and needed it—on Quine's killer, and the things that must be done to secure an arrest—to the seventeenth-century chapel in the Castle of Croy...

She would be getting dressed, no doubt in a bridal gown costing thousands. He could imagine her naked in front of the mirror, painting her face. He had watched her do it a hundred times; wielding the makeup brushes in front of dressing-table mirrors, hotel mirrors, so acutely aware of her own desirability that she almost attained unself-consciousness.

Was Charlotte checking her phone as the minutes slipped by, now that the short walk up the aisle was so close, now that it felt like the walk along a gangplank? Was she still waiting, hoping, for a response from Strike to her three-word message of yesterday?

And if he sent an answer now ... what would it take to make her turn her back on the wedding dress (he could imagine it hanging like a ghost in the corner of her room) and pull on her jeans, throw a few things in a holdall and slip out of a back door? Into a car, her foot flat to the floor, heading back south to the man who had always meant escape ...

"Fuck this," Strike muttered.

He stood up, shoved the mobile in his pocket, threw back the last of his cold tea and pulled on his overcoat. Keeping busy was the only answer: action had always been his drug of choice.

Sure though he was that Kathryn Kent would have decamped to a friend's now that the press had found her, and notwithstanding the fact that he regretted turning up unannounced on her doorstep, he returned to Clem Attlee Court only to have his suspicions confirmed. Nobody answered the door, the lights were off and all seemed silent within.

An icy wind blew along the brick balcony. As Strike moved away, the angry-looking woman from next door appeared, this time eager to talk.

"She's gawn away. You press, are you?"

"Yeah," said Strike, because he could tell the neighbor was excited at the idea and because he did not want Kent to know that he had been back.

"The things your lot've written," she said with poorly disguised glee. "The things you've said about her! No, she's gawn."

"Any idea when she'll be back?"

"Nah," said the neighbor with regret. Her pink scalp was visible through the sparse, tightly permed gray hair. "I could call ya," she suggested. "If she shows up again."

"That'd be very helpful," said Strike.

His name had been in the papers a little too recently to hand over one of his cards. He tore out a page of his notebook, wrote his number out for her and handed it over with a twenty-pound note.

"Cheers," she said, businesslike. "See ya."

He passed a cat on his way back downstairs, the same one, he was sure, at which Kathryn Kent had taken a kick. It watched him with wary but superior eyes as he passed. The gang of youths he had met previously had gone; too cold today if your warmest item of clothing was a sweatshirt.

Limping through the slippery gray snow required physical effort, which helped distract his busy mind, making moot the question of whether he was moving from suspect to suspect on Leonora's behalf, or Charlotte's. Let the latter continue towards the prison of her own choosing: he would not call, he would not text.

When he reached the Tube, he pulled out his phone and telephoned Jerry Waldegrave. He was sure that the editor had information that Strike needed, that he had not known he needed before his moment of revelation in the River Café, but Waldegrave did not pick up. Strike was not surprised. Waldegrave had a failing marriage, a moribund career and a daughter to worry about; why take a detective's calls too? Why complicate your life when it did not need complicating, when you had a choice?

The cold, the ringing of unanswered phones, silent flats with locked doors: he could do nothing else today. Strike bought a newspaper and went to the Tottenham, sitting himself beneath one of the voluptuous women painted by a Victorian set-designer, cavorting with flora in their flimsy draperies. Today Strike felt strangely as though he was in a waiting room, whiling away the hours. Memories like shrapnel, forever embedded, infected by what had come later ... words of love and undying devotion, times of sublime happiness, lies upon lies upon lies ... his attention kept sliding away from the stories he was reading.

His sister Lucy had once said to him in exasperation, "Why do you put up with it? Why? Just because she's beautiful?"

And he had answered: "It helps."

She had expected him to say "no," of course. Though they spent so much time trying to make themselves beautiful, you were not supposed to admit to women that beauty mattered. Charlotte *was* beautiful, the most beautiful woman he had ever seen, and he had never rid himself of a sense of wonder at her looks, nor of the gratitude they inspired, nor of pride by association.

Love, Michael Fancourt had said, *is a delusion.*

Strike turned the page on a picture of the Chancellor of the Exchequer's sulky face without seeing it. Had he imagined things in Charlotte that had never been there? Had he invented virtues for her, to add luster to her staggering looks? He had been nineteen when they met. It seemed incredibly young to Strike now, as he sat in this pub carrying a good two stone of excess weight, missing half a leg.

Perhaps he *had* created a Charlotte in her own image who had never existed outside his own besotted mind, but what of it? He had loved the real Charlotte too, the woman who had stripped herself bare in front of him, demanding whether he could still love her if she did *this*, if she confessed to *this*, if she treated him like *this* ... until finally she had found his limit and beauty, rage and tears had been insufficient to hold him, and she had fled into the arms of another man.

And maybe that's love, he thought, siding in his mind with Michael Fancourt against an invisible and censorious Robin, who for some reason seemed to be sitting in judgment on him as he sat drinking Doom Bar and pretending to read about the worst winter on record. *You and Matthew* ... Strike could see it even if she could not: the condition of being with Matthew was not to be herself.

Where was the couple that saw each other clearly? In the endless parade of suburban conformity that seemed to be Lucy and Greg's marriage? In the tedious variations on betrayal and disillusionment that brought a never-ending stream of clients to his door? In the willfully blind allegiance of Leonora Quine to a man whose every fault had been excused because "he's a writer," or the hero worship that Kathryn Kent and Pippa Midgley had brought to the same fool, trussed like a turkey and disemboweled?

Strike was depressing himself. He was halfway down his third pint. As he wondered whether he was going to have a fourth, his mobile buzzed on the table where he had laid it, facedown.

He drank his beer slowly while the pub filled up around him, looking at his phone, taking bets against himself. *Outside the chapel, giving me one last chance to stop it? Or she's done it and wants to let me know?*

He drank the last of his beer before flipping the mobile over.

Congratulate me. Mrs. Jago Ross.

Strike stared at the words for a few seconds, then slid the phone into his pocket, got up, folded the newspaper under his arm and set off home.

As he walked with the aid of his stick back to Denmark Street he remembered words from his favorite book, unread for a very long time, buried at the bottom of the box of belongings on his landing.

> ... *difficile est longum subito deponere amoren,*
> *difficile est, uerum hoc qua lubet efficias ...*
> ... it is hard to throw off long-established love:
> Hard, but this you must manage somehow ...

The restlessness that had consumed him all day had gone. He felt hungry and in need of relaxation. Arsenal were playing Fulham at three; there was just time to cook himself a late lunch before kick-off.

And after that, he thought, he might go round to see Nina Lascelles. Tonight was not a night he fancied spending alone.

42

MATHEO: ... an odd toy.
GIULIANO: Ay, to mock an ape withal.

Ben Jonson, *Every Man in His Humour*

Robin arrived at work on Monday morning feeling tired and vaguely battle-weary, but proud of herself.

She and Matthew had spent most of the weekend discussing her job. In some ways (strange to think this, after nine years together) it had been the deepest and most serious conversation that they had ever had. Why had she not admitted for so long that her secret interest in investigative work had long predated meeting Cormoran Strike? Matthew had seemed stunned when she had finally confessed to him that she had had an ambition to work in some form of criminal investigation since her early teens.

"I'd have thought it would've been the last thing..." Matthew had mumbled, tailing off but referring obliquely, as Robin knew, to the reason she had dropped out of university.

"I just never knew how to say it to you," she told him. "I thought you'd laugh. So it wasn't Cormoran making me stay, or anything to do with him as a—as a person" (she had been on the verge of saying "as a man," but saved herself just in time). "It was me. It's what I want to do. I love it. And now he says he'll train me, Matt, and that's what I always wanted."

The discussion had gone on all through Sunday, the disconcerted Matthew shifting slowly, like a boulder.

"How much weekend work?" he had asked her suspiciously.

"I don't know; when it's needed. Matt, I love the job, don't you understand? I don't want to pretend anymore. I just want to do it, and I'd like your support."

In the end he had put his arms around her and agreed. She had tried not to feel grateful that his mother had just died, making him, she could not help thinking, just a little more amenable to persuasion than he might usually have been.

Robin had been looking forward to telling Strike about this mature development in her relationship but he was not in the office when she arrived. Lying on the desk beside her tiny tinsel tree was a short note in his distinctive, hard-to-read handwriting:

No milk, gone out for breakfast, then to Hamleys, want to beat crowds. PS Know who killed Quine.

Robin gasped. Seizing the phone, she called Strike's mobile, only to hear the engaged signal.

Hamleys would not open until ten but Robin did not think she could bear to wait that long. Again and again she pressed redial while she opened and sorted the post, but Strike was still on the other call. She opened emails, the phone clamped to one ear; half an hour passed, then an hour, and still the engaged tone emanated from Strike's number. She began to feel irritated, suspecting that it was a deliberate ploy to keep her in suspense.

At half past ten a soft ping from the computer announced the arrival of an email from an unfamiliar sender called Clodia2@live.com, who had sent nothing but an attachment labeled *FYI*.

Robin clicked on it automatically, still listening to the engaged tone. A large black-and-white picture swelled to fill her computer monitor.

The backdrop was stark; an overcast sky and the exterior of an old stone building. Everyone in the picture was out of focus except the bride, who had turned to look directly at the camera. She was wearing a long, plain, slim-fitting white gown with a floor-length veil held in place by a thin diamond band. Her black hair was flying like the folds of tulle in what looked like a stiff breeze. One hand was clasped in that of a blurred figure in a morning suit who appeared to be laughing, but

375

her expression was unlike any bride's that Robin had ever seen. She looked broken, bereft, haunted. Her eyes staring straight into Robin's as though they alone were friends, as though Robin were the only one who might understand.

Robin lowered the mobile she had been listening to and stared at the picture. She had seen that extraordinarily beautiful face before. They had spoken once, on the telephone: Robin remembered a low, attractively husky voice. This was Charlotte, Strike's ex-fiancée, the woman she had once seen running from this very building.

She was *so* beautiful. Robin felt strangely humbled by the other woman's looks, and awed by her profound sadness. Sixteen years, on and off, with Strike—Strike, with his pube-like hair, his boxer's profile and his half a leg ... not that those things mattered, Robin told herself, staring transfixed at this incomparably stunning, sad bride ...

The door opened. Strike was suddenly there beside her, two carrier bags of toys in his hands, and Robin, who had not heard him coming up the stairs, jumped as though she had been caught pilfering from the petty cash.

"Morning," he said.

She reached hastily for the computer mouse, trying to close down the picture before he could see it, but her scramble to cover up what she was viewing drew his eyes irresistibly to the screen. Robin froze, shamefaced.

"She sent it a few minutes ago, I didn't know what it was when I opened it. I'm ... sorry."

Strike stared at the picture for a few seconds then turned away, setting the bags of toys down on the floor by her desk.

Robin hesitated, then closed the file, deleted the email and emptied the trash folder.

"Cheers," he said, straightening up, and by his manner informed her that there would be no discussion of Charlotte's wedding picture. "I've got about thirty missed calls from you on my phone."

"Well, what do you expect?" said Robin with spirit. "Your note— you said—"

"I had to take a call from my aunt," said Strike. "An hour and ten minutes on the medical complaints of everyone in St. Mawes, all because I told her I'm going home for Christmas."

He laughed at the sight of her barely contained frustration.

"All right, but we've got to be quick. I've just realized there's something we could do this morning before I meet Fancourt."

Still wearing his coat he sat down on the leather sofa and talked for ten solid minutes, laying his theory before her in detail.

When he had finished there was a long silence. The misty, mystical image of the boy-angel in her local church floated into Robin's mind as she stared at Strike in near total disbelief.

"Which bit's causing you problems?" asked Strike kindly.

"Er..." said Robin.

"We already agreed that Quine's disappearance might not've been spontaneous, right?" Strike asked her. "If you add together the mattress at Talgarth Road—convenient, in a house that hasn't been used in twenty-five years—and the fact that a week before he vanished Quine told that bloke in the bookshop he was going away and bought himself reading material—and the waitress at the River Café saying Quine wasn't really angry when he was shouting at Tassel, that he was enjoying himself—I think we can hypothesize a staged disappearance."

"OK," she said. This part of Strike's theory seemed the least outlandish to her. She did not know where to begin in telling him how implausible she found the rest of it, but the urge to pick holes made her say, "Wouldn't he have told Leonora what he was planning, though?"

"Course not. She can't act to save her life; he *wanted* her worried, so she'd be convincing when she went round telling everyone he'd disappeared. Maybe she'd involve the police. Make a fuss with the publisher. Start the panic."

"But that had never worked," said Robin. "He was always flouncing off and nobody cared—surely even he must have realized that he wasn't going to get massive publicity just for running away and hiding in his old house."

"Ah, but this time he was leaving behind him a book he thought was going to be the talk of literary London, wasn't he? He'd drawn as much attention to it as he could by rowing with his agent in the

377

middle of a packed restaurant, and making a public threat to self-publish. He goes home, stages the grand walkout in front of Leonora and slips off to Talgarth Road. Later that evening he lets in his accomplice without a second thought, convinced that they're in it together."

After a long pause Robin said bravely (because she was not used to challenging Strike's conclusions, which she had never known to be wrong):

"But you haven't got a single bit of evidence that there *was* an accomplice, let alone ... I mean ... it's all ... opinion."

He began to reiterate points he had already made, but she held up her hand to stop him.

"I heard all that the first time, but ... you're extrapolating from things people have said. There's no—no *physical* evidence at all."

"Of course there is," said Strike. "*Bombyx Mori.*"

"That's not—"

"It's the single biggest piece of evidence we've got."

"You're the one," said Robin, "who's always telling me: *means and opportunity.* You're the one who's always saying motive doesn't—"

"I haven't said a word about motive," Strike reminded her. "As it happens, I'm not sure what the motive was, although I've got a few ideas. And if you want more physical evidence, you can come and help me get it right now."

She looked at him suspiciously. In all the time she had worked for him he had never asked her to collect a physical clue.

"I want you to come and help me talk to Orlando Quine," he said, pushing himself back off the sofa. "I don't want to do it on my own, she's ... well, she's tricky. Doesn't like my hair. She's in Ladbroke Grove with the next-door neighbor, so we'd better get a move on."

"This is the daughter with learning difficulties?" Robin asked, puzzled.

"Yeah," said Strike. "She's got this monkey, plush thing, hangs round her neck. I've just seen a pile of them in Hamleys—they're really pajama cases. Cheeky Monkeys, they call them."

Robin was staring at him as though fearful for his sanity.

"When I met her she had it round her neck and she kept producing things out of nowhere—pictures, crayons and a card she sneaked off the kitchen table. I've just realized she was pulling it all out of the pajama case. She nicks things from people," Strike went on, "and she was in and out of her father's study all the time when he was alive. He used to give her paper to draw on."

"You're hoping she's carrying around a clue to her father's killer inside her pajama case?"

"No, but I think there's reasonable chance that she picked up a bit of *Bombyx Mori* while she was skulking around in Quine's office, or that he gave her the back of an early draft to draw on. I'm looking for scraps of paper with notes on them, a discarded couple of paragraphs, anything. Look, I know it's a long shot," said Strike, correctly reading her expression, "but we can't get into Quine's study, the police have already been through everything in there and come up with nothing and I'm betting the notebooks and drafts Quine took away with him have been destroyed. Cheeky Monkey's the last place I can think of to look, and," he checked his watch, "we haven't got much time if we're going to Ladbroke Grove and back before I meet Fancourt.

"Which reminds me..."

He left the office. Robin heard him heading upstairs and thought he must be going to his flat, but then the sounds of rummaging told her that he was searching the boxes of his possessions on the landing. When he returned, he was holding a box of latex gloves that he had clearly filched before leaving the SIB for good, and a clear plastic evidence bag of exactly the size that airlines provided to hold toiletries.

"There's another crucial bit of physical evidence I'd like to get," he said, taking out a pair of gloves and handing them to an uncomprehending Robin. "I thought you could have a bash at getting hold of it while I'm with Fancourt this afternoon."

In a few succinct words he explained what he wanted her to get, and why.

Not altogether to Strike's surprise, a stunned silence followed his instructions.

"You're joking," said Robin faintly.

"I'm not."

She raised one hand unconsciously to her mouth.

"It won't be dangerous," Strike reassured her.

379

"That's not what's worrying me. Cormoran, that's—that's *horrific*. You—are you really serious?"

"If you'd seen Leonora Quine in Holloway last week, you wouldn't ask that," said Strike darkly. "We're going to have to be bloody clever to get her out of there."

Clever? thought Robin, still fazed as she stood with the limp gloves dangling from her hand. His suggestions for the day's activities seemed wild, bizarre and, in the case of the last, disgusting.

"Look," he said, suddenly serious. "I don't know what to tell you except I can feel it. *I can smell it, Robin.* Someone deranged, bloody dangerous but efficient lurking behind all this. They got that idiot Quine exactly where they wanted him by playing on his narcissism, and I'm not the only one who thinks so either."

Strike threw Robin her coat and she put it on; he was tucking evidence bags into his inside pocket.

"People keep telling me there was someone else involved: Chard says it's Waldegrave, Waldegrave says it's Tassel, Pippa Midgley's too stupid to interpret what's staring her in the face and Christian Fisher—well, he's got more perspective, not being in the book," said Strike. "He put his finger on it without realizing it."

Robin, who was struggling to keep up with Strike's thought processes and skeptical of those parts she could understand, followed him down the metal staircase and out into the cold.

"This murder," said Strike, lighting a cigarette as they walked down Denmark Street together, "was months if not years in the planning. Work of genius, when you think about it, but it's over-elaborate and that's going to be its downfall. You can't plot murder like a novel. There are always loose ends in real life."

Strike could tell that he was not convincing Robin, but he was not worried. He had worked with disbelieving subordinates before. Together they descended into the Tube and onto a Central line train.

"What did you get for your nephews?" Robin asked after a long silence.

"Camouflage gear and fake guns," said Strike, whose choice had been entirely motivated by the desire to aggravate his brother-in-law, "and I got Timothy Anstis a bloody big drum. They'll enjoy that at five o'clock on Christmas morning."

In spite of her preoccupation, Robin snorted with laughter.

The quiet row of houses from which Owen Quine had fled a month previously was, like the rest of London, covered in snow, pristine and pale on the roofs and grubby gray underfoot. The happy Inuit smiled down from his pub sign like the presiding deity of the wintry street as they passed beneath him.

A different policeman stood outside the Quine residence now and a white van was parked at the curb with its doors open.

"Digging for guts in the garden," Strike muttered to Robin as they drew nearer and spotted spades lying on the van floor. "They didn't have any luck at Mucking Marshes and they're not going to have any luck in Leonora's flower beds either."

"So *you* say," replied Robin *sotto voce*, a little intimidated by the staring policeman, who was quite handsome.

"So *you're* going to help me prove this afternoon," replied Strike under his breath. "Morning," he called to the watchful constable, who did not respond.

Strike seemed energized by his crazy theory, but if by any remote chance he was right, Robin thought, the killing had grotesque features even beyond that carved-out corpse...

They headed up the front path of the house beside the Quines', bringing them within feet of the watchful PC. Strike rang the bell, and after a short wait the door opened revealing a short, anxious-looking woman in her early sixties who was wearing a housecoat and wool-trimmed slippers.

"Are you Edna?" Strike asked.

"Yes," she said timidly, looking up at him.

When Strike introduced himself and Robin Edna's furrowed brow relaxed, to be replaced by a look of pathetic relief.

"Oh, it's *you*, I've heard all about *you*. You're helping Leonora, you're going to get her out, aren't you?"

Robin felt horribly aware of the handsome PC, listening to all of it, feet away.

"Come in, come in," said Edna, backing out of their way and beckoning them enthusiastically inside.

"Mrs.—I'm sorry, I don't know your surname," began Strike,

wiping his feet on the doormat (her house was warm, clean and much cozier than the Quines', though identical in layout).

"Call me Edna," she said, beaming at him.

"Edna, thank you—you know, you ought to ask to see ID before you let anyone into your house."

"Oh, but," said Edna, flustered, "Leonora told me all about you ... "

Strike insisted, nevertheless, on showing her his driving license before following her down the hall into a blue-and-white kitchen much brighter than Leonora's.

"She's upstairs," said Edna when Strike explained that they had come to see Orlando. "She's not having a good day. Do you want coffee?"

As she flitted around fetching cups she talked nonstop in the pent-up fashion of the stressed and lonely.

"Don't get me wrong, I don't mind having her, poor lamb, but... " She looked hopelessly between Strike and Robin then blurted out, "But how long for? They've no family, you see. There was a social worker round yesterday, checking on her; she said if I couldn't keep her she'd have to go in a home or something; I said, you can't do that to Orlando, they've never been apart, her and her mum, no, she can stay with me, but... "

Edna glanced at the ceiling.

"She's very unsettled just now, very upset. Just wants her mum to come home and what can I say to her? I can't tell her the truth, can I? And there they are next door, digging up the whole garden, they've gone and dug up Mr. Poop ... "

"Dead cat," Strike muttered under his breath to Robin as tears bubbled behind Edna's spectacles and bounced down her round cheeks.

"Poor lamb," she said again.

When she had given Strike and Robin their coffees Edna went upstairs to fetch Orlando. It took ten minutes for her to persuade the girl to come downstairs, but Strike was glad to see Cheeky Monkey clutched in her arms when she appeared, today dressed in a grubby tracksuit and wearing a sullen expression.

"He's called like a giant," she announced to the kitchen at large when she saw Strike.

"I am," said Strike, nodding. "Well remembered."

Orlando slid into the chair that Edna pulled out for her, holding her orangutan tightly in her arms.

"I'm Robin," said Robin, smiling at her.

"Like a bird," said Orlando at once. "Dodo's a bird."

"It's what her mum and dad called her," explained Edna.

"We're both birds," said Robin.

Orlando gazed at her, then got up and walked out of the kitchen without speaking.

Edna sighed deeply.

"She takes upset over anything. You never know what she's—"

But Orlando had returned with crayons and a spiral-bound drawing pad that Strike was sure had been bought by Edna to try to keep her happy. Orlando sat down at the kitchen table and smiled at Robin, a sweet, open smile that made Robin feel unaccountably sad.

"I'm going to draw you a robin," she announced.

"I'd *love* that," said Robin.

Orlando set to work with her tongue between her teeth. Robin said nothing, but watched the picture develop. Feeling that Robin had already forged a better rapport with Orlando than he had managed, Strike ate a chocolate biscuit offered by Edna and made small talk about the snow.

Eventually Orlando finished her picture, tore it out of the pad and pushed it across to Robin.

"It's beautiful," said Robin, beaming at her. "I wish I could draw a dodo, but I can't draw at all." This, Strike knew, was a lie. Robin drew very well; he had seen her doodles. "I've got to give you something, though."

She rummaged in her bag, watched eagerly by Orlando, and eventually pulled out a small round makeup mirror decorated on the back with a stylized pink bird.

"There," said Robin. "Look. That's a flamingo. Another bird. You can keep that."

Orlando took her gift with parted lips, staring at it.

"Say thank you to the lady," prompted Edna.

"Thank you," said Orlando and she slid the mirror inside the pajama case.

"Is he a bag?" asked Robin with bright interest.

"My monkey," said Orlando, clutching the orangutan closer. "My daddy give him to me. My daddy died."

"I'm sorry to hear that," said Robin quietly, wishing that the image of Quine's body had not slid instantly into her mind, his torso as hollow as a pajama case . . .

Strike surreptitiously checked his watch. The appointment with Fancourt was drawing ever closer. Robin sipped some coffee and asked:

"Do you keep things in your monkey?"

"I like your hair," said Orlando. "It's shiny and yellow."

"Thank you," said Robin. "Have you got any other pictures in there?" Orlando nodded.

"C'n I have a biscuit?" she asked Edna.

"Can I see your other pictures?" Robin asked as Orlando munched.

And after a brief pause for consideration, Orlando opened up her orangutan.

A sheaf of crumpled pictures came out, on an assortment of different sized and colored papers. Neither Strike nor Robin turned them over at first, but made admiring comments as Orlando spread them out across the table, Robin asking questions about the bright starfish and the dancing angels that Orlando had drawn in crayon and felt tip. Basking in their appreciation, Orlando dug deeper into her pajama case for her working materials. Up came a used typewriter cartridge, oblong and gray, with a thin strip tape carrying the reversed words it had printed. Strike resisted the urge to palm it immediately as it disappeared beneath a tin of colored pencils and a box of mints, but kept his eye on it as Orlando laid out a picture of a butterfly through which could be seen traces of untidy adult writing on the back.

Encouraged by Robin, Orlando now brought out more: a sheet of stickers, a postcard of the Mendip Hills, a round fridge magnet that read *Careful! You may end up in my novel!* Last of all she showed them three images on better-quality paper: two proof book illustrations and a mocked-up book cover.

"My daddy gave me them from his work," Orlando said. "Dannulchar *touched* me when I wanted it," she said, pointing at a brightly colored picture that Strike recognized: Kyla the Kangaroo Who Loved to Bounce. Orlando had added a hat and handbag to Kyla and colored in the line drawing of a princess talking to a frog with neon felt tips.

Delighted to see Orlando so chatty, Edna made more coffee. Conscious of the time, but aware of the need not to provoke a row and a protective grab of all her treasures, Robin and Strike chatted as they picked up and examined each of the pieces of paper on the table. Whenever she thought something might be helpful, Robin slid it sideways to Strike.

There was a list of scribbled names on the back of the butterfly picture:

Sam Breville. Eddie Boyne? Edward Baskinville? Stephen Brook?

The postcard of the Mendip Hills had been sent in July and carried a brief message:

Weather great, hotel disappointing, hope the book's going well! V xx

Other than that, there was no trace of handwriting. A few of Orlando's pictures were familiar to Strike from his last visit. One had been drawn on the reverse of a child's restaurant menu, another on the Quines' gas bill.

"Well, we'd better head off," said Strike, draining his coffee cup with a decent show of regret. Almost absentmindedly he continued to hold the cover image for Dorcus Pengelly's *Upon the Wicked Rocks*. A bedraggled woman lay supine on the stony sands of a steep cliff-enclosed cove, with the shadow of a man falling across her midriff. Orlando had drawn thickly lined black fish in the seething blue water. The used typewriter cassette lay beneath the image, nudged there by Strike.

"I don't want you to go," Orlando told Robin, suddenly tense and tearful.

"It's been lovely, hasn't it?" said Robin. "I'm sure we'll see each other again. You'll keep your flamingo mirror, won't you, and I've got my robin picture—"

But Orlando had begun to wail and stamp. She did not want another good-bye. Under cover of the escalating furor Strike wrapped the type-writer cassette smoothly in the cover illustration for *Upon the Wicked Rocks* and slid it into his pocket, unmarked by his fingerprints.

They reached the street five minutes later, Robin a little shaken because Orlando had wailed and tried to grab her as she headed down the hall. Edna had had to physically restrain Orlando from following them.

"Poor girl," said Robin under her breath, so that the staring PC could not hear them. "Oh God, that was dreadful."

"Useful, though," said Strike.

"You got that typewriter ribbon?"

"Yep," said Strike, glancing over his shoulder to check that the PC was out of sight before taking out the cassette, still wrapped in Dorcus's cover, and tipping it into a plastic evidence bag. "And a bit more than that."

"You did?" said Robin, surprised.

"Possible lead," said Strike, "might be nothing."

He glanced again at his watch and sped up, wincing as his knee throbbed in protest.

"I'm going to have to get a move on if I'm not going to be late for Fancourt."

As they sat on the crowded Tube train carrying them back to central London twenty minutes later, Strike said:

"You're clear about what you're doing this afternoon?"

"Completely clear," said Robin, but with a note of reservation.

"I know it's not a fun job—"

"That's not what's bothering me."

"And like I say, it shouldn't be dangerous," he said, preparing to stand as they approached Tottenham Court Road. "But…"

Something made him reconsider, a slight frown between his heavy eyebrows.

"Your hair," he said.

"What's wrong with it?" said Robin, raising her hand self-consciously.

"It's memorable," said Strike. "Haven't got a hat, have you?"

"I—I could buy one," said Robin, feeling oddly flustered.

"Charge it to petty cash," he told her. "Can't hurt to be careful."

43

Hoy-day, what a sweep of vanity comes this way!

William Shakespeare, *Timon of Athens*

Strike walked up crowded Oxford Street, past snatches of canned carols and seasonal pop songs, and turned left into the quieter, narrower Dean Street. There were no shops here, just block-like buildings packed together with their different faces, white, red and dun, opening into offices, bars, pubs or bistro-type restaurants. Strike paused to allow boxes of wine to pass from delivery van to catering entrance: Christmas was a more subtle affair here in Soho, where the arts world, the advertisers and publishers congregated, and nowhere more so than at the Groucho Club.

A gray building, almost nondescript, with its black-framed windows and small topiaries sitting behind plain, convex balustrades. Its cachet lay not in its exterior but in the fact that relatively few were allowed within the members-only club for the creative arts. Strike limped over the threshold and found himself in a small hall area, where a girl behind a counter said pleasantly:

"Can I help you?"

"I'm here to meet Michael Fancourt."

"Oh yes—you're Mr. Strick?"

"That's me," said Strike.

He was directed through a long barroom with leather seats packed with lunchtime drinkers and up the stairs. As he climbed Strike reflected, not for the first time, that his Special Investigation Branch

387

training had not envisaged him conducting interviews without official sanction or authority, on a suspect's own territory, where his interviewee had the right to terminate the encounter without reason or apology. The SIB required its officers to organize their questioning in a template of *people, places, things* ... Strike never lost sight of the effective, rigorous methodology, but these days it was essential to disguise the fact that he was filing facts in mental boxes. Different techniques were required when interviewing those who thought they were doing you a favor.

He saw his quarry immediately he stepped into a second wooden-floored bar, where sofas in primary colors were set along the wall beneath paintings by modern artists. Fancourt was sitting slantwise on a bright red couch, one arm along its back, a leg a little raised in an exaggerated pose of ease. A Damien Hirst spot painting hung right behind his overlarge head, like a neon halo.

The writer had a thick thatch of graying dark hair, his features were heavy and the lines beside his generous mouth deep. He smiled as Strike approached. It was not, perhaps, the smile he would have given someone he considered an equal (impossible not to think in those terms, given the studied affectation of ease, the habitually sour expression), but a gesture to one whom he wished to be gracious.

"Mr. Strike."

Perhaps he considered standing up to shake hands, but Strike's height and bulk often dissuaded smaller men from leaving their seats. They shook hands across the small wooden table. Unwillingly, but left with no choice unless he wanted to sit on the sofa with Fancourt—a far too cozy situation, particularly with the author's arm lying along the back of it—Strike sat down on a solid round pouffe that was unsuited both to his size and his sore knee.

Beside them was a shaven-headed ex–soap star who had recently played a soldier in a BBC drama. He was talking loudly about himself to two other men. Fancourt and Strike ordered drinks, but declined menus. Strike was relieved that Fancourt was not hungry. He could not afford to buy anyone else lunch.

"How long've you been a member of this place?" he asked Fancourt, when the waiter had left.

"Since it opened. I was an early investor," said Fancourt. "Only club I've ever needed. I stay overnight here if I need to. There are rooms upstairs."

Fancourt fixed Strike with a consciously intense stare.

"I've been looking forward to meeting you. The hero of my next novel is a veteran of the so-called war on terror and its military corollaries. I'd like to pick your brains once we've got Owen Quine out of the way."

Strike happened to know a little about the tools available to the famous when they wished to manipulate. Lucy's guitarist father, Rick, was less famous than either Strike's father or Fancourt, but still celebrated enough to cause a middle-aged woman to gasp and tremble at the sight of him queuing for ice creams in St. Mawes—"ohmigod— *what are you doing here?*" Rick had once confided in the adolescent Strike that the one sure way to get a woman into bed was to tell her you were writing a song about her. Michael Fancourt's pronouncement that he was interested in capturing something of Strike in his next novel felt like a variation on the same theme. He had clearly not appreciated that seeing himself in print was neither a novelty to Strike, nor something he had ever chased. With an unenthusiastic nod to acknowledge Fancourt's request, Strike took out a notebook.

"D'you mind if I use this? Helps me remember what I want to ask you."

"Feel free," said Fancourt, looking amused. He tossed aside the copy of the *Guardian* that he had been reading. Strike saw the picture of a wizened but distinguished-looking old man who was vaguely familiar even upside down. The caption read: *Pinkelman at Ninety.*

"Dear old Pinks," said Fancourt, noticing the direction of Strike's gaze. "We're giving him a little party at the Chelsea Arts Club next week."

"Yeah?" said Strike, hunting for a pen.

"He knew my uncle. They did their national service together," said Fancourt. "When I wrote my first novel, *Bellafront*—I was fresh out of Oxford—my poor old Unc, trying to be helpful, sent a copy to Pinkelman, who was the only writer he'd ever met."

He spoke in measured phrases, as though some invisible third party were taking down every word in shorthand. The story sounded pre-rehearsed, as though he had told it many times, and perhaps he had; he was an oft-interviewed man.

"Pinkelman—at that time author of the seminal *Bunty's Big Adventure* series—didn't understand a word I'd written," Fancourt went on, "but to please my uncle he forwarded it to Chard Books, where it landed, most fortuitously, on the desk of the only person in the place who *could* understand it."

"Stroke of luck," said Strike.

The waiter returned with wine for Fancourt and a glass of water for Strike.

"So," said the detective, "were you returning a favor when you introduced Pinkelman to your agent?"

"I was," said Fancourt, and his nod held the hint of patronage of a teacher glad to note that one of his pupils had been paying attention. "In those days Pinks was with some agent who kept 'forgetting' to hand on his royalties. Whatever you say about Elizabeth Tassel, she's honest—in business terms, she's honest," Fancourt amended, sipping his wine.

"She'll be at Pinkelman's party too, won't she?" said Strike, watching Fancourt for his reaction. "She still represents him, doesn't she?"

"It doesn't matter to me if Liz is there. Does she imagine that I'm still burning with malice towards her?" asked Fancourt, with his sour smile. "I don't think I give Liz Tassel a thought from one year's end to the next."

"Why *did* she refuse to ditch Quine when you asked her to?" asked Strike.

Strike did not see why he should not deploy the direct attack to a man who had announced an ulterior motive for meeting within seconds of their first encounter.

"It was never a question of me asking her to drop Quine," said Fancourt, still in measured cadences for the benefit of that invisible amanuensis. "I explained that I could not remain at her agency while he was there, and left."

"I see," said Strike, who was well used to the splitting of hairs. "Why d'you think she let you leave? You were the bigger fish, weren't you?"

"I think it's fair to say that I was a barracuda compared to Quine's stickleback," said Fancourt with a smirk, "but, you see, Liz and Quine were sleeping together."

"Really? I didn't know that," said Strike, clicking out the nib of his pen.

"Liz arrived at Oxford," said Fancourt, "this strapping great girl who'd been helping her father castrate bulls and the like on sundry northern farms, *desperate* to get laid, and nobody fancied the job much. She had a thing for me, a *very* big thing—we were tutorial partners, juicy Jacobean intrigue calculated to get a girl going—but I never felt altruistic enough to relieve her of her virginity. We remained friends," said Fancourt, "and when she started her agency I introduced her to Quine, who notoriously preferred to plumb the bottom of the barrel, sexually speaking. The inevitable occurred."

"Very interesting," said Strike. "Is this common knowledge?"

"I doubt it," said Fancourt. "Quine was already married to his— well, his murderess, I suppose we have to call her now, don't we?" he said thoughtfully. "I'd imagine 'murderess' trumps 'wife' when defining a close relationship? And Liz would have threatened him with dire consequences if he'd been his usual indiscreet self about her bedroom antics, on the wild off-chance that I might yet be persuaded to sleep with her."

Was this blind vanity, Strike wondered, a matter of fact, or a mixture of both?

"She used to look at me with those big cow eyes, waiting, hoping..." said Fancourt, a cruel twist to his mouth. "After Ellie died she realized that I wasn't going to oblige her even when grief-stricken. I'd imagine she was unable to bear the thought of decades of future celibacy, so she stood by her man."

"Did you ever speak to Quine again after you left the agency?" Strike asked.

"For the first few years after Ellie died he'd scuttle out of any bar I entered," said Fancourt. "Eventually he got brave enough to remain in the same restaurant, throwing me nervous looks. No, I don't think we ever spoke to each other again," said Fancourt, as though the matter were of little interest. "You were injured in Afghanistan, I think?"

"Yeah," said Strike.

It might work on women, Strike reflected, the calculated intensity of the gaze. Perhaps Owen Quine had fixed Kathryn Kent and Pippa Midgley with the identical hungry, vampiric stare when he told them he would be putting them into *Bombyx Mori*...and they had been thrilled to think of part of themselves, their lives, forever encased in the amber of a writer's prose...

"How did it happen?" asked Fancourt, his eyes on Strike's legs.

"IED," said Strike. "What about Talgarth Road? You and Quine were co-owners of the house. Didn't you ever need to communicate about the place? Did you ever run into each other there?"

"Never."

"Haven't you been there to check on it? You've owned it—what—?"

"Twenty, twenty-five years, something like that," said Fancourt indifferently. "No, I haven't been inside since Joe died."

"I suppose the police have asked you about the woman who thinks she saw you outside on the eighth of November?"

"Yes," said Fancourt shortly. "She was mistaken."

Beside them, the actor was still in full and loud flow.

"...thought I'd bloody had it, couldn't see where the fuck I was supposed to be running, sand in my bloody eyes..."

"So you haven't been in the house since eighty-six?"

"No," said Fancourt impatiently. "Neither Owen nor I wanted it in the first place."

"Why not?"

"Because our friend Joe died there in exceptionally squalid circumstances. He hated hospitals, refused medication. By the time he fell unconscious the place was in a disgusting state and he, who had been the living embodiment of Apollo, was reduced to a sack of bones, his skin...it was a grisly end," said Fancourt, "made worse by Daniel Ch—"

Fancourt's expression hardened. He made an odd chewing motion as though literally eating unspoken words. Strike waited.

"He's an interesting man, Dan Chard," said Fancourt, with a palpable effort at reversing out of a cul-de-sac into which he had driven himself. "I thought Owen's treatment of him in *Bombyx Mori* was the biggest missed opportunity of all—though future scholars are hardly going to look to *Bombyx Mori* for subtlety of characterization, are they?" he added with a short laugh.

"How would you have written Daniel Chard?" Strike asked and Fancourt seemed surprised by the question. After a moment's consideration he said:

"Dan's the most *unfulfilled* man I've ever met. He works in a field where he's competent but unhappy. He craves the bodies of young men but can bring himself to do no more than draw them. He's full of inhibitions and self-disgust, which explains his unwise and hysterical response to Owen's caricature of him. Dan was dominated by a monstrous socialite mother who wanted her pathologically shy son to take over the family business. I think," said Fancourt, "I'd have been able to make something interesting of all that."

"Why did Chard turn down North's book?" Strike asked.

Fancourt made the chewing motion again, then said:

"I like Daniel Chard, you know."

"I had the impression that there had been a grudge at some point," said Strike.

"What gave you that idea?"

"You said that you 'certainly didn't expect to find yourself' back at Roper Chard when you spoke at their anniversary party."

"You were there?" said Fancourt sharply and when Strike nodded he said: "Why?"

"I was looking for Quine," said Strike. "His wife had hired me to find him."

"But, as we now know, she knew exactly where he was."

"No," said Strike, "I don't think she did."

"You *genuinely* believe that?" asked Fancourt, his large head tilted to one side.

"Yeah, I do," said Strike.

Fancourt raised his eyebrows, considering Strike intently as though he were a curiosity in a cabinet.

"So you didn't hold it against Chard that he turned down North's book?" Strike asked, returning to the main point.

After a brief pause Fancourt said:

"Well, yes, I did hold it against him. Exactly why Dan changed his mind about publishing it only Dan could tell you, but I think it was because there was a smattering of press around Joe's condition, drumming up middle-England disgust about the unrepentant book he was about to publish, and Dan, who had not realized that Joe now had full-blown AIDS, panicked. He didn't want to be associated with bathhouses and AIDS, so he told Joe he didn't want the book after all. It was an act of great cowardice and Owen and I—"

Another pause. How long had it been since Fancourt had bracketed himself and Quine together in amity?

"Owen and I believed that it killed Joe. He could hardly hold a pen, he was virtually blind, but he was trying desperately to finish the book before he died. We felt that was all that was keeping him alive. Then Chard's letter arrived canceling their contract; Joe stopped work and within forty-eight hours he was dead."

"There are similarities," said Strike, "with what happened to your first wife."

"They weren't the same thing at all," said Fancourt flatly.

"Why not?"

"Joe's was an infinitely better book."

Yet another pause, this time much longer.

"That's considering the matter," said Fancourt, "from a purely literary perspective. Naturally, there are other ways of looking at it."

He finished his glass of wine and raised a hand to indicate to the barman that he wanted another. The actor beside them, who had barely drawn breath, was still talking.

"…said, 'Screw authenticity, what d'you want me to do, saw my own bloody arm off?'"

"It must have been a very difficult time for you," said Strike.

"Yes," said Fancourt waspishly. "Yes, I think we can call it 'difficult.'"

"You lost a good friend and a wife within—what—months of each other?"

"A few months, yes."

"You were writing all through that time?"

"Yes," said Fancourt, with an angry, condescending laugh, "I was writing *all through that time*. It's my profession. Would anyone ask you whether you were *still in the army* while you were having private difficulties?"

"I doubt it," said Strike, without rancor. "What were you writing?"

"It was never published. I abandoned the book I was working on so that I could finish Joe's."

The waiter set a second glass in front of Fancourt and departed.

"Did North's book need much doing to it?"

"Hardly anything," said Fancourt. "He was a brilliant writer. I tidied up a few rough bits and polished the ending. He'd left notes about how he wanted it done. Then I took it to Jerry Waldegrave, who was with Roper."

Strike remembered what Chard had said about Fancourt's over-closeness to Waldegrave's wife and proceeded with some caution.

"Had you worked with Waldegrave before?"

"I've never worked with him on my own stuff, but I knew of him by reputation as a gifted editor and I knew that he'd liked Joe. We collaborated on *Towards the Mark*."

"He did a good job on it, did he?"

Fancourt's flash of bad temper had gone. If anything, he looked entertained by Strike's line of questioning.

"Yes," he said, taking a sip of wine, "very good."

"But you didn't want to work with him now you've moved to Roper Chard?"

"Not particularly," said Fancourt, still smiling. "He drinks a lot these days."

"Why d'you think Quine put Waldegrave in *Bombyx Mori*?"

"How can I possibly know that?"

"Waldegrave seems to have been good to Quine. It's hard to see why Quine felt the need to attack him."

"Is it?" asked Fancourt, eyeing Strike closely.

"Everyone I talk to seems to have a different angle on the Cutter character in *Bombyx Mori*."

"Really?"

"Most people seem outraged that Quine attacked Waldegrave at all. They can't see what Waldegrave did to deserve it. Daniel

Chard thinks the Cutter shows that Quine had a collaborator," said Strike.

"Who the hell does he think would have collaborated with Quine on *Bombyx Mori*?" asked Fancourt, with a short laugh.

"He's got ideas," said Strike. "Meanwhile Waldegrave thinks the Cutter's really an attack on you."

"But I'm Vainglorious," said Fancourt with a smile. "Everyone knows that."

"Why would Waldegrave think that the Cutter is about you?"

"You'll need to ask Jerry Waldegrave," said Fancourt, still smiling. "But I've got a funny feeling you think you know, Mr. Strike. And I'll tell you this: Quine was quite, quite wrong—as he really should have known."

Impasse.

"So in all these years, you've never managed to sell Talgarth Road?"

"It's been very difficult to find a buyer who satisfies the terms of Joe's will. It was a quixotic gesture of Joe's. He was a romantic, an idealist.

"I set down my feelings about all of this—the legacy, the burden, the poignancy of his bequest—in *House of Hollow*," said Fancourt, much like a lecturer recommending additional reading. "Owen had his say—such as it was—" added Fancourt, with the ghost of a smirk, "in *The Balzac Brothers*."

"*The Balzac Brothers* was about the house in Talgarth Road, was it?" asked Strike, who had not gleaned that impression during the fifty pages he had read.

"It was set there. Really it's about our relationship, the three of us," said Fancourt. "Joe dead in the corner and Owen and I trying to follow in his footsteps, make sense of his death. It was set in the studio where I think—from what I've read—you found Quine's body?"

Strike said nothing, but continued to take notes.

"The critic Harvey Bird called *The Balzac Brothers* 'wincingly, jaw-droppingly, sphincter-clenchingly awful.'"

"I just remember a lot of fiddling with balls," said Strike and Fancourt gave a sudden, unforced girlish titter.

"You've read it, have you? Oh yes, Owen was obsessed with his balls."

The actor beside them had paused for breath at last. Fancourt's words rang in the temporary silence. Strike grinned as the actor and his two dining companions stared at Fancourt, who treated them to his sour smile. The three men began talking hurriedly again.

"He had a real *idée fixe*," said Fancourt, turning back to Strike. "Picasso-esque, you know, his testicles the source of his creative power. He was obsessed in both his life and his work with machismo, virility, fertility. Some might say it was an odd fixation for a man who liked to be tied up and dominated, but I see it as a natural consequence ... the yin and yang of Quine's sexual persona. You'll have noticed the names he gave us in the book?"

"Vas and Varicocele," said Strike and he noted again that slight surprise in Fancourt that a man who looked like Strike read books, or paid attention to their contents.

"Vas—Quine—the duct that carries sperm from balls to penis—the healthy, potent, creative force. Varicocele—a painful enlargement of a vein in the testicle, sometimes leading to infertility. A typically crass Quine-esque allusion to the fact that I contracted mumps shortly after Joe died and in fact was too unwell to go to the funeral, but also to the fact that—as you've pointed out—I was writing under difficult circumstances around that time."

"You were still friends at this point?" Strike clarified.

"When he started the book we were still—in theory—friends," said Fancourt, with a grim smile. "But writers are a savage breed, Mr. Strike. If you want lifelong friendship and selfless camaraderie, join the army and learn to kill. If you want a lifetime of temporary alliances with peers who will glory in your every failure, write novels."

Strike smiled. Fancourt said with detached pleasure:

"*The Balzac Brothers* received some of the worst reviews I've ever read."

"Did you review it?"

"No," said Fancourt.

"You were married to your first wife at this point?" Strike asked.

"That's right," said Fancourt. The flicker of his expression was like the shiver of an animal's flank when a fly touches it.

"I'm just trying to get the chronology right—you lost her shortly after North died?"

"Euphemisms for death are so interesting, aren't they?" said Fancourt lightly. "I didn't 'lose' her. On the contrary, I tripped over her in the dark, dead in our kitchen with her head in the oven."

"I'm sorry," said Strike formally.

"Yes, well..."

Fancourt called for another drink. Strike could tell that a delicate point had been reached, where a flow of information might either be tapped, or run forever dry.

"Did you ever talk to Quine about the parody that caused your wife's suicide?"

"I've already told you, I never talked to him again about anything after Ellie died," said Fancourt calmly. "So, no."

"You were sure he wrote it, though?"

"Without question. Like a lot of writers without much to say, Quine was actually a good literary mimic. I remember him spoofing some of Joe's stuff and it was quite funny. He wasn't going to jeer *publicly* at Joe, of course, it did him too much good hanging around with the pair of us."

"Did anyone admit to seeing the parody before publication?"

"Nobody said as much to me, but it would have been surprising if they had, wouldn't it, given what it caused? Liz Tassel denied to my face that Owen had shown it to her, but I heard on the grapevine that she'd read it prepublication. I'm sure she encouraged him to publish. Liz was insanely jealous of Ellie."

There was a pause, then Fancourt said with an assumption of lightness:

"Hard to remember these days that there was a time when you had to wait for the ink and paper reviews to see your work excoriated. With the invention of the internet, any subliterate cretin can be Michiko Kakutani."

"Quine always denied writing it, didn't he?" Strike asked.

"Yes he did, gutless bastard that he was," said Fancourt, apparently unconscious of any lack of taste. "Like a lot of *soi-disant* mavericks, Quine was an envious, terminally competitive creature who craved adulation. He was terrified that he was going to be ostracized after Ellie died. Of course," said Fancourt, with unmistakable pleasure, "it happened anyway. Owen had benefited from a lot of reflected glory, being part of a triumvirate with Joe and me. When Joe died and I cut him adrift, he was seen for what he was: a man with a dirty imagination and an interesting style who had barely an idea that wasn't pornographic. Some authors," said Fancourt, "have only one good book in them. That was Owen. He shot his bolt—an expression he would have approved of—with *Hobart's Sin*. Everything after that was pointless rehashes."

"Didn't you say you thought *Bombyx Mori* was 'a maniac's masterpiece'?"

"You read that, did you?" said Fancourt, with vaguely flattered surprise. "Well, so it is, a true literary curiosity. I never denied that Owen could write, you know, it was just that he was never able to dredge up anything profound or interesting to write about. It's a surprisingly common phenomenon. But with *Bombyx Mori* he found his subject at last, didn't he? Everybody hates me, everyone's against me, I'm a genius and nobody can see it. The result is grotesque and comic, it reeks of bitterness and self-pity, but it has an undeniable fascination. And the language," said Fancourt, with the most enthusiasm he had so far brought to the discussion, "is admirable. Some passages are among the best things he ever wrote."

"This is all very useful," said Strike.

Fancourt seemed amused.

"How?"

"I've got a feeling that *Bombyx Mori*'s central to this case."

"'Case'?" repeated Fancourt, smiling. There was a short pause. "Are you *seriously* telling me that you still think the killer of Owen Quine is at large?"

"Yeah, I think so," said Strike.

"Then," said Fancourt, smiling still more broadly, "wouldn't it be more useful to analyze the writings of the killer rather than the victim?"

"Maybe," said Strike, "but we don't know whether the killer writes."

"Oh, nearly everyone does these days," said Fancourt. "The whole world's writing novels, but nobody's reading them."

"I'm sure people would read *Bombyx Mori*, especially if you did an introduction," said Strike.

"I think you're right," said Fancourt, smiling more broadly.

"When exactly did you read the book for the first time?"

"It would have been…let me see…"

Fancourt appeared to do a mental calculation.

"Not until the, ah, middle of the week after Quine delivered it," said Fancourt. "Dan Chard called me, told me that Quine was trying to suggest that I had written the parody of Ellie's book, and tried to persuade me to join him in legal action against Quine. I refused."

"Did Chard read any of it out to you?"

"No," said Fancourt, smiling again. "Frightened he might lose his star acquisition, you see. No, he simply outlined the allegation that Quine had made and offered me the services of his lawyers."

"When was this telephone call?"

"On the evening of the…seventh, it must have been," said Fancourt. "The Sunday night."

"The same day you filmed an interview about your new novel," said Strike.

"You're very well-informed," said Fancourt, his eyes narrowing.

"I watched the program."

"You know," said Fancourt, with a needle-prick of malice, "you don't have the appearance of a man who enjoys arts programs."

"I never said I enjoyed them," said Strike and was unsurprised to note that Fancourt appeared to enjoy his retort. "But I did notice that you misspoke when you said your first wife's name on camera."

Fancourt said nothing, but merely watched Strike over his wine-glass.

"You said 'Eff' then corrected yourself, and said 'Ellie,'" said Strike.

"Well, as you say—I misspoke. It can happen to the most articulate of us."

"In *Bombyx Mori*, your late wife—"

"—is called 'Effigy.'"

"Which is a coincidence," said Strike.

"Obviously," said Fancourt.

"Because you couldn't yet have known that Quine had called her 'Effigy' on the seventh."

"Obviously not."

"Quine's mistress got a copy of the manuscript fed through her letter box right after he disappeared," said Strike. "You didn't get sent an early copy, by any chance?"

The ensuing pause became overlong. Strike felt the fragile thread that he had managed to spin between them snap. It did not matter. He had saved this question for last.

"No," said Fancourt. "I didn't."

He pulled out his wallet. His declared intention of picking Strike's brains for a character in his next novel seemed, not at all to Strike's regret, forgotten. Strike pulled out some cash, but Fancourt held up a hand and said, with unmistakable offensiveness:

"No, no, allow me. Your press coverage makes much of the fact that you have known better times. In fact, it puts me in mind of Ben Jonson: 'I am a poor gentleman, a soldier; one that, in the better state of my fortunes, scorned so mean a refuge.'"

"Really?" said Strike pleasantly, returning his cash to his pocket. "I'm put more in mind of

> *"sicine subrepsti mi, atque intestina pururens*
> *ei misero eripuisti omnia nostra bona?*
> *Eripuisti, eheu, nostrae crudele uenenum*
> *Uitae, eheu nostrae pestis amicitiae."*

He looked unsmilingly upon Fancourt's astonishment. The writer rallied quickly.

"Ovid?"

"Catullus," said Strike, heaving himself off the low pouffe with the aid of the table. "Translates roughly:

> "So that's how you crept up on me, an acid eating away
> My guts, stole from me everything I most treasure?
> Yes, alas, stole: grim poison in my blood
> The plague, alas, of the friendship we once had.

"Well, I expect we'll see each other around," said Strike pleasantly. He limped off towards the stairs, Fancourt's eyes upon his back.

44

All his allies and friends rush into troops
Like raging torrents.

Thomas Dekker, *The Noble Spanish Soldier*

Strike sat for a long time on the sofa in his kitchen–sitting room
that night, barely hearing the rumble of the traffic on Charing
Cross Road and the occasional muffled shouts of more early
Christmas partygoers. He had removed his prosthesis; it was comfortable sitting there in his boxers, the end of his injured leg free
of pressure, the throbbing of his knee deadened by another double
dose of painkillers. Unfinished pasta congealed on the plate beside
him on the sofa, the sky beyond his small window achieved the
dark blue velvet depth of true night, and Strike did not move,
though wide awake.

It felt like a very long time since he had seen the picture of
Charlotte in her wedding dress. He had not given her another
thought all day. Was this the start of true healing? She had married
Jago Ross and he was alone, mulling the complexities of an elaborate
murder in the dim light of his chilly attic flat. Perhaps each of them
was, at last, where they really belonged.

On the table in front of him in the clear plastic evidence bag, still
half wrapped in the photocopied cover of *Upon the Wicked Rocks*, sat
the dark gray typewriter cassette that he had taken from Orlando. He
had been staring at it for what seemed like half an hour at least, feeling
like a child on Christmas morning confronted by a mysterious, inviting package, the largest under the tree. And yet he ought not to look,

or touch, lest he interfere with whatever forensic evidence might be gleaned from the tape. Any suspicion of tampering...

He checked his watch. He had promised himself not to make the call until half past nine. There were children to be wrestled into bed, a wife to placate after another long day on the job. Strike wanted time to explain fully...

But his patience had limits. Getting up with some difficulty, he took the keys to his office and moved laboriously downstairs, clutching the handrail, hopping and occasionally sitting down. Ten minutes later he reentered his flat and returned to the still-warm spot on the sofa carrying his penknife and wearing another pair of the latex gloves he had earlier given to Robin.

He lifted the typewriter tape and the crumpled cover illustration gingerly out of the evidence bag and set the cassette, still resting on the paper, on the rickety Formica-topped table. Barely breathing, he pulled out the toothpick attachment from his knife and inserted it delicately behind the two inches of fragile tape that were exposed. By dint of careful manipulation he managed to pull out a little more. Reversed words were revealed, the letters back to front.

YOB EIDDE WENK I THGUOHT DAH I DN

His sudden rush of adrenaline was expressed only in Strike's quiet sigh of satisfaction. He deftly tightened the tape again, using the knife's screwdriver attachment in the cog at the top of the cassette, the whole untouched by his hands, then, still wearing the latex gloves, slipped it back into the evidence bag. He checked his watch again. Unable to wait any longer, he picked up his mobile and called Dave Polworth.

"Bad time?" he asked when his old friend answered.

"No," said Polworth, sounding curious. "What's up, Diddy?"

"Need a favor, Chum. A big one."

The engineer, over a hundred miles away in his sitting room in Bristol, listened without interrupting while the detective explained what it was he wanted done. When finally he had finished, there was a pause.

"I know it's a big ask," Strike said, listening anxiously to the line crackling. "Dunno if it'll even be possible in this weather."

"Course it will," said Polworth. "I'd have to see when I could do it, though, Diddy. Got two days off coming up … not sure Penny's going to be keen … "

"Yeah, I thought that might be a problem," said Strike, "I know it'd be dangerous."

"Don't insult me, I've done worse than this," said Polworth. "Nah, she wanted me to take her and her mother Christmas shopping … but fuck it, Diddy, did you say this is life or death?"

"Close," said Strike, closing his eyes and grinning. "Life and liberty."

"And no Christmas shopping, boy, which suits old Chum. Consider it done, and I'll give you a ring if I've got anything, all right?"

"Stay safe, mate."

"Piss off."

Strike dropped the mobile beside him on the sofa and rubbed his face in his hands, still grinning. He might just have told Polworth to do something even crazier and more pointless than grabbing a passing shark, but Polworth was a man who enjoyed danger, and the time had come for desperate measures.

The last thing Strike did before turning out the light was to reread the notes of his conversation with Fancourt and to underline, so heavily that he sliced through the page, the word "Cutter."

45

Didst thou not mark the jest of the silkworm?

John Webster, *The White Devil*

Both the family home and Talgarth Road continued to be combed for forensic evidence. Leonora remained in Holloway. It had become a waiting game.

Strike was used to standing for hours in the cold, watching darkened windows, following faceless strangers; to unanswered phones and doors, blank faces, clueless bystanders; to enforced, frustrating inaction. What was different and distracting on this occasion was the small whine of anxiety that formed a backdrop to everything he did.

You had to maintain a distance, but there were always people who got to you, injustices that bit. Leonora in prison, white-faced and weeping, her daughter confused, vulnerable and bereft of both parents. Robin had pinned up Orlando's picture over her desk, so that a merry red-bellied bird gazed down upon the detective and his assistant as they busied themselves with other cases, reminding them that a curly-haired girl in Ladbroke Grove was still waiting for her mother to come home.

Robin, at least, had a meaningful job to do, although she felt that she was letting Strike down. She had returned to the office two days running with nothing to show for her efforts, her evidence bag empty. The detective had warned her to err on the side of caution, to bail at the least sign that she might have been noticed or remembered. He did not like to be explicit about how recognizable he thought her, even with her red-gold hair piled under a beanie hat. She was very good-looking.

"I'm not sure I need to be quite so cautious," she said, having followed his instructions to the letter.

"Let's remember what we're dealing with here, Robin," he snapped, anxiety continuing to whine in his gut. "Quine didn't rip out his own guts."

Some of his fears were strangely amorphous. Naturally he worried that the killer would yet escape, that there were great, gaping holes in the fragile cobweb of a case he was building, a case that just now was built largely out of his own reconstructive imaginings, that needed physical evidence to anchor it down lest the police and defense counsel blew it clean away. But he had other worries.

Much as he had disliked the Mystic Bob tag with which Anstis had saddled him, Strike had a sense of approaching danger now, almost as strongly as when he had known, without question, that the Viking was about to blow up around him. Intuition, they called it, but Strike knew it to be the reading of subtle signs, the subconscious joining of dots. A clear picture of the killer was emerging out of the mass of disconnected evidence, and the image was stark and terrifying: a case of obsession, of violent rage, of a calculating, brilliant but profoundly disturbed mind.

The longer he hung around, refusing to let go, the closer he circled, the more targeted his questioning, the greater the chance that the killer might wake up to the threat he posed. Strike had confidence in his own ability to detect and repel attack, but he could not contemplate with equanimity the solutions that might occur to a diseased mind that had shown itself fond of Byzantine cruelty.

The days of Polworth's leave came and went without tangible results.

"Don't give up now, Diddy," he told Strike over the phone. Characteristically, the fruitlessness of his endeavors seemed to have stimulated rather than discouraged Polworth. "I'm going to pull a sickie Monday. I'll have another bash."

"I can't ask you to do that," muttered Strike, frustrated. "The drive—"

"I'm offering, you ungrateful peg-legged bastard."

The Silkworm

"Penny'll kill you. What about her Christmas shopping?"

"What about my chance to show up the Met?" said Polworth, who disliked the capital and its inhabitants on long-held principle.

"You're a mate, Chum," said Strike.

When he had hung up, he saw Robin's grin.

"What's funny?"

"'Chum,'" she said. It sounded so public school, so unlike Strike.

"It's not what you think," said Strike. He was halfway through the story of Dave Polworth and the shark when his mobile rang again: an unknown number. He picked up.

"Is that Cameron—er—Strike?"

"Speaking."

"It's Jude Graham 'ere. Kath Kent's neighbor. She's back," said the female voice happily.

"That's good news," said Strike, with a thumbs-up to Robin.

"Yeah, she got back this morning. Got a friend staying with 'er. I asked 'er where she'd been, but she wouldn't say," said the neighbor.

Strike remembered that Jude Graham thought him a journalist.

"Is the friend male or female?"

"Female," she answered regretfully. "Tall skinny dark girl, she's always hanging around Kath."

"That's very helpful, Ms. Graham," said Strike. "I'll—er—put something through your door later for your trouble."

"Great," said the neighbor happily. "Cheers."

She rang off.

"Kath Kent's back at home," Strike told Robin. "Sounds like she's got Pippa Midgley staying with her."

"Oh," said Robin, trying not to smile. "I, er, suppose you're regretting you put her in a headlock now?"

Strike grinned ruefully.

"They're not going to talk to me," he said.

"No," Robin agreed. "I don't think they will."

"Suits them fine, Leonora in the clink."

"If you told them your whole theory, they might cooperate," suggested Robin.

Strike stroked his chin, looking at Robin without seeing her.

407

"I can't," he said finally. "If it leaks out that I'm sniffing up that tree, I'll be lucky not to get a knife in the back one dark night."

"Are you serious?"

"Robin," said Strike, mildly exasperated, "Quine was tied up and disemboweled."

He sat down on the arm of the sofa, which squeaked less than the cushions but groaned under his weight, and said:

"Pippa Midgley liked you."

"I'll do it," said Robin at once.

"Not alone," he said, "but maybe you could get me in? How about this evening?"

"Of course!" she said, elated.

Hadn't she and Matthew established new rules? This was the first time she had tested him, but she went to the telephone with confidence. His reaction when she told him that she did not know when she would be home that night could not have been called enthusiastic, but he accepted the news without demur.

So, at seven o'clock that evening, having discussed at length the tactics that they were about to employ, Strike and Robin proceeded separately through the icy night, ten minutes apart with Robin in the lead, to Stafford Cripps House.

A gang of youths stood again in the concrete forecourt of the block and they did not permit Robin to pass with the wary respect they had accorded Strike two weeks previously. One of them danced backwards ahead of her as she approached the inner stairs, inviting her to party, telling her she was beautiful, laughing derisively at her silence, while his mates jeered behind her in the darkness, discussing her rear view. As they entered the concrete stairwell her taunter's jeers echoed strangely. She thought he might be seventeen at most.

"I need to go upstairs," she said firmly as he slouched across the stairwell for his mates' amusement, but sweat had prickled on her scalp. *He's a kid*, she told herself. *And Strike's right behind you.* The thought gave her courage. "Get out of the way, please," she said.

He hesitated, dropped a sneering comment about her figure, and moved. She half expected him to grab her as she passed but he loped back to his mates, all of them calling filthy names after her as she climbed the stairs and emerged with relief, without being followed, on to the balcony leading to Kath Kent's flat.

The lights inside were on. Robin paused for a second, gathering herself, then rang the doorbell.

After some seconds the door opened a cautious six inches and there stood a middle-aged woman with a long tangle of red hair.

"Kathryn?"

"Yeah?" said the woman suspiciously.

"I've got some very important information for you," said Robin. "You need to hear this."

("Don't say 'I need to talk to you,'" Strike had coached her, "or 'I've got some questions.' You frame it so that it sounds like it's to her advantage. Get as far as you can without telling her who you are; make it sound urgent, make her worry she's going to miss something if she lets you go. You want to be inside before she can think it through. Use her name. Make a personal connection. Keep talking.")

"What?" demanded Kathryn Kent.

"Can I come in?" asked Robin. "It's very cold out here."

"Who are you?"

"You need to hear this, Kathryn."

"Who—?"

"Kath?" said someone behind her.

"Are you a journalist?"

"I'm a friend," Robin improvised, her toes over the threshold. "I want to help you, Kathryn."

"Hey—"

A familiar long pale face and large brown eyes appeared beside Kath's.

"It's her I told you about!" said Pippa. "She works with him—"

"Pippa," said Robin, making eye contact with the tall girl, "you know I'm on your side—there's something I need to tell you both, it's urgent—"

Her foot was two thirds of the way across the threshold. Robin put every ounce of earnest persuasiveness that she could muster into her expression as she looked into Pippa's panicked eyes.

"Pippa, I wouldn't have come if I didn't think it was really important—"

"Let her in," Pippa told Kathryn. She sounded scared.

The hall was cramped and seemed full of hanging coats. Kathryn led Robin into a small, lamplit sitting room with plain magnolia-painted walls. Brown curtains hung at the windows, the fabric so thin that the lights of buildings opposite and distant, passing cars shone through them. A slightly grubby orange throw covered the old sofa, which sat on a rug patterned with swirling abstract shapes, and the remains of a Chinese takeaway sat on the cheap pine coffee table. In the corner was a rickety computer table bearing a laptop. The two women, Robin saw, with a pang of something like remorse, had been decorating a small fake Christmas tree together. A string of lights lay on the floor and there were a number of decorations on the only armchair. One of them was a china disc reading *Future Famous Writer!*

"What d'you want?" demanded Kathryn Kent, her arms folded.

She was glaring at Robin through small, fierce eyes.

"May I sit down?" said Robin and she did so without waiting for Kathryn's answer. ("Make yourself at home as much as you can without being rude, make it harder for her to dislodge you," Strike had said.)

"What d'you want?" Kathryn Kent repeated.

Pippa stood in front of the windows, staring at Robin, who saw that she was fiddling with a tree ornament: a mouse dressed as Santa.

"You know that Leonora Quine's been arrested for murder?" said Robin.

"Of course I do. I'm the one," Kathryn pointed at her own ample chest, "who found the Visa bill with the ropes, the burqa and the overalls on it."

"Yes," said Robin, "I know that."

"Ropes and a burqa!" ejaculated Kathryn Kent. "Got more than he bargained for, didn't he? All those years thinking she was just some dowdy little...boring little—little *cow*—and look what she did to him!"

"Yes," said Robin, "I know it looks that way."

"What d'you mean, 'looks that'—?"

"Kathryn, I've come here to warn you: they don't think she did it."

("No specifics. Don't mention the police explicitly if you can avoid it, don't commit to a checkable story, keep it vague," Strike had told her.)

"What d'you mean?" repeated Kathryn sharply. "The police don't—?"

"And you had access to his card, more opportunities to copy it—"

Kathryn looked wildly from Robin to Pippa, who was clutching the Santa-mouse, white-faced.

"But Strike doesn't think you did it," said Robin.

"Who?" said Kathryn. She appeared too confused, too panicked, to think straight.

"Her boss," stage-whispered Pippa.

"Him!" said Kathryn, rounding on Robin again. "He's working for *Leonora!*"

"He doesn't think you did it," repeated Robin, "even with the credit card bill—the fact you even had it. I mean, it looks odd, but he's sure you had it by acci—"

"She gave it me!" said Kathryn Kent, flinging out her arms, gesticulating furiously. "His daughter—she gave it me, I never even looked on the back for weeks, never thought to. I was being *nice*, taking her crappy bloody picture and acting like it was good—I was being *nice!*"

"I understand that," said Robin. "We believe you, Kathryn, I promise. Strike wants to find the real killer, he's not like the police." ("Insinuate, don't state.") "*He's* not interested in just grabbing the next woman Quine might've—you know—"

The words *let tie him up* hung in the air, unspoken.

Pippa was easier to read than Kathryn. Credulous and easily panicked, she looked at Kathryn, who seemed furious.

"Maybe I don't care who killed him!" Kathryn snarled through clenched teeth.

"But you surely don't want to be arrest—?"

"I've only got your word for it they're interested in me! There's been nothing on the news!"

"Well … there wouldn't be, would there?" said Robin gently. "The police don't hold press conferences to announce that they think they might have the wrong pers—"

"Who had the credit card? *Her.*"

"Quine usually had it himself," said Robin, "and his wife's not the only person who had access."

"How d'you know what the police are thinking any more than I do?"

"Strike's got good contacts at the Met," said Robin calmly. "He was in Afghanistan with the investigating officer, Richard Anstis."

The name of the man who had interrogated her seemed to carry weight with Kathryn. She glanced at Pippa again.

"Why're you telling me this?" Kathryn demanded.

"Because we don't want to see another innocent woman arrested," said Robin, "because we think the police are wasting time sniffing around the wrong people and because," ("throw in a bit of self-interest once you've baited the hook, it keeps things plausible") "obviously," said Robin, with a show of awkwardness, "it would do Cormoran a lot of good if he was the one who got the real killer. Again," she added.

"Yeah," said Kathryn, nodding vehemently, "that's it, isn't it? He wants the publicity."

No woman who had been with Owen Quine for two years was going to believe that publicity wasn't an unqualified boon.

"Look, we just wanted to warn you how they're thinking," said Robin, "and to ask for your help. But obviously, if you don't want…"

Robin made to stand.

("Once you've laid it out for her, act like you can take it or leave it. You're there when she starts chasing you.")

"I've told the police everything I know," said Kathryn, who appeared disconcerted now that Robin, who was taller than her, had stood up again. "I haven't got anything else to say."

"Well, we're not sure they were asking the right questions," said Robin, sinking back onto the sofa. "You're a writer," she said, turning suddenly off the piste that Strike had prepared for her, her eyes on the laptop in the corner. "You notice things. You understood him and his work better than anyone else."

The unexpected swerve into flattery caused whatever words of fury Kathryn had been about to fling at Robin (her mouth had been open, ready to deliver them) to die in her throat.

"So?" Kathryn said. Her aggression felt a little fake now. "What d'you want to know?"

"Will you let Strike come and hear what you've got to say? He won't if you don't want him to," Robin assured her (an offer unsanctioned by her boss). "He respects your right to refuse." (Strike had made no such declaration.) "But he'd like to hear it in your own words."

"I don't know that I've got anything useful to say," said Kathryn, folding her arms again, but she could not disguise a ring of gratified vanity.

"I know it's a big ask," said Robin, "but if you help us get the real killer, Kathryn, you'll be in the papers for the *right* reasons."

The promise of it settled gently over the sitting room—Kathryn interviewed by eager and now admiring journalists, asking about her work, perhaps: *Tell me about* Melina's Sacrifice ...

Kathryn glanced sideways at Pippa, who said:

"That bastard *kidnapped* me!"

"You tried to attack him, Pip," said Kathryn. She turned a little anxiously to Robin. "*I* never told her to do that. She was—after we saw what he'd written in the book—we were both ... and we thought *he*—your boss—had been hired to fit us up."

"I understand," lied Robin, who found the reasoning tortuous and paranoid, but perhaps that was what spending time with Owen Quine did to a person.

"She got carried away and didn't think," said Kathryn, with a look of mingled affection and reproof at her protégée. "Pip's got temper issues."

"Understandable," said Robin hypocritically. "May I call Cormoran—Strike, I mean? Ask him to meet us here?"

She had already slipped her mobile out of her pocket and glanced down at it. Strike had texted her:

On balcony. Bloody freezing.

She texted back:

Wait 5.

In fact, she needed only three minutes. Softened by Robin's earnestness and air of understanding, and by the encouragement of the alarmed Pippa to let Strike in and find out the worst, when he finally knocked Kathryn proceeded to the front door with something close to alacrity.

The room seemed much smaller with his arrival. Next to Kathryn, Strike appeared huge and almost unnecessarily male; when she had swept it clear of Christmas ornaments, he dwarfed the only armchair. Pippa retreated to the end of the sofa and perched on the arm, throwing Strike looks composed of defiance and terror.

"D'you want a drink of something?" Kathryn threw at Strike in his heavy overcoat, with his size fourteen feet planted squarely on her swirly rug.

"Cup of tea would be great," he said.

She left for the tiny kitchen. Finding herself alone with Strike and Robin, Pippa panicked and scuttled after her.

"You've done bloody well," Strike murmured to Robin, "if they're offering tea."

"She's *very* proud of being a writer," Robin breathed back, "which means she could understand him in ways that other people ... "

But Pippa had returned with a box of cheap biscuits and Strike and Robin fell silent at once. Pippa resumed her seat at the end of the sofa, casting Strike frightened sidelong glances that had, as when she had cowered in their office, a whiff of theatrical enjoyment about them.

"This is very good of you, Kathryn," said Strike, when she had set a tray of tea on the table. One of the mugs, Robin saw, read *Keep Clam and Proofread.*

"We'll see," retorted Kent, her arms folded as she glared at him from a height.

"Kath, sit," coaxed Pippa, and Kathryn sat reluctantly down between Pippa and Robin on the sofa.

Strike's first priority was to nurse the tenuous trust that Robin had managed to foster; the direct attack had no place here. He therefore embarked on a speech echoing Robin's, implying that the authorities were having second thoughts about Leonora's arrest and that they were reviewing the current evidence, avoiding direct mention of the police yet implying with every word that the Met was now turning its attention to Kathryn Kent. As he spoke a siren echoed in the distance. Strike added assurances that he personally felt sure that Kent was completely in the clear, but that he saw her as a resource the police had failed to understand or utilize properly.

"Yeah, well, you could be right there," she said. She had not so much blossomed under his soothing words as unclenched. Picking up the *Keep Clam* mug she said with a show of disdain, "All they wanted to know about was our sex life."

The way Anstis had told it, Strike remembered, Kathryn had volunteered a lot of information on the subject without being put under undue pressure.

"I'm not interested in your sex life," said Strike. "It's obvious he wasn't—to be blunt—getting what he wanted at home."

"Hadn't slept with her in years," said Kathryn. Remembering the photographs in Leonora's bedroom of Quine tied up, Robin dropped her gaze to the surface of her tea. "They had nothing in common. He couldn't talk to her about his work, she wasn't interested, didn't give a damn. He told us—didn't he?"—she looked up at Pippa, perched on the arm of the sofa beside her—"she never even read his books properly. He wanted someone to connect to on that level. He could really talk to me about literature."

"And me," said Pippa, launching at once into a speech: "He was interested in identity politics, you know, and he talked to me for hours about what it was like for me being born, basically, in the wrong—"

"Yeah, he told me it was a relief to be able to talk to someone who actually understood his work," said Kathryn loudly, drowning Pippa out.

"I thought so," said Strike, nodding. "And the police didn't bother asking you about any of this, I take it?"

"Well, they asked where we met and I told them: on his creative writing course," said Kathryn. "It was just gradual, you know, he was interested in my writing..."

"... in our writing..." said Pippa quietly.

Kathryn talked at length, Strike nodding with every appearance of interest at the gradual progression of the teacher-student relationship to something much warmer, Pippa tagging along, it seemed, and leaving Quine and Kathryn only at the bedroom door.

"I write fantasy with a twist," said Kathryn and Strike was surprised and a little amused that she had begun to talk like Fancourt: in rehearsed phrases, in sound bites. He wondered fleetingly how many people who sat alone for hours as they scribbled their stories practiced talking about their work during their coffee breaks and he remembered what Waldegrave had told him about Quine, that he had freely admitted to role-playing interviews with a biro. "It's fantasy slash erotica really, but quite literary. And that's the thing about traditional publishing, you know, they don't want to take a chance on something that hasn't been seen before, it's all about what fits their sales categories, and if you're blending several genres, if you're creating something entirely new, they're afraid to take a chance... I know that *Liz Tassel*," Kathryn spoke the name as though it were a medical complaint, "told Owen my work was too *niche*. But that's the great thing about indie publishing, the freedom—"

"Yeah," said Pippa, clearly desperate to put in her two pennys' worth, "that's true, for genre fiction I think indie can be the way to go—"

"Except I'm not really genre," said Kathryn, with a slight frown, "that's my point—"

"—but Owen felt that for my memoir I'd do better going the traditional route," said Pippa. "You know, he had a real interest in gender identity and he was fascinated with what I'd been through. I introduced him to a couple of other transgendered people and he promised to talk to his editor about me, because he thought, with the right promotion, you know, and with a story that's never really been told—"

"Owen loved *Melina's Sacrifice*, he couldn't wait to read on. He was practically ripping it out of my hand every time I finished a chapter," said Kathryn loudly, "and he told me—"

She stopped abruptly in midflow. Pippa's evident irritation at being interrupted faded ludicrously from her face. Both of them, Robin could tell, had suddenly remembered that all the time Quine had been showering them with effusive encouragement, interest and praise, the characters of Harpy and Epicoene had been taking obscene shape on an old electric typewriter hidden from their eager gazes.

"So he talked to you about his own work?" Strike asked.

"A bit," said Kathryn Kent in a flat voice.

"How long was he working on *Bombyx Mori*, do you know?"

"Most of the time I knew him," she said.

"What did he say about it?"

There was a pause. Kathryn and Pippa looked at each other.

"I've already told him," Pippa told Kathryn, with a significant glance at Strike, "that he told us it was going to be different."

"Yeah," said Kathryn heavily. She folded her arms. "He didn't tell us it was going to be like that."

Like that…Strike remembered the brown, glutinous substance that had leaked from Harpy's breasts. It had been, for him, one of the most revolting images in the book. Kathryn's sister, he remembered, had died of breast cancer.

"Did he say what it was going to be like?" Strike asked.

"He lied," said Kathryn simply. "He said it was going to be the writer's journey or something but he made out … he told us we were going to be … "

"'Beautiful lost souls,'" said Pippa, on whom the phrase seemed to have impressed itself.

"Yeah," said Kathryn heavily.

"Did he ever read any of it to you, Kathryn?"

"No," she said. "He said he wanted it to be a—a—"

"Oh, *Kath*," said Pippa tragically. Kathryn had buried her face in her hands.

"Here," said Robin kindly, delving into her handbag for tissues.

"No," said Kathryn roughly, pushing herself off the sofa and disappearing into the kitchen. She came back with a handful of kitchen roll.

"He said," she repeated, "he wanted it to be a surprise. That bastard," she said, sitting back down. "*Bastard*."

She dabbed at her eyes and shook her head, the long mane of red hair swaying, while Pippa rubbed her back.

"Pippa told me," said Strike, "that Quine put a copy of the manuscript through your door."

"Yeah," said Kathryn.

It was clear that Pippa had already confessed to this indiscretion.

417

"Jude next door saw him doing it. She's a nosy bitch, always keeping tabs on me."

Strike, who had just put an additional twenty through the nosy neighbor's letter box as a thank-you for keeping him informed of Kathryn's movements, asked:

"When?"

"Early hours of the sixth," said Kathryn.

Strike could almost feel Robin's tension and excitement.

"Were the lights outside your front door working then?"

"Them? They've been out for months."

"Did she speak to Quine?"

"No, just peered out the window. It was two in the morning or something, she wasn't going to go outside in her nightie. But she'd seen him come and go loads of times. She knew what he l-looked like," said Kathryn on a sob, "in his s-stupid cloak and hat."

"Pippa said there was a note," said Strike.

"Yeah—'Payback time for both of us,'" said Kathryn.

"Have you still got it?"

"I burned it," said Kathryn.

"Was it addressed to you? 'Dear Kathryn'?"

"No," she said, "just the message and a bloody kiss. *Bastard!*" she sobbed.

"Shall I go and get us some real drink?" volunteered Robin surprisingly.

"There's some in the kitchen," said Kathryn, her reply muffled by application of the kitchen roll to her mouth and cheeks. "Pip, you get it."

"You were sure the note was from him?" asked Strike as Pippa sped off in pursuit of alcohol.

"Yeah, it was his handwriting, I'd know it anywhere," said Kathryn.

"What did you understand by it?"

"I dunno," said Kathryn weakly, wiping her overflowing eyes. "Payback for me because he had a go at his wife? And payback for him on everyone...even me. Gutless bastard," she said, unconsciously echoing Michael Fancourt. "He could've told me he didn't want...if he wanted to end it...why do that? *Why?* And it wasn't just me ... Pip ... making out he cared, talking to her about her life ... she's had an awful time ... I mean, her memoir's not great literature or anything, but—"

Pippa returned carrying clinking glasses and a bottle of brandy, and Kathryn fell silent.

"We were saving this for the Christmas pudding," said Pippa, deftly uncorking the cognac. "There you go, Kath."

Kathryn took a large brandy and swigged it down in one. It seemed to have the desired effect. With a sniff, she straightened her back. Robin accepted a small measure. Strike declined.

"When did you read the manuscript?" he asked Kathryn, who was already helping herself to more brandy.

"Same day I found it, on the ninth, when I got home to grab some more clothes. I'd been staying with Angela at the hospice, see ... he hadn't picked up any of my calls since bonfire night, not one, and I'd told him Angela was really bad, I'd left messages. Then I came home and found the manuscript all over the floor. I thought, Is that why he's not picking up, he wants me to read this first? I took it back to the hospice with me and read it there, while I was sitting by Angela."

Robin could only imagine how it would have felt to read her lover's depiction of her while she sat beside her dying sister's bed.

"I called Pip—didn't I?" said Kathryn; Pippa nodded, "—and told her what he'd done. I kept calling him, but he *still* wouldn't pick up. Well, after Angela had died I thought, Screw it. I'm coming to find *you*." The brandy had given color to Kathryn's wan cheeks. "I went to their house but when I saw her—his wife—I could tell she was telling the truth. He wasn't there. So I told her to tell him Angela was dead. He'd met Angela," said Kathryn, her face crumpling again. Pippa set down her own glass and put her arms around Kathryn's shaking shoulders, "I thought he'd realize at least what he'd done to me when I was losing ... when I'd lost ... "

For over a minute there were no sounds in the room but Kathryn's sobs and the distant yells of the youths in the courtyard below.

"I'm sorry," said Strike formally.

"It must have been awful for you," said Robin.

A fragile sense of comradeship bound the four of them now. They could agree on one thing, at least; that Owen Quine had behaved very badly.

"It's your powers of textual analysis I'm really here for," Strike told Kathryn when she had again dried her eyes, now swollen to slits in her face.

"What d'you mean?" she asked, but Robin heard gratified pride behind the curtness.

"I don't understand some of what Quine wrote in *Bombyx Mori*."

"It isn't hard," she said, and again she unknowingly echoed Fancourt: "It won't win prizes for subtlety, will it?"

"I don't know," said Strike. "There's one very intriguing character."

"Vainglorious?" she said.

Naturally, he thought, she would jump to that conclusion. Fancourt was famous.

"I was thinking of the Cutter."

"I don't want to talk about that," she said, with a sharpness that took Robin aback. Kathryn glanced at Pippa and Robin recognized the mutual glow, poorly disguised, of a shared secret.

"He pretended to be better than that," said Kathryn. "He pretended there were some things that were sacred. Then he went and..."

"Nobody seems to want to interpret the Cutter for me," said Strike.

"That's because some of us have some decency," said Kathryn.

Strike caught Robin's eye. He was urging her to take over.

"Jerry Waldegrave's already told Cormoran that he's the Cutter," she said tentatively.

"I like Jerry Waldegrave," said Kathryn defiantly.

"You met him?" asked Robin.

"Owen took me to a party, Christmas before last," she said. "Waldegrave was there. Sweet man. He'd had a few," she said.

"Drinking even then, was he?" interjected Strike.

It was a mistake; he had encouraged Robin to take over because he guessed that she seemed less frightening. His interruption made Kathryn clam up.

"Anyone else interesting at the party?" Robin asked, sipping her brandy.

"Michael Fancourt was there," said Kathryn at once. "People say he's arrogant, but I thought he was charming."

"Oh—did you speak to him?"

"Owen wanted me to stay well away," she said, "but I went to the Ladies and on the way back I just told him how much I'd loved *House of Hollow*. Owen wouldn't have liked that," she said with pathetic satisfaction. "Always going on about Fancourt being overrated, but *I* think he's marvelous. Anyway, we talked for a while and then someone pulled him away, but yes," she repeated defiantly, as though the shade of Owen Quine were in the room and could hear her praising his rival, "he was charming to *me*. Wished me luck with my writing," she said, sipping her brandy.

"Did you tell him you were Owen's girlfriend?" asked Robin.

"Yes," said Kathryn, with a twist to her smile, "and he laughed and said, 'You have my commiserations.' It didn't bother him. He didn't care about Owen anymore, I could tell. No, I think he's a nice man and a marvelous writer. People are envious, aren't they, when you're successful?"

She poured herself more brandy. She was holding it remarkably well. Other than the flush it had brought to her face, there was no sign of tipsiness at all.

"And you liked Jerry Waldegrave," said Robin, almost absent-mindedly.

"Oh, he's lovely," said Kathryn, on a roll now, praising anyone that Quine might have attacked. "Lovely man. He was very, *very* drunk, though. He was in a side room and people were steering clear, you know. That bitch Tassel told us to leave him to it, that he was talking gibberish."

"Why do you call her a bitch?" asked Robin.

"Snobby old cow," said Kathryn. "Way she spoke to me, to everyone. But I know what it was: she was upset because Michael Fancourt was there. I said to her—Owen had gone off to see if Jerry was all right, he wasn't going to leave him passed out in a chair, whatever that old bitch said—I told her: 'I've just been talking to Fancourt, he was charming.' She didn't like that," said Kathryn with satisfaction. "Didn't like the idea of him being charming to me when he hates her.

Owen told me she used to be in love with Fancourt and he wouldn't give her the time of day."

She relished the gossip, however old. For that night, at least, she had been an insider.

"She left soon after I told her that," said Kathryn with satisfaction. "Horrible woman."

"Michael Fancourt told me," said Strike, and the eyes of Kathryn and Pippa were instantly riveted on him, eager to hear what the famous writer might have said, "that Owen Quine and Elizabeth Tassel once had an affair."

One moment of stupefied silence and then Kathryn Kent burst out laughing. It was unquestionably genuine: raucous, almost joyful, shrieks filled the room.

"Owen and *Elizabeth Tassel?*"

"That's what he said."

Pippa beamed at the sight and sound of Kathryn Kent's exuberant, unexpected mirth. She rolled against the back of the sofa, trying to catch her breath; brandy slopped onto her trousers as she shook with what seemed entirely genuine amusement. Pippa caught the hysteria from her and began to laugh too.

"Never," panted Kathryn, "in ... a ... *million* ... years ... "

"This would have been a long time ago," said Strike, but her long red mane shook as she continued to roar with unfeigned laughter.

"Owen and Liz ... never. Never, ever ... you don't understand," she said, now dabbing at eyes wet with mirth. "He thought she was *awful*. He would've told me ... Owen talked about everyone he'd slept with, he wasn't a *gentleman* like that, was he, Pip? I'd have known if they'd ever ... I don't know *where* Michael Fancourt got that from. *Never*," said Kathryn Kent, with unforced merriment and total conviction.

The laughter had loosened her up.

"But you don't know what the Cutter really meant?" Robin asked her, setting her empty brandy glass down on the pine coffee table with the finality of a guest about to take their leave.

"I never said I didn't know," said Kathryn, still out of breath from her protracted laughter. "I *do* know. It was just awful, to do it to

Jerry. Such a bloody hypocrite...Owen tells me not to mention it to anyone and then he goes and puts it in *Bombyx Mori*..."

Robin did not need Strike's look to tell her to remain silent and let Kathryn's brandy-fueled good humor, her enjoyment of their undivided attention and the reflected glory of knowing sensitive secrets about literary figures do their work.

"All right," she said. "All right, here it is...

"Owen told me as we were leaving. Jerry was very drunk that night and you know his marriage is on the rocks, has been for years...he and Fenella had had a really terrible row the night before the party and she'd told him that their daughter might not be his. That she might be..."

Strike knew what was coming.

"...Fancourt's," said Kathryn, after a suitably dramatic pause. "The dwarf with the big head, the baby she thought of aborting because she didn't know whose it was, d'you see? The Cutter with his cuckold's horns...

"And Owen told me to keep my mouth shut. 'It's not funny,' he said, 'Jerry loves his daughter, only good thing he's got in his life.' But he talked about it all the way home. On and on about Fancourt and how much he'd hate finding out he had a daughter, because Fancourt never wanted kids...All that bullshit about protecting Jerry! Anything to get at Michael Fancourt. *Anything*."

46

Leander strived; the waves about him wound,
And pulled him to the bottom, where the ground
Was strewed with pearl ...

Christopher Marlowe, Hero and Leander

Grateful for the effect of cheap brandy and to Robin's particular combination of clearheadedness and warmth, Strike parted from her with many thanks half an hour later. Robin traveled home to Matthew in a glow of gratification and excitement, looking more kindly on Strike's theory as to the killer of Owen Quine than she had done before. This was partly because nothing that Kathryn Kent had said had contradicted it, but mainly because she felt particularly warm towards her boss after the shared interrogation.

Strike returned to his attic rooms in a less elevated frame of mind. He had drunk nothing but tea and believed more strongly than ever in his theory, but all the proof he could offer was a single typewriter cassette: it would not be enough to overturn the police case against Leonora.

There were hard frosts overnight on Saturday and Sunday, but during the daytime glimmers of sunshine pierced the cloud blanket. Rain turned some of the accumulated snow in the gutters to sliding slush. Strike brooded alone between his rooms and his office, ignoring a call from Nina Lascelles and turning down an invitation to dinner at Nick and Ilsa's, pleading paperwork but actually preferring solitude without pressure to discuss the Quine case.

He knew that he was acting as though he were held to a professional standard that had ceased to apply when he had left the Special

Investigation Branch. Though legally free to gossip to whomever he pleased about his suspicions, he continued to treat them as confidential. This was partly longstanding habit, but mainly because (much as others might jeer) he took extremely seriously the possibility that the killer might hear what he was thinking and doing. In Strike's opinion, the safest way of ensuring that secret information did not leak was not to tell anybody about it.

On Monday he was visited again by the boss and boyfriend of the faithless Miss Brocklehurst, whose masochism now extended to a wish to know whether she had, as he strongly suspected, a third lover hidden away somewhere. Strike listened with half his mind on the activities of Dave Polworth, who was starting to feel like his last hope. Robin's endeavors remained fruitless, in spite of the hours she was spending pursuing the evidence he had asked her to find.

At half past six that evening, as he sat in his flat watching the forecast, which predicted a return of arctic weather by the end of the week, his phone rang.

"Guess what, Diddy?" said Polworth down a crackling line.

"You're kidding me," said Strike, his chest suddenly tight with anticipation.

"Got the lot, mate."

"Holy shit," breathed Strike.

It had been his own theory, but he felt as astonished as if Polworth had done it all unaided.

"Bagged up here, waiting for you."

"I'll send someone for it first thing tomorrow—"

"And I'm gonna go home and have a nice hot bath," said Polworth.

"Chum, you're a bloody—"

"I know I am. We'll talk about my credit later. I'm fucking freezing, Diddy, I'm going home."

Strike called Robin with the news. Her elation matched his own.

"Right, tomorrow!" she said, full of determination. "Tomorrow I'm going to get it, I'm going to make sure—"

"Don't go getting careless," Strike talked over her. "It's not a competition."

He barely slept that night.

Robin made no appearance at the office until one in the afternoon, but the instant he heard the glass door bang and heard her calling him, he knew.

"You haven't—?"

"Yes," she said breathlessly.

She thought he was going to hug her, which would be crossing a line he had never even approached before, but the lunge she had thought might be meant for her was really for the mobile on his desk.

"I'm calling Anstis. We've done it, Robin."

"Cormoran, I think—" Robin started to say, but he did not hear her. He had hurried back into his office and closed the door behind him.

Robin lowered herself into her computer chair, feeling uneasy. Strike's muffled voice rose and fell beyond the door. She got up restlessly to visit the bathroom, where she washed her hands and stared into the cracked and spotted mirror over the sink, observing the inconveniently bright gold of her hair. Returning to the office, she sat down, could not settle to anything, noticed that she had not switched on her tiny tinsel Christmas tree, did so, and waited, absentmindedly biting her thumbnail, something she had not done for years.

Twenty minutes later, his jaw set and his expression ugly, Strike emerged from the office.

"Stupid fucking dickhead!" were his first words.

"No!" gasped Robin.

"He's having none of it," said Strike, too wound up to sit, but limping up and down the enclosed space. "He's had that bloody rag in the lockup analyzed and it's got Quine's blood on it—big effing deal, could've cut himself months ago. He's so in love with his own effing theory—"

"Did you say to him, if he just gets a warrant—?"

"*DICKHEAD!*" roared Strike, punching the metal filing cabinet so that it reverberated and Robin jumped.

"But he can't deny—once forensics are done—"

"That's the bleeding point, Robin!" he said, rounding on her. "Unless he searches *before* he gets forensics done, there might be nothing there to find!"

"But did you tell him about the typewriter?"

"If the simple fact that it's *there* doesn't hit the prick between the eyes—"

She ventured no more suggestions but watched him walk up and down, brow furrowed, too intimidated to tell him, now, what was worrying her.

"Fuck it," growled Strike on his sixth walk back to her desk. "Shock and awe. No choice. Al," he muttered, pulling out his mobile again, "and Nick."

"Who's Nick?" asked Robin, desperately trying to keep up.

"He's married to Leonora's lawyer," said Strike, punching buttons on his phone. "Old mate ... he's a gastroenterologist ... "

He retreated again to his office and slammed the door.

For want of anything else to do, Robin filled the kettle, her heart hammering, and made them both tea. The mugs cooled, untouched, while she waited.

When Strike emerged fifteen minutes later, he seemed calmer.

"All right," he said, seizing his tea and taking a gulp. "I've got a plan and I'm going to need you. Are you up for it?"

"Of course!" said Robin.

He gave her a concise outline of what he wanted to do. It was ambitious and would require a healthy dose of luck.

"Well?" Strike asked her finally.

"No problem," said Robin.

"We might not need you."

"No," said Robin.

"On the other hand, you could be key."

"Yes," said Robin.

"Sure that's all right?" Strike asked, watching her closely.

"No problem at all," said Robin. "I want to do it, I really do—it's just," she hesitated, "I think he—"

"What?" said Strike sharply.

"I think I'd better have a practice," said Robin.

"Oh," said Strike, eyeing her. "Yeah, fair enough. Got until Thursday, I think. I'll check the date now..."

He disappeared for the third time into his inner office. Robin returned to her computer chair.

She desperately wanted to play her part in the capture of Owen Quine's killer, but what she had been about to say, before Strike's sharp response panicked her out of it, was: "I think he might have seen me."

47

Ha, ha, ha, thou entanglest thyself in thine own work like a silkworm.

John Webster, *The White Devil*

By the light of the old-fashioned streetlamp the cartoonish murals covering the front of the Chelsea Arts Club were strangely eerie. Circus freaks had been painted on the rainbow-stippled walls of a long low line of ordinarily white houses knocked into one: a four-legged blonde girl, an elephant eating its keeper, an etiolated contortionist in prison stripes whose head appeared to be disappearing up his own anus. The club stood in a leafy, sleepy and genteel street, quiet with the snow that had returned with a vengeance, falling fast and mounting over roofs and pavements as though the brief respite in the arctic winter had never been. All through Thursday the blizzard had grown thicker and now, viewed through a rippling lamplit curtain of icy flakes, the old club in its fresh pastel colors appeared strangely insubstantial, pasteboard scenery, a *trompe l'œil* marquee.

Strike was standing in a shadowy alley off Old Church Street, watching as one by one they arrived for their small party. He saw the aged Pinkelman helped from his taxi by a stone-faced Jerry Waldegrave, while Daniel Chard stood in a fur hat on his crutches, nodding and smiling an awkward welcome. Elizabeth Tassel drew up alone in a cab, fumbling for her fare and shivering in the cold. Lastly, in a car with a driver, came Michael Fancourt. He took his time getting out of the car, straightening his coat before proceeding up the steps to the front door.

The detective, on whose dense curly hair the snow was falling thickly, pulled out his mobile and rang his half-brother.

"Hey," said Al, who sounded excited. "They're all in the dining room."

"How many?"

"'Bout a dozen of them."

"Coming in now."

Strike limped across the street with the aid of his stick. They let him in at once when he gave his name and explained that he was here as Duncan Gilfedder's guest.

Al and Gilfedder, a celebrity photographer whom Strike was meeting for the first time, stood a short way inside the entrance. Gilfedder seemed confused as to who Strike was, or why he, a member of this eccentric and charming club, had been asked by his acquaintance Al to invite a guest whom he did not know.

"My brother," said Al, introducing them. He sounded proud.

"Oh," said Gilfedder blankly. He wore the same type of glasses as Christian Fisher and his lank hair was cut in a straggly shoulder-length bob. "I thought your brother was younger."

"That's Eddie," said Al. "This is Cormoran. Ex-army. He's a detective now."

"Oh," said Gilfedder, looking even more bemused.

"Thanks for this," Strike said, addressing both men equally. "Get you another drink?"

The club was so noisy and packed it was hard to see much of it except glimpses of squashy sofas and a crackling log fire. The walls of the low-ceilinged bar were liberally covered in prints, paintings and photographs; it had the feeling of a country house, cozy and a little scruffy. As the tallest man in the room, Strike could see over the crowd's heads towards the windows at the rear of the club. Beyond lay a large garden lit by exterior lights so that it was illuminated in patches. A thick, pristine layer of snow, pure and smooth as royal icing, lay over verdant shrubbery and the stone sculptures lurking in the undergrowth.

Strike reached the bar and ordered wine for his companions, glancing as he did so into the dining room.

Those eating filled several long wooden tables. There was the Roper

Chard party, with a pair of French windows beside them, the garden icy white and ghostly behind the glass. A dozen people, some of whom Strike did not recognize, had gathered to honor the ninety-year-old Pinkelman, who was sitting at the head of the table. Whoever had been in charge of the *placement*, Strike saw, had sat Elizabeth Tassel and Michael Fancourt well apart. Fancourt was talking loudly into Pinkelman's ear, Chard opposite him. Elizabeth Tassel was sitting next to Jerry Waldegrave. Neither was speaking to the other.

Strike passed glasses of wine to Al and Gilfedder, then returned to the bar to fetch a whisky for himself, deliberately maintaining a clear view of the Roper Chard party.

"Why," said a voice, clear as a bell but somewhere below him, "are *you* here?"

Nina Lascelles was standing at his elbow in the same strappy black dress she had worn to his birthday dinner. No trace of her former giggly flirtatiousness remained. She looked accusatory.

"Hi," said Strike, surprised. "I didn't expect to see you here."

"Nor I you," she said.

He had not returned any of her calls for over a week, not since the night he had slept with her to rid himself of thoughts of Charlotte on her wedding day.

"So you know Pinkelman," said Strike, trying for small talk in the face of what he could tell was animosity.

"I'm taking over some of Jerry's authors now he's leaving. Pinks is one of them."

"Congratulations," said Strike. Still, she did not smile. "Waldegrave still came to the party, though?"

"Pinks is fond of Jerry. Why," she repeated, "are *you* here?"

"Doing what I was hired to do," said Strike. "Trying to find out who killed Owen Quine."

She rolled her eyes, clearly feeling that he was pushing his persistence past a joke.

"How did you get in here? It's members only."

"I've got a contact," said Strike.

"You didn't think of using me again, then?" she asked.

He did not much like the reflection of himself he saw in her large mouse-like eyes. There was no denying that he had used her repeat-edly. It had become cheap, shameful, and she deserved better.

"I thought that might be getting old," said Strike.

"Yeah," said Nina. "You thought right."

She turned from him and walked back to the table, filling the last vacant seat, between two employees whom he did not know.

Strike was in Jerry Waldegrave's direct line of vision. Waldegrave caught sight of him and Strike saw the editor's eyes widen behind his horn-rimmed glasses. Alerted by Waldegrave's transfixed stare, Chard twisted in his seat and he, too, clearly recognized Strike.

"How's it going?" asked Al excitedly at Strike's elbow.

"Great," said Strike. "Where's that Gilsomething gone?"

"Downed his drink and left. Doesn't know what the hell we're up to," said Al.

Al did not know why they were here either. Strike had told him nothing except that he needed entry to the Chelsea Arts Club tonight and that he might need a lift. Al's bright red Alfa Romeo Spider sat parked a little down the road. It had been agony on Strike's knee to get in and out of the low-slung vehicle.

As he had intended, half the Roper Chard table now seemed acutely aware of his presence. Strike was positioned so that he could see them reflected clearly in the dark French windows. Two Elizabeth Tassels were glaring at him over their menus, two Ninas were determinedly ignoring him and two shiny-pated Chards summoned a waiter each and muttered in their ears.

"Is that the bald bloke we saw in the River Café?" asked Al.

"Yeah," said Strike, grinning as the solid waiter separated from his reflected wraith and made his way towards them. "I think we're about to be asked whether we've got the right to be in here."

"Very sorry, sir," began the waiter in a mutter as he reached Strike, "but could I ask—?"

"Al Rokeby—my brother and I are here with Duncan Gilfedder," said Al pleasantly before Strike could respond. Al's tone expressed surprise that they had been challenged at all. He was a charming and privileged young man who was welcome everywhere, whose cre-dentials were impeccable and whose casual roping of Strike into the family pen conferred upon him that same sense of easy entitlement. Jonny Rokeby's eyes looked out of Al's narrow face. The waiter muttered hasty apologies and retreated.

"Are you just trying to put the wind up them?" asked Al, staring over at the publisher's table.

"Can't hurt," said Strike with a smile, sipping his whisky as he watched Daniel Chard deliver what was clearly a stilted speech in Pinkelman's honor. A card and present were brought out from under the table. For every look and smile they gave the old writer, there was a nervous glance towards the large, dark man staring at them from the bar. Michael Fancourt alone had not looked around. Either he remained in ignorance of the detective's presence, or was untroubled by it.

When starters had been put in front of them all, Jerry Waldegrave got to his feet and moved out from the table towards the bar. Nina and Elizabeth's eyes followed him. On Waldegrave's way to the bathroom he merely nodded at Strike, but on the way back, he paused.

"Surprised to see you here."

"Yeah?" said Strike.

"Yeah," said Waldegrave. "You're, er...making people feel uncomfortable."

"Nothing I can do about that," said Strike.

"You could try not staring us out."

"This is my brother Al," said Strike, ignoring the request.

Al beamed and held out a hand, which Waldegrave shook, seeming nonplussed.

"You're annoying Daniel," Waldegrave told Strike, looking directly into the detective's eyes.

"That's a shame," said Strike.

The editor rumpled his untidy hair.

"Well, if that's your attitude."

"Surprised you care how Daniel Chard feels."

"I don't particularly," said Waldegrave, "but he can make life unpleasant for other people when he's in a bad mood. I'd like tonight to go well for Pinkelman. I can't understand why you're here."

"Wanted to make a delivery," said Strike.

He pulled a blank white envelope out from an inside pocket.

"What is this?"

"It's for you," said Strike.

Waldegrave took it, looking utterly confused.

"Something you should think about," said Strike, moving closer to the bemused editor in the noisy bar. "Fancourt had mumps, you know, before his wife died."

"What?" said Waldegrave, bewildered.

"Never had kids. Pretty sure he's infertile. Thought you might be interested."

Waldegrave stared at him, opened his mouth, found nothing to say, then walked away, still clutching the white envelope.

"What was that?" Al asked Strike, agog.

"Plan A," said Strike. "We'll see."

Waldegrave sat back down at the Roper Chard table. Mirrored in the black window beside him, he opened the envelope Strike had given him. Puzzled, he pulled out a second envelope. There was a scribbled name on this one.

The editor looked up at Strike, who raised his eyebrows.

Jerry Waldegrave hesitated, then turned to Elizabeth Tassel and passed her the envelope. She read what was written on it, frowning. Her eyes flew to Strike's. He smiled and toasted her with his glass.

She seemed uncertain as to what to do for a moment; then she nudged the girl beside her and passed the envelope on.

It traveled up the table and across it, into the hands of Michael Fancourt.

"There we are," said Strike. "Al, I'm going into the garden for a fag. Stay here and keep your phone on."

"They don't allow mobiles—"

But Al caught sight of Strike's expression and amended hastily: "Will do."

48

Does the silkworm expend her yellow labors
For thee? For thee does she undo herself?

Thomas Middleton, The Revenger's Tragedy

The garden was deserted and bitterly cold. Strike sank up to his ankles in snow, unable to feel the cold seeping through his right trouser leg. All the smokers who would ordinarily have congregated on the smooth lawns had chosen the street instead. He plowed a solitary trench through the frozen whiteness, surrounded by silent beauty, coming to a halt beside a small round pond that had become a disc of thick gray ice. A plump bronze cupid sat in the middle on an oversized clam shell. It wore a wig of snow and pointed its bow and arrow, not anywhere that it might hit a human being, but straight up at the dark heavens.

Strike lit a cigarette and turned back to look at the blazing windows of the club. The diners and waiters looked like paper cutouts moving against a lit screen.

If Strike knew his man, he would come. Wasn't this an irresistible situation to a writer, to the compulsive spinner of experience into words, to a lover of the macabre and the strange?

And sure enough, after a few minutes Strike heard a door open, a snatch of conversation and music hastily muffled, then the sound of deadened footsteps.

"Mr. Strike?"

Fancourt's head looked particularly large in the darkness.

"Would it not be easier to go onto the street?"

"I'd rather do this in the garden," said Strike.

"I see."

Fancourt sounded vaguely amused, as though he intended, at least in the short term, to humor Strike. The detective suspected that it appealed to the writer's sense of theater that he should be the one summoned from the table of anxious people to talk to the man who was making them all so nervous.

"What's this about?" asked Fancourt.

"Value your opinion," said Strike. "Question of critical analysis of *Bombyx Mori*."

"Again?" said Fancourt.

His good humor was cooling with his feet. He pulled his coat more closely around him and said, the snow falling thick and fast:

"I've said everything I want to say about that book."

"One of the first things I was told about *Bombyx Mori*," said Strike, "was that it was reminiscent of your early work. Gore and arcane symbolism, I think were the words used."

"So?" said Fancourt, hands in his pockets.

"So, the more I've talked to people who knew Quine, the clearer it's become that the book that everyone's read bears only a vague resemblance to the one he claimed to be writing."

Fancourt's breath rose in a cloud before him, obscuring the little that Strike could see of his heavy features.

"I've even met a girl who says she heard part of the book that doesn't appear in the final manuscript."

"Writers cut," said Fancourt, shuffling his feet, his shoulders hunched up around his ears. "Owen would have done well to cut a great deal more. Several novels, in fact."

"There are also all the duplications from his earlier work," said Strike. "Two hermaphrodites. Two bloody bags. All that gratuitous sex."

"He was a man of limited imagination, Mr. Strike."

"He left behind a scribbled note with what looks like a bunch of possible character names on it. One of those names appears on a used typewriter cassette that came out of his study before the police sealed it off, but it's nowhere in the finished manuscript."

"So he changed his mind," said Fancourt irritably.

"It's an everyday name, not symbolic or archetypal like the names in the finished manuscript," said Strike.

His eyes becoming accustomed to the darkness, Strike saw a look of faint curiosity on Fancourt's heavy-featured face.

"A restaurant full of people witnessed what I think is going to turn out to be Quine's last meal and his final public performance," Strike went on. "A credible witness says that Quine shouted for the whole restaurant to hear that one of the reasons Tassel was too cowardly to represent the book was 'Fancourt's limp dick.'"

He doubted that he and Fancourt were clearly visible to the jittery people at the publisher's table. Their figures would blend with the trees and statuary, but the determined or desperate might still be able to make out their location by the tiny luminous eye of Strike's glowing cigarette: a marksman's bead.

"Thing is, there's nothing in *Bombyx Mori* about your dick," continued Strike. "There's nothing in there about Quine's mistress and his young transgendered friend being 'beautiful lost souls,' which is how he told them he was going to describe them. And you don't pour acid on silkworms; you boil them to get their cocoons."

"*So?*" repeated Fancourt.

"So I've been forced to the conclusion," said Strike, "that the *Bombyx Mori* everyone's read is a different book to the *Bombyx Mori* Owen Quine wrote."

Fancourt stopped shuffling his feet. Momentarily frozen, he appeared to give Strike's words serious consideration.

"I—no," he said, almost, it seemed, to himself. "Quine wrote that book. It's his style."

"It's funny you should say that, because everyone else who had a decent ear for Quine's particular style seems to detect a foreign voice in the book. Daniel Chard thought it was Waldegrave. Waldegrave thought it was Elizabeth Tassel. And Christian Fisher heard *you*."

Fancourt shrugged with his usual easy arrogance.

"Quine was trying to imitate a better writer."

"Don't you think the way he treats his living models is strangely uneven?"

Fancourt, accepting the cigarette Strike offered him and a light, now listened in silence and with interest.

"He says his wife and agent were parasites on him," Strike said. "Unpleasant, but the sort of accusation anyone could throw at the people who might be said to live off his earnings. He implies his mistress isn't fond of animals and throws in something that could either be a veiled reference to her producing crap books or a pretty sick allusion to breast cancer. His transgendered friend gets off with a jibe about vocal exercises—and that's after she claimed she showed him the life story she was writing and shared all her deepest secrets. He accuses Chard of effectively killing Joe North, and makes a crass suggestion of what Chard really wanted to do to him. And there's the accusation that you were responsible for your first wife's death.

"All of which is either in the public domain, public gossip or an easy accusation to sling."

"Which isn't to say it wasn't hurtful," said Fancourt quietly.

"Agreed," said Strike. "It gave plenty of people reason to be pissed off at him. But the only real revelation in the book is the insinuation that you fathered Joanna Waldegrave."

"I told you—as good as told you—last time we met," said Fancourt, sounding tense, "that that accusation is not only false but impossible. I am infertile, as Quine—"

"—as Quine should have known," agreed Strike, "because you and he were still ostensibly on good terms when you had mumps and he'd already made a jibe about it in *The Balzac Brothers*. And that makes the accusation contained in the Cutter even stranger, doesn't it? As though it was written by someone who didn't know that you were infertile. Didn't any of this occur to you when you read the book?"

The snow fell thickly on the two men's hair, on their shoulders.

"I didn't think Owen cared whether any of it was true or not," said Fancourt slowly, exhaling smoke. "Mud sticks. He was just flinging a lot around. I thought he was looking to cause as much trouble as possible."

"D'you think that's why he sent you an early copy of the manuscript?" When Fancourt did not respond, Strike went on: "It's easily checkable, you know. Courier—postal service—there'll be a record. You might as well tell me."

A lengthy pause.

"All right," said Fancourt, at last.

"When did you get it?"

"The morning of the sixth."

"What did you do with it?"

"Burned it," said Fancourt shortly, exactly like Kathryn Kent. "I could see what he was doing: trying to provoke a public row, maximize publicity. The last resort of a failure—I was not going to humor him."

Another snatch of the interior revelry reached them as the door to the garden opened and closed again. Uncertain footsteps, winding through the snow, and then a large shadow looming out of the darkness.

"What," croaked Elizabeth Tassel, who was wrapped in a heavy coat with a fur collar, "is going on out here?"

The moment he heard her voice Fancourt made to move back inside. Strike wondered when was the last time they had come face to face in anything less than a crowd of hundreds.

"Wait a minute, will you?" Strike asked the writer.

Fancourt hesitated. Tassel addressed Strike in her deep, croaky voice.

"Pinks is missing Michael."

"Something you'd know all about," said Strike.

The snow whispered down upon leaves and onto the frozen pond where the cupid sat, pointing his arrow skywards.

"You thought Elizabeth's writing 'lamentably derivative,' isn't that right?" Strike asked Fancourt. "You both studied Jacobean revenge tragedies, which accounts for the similarities in your styles. But you're a very good imitator of other people's writing, I think," Strike told Tassel.

He had known that she would come if he took Fancourt away, known that she would be frightened of what he was telling the writer out in the dark. She stood perfectly still as snow landed in her fur collar, on her iron-gray hair. Strike could just make out the contours of her face by the faint light of the club's distant windows. The intensity and emptiness of her gaze were remarkable. She had the dead, blank eyes of a shark.

"You took off Elspeth Fancourt's style to perfection, for instance."

Fancourt's mouth fell quietly open. For a few seconds the only sound other than the whispering snow was the barely audible whistle emanating from Elizabeth Tassel's lungs.

"I thought from the start that Quine must've had some hold on you," said Strike. "You never seemed like the kind of woman who'd let herself be turned into a private bank and skivvy, who'd choose to keep Quine and let Fancourt go. All that bull about freedom of expression... *you* wrote the parody of Elspeth Fancourt's book that made her kill herself. All these years, there's only been your word for it that Owen showed you the piece he'd written. It was the other way round."

There was silence except for the rustle of snow on snow and that faint, eerie sound emanating from Elizabeth Tassel's chest. Fancourt was looking from the agent to the detective, open-mouthed.

"The police suspected that Quine was blackmailing you," Strike said, "but you fobbed them off with a touching story about lending him money for Orlando. You've been paying Owen off for more than a quarter of a century, haven't you?"

He was trying to goad her into speech, but she said nothing, continuing to stare at him out of the dark empty eyes like holes in her plain, pale face.

"How did you describe yourself to me when we had lunch?" Strike asked her. "'The very definition of a blameless spinster'? Found an outlet for your frustrations, though, didn't you, Elizabeth?"

The mad, blank eyes swiveled suddenly towards Fancourt, who had shifted where he stood.

"Did it feel good, raping and killing your way through everyone you knew, Elizabeth? One big explosion of malice and obscenity, revenging yourself on everyone, painting yourself as the unacclaimed genius, taking sideswipes at everyone with a more successful love life, a more satisfying—"

A soft voice spoke in the darkness, and for a second Strike did not know where it was coming from. It was strange, unfamiliar, high-pitched and sickly: the voice a madwoman might imagine to express innocence, kindliness.

"No, Mr. Strike," she whispered, like a mother telling a sleepy child not to sit up, not to struggle. "You poor silly man. You poor thing."

She forced a laugh that left her chest heaving, her lungs whistling.

"He was badly hurt in Afghanistan," she said to Fancourt in that eerie, crooning voice. "I think he's shell-shocked. Brain damaged, just like little Orlando. He needs help, poor Mr. Strike."

Her lungs whistled as she breathed faster.

"Should've bought a mask, Elizabeth, shouldn't you?" Strike asked.

He thought he saw the eyes darken and enlarge, her pupils dilating with the adrenaline coursing through her. The large, mannish hands had curled into claws.

"Thought you had it all worked out, didn't you? Ropes, disguise, protective clothing to protect yourself against the acid—but you didn't realize you'd get tissue damage just from inhaling the fumes."

The cold air was exacerbating her breathlessness. In her panic, she sounded sexually excited.

"I think," said Strike, with calculated cruelty, "it's driven you literally mad, Elizabeth, hasn't it? Better hope the jury buys that anyway, eh? What a waste of a life. Your business down the toilet, no man, no children... Tell me, was there ever an abortive coupling between the two of you?" asked Strike bluntly, watching their profiles. "This 'limp dick' business... sounds to me like Quine might've fictionalized it in the real *Bombyx Mori*."

With their backs to the light he could not see their expressions, but their body language had given him his answer: the instantaneous swing away from each other to face him had expressed the ghost of a united front.

"When was this?" Strike asked, watching the dark outline that was Elizabeth. "After Elspeth died? But then you moved on to Fenella Waldegrave, eh, Michael? No trouble keeping it up there, I take it?"

Elizabeth emitted a small gasp. It was as though he had hit her.

"For Christ's sake," growled Fancourt. He was angry with Strike now. Strike ignored the implicit reproach. He was still working on Elizabeth, goading her, while her whistling lungs struggled for oxygen in the falling snow.

"Must've really pissed you off when Quine got carried away and started shouting about the contents of the real *Bombyx Mori* in the

River Café, did it, Elizabeth? After you'd warned him not to breathe a word about the contents?"

"Insane. You're insane," she whispered, with a forced smile beneath the shark eyes, her big yellow teeth glinting. "The war didn't just cripple you—"

"Nice," said Strike appreciatively. "There's the bullying bitch everyone's told me you are—"

"You hobble around London trying to get in the papers," she panted. "You're just like poor Owen, just like him...how he loved the papers, didn't he, Michael?" She turned to appeal to Fancourt. "Didn't Owen adore publicity? Running off like a little boy playing hide-and-seek..."

"You encouraged Quine to go and hide in Talgarth Road," said Strike. "That was all your idea."

"I won't listen to any more," she whispered and her lungs were whistling as she gasped the winter air and she raised her voice: "*I'm not listening, Mr. Strike, I'm not listening. Nobody's listening to you, you poor silly man...*"

"You told me Quine was a glutton for praise," said Strike, raising his voice over the high-pitched chant with which she was trying to drown out his words. "I think he told you his whole prospective plot for *Bombyx Mori* months ago and I think Michael here was in there in some form—nothing as crude as Vainglorious, but mocked for not getting it up, perhaps? 'Payback time for both of you,' eh?"

And as he had expected, she gave a little gasp at that and stopped her frantic chanting.

"You told Quine that *Bombyx Mori* sounded brilliant, that it would be the best thing he'd ever done, that it was going to be a massive success, but that he ought to keep the contents very, very quiet in case of legal action, and to make a bigger splash when it was unveiled. And all the time you were writing your own version. You had plenty of time on your hands to get it right, didn't you, Elizabeth? Twenty-six years of empty evenings, you could have written plenty of books by now, with your first from Oxford...but what would you write about? You haven't exactly lived a full life, have you?"

Naked rage flickered across her face. Her fingers flexed, but she controlled herself. Strike wanted her to crack, wanted her to give in, but the shark's eyes seemed to be waiting for him to show weakness, for an opening.

"You crafted a novel out of a murder plan. The removal of the guts and the covering of the corpse in acid weren't symbolic, they were designed to screw forensics—but everyone bought it as literature.

"And you got that stupid, egotistical bastard to collude in planning his own death. You told him you had a great idea for maximizing his publicity and his profits: the pair of you would stage a very public row—you saying the book was too contentious to put out there—and he'd disappear. You'd circulate rumors about the book's contents and finally, when Quine allowed himself to be found, you'd secure him a big fat deal."

She was shaking her head, her lungs audibly laboring, but her dead eyes did not leave his face.

"He delivered the book. You delayed a few days, until bonfire night, to make sure you had lots of nice diversionary noise, then you sent out copies of the fake *Bombyx* to Fisher—the better to get the book talked about—to Waldegrave and to Michael here. You faked your public row, then you followed Quine to Talgarth Road—"

"No," said Fancourt, apparently unable to help himself.

"Yes," said Strike, pitiless. "Quine didn't realize he had anything to fear from Elizabeth—not from his coconspirator in the comeback of the century. I think he'd almost forgotten by then that what he'd been doing to you for years was blackmail, hadn't he?" he asked Tassel. "He'd just developed the habit of asking you for money and being given it. I doubt you ever even talked about the parody any-more, the thing that ruined your life ...

"And you know what I think happened once he let you in, Elizabeth?"

Against his will, Strike remembered the scene: the great vaulted window, the body centered there as though for a grisly still life.

"I think you got that poor naive, narcissistic sod to pose for a public-ity photograph. Was he kneeling down? Did the hero in the real book plead, or pray? Or did he get tied up like *your* Bombyx? He'd have liked that, wouldn't he, Quine, posing in ropes? It would've made it nice and easy to move behind him and smash his head in with the metal doorstop, wouldn't it? Under cover of the neighborhood fireworks, you knocked Quine out, tied him up, sliced him open and—"

Fancourt let out a strangled moan of horror, but Tassel spoke again, crooning at him in a travesty of consolation:

"You ought to see someone, Mr. Strike. *Poor* Mr. Strike," and to his surprise she reached out to lay one of her big hands on his snow-covered shoulder. Remembering what those hands had done, Strike stepped back instinctively and her arm fell heavily back to her side, hanging there, the fingers clenching reflexively.

"You filled a holdall with Owen's guts and the real manuscript," said the detective. She had moved so close that he could again smell the combination of perfume and stale cigarettes. "Then you put on Quine's own cloak and hat and left. Off you went, to feed a fourth copy of the fake *Bombyx Mori* through Kathryn Kent's letter box, to maximize suspects and incriminate another woman who was getting what you never got—sex. Companionship. At least one friend."

She feigned laughter again but this time the sound was manic. Her fingers were still flexing and unflexing.

"You and Owen would have got on so well," she whispered. "Wouldn't he, Michael? Wouldn't he have got on marvelously with Owen? Sick fantasists...people will laugh at you, Mr. Strike." She was panting harder than ever, those dead, blank eyes staring out of her fixed white face. "A poor cripple trying to recreate the sensation of success, chasing your famous fath—"

"Have you got proof of any of this?" Fancourt demanded in the swirling snow, his voice harsh with the desire not to believe. This was no ink-and-paper tragedy, no greasepaint death scene. Here beside him stood the living friend of his student years and whatever life had subsequently done to them, the idea that the big, ungainly, besotted girl whom he had known at Oxford could have turned into a woman capable of grotesque murder was almost unbearable.

"Yeah, I've got proof," said Strike quietly. "I've got a second electric typewriter, the exact model of Quine's, wrapped up in a black burqa and hydrochloric-stained overalls and weighted with stones. An amateur diver I happen to know pulled it out of the sea just a few days ago. It was lying beneath some notorious cliffs at Gwithian:

Hell's Mouth, a place featured on Dorcus Pengelly's book cover. I expect she showed it to you when you visited, didn't she, Elizabeth? Did you walk back there alone with your mobile, telling her you needed to find better reception?"

She let out a ghastly low moan, like the sound of a man who has been punched in the stomach. For a second nobody moved, then Tassel turned clumsily and began running and stumbling away from them, back towards the club. A bright yellow rectangle of light shivered then disappeared as the door opened and closed.

"But," said Fancourt, taking a few steps and looking back at Strike a little wildly, "you can't—you've got to stop her!"

"Couldn't catch her if I wanted to," said Strike, throwing the butt of his cigarette down into the snow. "Dodgy knee."

"She could do anything—"

"Off to kill herself, probably," agreed Strike, pulling out his mobile.

The writer stared at him.

"You—you cold-blooded bastard!"

"You're not the first to say it," said Strike, pressing keys on his phone. "Ready?" he said into it. "We're off."

49

Dangers, like stars, in dark attempts best shine.

Thomas Dekker, *The Noble Spanish Soldier*

Out past the smokers at the front of the club the large woman came, blindly, slipping a little in the snow. She began to run up the dark street, her fur-collared coat flapping behind her.

A taxi, its "For Hire" light on, slid out of a side road and she hailed it, flapping her arms madly. The cab slid to a halt, its headlamps making two cones of light whose trajectory was cut by the thickly falling snow.

"Fulham Palace Road," said the harsh, deep voice, breaking with sobs.

They pulled slowly away from the curb. The cab was old, the glass partition scratched and a little stained by years of its owner's smoking. Elizabeth Tassel was visible in the rearview mirror as the streetlight slid over her, sobbing silently into her large hands, shaking all over.

The driver did not ask what was the matter but looked beyond the fare to the street behind, where the shrinking figures of two men could be seen, hurrying across the snowy road to a red sports car in the distance.

The taxi turned left at the end of the road and still Elizabeth Tassel cried into her hands. The driver's thick woolen hat was itchy, grateful though she had been for it during the long hours of waiting. On up the King's Road the taxi sped, over thick powdery snow that resisted tires' attempts to squash it to slush, the blizzard swirling remorselessly, rendering the roads increasingly lethal.

"You're going the wrong way."

"There's a diversion," lied Robin. "Because of the snow."

She met Elizabeth's eyes briefly in the mirror. The agent looked over her shoulder. The red Alfa Romeo was too far behind to see. She stared wildly around at the passing buildings. Robin could hear the eerie whistling from her chest.

"We're going in the opposite direction."

"I'm going to turn in a minute," said Robin.

She did not see Elizabeth Tassel try the door, but heard it. They were all locked.

"You can let me out here," she said loudly. "Let me out, I say!"

"You won't get another cab in this weather," said Robin.

They had counted on Tassel being too distraught to notice where they were going for a little while longer. The cab was barely at Sloane Square. There was over a mile to go to New Scotland Yard. Robin's eyes flickered again to her rearview mirror. The Alfa Romeo was a tiny red dot in the distance.

Elizabeth had undone her seatbelt.

"Stop this cab!" she shouted. "Stop it and let me out!"

"I can't stop here," said Robin, much more calmly than she felt, because the agent had left her seat and her large hands were scrabbling at the partition. "I'm going to have to ask you to sit down, madam—"

The screen slid open. Elizabeth's hand seized Robin's hat and a handful of hair, her head almost side by side with Robin's, her expression venomous. Robin's hair fell into her eyes in sweaty strands.

"Get off me!"

"Who are you?" screeched Tassel, shaking Robin's head with the fistful of hair in her hand. "Ralph said he saw a blonde going through the bin—*who are you?*"

"Let go!" shouted Robin, as Tassel's other hand grabbed her neck.

Two hundred yards behind them, Strike roared at Al:

"Put your fucking foot down, there's something wrong, look at it—"

The taxi ahead was careering all over the road.

"It's always been shit in ice," moaned Al as the Alfa skidded a little and the taxi took the corner into Sloane Square at speed and disappeared from view.

Tassel was halfway into the front of the taxi, screaming from her ripped throat—Robin was trying to beat her back one-handed while maintaining a grip on the wheel—she could not see where she was going for hair and snow and now both Tassel's hands were at her throat, squeezing—Robin tried to find the brake, but as the taxi leapt forwards realized she had hit the accelerator—she could not breathe—taking both hands off the wheel she tried to prize away the agent's tightening grip—screams from pedestrians, a huge jolt and then the ear-splitting crunch of glass, of metal on concrete and the searing pain of the seatbelt against her as the taxi crashed, but she was sinking, everything going black—

"Fuck the car, leave it, we've got to get in there!" Strike bellowed at Al over the wail of a shop alarm and the screams of the scattered bystanders. Al brought the Alfa to an untidy skidding halt in the middle of the road a hundred yards from where the taxi had smashed its way into a plate-glass window. Al jumped out as Strike struggled to stand. A group of passersby, some of them Christmas partygoers in black tie who had sprinted out of the way as the taxi mounted the curb, watched, stunned, as Al ran, slipping and almost falling, over the snow towards the crash.

The rear door of the cab opened. Elizabeth Tassel flung herself from the backseat and began to run.

"Al, get her!" Strike bellowed, still struggling through the snow. "Get her, Al!"

Le Rosey had a superb rugby team. Al was used to taking orders. A short sprint and he had taken her down in a perfect tackle. She hit the snowy street with a hard bang over the screamed protests of many women watching and he pinned her there, struggling and swearing, repelling every attempt of chivalrous men to help his victim.

Strike was immune to all of it: he seemed to be running in slow motion, trying not to fall, staggering towards the ominously silent and still cab. Distracted by Al and his struggling, swearing captive, nobody had a thought to spare for the driver of the taxi.

"Robin..."

She was slumped sideways, still held to her seat by the belt. There was blood on her face, but when he said her name she responded with a muddled groan.

"Thank fuck … thank fuck … "

Police sirens were already filling the square. They wailed over the shop alarm, the mounting protests of the shocked Londoners, and Strike, undoing Robin's seatbelt, pushing her gently back into the cab as she attempted to get out, said:

"Stay there."

"She knew we weren't going to her house," mumbled Robin. "Knew straightaway I was going the wrong way."

"Doesn't matter," panted Strike. "You've brought Scotland Yard to us."

Diamond-bright lights were twinkling from the bare trees around the square. Snow poured down upon the gathering crowd, the taxi protruding from the broken window and the sports car parked untidily in the middle of the road as the police cars came to a halt, their flashing blue lights sparkling on the glittering glass-strewn ground, their sirens lost in the wail of the shop alarm.

As his half-brother tried to shout an explanation as to why he was lying on top of a sixty-year-old woman, the relieved, exhausted detective slumped down beside his partner in the cab and found himself—against his will and against the dictates of good taste—laughing.

One week later

50

CYNTHIA: How say you, Endymion, all this was for love?
ENDYMION: I say, madam, then the gods send me a
  woman's hate.

John Lyly, *Endymion: or, the Man in the Moon*

Strike had never visited Robin and Matthew's flat in Ealing before. His insistence that Robin take time off work to recover from mild concussion and attempted strangulation had not gone down well.

"Robin," he had told her patiently over the phone, "I've had to shut up the office anyway. Press crawling all over Denmark Street... I'm staying at Nick and Ilsa's."

But he could not disappear to Cornwall without seeing her. When she opened her front door he was glad to see that the bruising on her neck and forehead had already faded to a faint yellow and blue.

"How're you feeling?" he asked, wiping his feet on the doormat.

"Great!" she said.

The place was small but cheerful and it smelled of her perfume, which he had never noticed much before. Perhaps a week without smelling it had made him more sensitive to it. She led him through to the sitting room, which was painted magnolia like Kathryn Kent's and where he was interested to note the copy of *Investigative Interviewing: Psychology and Practice* lying cover upwards on a chair. A small Christmas tree stood in the corner, the decorations white and silver like the trees in Sloane Square that had formed the background of press photographs of the crashed taxi.

"Matthew got over it yet?" asked Strike, sinking down into the sofa.

"I can't say he's the happiest I've ever seen him," she replied, grinning. "Tea?"

She knew how he liked it: the color of creosote.

"Christmas present," he told her when she returned with the tray, and handed her a nondescript white envelope. Robin opened it curiously and pulled out a stapled sheaf of printed material.

"Surveillance course in January," said Strike. "So next time you pull a bag of dog shit out of a bin no one notices you doing it."

She laughed, delighted.

"Thank you. *Thank you!*"

"Most women would've expected flowers."

"I'm not most women."

"Yeah, I've noticed that," said Strike, taking a chocolate biscuit.

"Have they analyzed it yet?" she asked. "The dog poo?"

"Yep. Full of human guts. She'd been defrosting them bit by bit. They found traces in the Doberman's bowl and the rest in her freezer."

"Oh God," said Robin, the smile sliding off her face.

"Criminal genius," said Strike. "Sneaking into Quine's study and planting two of her own used typewriter ribbons behind the desk . . . Anstis has condescended to have them tested now; there's none of Quine's DNA on them. He never touched them—ergo, he never typed what's on there."

"Anstis is still talking to you, is he?"

"Just. Hard for him to cut me off. I saved his life."

"I can see how that would make things awkward," Robin agreed. "So they're buying your whole theory now?"

"Open and shut case now they know what they're looking for. She bought the duplicate typewriter nearly two years ago. Ordered the burqa and the ropes on Quine's card and got them sent to the house while the workmen were in. Loads of opportunity to get at his Visa over the years. Coat hanging up in the office while he went for a slash … sneak out his wallet while he was asleep, pissed, when she drove him home from parties.

"She knew him well enough to know he was slapdash on checking things like bills. She'd had access to the key to Talgarth Road—easy to copy. She'd been all over the house, knew the hydrochloric acid was there."

"Brilliant, but over-elaborate," said Strike, sipping his dark brown tea. "She's on suicide watch, apparently. But you haven't heard the most mental bit."

"There's more?" said Robin apprehensively.

Much as she had looked forward to seeing Strike, she still felt a little fragile after the events of a week ago. She straightened her back and faced him squarely, braced.

"She kept the bloody book."

Robin frowned at him.

"What do you—?"

"It was in the freezer with the guts. Bloodstained because she'd carried it away in the bag with the guts. The real manuscript. The *Bombyx Mori* that Quine wrote."

"But—why on earth—?"

"God only knows. Fancourt says—"

"You've seen him?"

"Briefly. He's decided he knew it was Elizabeth all along. I'll lay you odds what his next novel's going to be about. Anyway, he says she wouldn't have been able to bring herself to destroy an original manuscript."

"For God's sake—she had no problem destroying its author!"

"Yeah, but this was *literature*, Robin," said Strike, grinning. "And get this: Roper Chard are very keen to publish the real thing. Fancourt's going to write the introduction."

"You *are* kidding?"

"Nope. Quine's going to have a bestseller at last. Don't look like that," said Strike bracingly as she shook her head in disbelief. "Plenty to celebrate. Leonora and Orlando will be rolling in money once *Bombyx Mori* hits the bookshelves.

"That reminds me, got something else for you."

He slid his hand into the inside pocket of the coat lying beside him on the sofa and handed her a rolled-up drawing that he had been keeping safe there. Robin unfurled it and smiled, her eyes filling with tears. Two curly haired angels danced together beneath the carefully penciled legend *To Robin love from Dodo*.

"How are they?"

"Great," said Strike.

He had visited the house in Southern Row at Leonora's invitation. She and Orlando had met him hand in hand at the door, Cheeky Monkey dangling around Orlando's neck as usual.

"Where's Robin?" Orlando demanded. "I wanted Robin to be here. I drew her a picture."

"The lady had an accident," Leonora reminded her daughter, backing away into the hall to let Strike in, keeping a tight hold on Orlando's hand as though frightened that someone might separate them again. "I told you, Dodo, the lady did a very brave thing and she had a crash in a car."

"Auntie Liz was *bad*," Orlando told Strike, walking backwards down the hall, still hand in hand with her mother but staring at Strike all the way with those limpid green eyes. "She was the one who made my daddy die."

"Yes, I—er—I know," Strike replied, with that familiar feeling of inadequacy that Orlando always seemed to induce in him.

He had found Edna from next door sitting at the kitchen table.

"Oh, you were clever," she told him over and again. "Wasn't it *dreadful*, though? How's your poor partner? *Wasn't* it terrible, though?"

"Bless them," said Robin after he had described this scene in some detail. She spread Orlando's picture out on the coffee table between them, beside the details of the surveillance course, where she could admire them both. "And how's Al?"

"Beside himself with bloody excitement," said Strike gloomily. "We've given him a false impression of the thrill of working life."

"I liked him," said Robin, smiling.

"Yeah, well, you were concussed," said Strike. "And Polworth's bloody ecstatic to have shown up the Met."

"You've got some very interesting friends," said Robin. "How much are you going to have to pay to repair Nick's dad's taxi?"

"Haven't got the bill in yet," he sighed. "I suppose," he added, several biscuits later, with his eyes on his present to Robin, "I'm going to have to get another temp in while you're off learning surveillance."

"Yeah, I suppose you will," agreed Robin, and after a slight hesitation she added, "I hope she's rubbish."

Strike laughed as he got to his feet, picking up his coat.

"I wouldn't worry. Lightning doesn't strike twice."

"Doesn't anyone ever call you that, among all your many nicknames?" she wondered as they walked back through to the hall.

"Call me what?"

"'Lightning' Strike?"

"Is that likely?" he asked, indicating his leg. "Well, merry Christmas, partner."

The idea of a hug hovered briefly in the air, but she held out her hand with mock blokeyness, and he shook it.

"Have a great time in Cornwall."

"And you in Masham."

On the point of relinquishing her hand, he gave it a quick twist. He had kissed the back of it before she knew what had happened. Then, with a grin and a wave, he was gone.

Acknowledgments

Writing as Robert Galbraith has been pure joy and the following people have all helped make it so. My heartfelt thanks go to:

SOBE, Deeby and the Back Door Man, because I'd never have got as far without you. Let's plan a heist next.

David Shelley, my incomparable editor, stalwart support and fellow INFJ. Thank you for being brilliant at your job, for taking seriously all the things that matter and for finding everything else as funny as I do.

My agent, Neil Blair, who cheerfully agreed to help me achieve my ambition of becoming a first-time author. You are truly one in a million.

Everyone at Little, Brown who worked so hard and enthusiastically on Robert's first novel without having a clue who he was. My special gratitude to the audiobook team, who took Robert to number one before he was unmasked.

Lorna and Steve Barnes, who enabled me to drink in The Bay Horse, examine the tomb of Sir Marmaduke Wyvill and find out that Robin's hometown is pronounced "Mass-um" not "Mash-em," saving me much future embarrassment.

Fiddy Henderson, Christine Collingwood, Fiona Shapcott, Angela Milne, Alison Kelly and Simon Brown, without whose hard work I would not have had time to write *The Silkworm*, or indeed anything else.

Mark Hutchinson, Nicky Stonehill and Rebecca Salt, who can take a great deal of credit for the fact that I still have some marbles left.

My family, especially Neil, for much more than I can express in a few lines, but in this case for being so supportive of bloody murder.